'What a terrific novel – wickedly sharp, wildly entertaining – I was gripped from start to finish. With its twisty plots and interwoven characters it paints a vivid portrait of a crucial decade. It's laugh-out-loud funny, too. And with property porn thrown in, what's not to like?' **Deborah Moggach**

'Wickedly funny and deeply humane. I loved this book.' **Sadie Jones**

'Tim Lott revisits the years between millennium fever and the financial crisis, and brings this already long-lost era back to life in a novel every bit as evocative and compelling as we would expect from this prodigiously gifted author.' **Jonathan Coe**

'Lott delivers many hilarious and sad scenes of life in a long-term relationship. He also explores the poignancy and fragility of male friendships, in a manner reminiscent of Graham Swift's *Last Orders* . . . [He is,] crucially, careful to linger over moral difficulty and vulnerability rather than evading it.' *TLS*

'Lott's carefully observed period piece captures the mood of an era that now seems like a lost world.' *Daily Mail*

'A sharp and very funny portrait of a brash era which is also a surprisingly tender take on flawed masculinity.' **i paper**

Now We
Are Forgiven

TIM LOTT

SCRIBNER

LONDON NEW YORK SYDNEY TORONTO NEW DELHI

First published in Great Britain by Scribner, an imprint of
Simon & Schuster UK Ltd, 2022
This edition published 2023

1 3 5 7 9 10 8 6 4 2

Simon & Schuster UK Ltd
1st Floor
222 Gray's Inn Road
London WC1X 8HB

Simon & Schuster Australia, Sydney
Simon & Schuster India, New Delhi

www.simonandschuster.co.uk
www.simonandschuster.com.au
www.simonandschuster.co.in

A CIP catalogue record for this book is available from the British Library

Paperback ISBN: 978-1-3985-0559-9
eBook ISBN: 978-1-3985-0558-2
Audio ISBN: 978-1-3985-1444-7

Typeset by M Rules
Printed and Bound in the UK using 100% Renewable
Electricity at CPI Group (UK) Ltd

For Esme, Lydia, Cissy and Ruby

'He maketh his sun rise on the evil and on the good, and sendeth rain on the just and on the unjust.'

Matthew 5:45

PART ONE

Immunity

Chapter One

The seafront on the south coast in winter is not a hospitable place. A few hours after dawn, a frail but clearly determined teenage girl wearing Lycra tights, a red long-sleeved tech shirt and running gloves makes steady progress along the front, her face dashed by the wind and punctured by needles of sharp cold. Her wavy brown hair is not fully restrained by an elasticated headband, so scraps blow occasionally into her eyes, which are watering. The headband has imprinted in large white letters the breezy legend 'I'm Fine!'.

One of the dog walkers she occasionally passes might conclude that she is crying, but it is hard to tell, since the sea spray spits at her eyes, her cheeks, her mouth. She has three silver studs in her left ear – a star, a flower and a simple pearl pin. Her teeth, when she grimaces, show a single gold tooth with the letter 'C' hollowed out. On her back, just above the waistline, a fresh tattoo is visible of a small tree, very dark blue,

3

almost black, bare but for one leaf falling. The surrounding skin is still livid from the needle. The tat shows a single bird taking flight from the top branch as the leaf falls towards the ground. Beneath her waistline, delicate roots coiling into earth are etched.

She is on the return leg of her route, making her way from Roedean, east of Brighton, towards the shuttered entrance of the Palace Pier. She barely notices the pavilion roofs, towers and flags that decorate the boardwalk. Concentrating on her breathing and the music that seeps from her earbuds – a loop of Little Mix – her thoughts are as scattered as the distant clouds born out of the night, gathering on the horizon. Her eyes, although open, might as well be closed for all that they register.

Half dreaming, trancing to the music, she senses invisible forces around her. The pull of the moon that drags at the waves. The unheard whisper of the wind scattering detritus along Marine Parade. The secret rhythms of her own body, the movement of blood in artery, vein and synapse.

She passes a seafood stall, smells a trace of mussels and whelks, then a whiff of burned doughnuts. There is tar and ozone. Then salt, though she can't say for sure what salt smells like. Perhaps nothing.

She has a sense that she can detect particles penetrating her skin. Neutrinos? Photons? Scanning half-remembered shadows of her science lessons, fading now that she has finished school for ever, she can barely call to mind the details. She knows that whatever they are, they perpetually crash into Earth at near light speed. Little bits of almost nothing, falling as endless rain on the planet. She feels, momentarily, utterly transparent, entirely permeable.

She accelerates her pace – running, in her mind, away from something she hates, towards something she fears. The cold air singes her lungs. She passes what appears to be a woman – the sleeper is nested under some thick reflective fabric so thoroughly it is hard to tell – prone on a bench. A large bright blue nylon laundry bag is stuffed underneath the seat. The sleeper's hand is tangled with one of the handles of the bag, as if to protect it from thieves.

The running girl notices flaked traces of purple varnish on two of the fingernails. Unmoved at first by the sight of the prostrate figure – rough sleepers are an everyday sight on this part of the south coast – the remnants of decoration on the nails skewer her with unexpected pity. She slows, almost stops. Then, assessing her own helplessness – she isn't even carrying any money to offer – she picks up her pace again, mood curdled with a faint vinegar of guilt.

Turning at her designated point – the doughnut-on-a-stick of the British Airways observation tower facing the burned-out West Pier – she makes her way towards home. She prefers the carbon skeleton of the West Pier to the gaudy, inescapable there-ness of the Palace Pier. The West Pier seems to her more essentially honest in its tragedy, blackened stumps which appear at high tide as a hesitant semicircle spiking out from beneath the grey-green torpor of the English Channel. They stand in sober reproach to the *Carry On* knockabout of the pier's younger counterpart, a pocket-picking carnival of funhouse mirrors, pulsing slot machines, slides, wheels and dodgems.

Minutes later she arrives home, a marshmallow-pink three-bedroom terrace near the North Laines. Making her way up the short garden path chequered with black and white tiles, she lets herself in through the heavy panelled front door with its frowning brass lion door knocker.

Entering, she continues jogging on the spot in the hallway, then continues upstairs to her bedroom with its hand-lettered sign on the door:

'Tips for Entering My Bedroom Properly: 1. <u>Do Not.</u>'

Inside the room there are traces that suggest the occupant is some years younger than her height, piercings and unapologetic tattoo might suggest. The bed is draped with curtains of white muslin on all four sides, supported by horizontal metal struts which connect four upright vertical poles. There is a picture of a pony imprinted on the pillow, although she has never so much as sat on a pony, and, resting upon it, a ragged and puzzled toy monkey. To the right of the bed, there is an orange egg chair suspended on a chain from the ceiling – her favourite item in the otherwise sparsely furnished but persistently cluttered room.

On the egg chair squats Kardashian – Kardy – her step-father's obese black cat. Not bothering to undress or shower, she tosses Kardashian out of the chair and throws herself into the womblike space. Here, she weeps – unmistakeably this time. She doesn't know if the tears come because of the previous night's election result or because of the painted fingernails of the sleeping woman. Or then again, perhaps it is because during the course of her run she feels she has cemented a long-deferred decision into place.

Kardashian has made no noise of protest. Pragmatically, the cat has resumed her sleep on the girl's cloistered single bed. Restless, the girl pulls herself out of the egg chair, as if burdened not by gravity but the future.

She doesn't know when she will put her decision into effect, but the trigger — she feels in her gut — must come soon. With Christmas so close, the stresses building within this house will coalesce and, somehow or other, force her hand. Of this, China Blue is sure.

December 2019: London

A woman's voice floats up like vapour from the pillow next to where Frankie Blue is vainly trying to pursue some final, scattered wisps of sleep. The interior of his skull feels musty and vague, while the exterior is braided around the crown with thin pepper-and-salt hair and the features below tarpaulined with sallow skin. His mind is hung with cobwebs that sag with the toiling flies he imagines his thoughts to resemble. This sense of malaise, as well as the appearance of sallowness, is the consequence of staying up the previous night, until 4 a.m., watching the coverage of the general election.

'Hosh. The bears are. The beers ARE. They're not? Ok then. You stupid.'

Roxy, his girlfriend of six months, is talking in her sleep again. Most of the mumblings are indistinct, but Frankie's brain automatically converts the sounds into words. The outpouring of nonsense is bookended with a random giggle.

Still muttering, Roxy turns over to face him, eyes still closed, eyeballs visibly roaming under the powdered skin. Other traces of makeup blur her features. Frankie, who has given up on sleep now, idly examines them, with the sudden, uncomfortable feeling that he is seeing the face of an alien species. He senses the weirdness of the slope of a human nose, of the bizarrely comic protrusion of ears, of the slow exhalation of hair from the minutely perforated scalp.

'Sofa it's coming and I'm chuffed. Isn't it? Same, mate.'

Outside, on the Golborne Road, North Kensington, the street traders are busy at their stalls. Moroccans, Tunisians, cockneys, Ethiopians, Somalis — just to name a few of the patchwork of creeds and nationalities Frankie is able to make a stab at identifying. Food, furniture, junk and second-hand clothes are laid out for inspection. He finds the buzz of shoppers and the calls of the traders briefly comforting. His affection for London's perpetual chaos surges over him in a wave, then crests and disappears into light froth. It finally settles into a vague, contradictory trough of resentment at what he suddenly experiences as mere cacophony.

He reaches to the bedside table on his left. His fingers — the nails clean and manicured — feel their way towards two gelatinous pink lumps resting on the glass top of a scratched walnut 1930 nightstand, picked up from a stall outside a month ago for £50, a figure reached by an epic bout of haggling with the dealer. Frankie, taking pride in his skills as an estate agent, was not prepared to let himself be bested in a negotiation and felt sure that he had walked away with a bargain. But the door of the nightstand is now falling off while the cupboard catch is faulty and refuses to keep the door closed.

The lumps his fingers eventually discover are wax earplugs, with which he tries to block out not only the sleep talking but Roxanne's persistent, unmaidenly snoring. He works them like putty deeper and deeper into the auditory canal, wondering, not for the first time, if his relationship with Roxy has any future. He suspects that he is only with her because he is lonely. Perhaps that was a good enough reason. Why was anyone with anyone? Not for fun, surely.

'Blurgh, hff, sngl.'

The plugs are effective to the extent that he can no longer make out Roxy's words. But enough vibration penetrates the wax to confirm that she is still babbling. He wonders what kind of dreams she has. As dreams go, they seem – when later and inevitably related to Frankie – mundane, often focusing on expensive consumer goods, missed buses and public exposure to mild embarrassment rather than the realms of the truly fantastical. But then – he reflects – it is probably unfair to judge others for their dreams.

He rests his hand on her bare hip. Her skin is hot. How many relationships, he wonders, are founded on this simple desire for skin to touch skin, the fundamental urge for physical connection? He thinks of the places this urge has led him, the bodies it has thrown him up against, human flotsam crashing into one another on a relentless wave of need.

It is a deeper form of connection that Frankie craves. Checking his phone for the third time that morning – it is already 11 a.m. – to see if his daughter has replied to his texts, he feels a soft stab of disappointment. Ten years divorced now, his parents are long dead, and his relationship with Roxy is fledgling and unpromising. His father substitute, old mentor and erstwhile employer Ralph Gwynne is also gone, taken by heart disease. Apart from Jon – 'Nodge' – Drysdale, his best friend since schooldays, his daughter is his only real potential remaining link to intimacy, the intimacy that he feels sure should properly and naturally exist between a father and his child.

The trouble being – he reflects bitterly – that his daughter hates him. Sometimes, shamefully, he can't help but hate her back for it, even though he knows it isn't her fault. The children of divorce are always hurt, brutally, savagely. Sooner or later, they exact their revenge.

Frankie feels muddy layers of still more unwelcome thoughts and questions accrue inside him. What does his life amount to? The answers torment him with their banality. Work. Five-a-side football on a Sunday. Occasional sex, usually mediocre. A drink out with Nodge. Hard to get proper bitter nowadays. Work. Cycling in Lycra on the latest fancy bike before it gets stolen. Nine holes of golf on a municipal golf course. TV. Work. Brief, unsatisfying masturbation. A Diavolo pizza, extra chillies. Work. Shopping for clothes he can't afford and artwork he doesn't like but which makes his sparse, dull flat seem more distinguished, more *aesthetic*. Work. A fortnight's holiday abroad once a year, a weekend city break now and then.

Sleep. Work. Sleep. Work. Sleep . . . With this incantation still ticking over, Frankie becomes aware of a distant voice as if heard through veils of cotton wool.

'Frankie! It's nearly midday.'

Frankie reluctantly surfaces into consciousness. He prises the earplugs out of their gristly caves and balances them in his palm. They are ranged there, coated now with traces of brown earwax.

'Disgusting,' says Roxy mildly. 'Like giant hamster droppings.'

She is propped up on her pillow holding a cup of tea. Given

the missing frame of time, Frankie realises he must have drifted asleep without registering the fact.

'I'm sorry you have to witness the distressing fact of their existence,' he says, replacing the earplugs delicately on the bedside table, as if they still carried precious remnants of his inner life. 'But you talk even more when you're asleep than when you're awake.' *Sometimes I wish I could wear them then as well*, he adds, silently to himself.

He pulls his own pillow up behind him to bring him level with Roxy, who is naked apart from an oversized 'Make America Great Again' T-shirt. She wears it, she insists, as a joke, a windup. 'Anything for a laugh' is her one-time motto that has evolved somehow into what passes for a life philosophy. But Frankie isn't so sure it's a joke at all. After all, she had voted for Brexit – made no bones about it, told everyone who cared to listen. Frankie stretches out, hands above his head, feeling a slight crick of protest in his neck.

'Did you make me a cup?'

'You were asleep.'

'You knew I was going to wake up.'

'Sooner or later.'

'I could have done with a cup. Anyway, you woke me deliberately.'

'I'll go and make you one now if you like.'

'I don't want one now.'

'You just said you did.'

'Now I don't.'

'Stop being a martyr.'

Roxy puts the cup down on her side table, then leans over and rests her head gently on his bare shoulder. Her straight chestnut hair, interrupted with irrepressible grey strands, trails of winding mist, continues halfway down her back. It is too long now for Frankie's liking – she is too old for it in his uncharitable view – and it now carpets his chest like a dry flannel.

Her brown eyes, soft when Frankie first met her at a Millennium night party in the West End, have hardened into a corona of darkness at the edges while seeming to devolve into sticky caramel at the centre. It was at that Millennium celebration she had met her tragic husband. Tragic, thought Frankie, long before he was scattered across the Piccadilly Line by the detonation of a home-made brew of hydrogen peroxide and liquid oxygen.

'Don't be mean to me, Frankie. Don't be a wanky, Frankie.'

She delivers this plea in a baby voice, which darkens Frankie's mood afresh. He drapes his arm round her shoulders but says nothing.

'Do you still love me?' she whispers.

'I've still got wax in my ears.'

He digs into his ear to remove fictional remnants of the plugs. His responding to Roxy's drunken announcement a few weeks previously that she was in love with him with a reciprocal tribute – largely uttered through courtesy and drunkenness – seems to have resulted in the unspoken signing of an unspecified yet binding contract.

'It doesn't matter,' says Roxy.

'Shall we have some breakfast?'

'Why are you in such a bad mood?'

'What makes you think I'm in a bad mood?'

Roxy shrugs, picks up her phone and starts scrolling.

Frankie closes his eyes. Immediately drifting off, he tries to force his thoughts to straighten out, but whatever it is within him that does the thinking isn't listening to whatever does the willing. His mind chatters like a radio trying to find a signal. He has never really succeeded in making peace with what Veronica, his therapist ex-wife, would call his 'internal narrator'. Instead, the unseen voice badgers him, mocks him, criticizes him, rebukes him. As he sinks further towards sleep, images and memories are mixed with the scattered words chasing one another around inside his skull, mongrels pursuing their own tails. They are random, with no narrative glue to hold them together.

Roxy, ten years younger, dressed as a bowl of popcorn when she opened her short-lived gourmet popcorn shop in Portobello Road.

A ghostly bulletin seeps into the dreamworld from the office: Would the contract on Coningham Road go through?

Cue music.

My girl's name is Senora.

Had he made the follow-up call to the vendor? He can't remember.

I tell you friends, I adore her.

In an unconscious response to a physical hunger pang, a preview of that day's intended breakfast manifests — rashers of bacon, sausages, fried bread.

China, grown up now, the face she makes when she criticizes him for continuing to eat meat.

'It's a corpse dad. *A corpse.*'

Shake, shake, shake, Senora.

Harry Belafonte?

13

China's voice, five years old: *bungalow, bung bung a low.*

An image of Colin Burden, his childhood friend as well as Roxy's former husband, exploding into a thick mist of blood and bone.

Would he have baked beans?

My hands are high my feet are low and this is how I bungalow . . .

Probably, if they had a tin left. Didn't Roxy finish them for supp—

He is woken by the awareness of a faint sensation of movement to the side of his face. Opening his eyes, he sees that Roxy is gazing at Frankie's phone which had been resting in the space between their pillows.

'Give me that.'

'Madam hasn't been answering your texts again. That explains the sour mood.'

Frankie snatches the phone back. Roxy calmly picks up her tea and drains it.

'Don't call her "madam".'

'You're so touchy. And so needy. No wonder . . . '

'No wonder *what?*'

Roxy stares into the tea dregs as if searching for fortune.

'No wonder she tries to avoid you.'

Frankie taps at his phone, changing the password. He slams the phone on the side table, rattling the glass surface.

'I miss her. That's all it is.'

'I wasn't trying to get at you, Frankie.'

'Why do you think she's so angry with me?'

Roxy slides off the bed and stands up. There is a tea stain across the state of California on the American map that decorates the MAGA T-shirt. She makes her way across the

14

room to a chair which has a pair of Frankie's suit trousers folded over it. She sits on the chair and leans back.

'Apart from the fact that she's nineteen and nineteen-year-old girls are usually angry with one or both parents along with the world generally?'

'Apart from that. Can you try and not crease those trousers?'

Roxy stands again, then pulls off her T-shirt, depositing it in what she calls the 'ali' – the Ali Baba-styled laundry basket that stands under the window looking out on Golborne. Her body was still good, her breasts not sagging, her belly round but firm. Having no children does wonders for your figure, thinks Frankie, then reprimands himself, wondering if he has made a sexist remark, even if the remark is made only to himself.

Often nowadays, it feels to him like he was in church school in White City when he was a boy again and being told that everything he thought and felt, God could see and hear – and judged, largely, to be sinful. Only this time, it was a different god – equally judgemental but coming from the social ether around him rather than heaven. This god was less powerful, but more real, and did not make offers of forgiveness.

Roxy arches her back – ostensibly to yawn, but Frankie thinks it is really to preen herself in front of him. He feels no answering twitch from his loins. The blue pills that Roxy has been pressing him to purchase seem to be an option he cannot avoid for much longer. But he doesn't want a fake hard-on. Sometimes he wonders if he even wants a real one. It was all so much effort now that women had discovered their sexuality. Hard slog, the female orgasm, if the truth be known.

Was that thought sexist too? He pushes the speculation into a remote chamber in his mind marked 'Don't Know', an imagined vault where countless strata of unanswerable questions lay in tumbling, disordered piles. Some were merely dormant, waiting to once more rise up, prompted by the right word or circumstance. Others eventually decayed into non-existence or sank to the unreachable bottom of the pile, propelled by the force of time and events.

He watches as Roxy pushes her size 5 feet into a pair of green novelty crocodile slippers. They disconcert Frankie, as the jaws of the crocodile appear to be where the feet enter, leaving the impression that the sharp white felt teeth at each ankle are in the process of consuming the wearer's leg, having already begun digesting the feet.

'So, are you going to answer my question?'

'What question?'

'Why is China so angry with me?'

'You left her mother.'

'I didn't want to leave. Veronica threw me out.'

'Can you blame her? You made yourself and your family bankrupt.'

'She slept with my *friend*. No one ever mentions that, do they?'

'Tony wasn't your friend.'

'So it transpired. Anyway, that's hardly the point.'

'What is the point, then?'

'The point is, it wasn't *all* my fault. Nothing is ever completely one person's fault. Ask any marriage counsellor.'

'You can hardly expect China to see it that way.'

'Thanks for the support,' says Frankie sulkily.

Roxy stares out the sash window overlooking the busy street. On either side of the window are two posters, one an old movie poster of Henry Fonda in *12 Angry Men*, the other a framed photo of a green Lamborghini Huracan.

'I'm just being honest,' she says.

'Honesty is overrated.'

'You *would* think that. Because you're an estate agent, isn't it?'

Frankie exhales loudly and throws the yellowing white duvet off his side of the bed, suddenly aware of an acute need to piss. He feels pressure on his bladder more and more often nowadays. As often as not, he has to get up in the night. Prostate cancer, probably. He discards the thought quickly. The prospect of death pursues him nowadays like a predatory shadow. He wishes that, like Peter Pan, he could tear the shadow away.

He glances at the digital clock on the wall. At the second he does so, the minute counter slides from forty-five to forty-six minutes past the hour of eleven. He stretches, thinking how pleasant it is to be at home on a Friday. He has taken the day off work in anticipation of a hangover.

'She won't always be angry with you, Frankie.'

'She's managed it quite well for the last five years. When did she even come and stay with me last? August? I've managed to see her twice in the last six months, and on both those occasions it involved a 100-mile round trip in order to sit in a vegetarian restaurant and be used as an emotional dartboard.'

'She's busy. She has school. Or I suppose its uni now.'

'She doesn't have either. She's on a gap year. You know that.'

'I forgot. She has a job anyway.'

'Don't talk to me about jobs. She keeps quitting them. Never has one she considers good enough for her. Last I heard she was delivering pizza leaflets. The fact I give her fifty quid a week which I can ill afford cuts me no slack at all.'

'Can't buy me love.'

'Colin did.'

Roxy stares at him in disbelief. Frankie feels a gobbet of regret rise in his throat. He struggles to grasp the reason behind his casual spite.

'Sorry, Rocks. I didn't mean that.'

Roxy grabs her bathrobe – hooded with a fake leopard-skin collar – from the hook behind the bedroom door, walks into the hall and then into the bathroom, slamming the door behind her. Frankie drags himself out of bed, grabs his own bathrobe and pursues her.

'Rocks! I'm sorry. And I'm desperate to go. Let me in, would you?'

There is no answer. Frankie jiggles on the spot, checks his phone again to distract himself from the irresistible pressure on his bladder. Still no messages. It isn't for another four or five deeply uncomfortable minutes that Roxy leaves the bathroom. She walks past Frankie, who has been squirming and jumping up and down on the landing, then makes her way silently down the stairs.

Taking her place in the bathroom, Frankie squats on the toilet, pisses violently and then strains to evacuate his bowels. As so often happens lately, his colon refuses to co-operate. He briefly wonders if he has colon cancer as well as the hypothetical prostate cancer which he imagines is forcing him to urinate so frequently. He instructs himself to eat more fibre, while at the same time knowing that he will do nothing of the sort.

Anticipating a lengthy stretch of confinement, he picks up a *What Car?* magazine from the pile he has stacked on top of the cistern. He grabs one of the pairs of reading glasses from Poundland he leaves distributed randomly about the house and perches them on his nose.

Several of the cars in the latest issue have been circled by him in ballpoint pen. Frankie has decided to go for something around the 60K mark. He's almost saved enough. Loans are hard to come by for a former bankrupt, and anyway he never wants to get into debt again. His dream is to walk into a Mercedes showroom and pay in cash. A great thick wad, bulging inside an immaculate buff envelope. The salesman's eyes would widen when Frankie brought out the swathe of green.

Ten minutes later, finally having given up on any hope of evacuation, he wipes himself, then stands and washes his hands desultorily, staring at his face blankly in the mirror over the basin. The face that stares back at him seems to be disappointed at something or other. He notes that flecks of grey are starting to appear in the stubble. He dries his hands, then leaves the bathroom and heads down the stairs into the living room. Roxy is sitting reading, absorbed in that month's copy of *Vogue*. Frankie still carries his copy of *What Car?* in one hand and with the other idly scratches his balls.

'That's not very attractive,' says Roxy, without looking up.

'Sorry,' says Frankie.

'Stop doing it, then.'

'No. I mean I'm sorry for what I said.'

'It's fine,' says Roxy, turning the page of an ad for laboratory diamonds. She notices the magazine he is holding.

'Why are you so obsessed with getting a fancy car?'

Frankie puts the magazine on the table while he goes into the kitchen and starts to make himself coffee and toast.

'Why are you so obsessed with staring at fashion magazines? Anyway, I'm not obsessed.'

'You've been saving up for a flash wagon for years. What's the point?'

'I just think it will make me happy. Isn't that a good enough reason?'

'Hey, have you heard this one? What do you do with an old German car?'

'Don't know.'

'Put it in an old Volks home.'

Roxy stares at him expectantly, waiting for a response. He remains stony-faced. Usually he at least pretends to humour her. He pours the coffee from the French press and adds some milk.

'Look, Frankie. Happiness is like love. You can't buy it.'

The toast pops up and Frankie throws the slices onto his plate, careful not to singe his fingers.

'Any more clichés to offer up this morning? How about "what goes around comes around"? Or "time flies when you're having fun"?'

'The reason clichés are clichés is because . . . '

'Because they're true. That's *another* cliché. Yes, it's true money can't buy me happiness. But it can buy me a fuck-off Mercedes. That's close enough for me.'

'I think this obsession is a substitute for something else.'

'If I'd wanted a therapist for a partner I would have stayed married. I just always wanted a Mercedes. Simple as. Lots of men do. And now that I'm finally going to be getting a partnership at Farley & Ratchett, I'll be able to afford it. I'm fifty years old. Time to stop thinking about tomorrow and start enjoying myself.'

He scrapes butter and Marmite on the two slices of white bread. Thinking of his daily struggle to empty his bowels, he resolves, weakly, to substitute wholemeal in future.

'Time to think about yourself for a change?'

'Exactly.'

Roxy laughs, not unpleasantly but in genuine amusement. Frankie sits down and takes a bite from one of the slices of toast, chews and swallows quickly. Nothing to it but air and chemicals.

'What's so funny?'

'Nothing. I have to go. I'm late for the salon.'

'No but, what are you laughing about?'

'You should do stand-up, Frankie.'

She slides her copy of *Vogue* into the magazine rack, then makes her way back upstairs to get dressed, her gentle laughter tumbling down the stairs in her wake like bright polythene confetti.

On a bench on the Brighton seafront, a ragged figure moves herself slowly as she becomes aware of the policeman standing over her on the bench, coughing politely. She opens her eyes and recognizes the intractability of the situation. Daytrippers are beginning to appear, even on this winter's day. They – whoever 'they' are, although they clearly include the police – don't like rough sleepers near the main attraction of the Palace Pier.

The woman feels for the laundry bag under the bench. It is there, stuffed and zipped, untouched overnight. She throws the sleeping bag off and sits up. The policeman says nothing. He does not look unkind, but he does not move either.

She catches the odour of herself and grimaces, then belches, sending out a cloud of foul air which dissipates quickly in the ozone. She sees the policeman, who is swaying back and forth on his heels, open his mouth to speak, but pre-empts him.

'I'm going.' Her voice is classless, raspy, low but oddly penetrating.

'I was going to ask you if you wanted a cup of tea,' says the policeman, ending his rocking motion. He gestures towards a refreshment stall ten yards away.

'Alright.'

The man turns and walks to the kiosk. The woman stretches and yawns, briefly unzips her bag to see that every-thing is still there. There are unwashed clothes, a toilet bag, a pair of shoes, an unread book – a novel by Minette Walters that she found in the rubbish bin – an uncharged mobile phone and a mess of clutter that she can't be bothered to identify. She gathers up her sleeping bag and secures it into the shape of a Swiss roll.

The policeman returns with the tea. He also has what looks like a chocolate muffin in a paper bag. He hands both to her and she takes them without meeting his eyes.

'Rough night?'

'Had better.'

She bites into the muffin. It tastes stale, but the hot tea is good, although she could have used a bit more sugar.

'Do you want the address of a hostel?'

The woman shakes her head, producing a spray of crumbs from her still-full mouth.

'Not staying.'

She wonders what the hell she is doing here in the first place, then remembers. Her friend of three weeks, Ugly Sue, decided during a drunken binge that she wanted to go to the seaside. The woman, also drunk, agreed, and they begged some money and got the coach from London to Brighton, partly because the woman knew the streets and partly because Ugly Sue, once she got an idea in her head, never would shake it off. They even started to paint their nails purple as if it was some kind of party, but got quickly bored and threw the varnish bottle at a brick wall, just to watch it shatter.

An hour after they had arrived on the coach from Victoria, Sue had met with another rough sleeper on the esplanade who fancied himself a dandy. He had a folded handkerchief in the top pocket of what once might have been an expensive jacket and a whole bottle of Grey Goose. That was the last she had seen of Ugly Sue.

That had been two days ago, and although she'd hung around, half hoping to reconnect with Sue, she didn't much like Brighton. Too many memories. Also hard to find a connection. Also too small, the police and the do-gooders could find her easily and try to rouse her out of her sodden blur. But she had no wish to be resurrected. Why couldn't they understand that, whoever they were?

'Do you have somewhere to go?' asks the policeman.

The woman nods and takes a swig of the tea. She stares past him at the sea. It is the colour of dough.

'Alright, then. I'm watching you, though,' he says pleasantly. It doesn't sound like a threat, but, the woman thinks, it probably is.

Once the policeman is out of sight, she finishes her tea, drops the paper bag the muffin came in and the empty polystyrene cup on the pavement, although there is a rubbish bin ten feet away, and heads for Brighton coach station. A few hours later, she is in Victoria again and heading for her old haunts.

The ping of a message alert on her iPhone interrupts the remnants of China Blue's crying jag. She is now spreadeagled like a starfish on her single bed, having displaced Kardashian once more. The struts and posts themselves are decorated with outdated and peeling stickers – Powerpuff Girls, *The Amazing World of Gumball*, One Direction, red hearts, fluorescent plastic stars and cute cartoon animals with enormous eyes. She had wanted the fancy bed for her twelfth birthday, has long outgrown it but somehow cannot bring herself to replace it.

Face stuffed down into the pillow, she can hardly be bothered to check who the text is from, let alone trouble herself to respond. She assumes the message is another condolence text. Her friends have been sending them all morning, decorated with weeping or nauseous or furious emojis. She is tired of them. They won't make any difference to anything. Her mood is not helped by the sharp intrusions of period cramps. Her cycle started the previous day, and she knows that she can expect three more days of discomfort and dull aching in her lower back and abdomen.

She drags herself out of bed, removes and discards a bloody tampon, replaces it with a fresh one, then returns to her soft cave under the covers. The phone sounds again, then again. Reluctantly, she hauls herself into a partially upright position and inspects the screen through the map of spidery cracks it acquired when it fell out of her pocket during her daily run two weeks ago. There were three texts displayed.

Are you OK? – Dad.

Can we talk? – Dad.

The third was yet another crying emoji – also from her father.

She tosses the phone to one side and buries her face back into her pillow. It smells of tobacco smoke and hydroponic weed from the joint she had sucked on last night, her face pushed out of her bedroom window, as the results for the Labour Party dipped to catastrophic levels.

Her mother wouldn't be angry about the spliff – she knows Veronica and Frankie used to smoke weed sometimes – but Silas, her stepfather, will make some kind of embarrassing joke if he notices it. And he will notice it, since while cultivating the demeanour of an 'Occupy' activist – which he once was – he retains the puritanical sensibility of a volunteer policeman.

The pungent vapour of the weed gets everywhere, penetrates everything. At least the odour in the room will dissipate eventually. If only she could flush a different toxicity out of herself. Be cleansed of Englishness – of shame, of self-pity, of guilt, of bombast, of atomization. But it is impossible.

She presumes that her father is going to pretend he is upset the Conservatives have triumphed. She decides in advance not to believe him. She hasn't believed anything he says about anything for years. 'Frankie the Fib', her mother, Veronica, once told her, was her father's nickname when she met him back in the 1990s. Veronica thinks it is funny. China finds it disgusting – another flake torn from the pristine varnish with which she had once lovingly coated a private hagiography of her father.

Now if she imagines a depiction of him, it is vandalized and torn – the only difference from actual vandalism being that the damage has come from within. Her father has defaced his own image simply by being who he is and being unable to hide it – as China emerged, painfully, year by year, from the bright, false amusement park of childhood.

Apart from anything else, her father was an estate agent. It was embarrassing. Estate agents, China knew, were among the prime beneficiaries of capitalism. So he would hardly have voted for Jeremy Corbyn. Perhaps the Lib Dems at a stretch. Not that, in her mind, they were any better than the Tories. The university fees that she was going to have to take loans to cover the following September when her gap year ended were causing her anxiety already, and she held the Lib Dems responsible.

Interrupting her thoughts, from somewhere beneath the uncarpeted floorboards of her first-floor bedroom comes the cry of a complaining child – answered with the soft response of his ever-patient, ever-pleading, ever-negotiating father. The bleater is Mason Foale, twelve, and the pleader, Silas Foale, age unconfirmed (China guesses fifty-five rather than the fifty he claims). They are her stepbrother and stepfather in effect, since her mother and Silas have been cohabiting for seven years.

If she applied blinkers carefully enough, China can imagine what her mother saw in Silas. He was cookie-cutter. The careful use of sentences trimmed to remove offence or controversy. The copies of Bernardine Evaristo and Rebecca Solnit on his homemade bookcase – unread so far as China could make out, stored next to well-thumbed carpentry manuals as well as books on British military history, guides on running a successful small business and several volumes of popular science.

Silas Foale was tall, he was athletic, he cycled and swam, and meditated for twenty minutes every day. He supported the right causes, marched on the appropriate marches. He volunteered at a food bank once a fortnight. He was a guitarist in a pub band that had a good local reputation. The band, 'Black Axis', although all white (except for a Hispanic – no, *LatinX* – keyboard player), were known for their reggae covers, which included obscure Ska rarities, some Burning Spear reworks and a couple of Linton Kwesi Johnson tributes.

Silas avoided charges of cultural appropriation with a deft manoeuvre. He claimed to be black, although his skin was verging on the pasty. According to Silas, his father, Vitalis – whom neither Veronica nor China had ever met – had come to escape the sugar cane fields of St Lucia, only to find himself in the West of England, Bristol, home of slave traders, half a mile under the earth toiling for industrialists who sought profit from coal, instead of plantation owners extracting sugar from the land.

Vitalis, having married Carol, a white laundry worker from Knowle, the toughest part of an otherwise prosperous town, eventually set himself up in a hardware shop, and by the time he died, ten years ago, had three branches in the West of

England and had accrued enough resources to send his only child, Silas, to private school. Carol, apparently grief-stricken, died six months after Vitalis.

Silas had moved to Brighton after his father died and started work as a 'gentleman carpenter', as he would have it, in and around London. His inheritance from his father purchased the Brighton house. Despite his expensive education, he was not academically minded and preferred to work with his hands. It was on one of his carpentry jobs that he had met China's mother, at her grandmother's house in Buckinghamshire, where China and Veronica had landed up with the ever-bickering Cordelia and Michael, after Frankie had rendered them penniless. Silas was building wardrobes and Veronica made him cups of tea, then brought him glasses of wine, and, as she usually abbreviated the subsequent process when reminiscing, *one thing led to another.*

The altercation taking place on the ground floor beneath China's bedroom increases in volume – the only noise insulation being a cheap, once-fluffy white rug that extended from the door to the foot of the bed. Or it had been white before China's indifference to hygiene and personal organization had transformed it. Now there are faint stains from herbal tea, kimchi, carrot juice and pesto, none of which can quite be erased by the repeated journeys to the washing machine, which have more or less flattened most of the fluff into a matted, smooth veldt. Elsewhere, distributed across the floor are hair straighteners, several pairs of jogging trousers, scattered trainers, a half-eaten packet of plain chocolate digestives, a scattered box of tampons, three empty coffee cups and a dozen or so pens and pencils sprinkled across virgin A4 cartridge paper. Each of the three drawers in the pine wooden chest hangs half open, with items of clothing – knickers, tights, T-shirts – overflowing.

Silas's pleading, although the words cannot be made out through the barrier of the floorboards, displays its infuriating tone of quiet, rational, patient common sense. Irritated, China rises reluctantly from her bed and takes her diary out of the back of the drawer of the nightstand where it lies vaguely concealed under several layers of buff folders. Taking a Uni-ball, she opens the diary and starts to write, pressing too hard on the paper, making scarifications in the wood pulp. There is a tap on the door. China puts the diary and pen back in her drawer, closes it, jumps back into bed and pulls the covers over her head.

'China? China girl? Can I come in?'

China remains silent and inert, hoping this will discourage the visitor. Disappointingly, she hears the door creak open and then her mother pacing across the room. She knows it is Veronica without hearing her voice, because even at this distance, under these layers, she can detect the faint scent of the pungent neem and turmeric soap her mother uses to wash her hands.

What is neem anyway? thinks China randomly, then burrows further into the bedclothes. There is a creak as Veronica seats herself on the vintage armchair, recovered from the skip and painstakingly restored by Silas, that stands to the left of her bed. Beyond the chair is a dark wood Ercol-inspired John Lewis dressing table, out of place among the childish trappings of the rest of the room. The table has a mirror built in and it reflects a lava lamp that sits forlornly on the surface.

The lava lamp is broken. Mason broke it in the summer, trying to take it apart so he could examine the mixture of water, dye and paraffin wax. Silas had had one of his *little chats* with him afterwards, but had been sympathetic to his son, putting the transgression down to the workings of a curious, probing mind rather than the act of pure mischief that China frames it as. To China, Mason's mind was as curious and probing as one of the Mars Bars he compulsively helped himself to, contributing to his ever-swelling physique. Not that she was fat-shaming, but the kid was a whale.

Veronica, having entered, regards the gently rising and falling hillock under the bedclothes through the semi-transparency of the pale muslin curtain. She has little doubt about the reason for China's reluctance to face the world. She had felt much the same when she had awoken four hours previously, but with five therapy sessions to conduct that afternoon, she has too many commitments to allow the disappointment to immobilize her.

'It's not so bad,' says Veronica, just loud enough for China to make out through the bedcovers. She pulls back one of the wispy curtains to clarify the image of her daughter's silhouette.

'Isn't it?' says China audibly, albeit into her pillow which is damp from tears and spittle.

'It's not *great*. But everything will keep ticking over. I've brought you a cup of green tea. I've put some Manuka in it.'

Throwing back the covers and raising herself from the pillow, China accepts the mug, which announces its colour as Pantone Blue 19-4052. Her father bought it for Veronica as a birthday present two years ago. He still bought her birthday presents even though they had been divorced for nearly a decade. Frankie got a lot of mileage out of their surname when it came to gifts – *Kind of Blue* by Miles Davis, *The Blue Room* poster by Picasso, and most recently *The Bluest Eye* by Toni Morrison. Veronica, however, had long since reverted to her maiden name, Tree – part of the reason China had the arboreal tattoo etched on her lower back.

'Don't forget that . . .' begins Veronica, not sure how she is going to finish, but determined to trick China out of her despair.

'It's my *future*.'

'I'm just saying that . . .'

'*What?* What *are* you saying?'

'That we live in a democracy and we have to . . .'

'The trouble with democracy is that most voters are cunts.'

Veronica checks the time on China's novelty clock, which is faced with a tumble of random numbers and the legend 'Whatever, I'm Late Anyway'. Veronica, after a few moments trying to decode the time through the jumble of numbers, registers that she is going to have to leave for work shortly.

'I take your point.'

Veronica has been no less upset than her daughter by the ascendancy and then triumph of Boris Johnson, but, unlike China, had struggled mightily to put her cross next to the party of Jeremy Corbyn. But she had done so in the end. What was the alternative? The Greens? The way they ran Brighton, their only parliamentary seat, was chaotic. Anyway, it turns out that – she reflects – for the overwhelming majority of voters, Boris Johnson *was* the alternative.

China takes another sip of the tea. It is so weak as to be taste-less, apart from the honey. This is not, in her mind, an entirely bad thing. It indicates to China that it is probably good for her. Things that were bland or unpleasant usually were, or so she has come to believe. After sipping the tea, she takes a draught of water from the HydrateM8 bottle on her side table, starting her fulfilment of her two litres a day of pure water minimum.

'What's going on with Silas and the Beelzebrat?' she mutters, swallowing another teaspoon's worth of the tea.

'He has a name.'

'Mason. Macy. Mad Macy.'

'Going on in what sense?'

'It sounded like he was having another one of his tantrums.'

'He's calmed down.'

'What's his problem this time?'

'He's only twelve years old. That's his problem. He has issues.'

'*Ish-shoos.*'

'He hasn't got a mother.'

'So?'

'Come on, China, you're better than this.'

Veronica pats China on the back of the hand. China carelessly puts down the tea on the side table on the other side of the bed, spilling part of it in the process. She flings her head back into the pillow, face first. Veronica can just make out a muffled complaint.

'I'm not better than this! I *am* this!'

Veronica rises and dabs at the spilled tea with a Kleenex taken from a box on the dressing table, sits down again, then waits in silence. After thirty seconds, China emerges from the pillow. Veronica is now breathing with such forced deliberation that China feels sure her mother is putting into practice one of the relaxation techniques she has recently learned on her Headspace app.

'Dad texted me,' says China, obscurely annoyed by her mother's regular, accentuated breathing. 'He claims to be disappointed with the election results.'

'Oh yes?'

'Just trying to curry favour,' says China. 'I'm sure he's delighted at the result.'

'Not necessarily. Your father is – well, politically neutral. More or less. As far as I can gather.'

'You mean he couldn't care less, so long as he gets his pay cheque. He's not exactly going to be manning the barricades when the time comes.'

'Selling them, more like,' says Veronica.

'At unreasonably inflated prices,' says China. She manages a faint laugh. 'Sorry, I'm being such a bitch.'

'You're not. It's okay.'

China looks at her mother's face full on. The face is drawn, but she still looks okay for her fifty years. Did the creases on your face really reveal your accrued personality? There are laugh lines at the corner of Veronica's eyes. Or were they frown lines? China finds it hard to tell. But her overall impression is of someone stoic and unbowed, if somewhat weary and, China guesses, not as fulfilled as she had once hoped to be by this age.

The door opens again – no knock this time – and Silas enters, wearing faded blue OshKosh overalls, a Muji collarless jerkin, rubber-soled boots, and looking like the overgrown infant China casts him as in her private family melodrama. His expression is open as usual, but somehow, thinks China, artificially so, like a full-blown plastic flower. His eyes slide about like eels, never quite meeting those of whoever he is talking to, except fitfully. The only exception is when he is angry. Then he looks right at you and his eyes blaze.

He stops and sniffs the air shaking his head, his still-plentiful brown curls flopping around flaccidly as if defeated by the perpetual effort to remain as pert, shiny and tight as they had been when Veronica and China had first encountered him, planing planks of wood in Grandma's garden in Buckinghamshire.

'Been at the waccy baccy again, bud?' he says, glancing amiably at China.

Policeman, thinks China. Veronica shoots Silas a glance. She, too, has smelled the pungency of the extinguished joint, but has mustered the tact to say nothing. They will discuss it later. Veronica and Silas talk with a frequency and depth she and Frankie never managed, but somehow don't seem to understand one another any better for it.

'No problem, Chi Chi. Just save a sprig for *moi*.'

He grins, showing crooked teeth, two of which on the lower rack are missing, although the gaps can only be seen when he smiles.

'I thought you hated smoking,' says Veronica. She has given up her enjoyment of the occasional cigarette – at least when Silas was around – to pacify his hatred of smokers, whom he categorizes as anti-social, pollution-spreading vandals.

'I hate tobacco, to be specific. Ganja is part of my culture.'

China, discomfited by this attempt by Silas to forge camaraderie with her, simply stares at him mutely. He continues to grin back, the smile eventually taking on an unsettling fixity. Then Silas slides his eyes critically over her bed. The stickers were peeling as well as the pink paint.

'You should get rid of that bed. What are you, twelve?' says Silas. 'I could make you a new one.'

'No, thanks.'

'It's a bit – you know – *young* for you?'

'My heritage.'

A sound of thumping starts from downstairs. Mason, China speculates, is taking his frustration out on the sofa cushions.

'What were you fighting with Mason about?' she says. 'And why isn't he at school, anyway?'

'We weren't fighting. We were just working something out between us. He's not at school because he's taking a mental health day off. The school allows it. He's feeling a bit edgy. I'm going to take him on my current job. Try and get him to learn a bit of carpentry. Physical activity calms him.'

'Anything you'd like to share? About the argument?'

'No secrets in this household.'

Silas just continues smiling, though, as if it solves all puzzles, dissolves all mysteries. China knows that any important information will have to be painstakingly excavated.

'Carry on.'

'It's not really important.'

'I thought you just said no secrets.'

'It's not a secret.'

'Just tell her what you were arguing about, Si,' interjects Veronica, an edge in her voice. She finds herself snapping at him far more than she used to. She dismisses this as inevitable. People are always annoying when you get to know them well enough.

Silas looks only mildly hurt. He turns to China with a serious, concerned expression.

'Mason was just a little disappointed about Christmas.'

'In what sense?'

She sees a dark ember, dully glowing in the back of his eyes.

'I had to break it to him that I wasn't going to get him the Nerf Super Soaker.'

China stares back blankly.

'It's a water cannon. You know – a toy one,' says Silas.

'I presumed you didn't mean one of those that the riot police use.'

'No, no, of course not,' says Silas, his smile disappearing.

'Why not?'

'Why not what?' said Silas pleasantly, hitching up his overalls, then scratching his butt unashamedly. To conceal one's animality was against Silas's liberal, green, grassroots principles. He sometimes left the door open when he was doing a shit.

'Why aren't you . . . ?'

'Why isn't *Santa*,' corrects Silas conspiratorially.

'Why isn't *Santa*, who Mason hasn't believed in since he was five, going to bring him a toy water cannon?'

Silas stops scratching himself and instead tugs at his left ear, a tic that often appears when sensing any imminent conflict.

'It's a bit aggressive, wouldn't you say?'

'He's twelve. He's not going to go out and buy an Uzi and start spraying year 8.'

'It is what it is. But it's the principle.' Silas smiles again. He has such a wide palette of smiles, all of them, to China, unconvincing – encouraging, sympathetic, curious, engaged. 'I had a long talk with him about aggression, and war, and weapons of war, and I think I deepened his understanding. He's taking it on board. He can be surprisingly receptive for someone with learning difficulties.'

More thumping can be heard from downstairs, more urgent this time.

'Sounds like it. So what are you getting him instead?'

'A punchbag.'

'No, but really, though. What are you getting him?'

'Like I said – I'm getting him a punchbag.'

China examines Silas's face to see if she can find traces of irony. But he is deadpan.

'He can't have a water pistol, but he can have a punchbag?'

'There are healthy ways to channel aggression, Chi.'

'Can you not call me "Chi" please? My name's China.'

'I didn't mean to offend you.'

'It's not offensive, "Si". It's simply annoying.'

'I didn't mean to annoy you, then. Sorry.'

'That's annoying too.'

'What is?'

'The way that you're always apologizing when you don't really mean it.'

Silas looks at Veronica, dredging her face with his eyes, looking, apparently, for support. Veronica, trapped as ever between poles of her life, keeps her expression neutral. Silas turns back to China and holds his raised hands out towards her, palms open, elbows bent. Even his body language, thinks China, manages to be patronizing.

'I'm just doing my best. It's not easy trying to keep the peace and at the same time inculcate the sense of some kind of values in Macy.'

Veronica picks up the now-empty tea mug from the chair, and moves towards the door. Silas, considering the matter settled now, turns to follow her.

Just before he closes the door gently behind him, he turns and looks at China.

'Don't forget to save me some of that sprig, bud.'

He winks.

'By the way, you haven't got that £20 I lent you last week, have you?' he adds.

'Not on me.'

'No worries. But if I could have it sometime today, that would be good. I'm a bit pinched for funds at the moment.'

With that he goes, closing the door behind him. China considers her next move. Veronica and Silas will both leave for work soon. Silas is taking Mason with him on the job. She starts to ruffle though her bag. Makeup. Credit cards. A packet of Mentos. Crumbs. Eventually she finds at the bottom her wrap of grass. She digs it out along with papers and a plastic grinder. Putting the hook into the ring that lightly secures her bedroom door from the inside, she takes a lump of green and begins to grind it.

Downstairs, Silas checks his watch – still fifteen minutes before he has to leave – sits at the kitchen table and opens his computer, a cheap PC plagued with viruses, while Veronica clears up. China has left a mess after last night's TV marathon. He squints at the computer screen. He has long needed reading glasses, but is too vain to get his eyes tested, insisting against all the evidence that he has 20/20 vision.

'What are you doing?' says Veronica, swilling out China's teacup. She grimaces as she spots a curd of mould at the bottom.

'Finishing off the monthly accounts.'

Veronica tenses slightly as Silas looks up. She recognizes the cast of his expression. Such pointed glances are most common this time of the month, when the nitty gritty of finances are routinely picked over, and particularly apparent at Christmas when money is especially tight.

'I don't want to make a fuss, Veronica, but you've barely used the gym membership that you paid for out of the joint account.'

'You told me to get myself a present for my birthday.'

'I didn't think it was going to be a present that cost £300 that was never going to get used. It is what it is, but it seems a bit of a waste.'

'Are you saying you think I need to go to the gym?'

His slightly bulging eyes bulge further. The light from the steel hanging lamp above him, switched on because of the poor light of the now-overcast day, gives his face a saturnine appearance.

'I didn't mean that.'

'You're saying I'm fat.'

'Not at all. Although . . . '

He picks up a circular table mat made of recycled paper and picks at the edge of it with a cracked fingernail. Then he brings the nail to his teeth and bites off the end, leaving a ragged strip. The detached scrap of nail he swallows.

'Although *what*?'

'When you asked for gym membership you told me you were getting out of shape.'

'There's nothing wrong with my shape. A gym membership is about getting fit, not your shape.'

'No, I know, but . . . '

'So you only gave me gym membership so that you could have

something smaller to look at. For yourself, in other words. Just keep digging, Silas, why don't you. Here's a shovel.'

Silas's eyes flick back to the computer and he squints again to make out the figures that fill his screen. He tries to Google search 'Gym Membership Fees' but gets a message 'Unfortunately Google Search is Not Working, Please Contact Your Server'.

'Sugar. This fricking thing is glitching again.'

'Is that all you've got to say?'

'You're perfect just as you are, Vronky,' says Silas, without looking up from his screen. His eyebrows are knitted, his eyes milky. Veronica, pretending to be appeased, leaves the kitchen and heads back upstairs to prepare for the afternoon therapy sessions. Silas labours at getting the Google search to work. The wasted £300 still niggles. So does the £20 that China owes him. He tries to make a note on his computer to pursue her for it, but the Notes app isn't working.

'Frick,' breathes Silas, returning his gaze to the Excel spreadsheet which, despite refreshing successfully, stubbornly refuses to improve the financial picture it presents.

December 2019: London

There are only three people using the outdoor gym on Tiverton Green in Brondesbury. It is otherwise deserted, since it is cold and there is rain in the air which has chased most of the other regulars away.

The middle-aged man on the sit-up bench is panting heavily as he pulls himself vertical once more. He is maybe ten pounds overweight with a round, doughy face made rounder by the fact that his hair, entirely receded, is cropped close to the skull. Next to him, on a Sky Stepper, which mimics the activity of walking, is his husband, about the same age. This man is taller, heavily bearded and humming 'Three Little Maids From School Are We' from *The Mikado*. A third, older man, in his early sixties, labours on a fixed bicycle. He is elegant, with sharp cheekbones, long thick white hair brushed back and an abstracted, kindly expression.

'Driscoll and Drysdale. Sounds like a firm of dodgy lawyers,' says the man on the bicycle, pausing for breath and regarding his two companions fondly. He dismounts from the bicycle and fumbles for his cigarettes.

'What's that, JJ?' says Jon – known to all his friends as 'Nodge' – as he struggles to raise his body again from its prone position. JJ, the older man, habitually speaks in a lazy semi-mumble and constantly has to repeat himself.

'I said, Owen Driscoll and Jon Drysdale – it sounds like a firm of lawyers.'

JJ is tall – 6'2". He has a soft, musical voice and is slightly theatrical in his presentation, a residue of the now-defunct gay culture in which he came of age. He has a Nat Sherman cigarette, imported from New York, hanging out the side of his mouth, and a tattoo of a merman with a bulging, muscled torso, a long tail and a sailor hat on his left bicep.

Owen met JJ some years ago at the local amateur dramatic society he belongs to. He is a GP, retired, not been on the scene for years, perfectly happy on his own as far as either Nodge or Owen can make out, living in a tidy little cottage overlooking Queen's Park in north-west London with three cats – Bibbety, Bobbety and Boo – and a terrified rabbit in the garden, constantly in fear of feline attack.

He isn't a particularly good-looking man, his beaky nose and thin white lips sabotage any potential charm, but his eyes are kindly and intelligent. He has a very faint Irish burr and cadence to his voice, although his family left County Down before he was born, sixty-five years ago.

JJ lights his Nat Sherman and takes a deep inhalation.

'God, JJ, you're a *doctor*,' says Nodge, pausing in his exertions as JJ blows out smoke into the cold air. 'What are you doing smoking anyway?'

'Ah, I don't know. It's sort of a habit,' he says, blowing a perfect smoke ring.

'We get that.'

'When you get to nearly seventy you sort of can't be arsed anymore. Being born and dying, it's all the same as my old mother used to say, haha.' JJ has a nervous habit of laughing mirthlessly at the end of his sentences. 'Anyway – I'm not a doctor anymore, am I?'

'That's stupid,' says Owen. 'Birth isn't the same as death. And you aren't nearly seventy. And you are still a doctor even if you've retired.'

'I dare say,' breathes JJ, unoffended. He sucks on the cigarette again, checks his 1930s Rolex. 'But it's part of the same thing, process, whatever. Yin and yang, you know, all that.'

'Death is death and birth is birth,' says Owen.

'If you say so,' responds JJ, moving further away out of earshot, worrying that his smoke will disturb the other two. Neither Owen nor Nodge can quite make out his words. Owen stops pedalling and looks meaningfully at Nodge, who has gone back to lowering and raising himself.

'What shall I do with the fag end?' calls JJ, holding up a

filter blackened by nicotine and tar. 'I don't want to besmirch the immaculation of the recreation ground.'

Owen indicates the litter bin in the corner of the exercise area. JJ walks over, flicks it in and looks back at them. There is fondness in his gaze. Owen climbs off the Sky Stepper as Nodge disentangles himself from the sit-up bench. He stands stiffly at Nodge's side. JJ walks slowly towards them.

'What the Jesus is wrong with the two of you? You look like a pair of stuffed dummies. And you, Owen, it's your face that's gone red.'

'Something about that death and birth thing. I can't really explain.'

'What about it, haha? You're making no sense.'

'We're going to be fathers.'

Nodge glances at him sharply. Owen catches the look and shrugs.

'That just sort of slipped out. You're the first to know,' says Owen.

There is a heavy silence. Owen reaches for Nodge's hand, but he can't find it. JJ speaks again in barely a whisper.

'Well, I'm nothing special. I don't know what you want to be telling me for.'

'You said that birth and death are the same. And they're not. And you *are* special. You're our friend. The only one we really share.'

'Apart from Frankie,' says Nodge.

'He's *your* friend, Nodge.'

JJ looks puzzled. He thrusts his hands into his lilac tracksuit bottoms and grabs his groin from the inside, exploring it as if it were uncharted territory.

'I need to get some sweatproof underpants, I reckon,' he mutters.

JJ seems to realize that his remark is insufficient and trite.

'You're going to be fathers, then, are you?' he says even more softly than usual. But giving their full attention now, Owen and Nodge clearly hear what he says.

'We're going to adopt,' says Owen. 'We've got the papers and everything. Just fighting our way through all the bureaucracy.'

Now JJ breaks into a broad, if – Nodge thinks – slightly forced grin, showing nicotine-stained teeth that are nevertheless regular and all intact.

'Now then. That's extremely terrific.'

He walks over and hugs each of them in turn.

'I love the smell of that perfume you wear. It goes so well with perspiration,' says Owen.

'Eau de toilette. Terre d'Hermès. When was this decided upon, then?'

'Months ago,' says Owen.

'Yes,' says Nodge.

'I nagged Nodge until he finally gave in.'

'That's not fair,' says Nodge.

Owen searches for Nodge's hand again and finds it this time.

'Come on now, Nodge. You can't say it's been a lifelong ambition for you.'

'I'm fine with it.'

'"I'm fine with it" isn't exactly a ringing declaration of enthusiasm.'

'I want you to be happy, Owen. That's all that matters to me.'

Nodge squeezes Owen's hand. Owen does not return the pressure.

'That's all very touching. In fact – it's very fantastic,' says JJ. 'I'm happy for you both. Tell you what. Why don't I nip out on the way back to the ranch and buy us a bottle of bubbles? I'll get myself a shower and drop by after. If you're allowed to drink when you're expecting, haha.'

'That would be great,' says Nodge.

JJ nods and picks up his steel-grey goosedown jacket, hung over an exercise bar, and strides towards the park exit where his bike is chained, a clunky Dutch number which sits incongruously next to Nodge and Owen's carbon road bikes. As soon as he is out of earshot, Owen turns towards Nodge.

'Are you annoyed with me?'

Nodge is feeling his midriff, trying to work out if his stomach muscles have hardened at all.

'A little bit. I haven't even told Frankie yet. It feels a bit of a betrayal to tell you the truth. I didn't think we were ready to go public.'

Owen settles his leg on the low wall that borders the gym and stretches out his calf muscles.

'Just got the urge. Don't know what came over me. Keeping it a secret too long. Somehow speaking the words makes it more real. You can phone Frankie and tell him now if you like. I don't want to cause ripples.'

'Doesn't matter. Yeh, I will do later. I should. No, but – I thought you were annoyed with *me*. I'm sure I felt tension – after I said I just wanted you to be happy.'

'I didn't notice. Well – I did notice a *bit* of tension. But I thought it came from JJ.'

'JJ? Why would it come from JJ?'

Owen, finishing his stretches, looks at Nodge, scrunching his face up. Nodge always thinks he looks like a walnut when he does this, brown, crinkled, expressionless.

'JJ's always wanted to adopt. He doesn't want to do it alone, but he's never found the right person to do it with. And he's old. And lonely.'

'Who isn't?'

'Us.'

Owen touches the back of Nodge's hand. They hold one another, chest to chest, and kiss. A passing teenager on a stunt bike wolf-whistles. Owen gives him the finger and they carry on kissing.

Back at their flat, a gated development in Kensal Rise, all flowered courtyards and Japanese-style balconies, Owen and Nodge have showered and are now dressed in pristine Selvedge jeans and bright white T-shirts. There is absolutely no clutter in their flat. Everything within is placed with an exact purpose. French windows lead to a balcony looking over the London skyline. Books cover half of one wall, perfectly catalogued and in order. The sofas are not bulgy and welcoming but have clean, geometric lines. An expensive early twentieth-century rug is the only real colour. The rest is white, brown and grey. Even the prints on the wall – prints of Rothko – are largely black with a red bordering.

There is a ring at the doorbell. When Owen opens it, JJ stands there with two bottles of Krug. He wears a bespoke tweed suit that hangs on his bony frame perfectly, and a pair of polished brown brogues.

'Nice whistle,' says Owen.

'I thought I should honour the occasion. I've even combed my hair.'

He lopes into the room, pushes his fingers through his luxurious white locks.

'You've still got plenty to comb. More than me and Nodge put together.'

'Hard to measure something like that, I expect. Anyway, hair envy notwithstanding, haha, this should put us all in the mood for celebration.'

'We haven't got approval yet,' says Owen. 'We're just in the system.'

'Ah, it'll be a shoo-in. I know a little bit about adoption, because GPs often have to be involved. You two are prime candidates. Far as I can make out they're all desperate to show their liberal credentials by signing up a few queers. How long does the process take?'

'Be grateful if you could keep this to yourself anyway,' says Nodge. 'We were a bit premature in making the announcement.'

'They reckon we could have our tiny lodger in three to six months,' says Owen. 'We have a key meeting about it in the New Year. Then we'll know one way or another, but it's all looking good from what we can tell.'

Nodge fetches three crystal champagne flutes from the glass-fronted cabinet next to the Corian sink and gives one to Owen as JJ gets ready to open the bottle.

'Never mind about hair, lovely though mine is. It's you that I have the envy for,' says JJ. He pops the bottle and the cork slams into the ceiling. They laugh as it rebounds and bounces off Owen's head like a ping-pong ball on a melon. Owen finds the cork and puts it in a steel litter bin under a nest of Deco coffee tables. JJ fills the glasses.

'I envy whoever your child turns out to be. They are very, very lucky to have a couple like you fellers raising them up.'

'You're kind,' says Nodge.

JJ downs his champagne in a single swallow then immediately pours himself another glass.

'Down the hatch.'

'Slow down, JJ,' says Owen.

'I'm a little nervous to tell you the truth, haha. Not sure why. It's not me who's having a kid.'

'Don't worry – we're not going to force you to babysit,' says Nodge.

'Thanks Jesus for that mercy. No, it's not that. Look. I just wanted to ask you fellers to do me a little favour. Or I planned to anyway, before you gave me the news. It may not be the best time to ask. I don't want to take advantage of your good mood. But, then, it's been playing on my mind.'

He thrusts his hands into the pockets of his tweed jacket as if the touch of the lining will give him reassurance.

'Ask us anything,' says Owen.

'More than happy to be taken advantage of,' says Nodge.

'I'm having some works done at my house sometime towards the early spring. Just a week or three it should be, but they are going to pull down some inner walls and it's going to be a total crime scene. So I've got to relocate temporarily.'

Instead of speaking any further, JJ simply stands there, clenching and unclenching his fists inside the pockets.

'You want to stay here?' says Owen.

'Would it be an awful imposition? I hate to ask, but I don't fancy a hotel. Obviously only if it's before your new arrival.'

'We'd welcome it,' says Nodge, putting his hand on JJ's narrow left shoulder and giving it a slight squeeze. 'Really we would. You can sleep in the nursery. I'll set up a cot for you.'

'You are princes. Princes among men. Would you have one of them mobiles that hang from the ceiling I could tinkle by any chance? And a nightlight perhaps. I do get scared of that dark. It's the monsters that concern me, the ones under the bed.'

'No such thing,' says Owen.

'As my old mother used to say, there's plenty of monsters you can't see. They're the worst ones.'

JJ examines Owen and Nodge closely, darting his small bright dappled eyes with their heavy thatch of greying brow and wrinkles piled below like blown desert sandbanks, from one to another in quick succession as if looking for signs that they might have been forced into polite acceptance of his request. Finally, convinced that they are being sincere, he nods firmly as if to seal the contract.

'Thank you, boys. I'm very much appreciative.'

His smile holds firm, but his hands remain inside his pockets, fists gripped tight as if trying to throttle something invisible.

Chapter Two

December 2019: Brighton

The therapy consultation room, part of a shared work hub in an anonymous office building in Hove, is designed to be neutral. There are two straight-backed armchairs, upholstered in grey wool, the therapist's slightly larger but no higher than the client's.

The room is filled with light from two large windows and there is an unused fireplace, the entrance to its flue blocked with fresh flowers. In between the two chairs, there is a glass coffee table with a pot plant on it, a beaker of water and a box of paper tissues.

On the wall are three small prints of rural scenes. There is pastel wallpaper, pale grey showing white flowers in relief, leaving the impression of a diluted William Morris print. On a small desk facing the rear window sits Veronica's Apple Mac. The only slightly jarring element is the carpet of hard brown coir, which responds with a harsh scratching sound to any shoe sole dragged too heavily across it.

On the smaller of the chairs sits Vincent Canby, a stubby, pugnacious, overweight figure resembling a fair-haired Tony Soprano. His tidy grey suit trousers are oddly short for his truncated legs. He is sporting a fresh black eye on the left side of his face. He crosses his fat arms, which are hidden under a sharp blue shirt – expensive, Veronica guesses – with a brilliant white collar.

Veronica, dressed in a simple black business suit, no makeup and pinned hair, is looking down at her notepad and prepares herself to ask the Question, which lately has come to seem pointless and unilluminating. But she finds herself with nothing else in her head left to say after three quarters of an hour of diligent inquiry and careful listening.

'How does that make you feel, Vincent?'

Vincent squirms, crosses his arms and leans forward. 'Defensive body language,' writes Veronica in her small plain notepad.

'I don't know how it makes me feel. How am I supposed to answer that?'

'You seem angry.'

Vincent shifts in his chair, making his trouser hems shift further up his calves, revealing novelty socks that are decorated with depictions of small chipolata sausages. It was an oddly whimsical choice, thinks Veronica, for a successful architect, one who is struggling with his ten-year marriage and is full of unnameable dreads and anxieties. He first came into the consulting room six months previously, demanding to be 'fixed' and staring at Veronica defiantly as if he was on to her scam. But he had attended faithfully twice weekly ever since.

'Most feelings don't *have* names, do they?' says Vincent. 'You can call them sadness, or excitement, or irritation, or disappointment or frustration; you can *give* them names. But that's not what they are – is it? Apart from anything else, I don't know where my thoughts end and my feelings begin. They sort of – bleed into one another. Do my thoughts make me angry or does my anger produce my thoughts? I don't know. It's all a mess in here.'

He taps his head violently with one finger, takes a sip of the water in front of him, replaces it on the coaster then cradles his arms once more across his chest.

'Events seem to connect to my emotions – and my emotions to events – in a very unpredictable way. As I told you, my dog died last week. I felt okay about it – I'm not sentimental about animals like my wife is – and then two days later I got in a fight in a pub. My fault entirely. Hence this black eye. I don't know what the hell is going on. Do emotions just sit there and suddenly explode without warning?'

'Sometimes.'

'I paid you to fix me,' says Vincent suddenly. 'And you haven't.'

'Have I upset you?' says Veronica, glancing at the clock behind Canby's head, urging the minute hand onward.

'Have you? Or is that simply your perception?'

'Why don't you tell me?'

'That's what I'm trying to say. I don't know if you've upset me. Or if I'm just upset.'

His small hard eyes dart back and forth, avoiding contact with Veronica's.

'What do you think?'

53

'I don't know *what* I think.'

Veronica feels her stomach muscles tighten slightly. She says nothing.

'If you're waiting for me to say something, I'm afraid haven't got anything left to say,' says Vincent.

His left foot is tapping incessantly on the floor and he is wringing his hands. Veronica nods but still says nothing. This is what she is trained to do. Allowing another thirty seconds to tick away, she finally speaks the incantation, the spell of release.

'I think our time is up now.'

Vincent, who has been torpid and lackadaisical throughout most of the session, abruptly rises from the chair, grabs his raincoat from the distressed white-painted coat stand and thrusts his arms, one by one, violently into the sleeves.

'At last something we can agree on.'

He takes his wallet from his coat pocket, fishes out three twenty-pound notes, screws them into a ball and throws them, as if soiled, onto the table that separates client from therapist.

'I can tell you what emotion I'm having now. I'm feeling like a total fool. Does that have a proper name? The feeling of being foolish?'

'Vincent. I don't think it would be a good idea for you to end our sessions before . . . '

'I've had enough. Six months, more than a grand down the drain, and I'm more confused than when I came in the first place.'

'If you're having financial difficulties . . . '

'I'm not having financial difficulties. I'm having therapy difficulties. I'm having *you* difficulties.'

He waves his hands in front of him, as if seeking to pull words out of the air.

'Don't you . . . you must sometimes wonder whether all this that you do is just snake oil?'

'I'm not out to "cure" you, Vincent. It's an . . . '

' . . . "Exploration". I know. And we've ended up in . . . I don't know – darkest fucking Borneo, drifting along shit creek without a paddle. Or at least I have. Meanwhile, you're on easy street.'

Before Veronica can reply Vincent turns, yanks open the door to the room and leaves, not quite slamming the door behind him, but hard enough to make a clear enough parting statement. Veronica turns her gaze on the twenty-pound notes. Two are on the table, one has fallen onto the carpet. She bends and picks up each note as if it were unaccountably heavy. She feels tears well up and fights them back. It is important not to get too involved. This is what her training tells her. Unfortunately this distancing lately appears to be increasingly impossible. She had really thought she was getting somewhere with Vincent – with his depression, his anxiety, his inappropriate emotional outbursts. She had thought they had gone on an interesting journey together. Maybe they had. But it had ended up, as he said, nowhere. If he said it was nowhere, perhaps that was where it was. Maybe she should have just told him to go and get a prescription for Prozac from his doctor.

Vincent is right – in a way. She doesn't understand him. People cannot be understood. She doesn't even understand herself. Harrowed by this thought, Veronica reaches into her plain black leather handbag, big enough to hold the Mac, and finds a packet of cigarettes in a zip pouch at the back. She gave up years ago, for Silas's sake as much as her own, but earlier in the year she started again. She doesn't know why. An act of rebellion, perhaps.

She opens the window, lights the cigarette and puts her head outside the window. She smokes half the cigarette, then tosses it to the car park below, finding the taste simultaneously disgusting and appealing.

She visits the bathroom that is adjacent to her office and brushes her teeth to prevent Silas noticing any odour, then slips a Mento into her mouth. Then she locks the cigarettes in her drawer, slides the laptop into her bag, switches off the lights, secures the door and heads down two flights of stairs to the car park. Arriving, she locates and picks up the cigarette butt with a tissue before disposing of it in a municipal litter bin.

As Veronica makes the short drive home in her racing green Mini Cooper from Hove back to the house in Brighton, the session with Vincent continues to nag at her. She enjoys the process of therapy; she has worked hard to build up a good practice; she gets reliably paid for it – but could she actually point to any of her clients and say, with certainty, that she had made them 'better'? What did that even mean? Better than what? She had heard older colleagues warn her about wanting to 'fix' her clients, but if she couldn't help them – or at least help them to help themselves – what was the point?

Certainly, some clients improved, the majority even, but that might have happened anyway without her intervention. She was meant to be the expert but sometimes she felt she didn't have a clue what she was doing. Not about anything. Not even in her own life. Silas, for a start. Why was she with him? Come to that, why did she marry Frankie before that? Her long-time therapeutic supervisor, Elizabeth Pember, suggested that it was because Veronica had wanted to get back at her cold, snobbish mother by marrying a rough-at-the-edges estate agent from Shepherd's Bush.

Perhaps Elizabeth was right, but she had loved Frankie, she was sure of it. Even after she slept with *that person* – she cannot bring herself to name her ex-husband's friend, the worthless man whom she had so impulsively thrown herself at – she had loved Frankie. But somehow, his neediness, his desperation to be loved, pushed her away, even as at the same time she loved him for his helplessness, for the sincerity of that helplessness, for the transparent disguises he plastered over the fear, the sorrowful, spirited mask of the hustler.

The damage was done now anyway. Even though Frankie had wanted to stay in the marriage, despite finding out that she had been unfaithful. She knew she had broken it beyond repair. She was pretty sure she had done so deliberately. The fact that Frankie had gone bankrupt as a result of his lying and cheating – the reason she told everyone she had ended the marriage – was incidental to the fact that something deeper in her had demanded a change. Now she had ended up with Silas. He was certainly different from Frankie. Middle-class, privately educated, excellent manners, ticked all the right boxes. Above all, took a pride in his honesty. There was to be no more lying.

But did she actually love him? It was hard to say, since you couldn't strip wishful thinking out of the equation, or denial for that matter, or selective memory, or confirmation bias, or projection, or transference – all the things she had learned about while studying to be a therapist. At least Silas was not helpless, not by any definition – he was capable, confident, compassionate. He could put up a shelf, cook a meal, build a fence, change a fuse. He was straightforward, in touch with his feminine side, a good father to Mason and a decent stepfather to China, however much China resented him (which was only natural). But what was it to love a man, or for a man to love a woman? The question remained unanswerable. Vincent was right. The language of feeling was hopelessly impoverished.

At the end of the ten-minute journey, Veronica pulls into a residents' parking bay outside the pink house behind Silas's five-year-old silver grey Volvo S-90, takes her handbag from the seat, locks the car and walks slowly up to the front door of the house, still lost in her thoughts. She keys the lock and steps into the hall. In front of her to the left are stairs leading to three bedrooms and a bathroom. Ahead of her there is a corridor leading to the kitchen. To her right, a door leads to a living room that extends from the front of the house to a second connecting door at the back of the room, also leading into the kitchen.

She hangs up her coat and makes her way along the short corridor, containing a small privy to the left, until she reaches the main kitchen door. As she enters, she sees Silas standing at the stove wearing a pinafore. The slogan on it reads 'This is what a real feminist looks like' in spidery pastel script. Three copper pots are steaming on the hob. The Verve are playing from a Bose speaker.

'Hi, bud.' He glances up at her, shoots a quick smile and returns to the cooking. 'How was your day?'

'I've had better.'

'Me too,' he says, sprinkling some herbs into one of the

pots. 'I drove all the way to Saltdean because I heard there was a half-price deal on firewood. They'd sold out. So instead of saving money I spent it on petrol.'

'Sad story.'

Silas stops working at the stove and switches the music off.

'What's the matter, Vronky?'

'I don't know. Tired, I suppose.'

He wipes his hands on a tea towel and takes a step toward her.

'*Bud*. Have you been crying?'

Silas takes off his pinafore, moves another step towards Veronica, grasps her hand and leads her through the door into the sitting room. He pulls her towards the three-seater sofa, which isn't nearly as comfortable as it looked when they saw it in the showroom. Silas had insisted on it because it was reduced by 20 per cent. He sits down, dragging at her hand. She reluctantly lowers herself onto the space next to him.

'Ouch! Fuck!'

She looks under her rump. A sharp metal toy has been left there by Mason, some kind of retro robot.

'I wish that bloody kid . . . '

She checks herself. She puts the toy on the rustic yew coffee table, crafted by Silas and retaining its original knots and boles. Small items frequently fall through two small naturally occurring gaps in the wood and onto the floor beneath.

'Sorry. I'll have a word with him. Now – tell me about what's upsetting you.'

Veronica stares into his watery, bulging eyes – she finds them off-putting, but tries to ignore the vague frogginess they suggest – and regards, objectively, the mottled, calloused, pasty hand that is holding hers. The manual worker's skin seems incongruous with its fruity-voiced, soft-spoken owner. She looks up at his face again. He has a galaxy of dark brown freckles running across the bridge of his nose and across his cheeks. Silas claims that the copious freckles are to do with his mixed-race background.

Veronica searches for the right words to express what she has been feeling. In the end, 'I wish you'd stop calling everyone "bud", Silas' is all she can manage. Silas nods. Veronica knows that he is 'holding the space'. He has done his homework. He has been on men's personal growth weekends and removed his shirt and beat his chest and screamed his male rage at the skies until it was exorcised. He smells of Fairy Liquid and cumin.

'I'll try,' says Silas, his voice dripping empathy, like spilled cleaning fluid.

'Thank you.'

'So what's *really* the problem?'

He squeezes her hand gently. Veronica can detect the faint sheen of sweat. Or was it the washing-up liquid?

'Can we talk about it later?'

Silas pauses. His eyes seem to expand slightly more as if some pressure from behind was suddenly going to force them out of his head completely and send them flying across the room. She imagines them sticking to the wall opposite, then slowly descending like slugs to the floor.

'Of course, hon. Whenever you like.'

'I'm going to take a shower.'

'I'll get back to making the supper, then,' says Silas with a jarring cheerfulness. 'It'll spoil.'

Veronica makes her way along the corridor to the stair. As she does so she hears the Verve again, Silas lustily singing along.

China is standing by the window in her room, facing the small patch of rear garden that shows through a gap in the curtains. Scrolling down the contacts on her phone, she comes to one entry that simply says 'Fairy Godfather', filed under 'F'. She deletes the word 'Fairy' and re-files it under 'N'. It isn't funny anymore. It never was. Not that Nodge would have minded. He doesn't really mind anything. His inability to be offended is one of the things she loves about him.

She is wearing mismatched baggy clothes from the charity shop — a paisley shirt, a frilly white lace skirt, junk necklaces and rings. She doesn't believe in chain store shopping, all sweatshops and boring and ugly anyway and bad for the environment. She takes a selfie of her outfit, brandishing a pout, and posts it on Insta. Caption *'nouveau normcore, mixed with Downton vibe'*. She waits a minute for likes. None appear.

Sighing, she makes her way across the room, past the rarely played cheap guitar — a birthday present from Silas — and a beanbag designed to look like a trainer. She throws herself into the hanging egg chair, dislodging Kardashian, who squeals then falls immediately asleep again, this time on the beanbag. She goes to her FaceTime app and rings Nodge. After a couple of buzzes, the screen flickers and Nodge materializes, blinking, cheerful, solid. He is wearing Cubitts designer glasses with super thick black frames that make him look more like a philosopher than a taxi driver.

'Come in, London,' says China in a 1930s BBC announcer's voice.

'Reading you, Brighton,' says Nodge. 'All tickety-boo?'

His face almost fills the screen. She can see the large pores of his skin, like the peel of an orange.

'Can you stand back from the phone a bit. It's like you're going to burst through the screen and devour me.'

Nodge retreats and the rest of the apartment comes into view, as ever immaculately tidy. She notices a spray of mixed wild flowers in a blue fluted glass vase on the industrial steel coffee table. Otherwise it seems there is little colour or decoration. She assumes this is deliberate to emphasize the clean lines of the furniture.

'That's better. No work today? Have the unregulated goblins of the Uber brigade finally brought you to penury?'

Nodge glances at his watch.

'I start a shift in thirty, so I have to be quick. What's happening?'

'The wicked stepfather is being annoying.'

'*Quelle surprise.*'

The picture wobbles as Nodge starts to move about the room. He adjusts a photo of him and Owen on their wedding day on the shelf above the grey-veined soapstone fireplace then heads into the en-suite kitchen area, where he pours himself a coffee from a cafetière.

'What about your real father?' says Nodge, taking a swallow of the black liquid and grimacing. It is cold and bitter. 'Have you spoken to him?'

He pours the rest of the coffee down the sink and puts the grey porcelain mug into the dishwasher. China notices that her old school pencil case is down the side of the cushion of the egg chair. She fishes into the unzipped top, takes out a compass, opens it and traces out an invisible circle on her thigh.

'Uncle Jon, you're not going to give me grief, are you? I haven't spoken to him.'

Nodge reaches into the fridge and takes out the packed lunch he prepared the night before — focaccia with mozzarella and tomato, a brownie, some quinoa crisps, and a can of Fanta, which Nodge has never really lost the childhood taste for.

'One of your shirt buttons is undone.'

Nodge reaches down and closes the button. It pops open again immediately.

'You should cut down on the Fanta.'

'Frankie worries about you,' says Nodge, fastening the button again and putting the snacks and drinks into a Tupperware container, snapping the top closed.

'What are you? His representative on earth?'

'I'm his friend.'

China becomes aware of a hammering from downstairs. It will be Silas, she supposes, on one of his endless DIY missions. His latest project is to build bookcases on the landing.

'He *should* be worried about me. I can't get a proper job. Working at Nando's is rubbish. I'm reliant on Mum for cash. But she hasn't got hardly any because she spends most of it on Silas and the Beelzebrat.'

She turns the phone to show her Nando's uniform from where it is draped on her bed. To her annoyance, the inescapable Kardashian now rests on it, shedding hair.

'I happen to know that Frankie gives you quite a generous allowance. Anyway, why did you take a gap year if you couldn't afford it?'

China rises from the chair, still holding her compass. She places it on her work desk, which sits on the other side of her bed from the dressing table, turfs the cat off the bed then starts trying to remove the hair from her uniform. Kardashian jumps into the space she has left in the egg chair, settles and closes her eyes again.

'I was sick of studying. Fourteen years of it without a break. And as you know I was meant to be travelling the world. Until, you know, Sophie pulled out at the last minute. Me and her are so fucking over.'

Removing as much of the cat hair as she can, she sits down at her desk and starts fiddling with her compass again, propping the phone up against her desktop computer screen.

'You've got other friends.'

'Not ones that are going to fill in on a global tour at a week's notice. Anyway, I don't have *any* friends anymore – not since I left school. They've all gone off to uni. All I've got is Instagram posts of what fun they are having, or TikTok videos of them and their new buddies. I'm *unhappy*, Nodge.'

Nodge's face becomes severe. He brings it close to the phone camera again. This time the pores look like the surface of the moon.

'This is a conversation you should be having with Frankie.'

China taps idly at the switched-off keyboard of the computer, spelling out f. u. c. k.

'I can't communicate with him. We rub each other up the wrong way. Every single time.'

Nodge has moved to the bedroom he shares with Owen, dominated by a king-size bed draped in pure white Egyptian cotton with a Keith Haring 'Safe Sex' poster above it featuring two anonymous pale pink male figures in outline, holding one another's cocks. Each has a green cross instead of facial features. Picking up the rest of the gear he needs to take on the shift – a spare pair of glasses, a book, a pair of leather gloves – Nodge places them in his canvas shoulder bag.

'Apart from anything else, he's pretty much a fascist,' continues China.

Moving close up to the camera eye again, Nodge raises a heavy knitted unibrow.

'No, he's not.'

'He *is*.'

'You don't even know what a fascist is.'

'He is one anyway. Do you know what he said to me the other day?'

China does a passable impression of Frankie's west London, sub-cockney brogue. '"Colonialism wasn't all bad, China."'

China puts a finger to her head, pulls an imaginary trigger and blows her imaginary brains out.

'He also told me that he "loves England". *Loves "England"*! Not even Britain. But *England*.'

'He's hardly Nigel Farage.'

'He's Tommy fucking Robinson.'

'He voted Labour. He's a Remainer. I've never heard him say anything racist in my life. Not intentionally, anyway.'

'Intention doesn't *count*. It's how the person who experiences it feels about it that matters.'

China hears a piping sound offscreen. It is a high tenor voice singing:

'Three little maids who all unwary /come from a ladies' seminary.'

'Did you ring me up for a political debate? One of your re-education sessions?' says Nodge.

65

Owen drifts into view at the corner of the screen. He is wearing a gold Japanese kimono and carrying a floral fan. He drapes his arm around Nodge's shoulders and puts his face next to Nodge's so they together fill China's screen. Owen is wearing a black wig with bunches on either side and pancake-white makeup with thin pencilled eyebrows. He flutters a yellow paper floral fan in front of his face.

'Hey! Jiang Qing! When you coming to see us?'

'Why are you in drag, Owen?' says China.

'*Mikado*.'

'Mick who?'

'He's in a gender-blind version of *The Mikado*. Am-dram,' says Nodge.

'The ignorance of Zoomers is fucking terrifying,' says Owen. 'I'm Yum-Yum.'

'Who's Jiang Qing? Is he in *The Mikado*?' says China.

'Christ, China,' says Owen, raising both pencilled eyebrows. 'She was the leader of the Gang of Four.'

'That Indie band?'

'No, the Chinese communist who . . . the wife of Mao . . . she . . . '

Owen sees China yawning theatrically on the screen.

'Never mind.'

Owen, rolling his eyes, starts singing again, then disappears from the edge of the screen with a wave of his fan. As if in replacement, JJ briefly moves across the background carrying a bone-china teacup with an unlit cigarette hanging out the side of his mouth. He is dressed in purple pyjamas, his grey hair is tied up in a knot and he is carrying a small trumpet.

'Now what? Who's that? What's going on?' says China as JJ wanders offscreen.

'JJ. A friend of ours. Or rather, Nanki-Poo. Also in *The Mikado*. He's a player in the Titipu big band. He's going to be staying with us for a few days in a little while. He's having the builders in.'

The strains of 'A Wand'ring Minstrel, I' come from off camera, delivered in a faltering tenor by JJ.

'It's like one big crazy party down there. What is your part in this carnival of cultural appropriation?'

'Not one of my talents, I'm afraid.'

China turns the compass around in her right hand, and punches more letters on the computer keyboard. B. O. R. E. D.

'Nodge, to get back to the point. I didn't ring for a political debate. There's no point since you'd agree with me anyway.'

'I wouldn't be so sure.'

'I need an ally somewhere who isn't away at uni. You'll have to do.'

'I'm in London and you're in Brighton, so it's not much of a geographical improvement. I've got to go in a minute, China. Are you okay, though?'

'Of course. I have everything. Except a life. Or a father who is actually living in the twenty-first century.'

'No one has a life, China. Or at least not a life like you see on your Instagram feed.'

Hearing a faint purring behind her, China turns and sees Kardashian looking immensely self-satisfied stretching herself out on her egg chair. She wonders what it would be like to be a cat, or any animal, living entirely in the present, without anxiety for the future or suffering the ache of the past.

Nodge slips on his jacket and turns away from the screen. China can hear him calling goodbye to Owen and JJ. China stares at her wrists. Still playing with the compass, she begins gently prodding at the skin. A small puncture appears and a globule of blood.

'What are you doing, China?'

Taken aback, she realizes that Nodge has returned to the screen and that her bleeding wrist is in view of the camera.

'Nothing.'

'You just put that point into your arm.'

'So?'

'Are you self-harming?'

'Christ, Nodge, I was barely thinking what I was doing.'

'China . . . ?'

'I'm fine! Honestly.'

She puts down the compass and wipes away the drop of blood with the palm of her hand, but it simply spreads it into a pink stain on her skin.

'I have to go. Can we talk about this later?'

'No,' says China firmly. 'It's nothing. Nothing to talk about.'

Nodge looks sceptical. The image on his phone wobbles as he makes his way towards the door.

'Bye, then,' he says, looking worried but with a final wave. Then he vanishes from the screen.

Feeling, for no reason she can understand, unfairly abandoned, China stares at the blank screen and becomes once again conscious of the hammering that continues downstairs. She checks her Insta account. Still no likes. She picks up the compass again, deliberately this time rather than absently. She turns it around in her fingers, as if uncertain what its purpose is. She tests the thin skin around her wrist with the point, pushing the skin until deep and concave, to the point of breaking.

Christmas Day 2019: Brighton

The Christmas lunch, cooked by Silas, has been meticulously prepared. He is meticulous about everything. The meal is more sociable than either Veronica or China anticipated. Despite Mason receiving gracelessly some of the presents that 'Santa' has brought him – along with the punchbag, he received a pair of off-message trainers, an eco-friendly box of naturally fla-voured jelly sweets and a voucher securing a goat for a family in Africa – he has been unusually well behaved, cheerfully anticipating the 'tree presents' that tradition, such as it is, demands. These are the non-Santa gifts – family offerings – which are distributed after the Christmas meal.

After the turkey and trimmings – China has waived her vegetarianism for Christmas Day, temporarily adopting the mantle of flexitarian – there is Christmas pudding with a sprig of holly and served with brandy butter plus an enormous trifle, concocted by China, without alcohol in consideration of Silas, who is a strict teetotaller. The women have drunk deeply of the good Primitivo that Veronica had been gifted by one of her grateful clients. Silas sticks to G&T made with fake herbal gin.

Mason, having that morning spent thirty minutes ham-mering at the punchbag, has usefully consumed a great deal of pent-up energy. His perpetual restlessness is becoming a cause of concern – there has been talk of setting up an ADHD diagnosis. *The sooner he's drugged up and locked in a room the better* has been China's contribution to the debate about his behavioural difficulties. Silas, meanwhile, has been complaining to whoever will pretend to listen about the cost of all the presents and the waste involved – he is always mindful of money and landfill. His justification for this grousing is that his work is intermittent and he does not know how much he will earn from one month to another. China simply thinks him a miser. Generosity, Veronica confirms secretly to China, does not come to Silas readily.

The family snap the crackers, slap on the paper hats and tell the jokes contained within. They are reliably unfunny. They phone absent relatives and friends then settle into armchairs and the sofa – threadbare, but redeemed by a colourful woollen throw – in the living room. The room is in chaos, but then it is a relaxed, comfortable and jumbled house, which is the way Veronica likes it. The Christmas tree, which stands six foot high, is close enough, with the teetering silver angel on top, to touch the vintage chandelier hanging from the ceiling rose. The tree was dressed by all of them a week ago with baubles, tinsel and foil-wrapped chocolates. There is a spreading pile of gifts underneath, most of them for Mason – another reason, perhaps, for his temperate mood. The wood-burning stove in the fireplace forces out heat and for once China does not berate her stepfather for its polluting presence.

Kardashian sleeps on top of the bookcase pushed against the party wall that joins the house to the neighbour, insensible to the celebrations as she seems insensible to everything else. China lowers her gaze to the book spines, her eye briefly resting on *The End of Your World* by someone called Adyashanti

(Veronica's), *Rum Punch* by Elmore Leonard (Silas) and *Watchmen* (Mason). Mason only reads graphic novels, and then rarely, preferring *Minecraft* or, when visiting certain friends with more liberal parents, *Call of Duty: Black Ops*.

'That animal is fat, lazy and largely useless as a pet,' says China to no one in particular, sitting on the sofa next to her mother, staring at the inert furry blob breathing quietly on the bookcase. She is only slightly drunk. She has removed her paper hat and replaced it with a soft conical red velveteen one. Her top is an outsize sweater with Jeremy Corbyn's face, topped by a red and white bobble hat, festooned across the front. It reaches almost to her knees. Underneath she is wearing expensive thick white tights, a Christmas gift to herself, which have remained miraculously unsoiled during the messy Christmas lunch.

'Very body confident, though,' says Silas, who is sunk into a faded red shabby-chic armchair. He is wearing black trousers, a white collarless linen shirt and a festive waistcoat decorated with holly sprigs. He sips at his alcohol-free G&T while at the same time surreptitiously checking his bank accounts on his brand-new iPhone – a generous Christmas present to himself – under the pretence of texting relatives.

'Does she ever wake up?'

'Occasionally. To eat. And shit probably,' says Silas, not looking up. 'Although she could probably do that in her sleep.'

'Don't you worry about her health?'

'It is what it is,' says Silas. 'She's got plenty of lives anyway.'

'Who wants to start?' says Veronica, waving in the direction of the pile of presents woozily, paper hat askew on her head.

'Me!' yells Mason, leaping to his feet from the embroidered

Indian footstool upon which he has been sitting and fidgeting, foot tapping relentlessly, a soft jackhammer. He is still wearing his red paper Christmas hat. Somehow it has become stained by gravy. China earlier noticed him taking furtive sips of wine from Veronica's glass. His cheeks are flushed and eyes slightly fogged. Silas looks at Veronica questioningly. Veronica smiles and nods. She feels relaxed, even content. Pine needles thrown onto the burner fills the room with a festive scent. A carol seeps out of the radio like incense in a thurible.

'I want to open THIS ONE,' shouts Mason, jumping up from the footstool and grabbing a long parcel wrapped in foil from the back of the pile. He starts tearing violently at the wrapping.

'Read the tag first, Mason,' says Silas evenly.

'It's from . . . ' He strains impatiently to read the handwriting. 'China to ME.'

He rips off the rest of the foil to reveal the blazing, brash packaging of a Nerf Super Soaker. His normally restless, twitchy demeanour is torn by a vast grin.

'THANK YOU, CHINA.'

He runs to China, throws his arms round her throat, quickly lets go, then mysteriously disappears from the room, clutching his plastic booty.

'Mason!' calls Silas.

Mason is gone. No one can be bothered to find out where. The three remaining celebrants sit staring at the tree. China feels an invisible force pushing the air out of the room. She has little doubt about its source.

'It made him happy, Silas,' says China in a quiet voice, then takes a deep draught of wine. Silas nods, but does not respond.

'Come on, Silas. It's just a glorified water pistol,' adds
Veronica, smiling groggily. 'Shall we do another present?
Mason will be back in a moment from – wherever he's gone.'

Silas nods again. His lips are pressed together. He clutches
his glass of fake gin and tonic. White skin shows at the
knuckle. He is making China nervous. She has always sensed
something dark in Silas. Perhaps by provoking him with her
forbidden gift, she is testing him to see if she can force it out
into the open. There is a thrill to the fear.

'Come on, Silas, don't be a dick,' she says in a slightly wary
voice. Gently though, hoping to lighten the heavy air. 'You
don't mind having a wood-burning stove in the corner spewing
out poisonous particles for him to inhale, but you worry about
the kid having a water pistol?'

At that moment, Mason re-enters the room, holding the
Super Soaker. It suddenly occurs to them all where he has been.

'Mason . . .' begins Silas, but it is too late. With a cackle,
Mason fires a torrent of water in all directions, head stoked
with *Call of Duty* fantasies.

'Eat liquid death, suckers!' he cries. Within a matter of
seconds China, Silas and Veronica are all drenched. Kardashian
too, but she isn't aroused from her slumbers.

Silas slowly examines his brand-new but now drenched iPhone.
Its screen has gone dark already. He wipes at it with his shirt
sleeve, trying to clean off the puddles of water. Veronica laughs
nervously. China dries herself with a holly-decorated napkin.

Eventually, Silas stops trying to save his phone. Mason
stands rooted to the spot, entertained by the devastation he has
wrought, but growing increasingly anxious about his father's
apparent lack of reciprocal amusement.

Silas slowly stands. Nobody moves. Then, with a burst of speed and precision, Silas snatches the Super Soaker out of Mason's hands. There is one more moment's pause. Then he raises the water pistol in the air and smashes it against the tiled fireplace. Water leaks onto the floor and chips of black plastic scatter like shrapnel.

'I explained to you why you couldn't have a water cannon, Mason,' says Silas, very quietly. Mason, the shock of the performance wearing off, screams and starts punching Silas ineffectively in the stomach.

'Happy now?' says Silas, now addressing himself to China. He ignores the punches from Mason, which fall on him with all the effect of faint sleet against a heavy door. China unsteadily rises from her chair. Mason gives up on his futile pounding and runs out of the room into the kitchen. China, not sure what else to do, but certain she doesn't want to stay in the immediate orbit of Silas, follows him.

Veronica picks idly at her wet clothes, still insulated from the drama by her lining of alcohol. She regards the pool of water spreading across the wooden floor and the damp stain now gathering on the Turkish rug. She raises her gaze to Silas, who is bending down, picking up fragments of the Super Soaker. He seems to be working at controlling his breathing. The gallery of freckles on his face is backed with an angry red blush.

'Is there any more wine, do you think?' says Veronica.

In the kitchen, China stands against the sink, drinking water directly from the tap, as much as she can stand to swallow. In the corner Mason sits on the floor, weeping.

'I hate my dad,' he says under his breath, more to himself than China.

'No, you don't,' says China, finally switching off the tap. To her surprise, she feels the urge to put her arm around Mason, but cannot bring herself to do it. She steels herself nonetheless and moves towards him, offering her hand so she can pull him up. He stares sullenly at her outstretched palm, unmoving.

'Look,' says China, dropping her arm. 'Let's have a bit of fun, shall we?'

Next to Mason, on the floor, there are three separate waste bins. One is for recyclable paper and plastic, one is for organic waste and one for general waste. She opens the recycling bin, takes a couple of plastic bottles out, and puts them in the general waste compartment.

'This always drives your dad mad.'

Summarily revived, Mason joins in, tentatively at first then with increasing vigour. Glass jars are put in among rotting vegetables. Clingfilm finds its way into recyclables. Before long, they giggle together. Then, carried away by the excitement, Mason flings the remnants of a huge squashed tomato at China. It lands on her new white tights, leaving a tennis ball-sized stain.

'For fuck's sake, Mason,' says China, more angrily than she had intended. Mason, stung by the dissolution of their temporary alliance, unleashes a cry of anguish. China takes a paper towel from the worktop and tries to remove the stain, but just succeeds in spreading the mush across her thigh.

'I hate you,' says Mason.

'I hate you too, you little fucker,' says China, and stamps out of the room still dabbing at her leg. Behind her, she hears

Mason, now sobbing and muttering. She stops and strains to hear what he is saying. Four words, repeated again and again.

'I want my *mummy*.'

Stung by sudden pity, she tries to muster the resources to go back and apologize, take him in her arms and console him. But she cannot disinter the necessary humility. Instead, she marches upstairs to her bedroom where she tears off the tights and puts them to soak in the small enamel wash basin. Her pale legs provoke her. She sees the open compass on her desk, sees the light reflect from the steel point.

January 2020: London

'The thing I most struggle with,' says Veronica, staring at her handbag and thinking longingly of the unopened pack of Silk Cut nesting next to her keys, 'is guilt.'

She is with her therapeutic supervisor, Elizabeth Pember, at Elizabeth's studio in London, an expensively decorated room in a cottage block in Primrose Hill. There are three large framed Rorschach blots on the wall, but otherwise it is a space with no language of its own.

'Most people do,' says Elizabeth.

Veronica looks up at Elizabeth's placid, plain features which, she knows, conceal an acute intelligence. However, something is bothering her about Elizabeth's face. Then she realizes what it is. Elizabeth is slowly becoming cross-eyed over the years. This disconcerts her, since now she realizes she isn't sure where the therapist is looking. At the same time, she wonders if the crossed eyes are a morbid feature of her own imagination. The thought drifts away from her as Veronica's phone vibrates in her bag.

'Sorry,' she says, taking it out and examining the text. It is from Frankie, confirming their meeting later in the afternoon. She switches the phone off.

'Did anything instigate this particular bout of guilt?' says Elizabeth.

'I think it's been triggered by one of my clients. Vincent Canby. When he first came to see me, maybe six months ago, he was one of those "okay, I've got a problem, now fix me" cases. Then, a few weeks before Christmas, he just stormed out. He practically threw my fee at me like I was a prostitute. It was clear that he hated me. It made me feel terrible. Now he's filed a complaint to the BACP accusing me of negligence.'

'Anything else you feel guilty about?' says Elizabeth, who has the disconcerting habit – for a therapist – of occasionally picking her nose during a session, something she is currently attempting before becoming conscious of the action then lowering her hand.

'Everything. Particularly my daughter.'

She falls silent. Elizabeth rotates her finger in front of her chest, prompting her to continue.

'It's called "being a woman", isn't it? Being angry, feeling guilty. Whatever the reason, I appear to be racked by it more than usual lately.'

'A lot of irrational guilt is born out of a feeling of powerlessness that many people experience in childhood. You know this. You had a difficult, distant, judgemental mother, didn't you, Veronica? Blaming yourself for everything is a form of hope. Because if it's your fault, then you can change it. Except that it isn't your fault and you can't change it. Because it already happened.'

'Strange kind of hope, then.'

'But difficult to resist – even for someone schooled, like you, in how these things tend to work.'

Elizabeth scribbles briefly in her notebook, crosses and uncrosses her legs. Veronica finds herself momentarily touched with a feeling of arousal, and wonders if she is unconsciously in love with Elizabeth. She has, after all, shared with her supervisor her most intimate secrets. Nobody knows her so well. On the other hand, Veronica knows virtually nothing outside the professional sphere about Elizabeth, while real love must encompass mutuality. She is fully sensitive of the dangers of transference.

'Try and break down your personal experience of guilt for me,' says Elizabeth, briskly clipping her pen to the front of the pad. Perhaps sensing something, she pulls down the hem of her skirt. Veronica takes a tissue from the box in front of her and begins to slowly tear it purposelessly into ragged scraps.

'Why do I feel guilty? Because China feels her separation from her father so keenly and it makes her suffer – and I can't do anything about it. At the same time, she is full of anger towards him. So he suffers too. Of course – she has a right to her feelings. They're justified to some extent. But there's no end to it. It's probably more punishment than he deserves.'

'Unpack that a little for me? It doesn't seem to follow why this should arouse these feelings in you.'

Veronica stops tearing at the tissue and takes a sip of the water. It is warm and slightly soapy-tasting. Her voice lowers as if she doesn't want Elizabeth to properly hear her.

'I *did* have sex with Frankie's . . . friend after all. Which is another reason I feel guilty. Even though it was so long ago. It wasn't *all* Frankie's fault our marriage broke up. And I let

China think it is. He didn't *want* it to break up. He just took the rap for it, for China's sake. And for my sake. Which was good of him, actually. That makes me feel bad too. That he did that. You know?'

'Does China know about this . . . man you slept with?'

She checks her notes.

'Tony something or other, wasn't it? Tony Diamond?'

'Diamond Tony. I can't bear to tell her. She needs at least one parent she looks up to. I think she would be crushed if she thought I was capable of such a thing. I think she has come to even idealize me to some extent. Which is to my advantage, I suppose. Of course, we argue sometimes, it would be strange if we didn't, but she almost needs to . . . I don't know. Keep me pure.'

'So – you feel guilty about China being in a single-parent family. Surely you must acknowledge that this isn't at all unusual. Neither the guilt nor the single-parent family.'

'No. It isn't unusual.'

'But what exactly do you feel guilty about, then?'

Veronica stares at a patch of wall above Elizabeth's head. She can think of nothing that might satisfy her supervisor. She notices Elizabeth's thigh again, checks herself. Then, out of nowhere, her mind fills. It releases its contents in a blind torrent.

'Guilty because I still care about Frankie and I think he's having a rotten time and because I cheated on him. Even if it was ten years ago. Guilty because I'm working so hard, I can't give China all the attention she needs. Guilty that I don't love Silas as much as he appears to love me. Guilty that I can't love his son at *all*. Guilty that I can't tell Silas that I can't love his son. That, in fact, I can't *stand* his fucking son. Guilty because the reason I can't stand his son may be because he has a developmental disorder that isn't his fault. Guilty because I feel guilty and it's pointless and self-indulgent and I should know better. Guilty because in the spare time I *do* have, I give more time to Mason than I do to China because he is so demanding and she's a grown-up now. Guilty because I'm angry at Silas because he isn't making more money, yet I know he's trying really hard by economizing. Always economizing. Or perhaps he's just mean. I don't know. Guilty that I can't cook as well as him. Guilty that I don't want to have as much sex as Silas does. Guilty that I'm angry with him because he doesn't always want to have sex with me when I want it. Guilty that I had too many Choco Leibniz last night. Guilty that I can't be the mother Mason hasn't got. Guilty that I feel I'm running out of time and my life hasn't turned out to be perfect. Just, you know. Guilty.'

Elizabeth scribbles in her pad so hard the pencil tip breaks.

'I don't think you've ever told me what happened to Mason's mother,' she says, picking up a sharpener and rotating the pencil within, a perfect curl of thin wood emerging from the blade.

'She died when he was a baby. He can't remember anything about her. Breast cancer apparently.'

Now the pencil has a sharp point again, Pember starts to scribble once more. She writes:

'Mason: Mother dead.'

'Do you understand what I meant when I said that guilt can be a form of hope?' she says, looking up from the pad. She *has* gone cross-eyed; Veronica is sure of it.

'It's not exactly a novel observation, Elizabeth.'

'Doesn't this understanding give you any relief from your negative feelings?'

'No.'

'Why not?'

'Because I'm a bad person — obviously. I don't think it's my self-defence mechanism or whatever you say it is. And I want to be a good person.'

She nods furiously as if to confirm the point. Elizabeth peers at her with kind eyes over rimless spectacles.

'You're familiar with the formula, "I'm so good, only I can see how bad I am"?'

'I'm familiar with it, yes.'

'Self-hatred can be a form of narcissism.'

Veronica considers this, thinks again of the cigarettes in her bag.

'That makes me feel a *lot* better,' she says eventually, unwilling to hide the bitterness in her voice. She gets up from her chair and begins picking up the pieces of the tissue she has strewn there and putting them in the bin.

'What *would* make it better? Leave that alone, please.'

Veronica continues and finishes the job before sitting back down. Now she leans forward in her chair.

'Honestly? I can think of one thing. If Saint Silas actually turned out to be even worse than me.'

Elizabeth raises a plucked eyebrow.

'You want *him* to be a bad person?'

'No. Not exactly. But in a strange way — yes. More flawed. Like me. Over Christmas he lost his temper over something for once and instead of feeling angry with him, I felt vaguely triumphant.'

81

Elizabeth adjusts the arrangement in the flower vase slightly before continuing, moving a tulip further from a second tulip to create a harmony between the objects.

'What do you value most about him?'

Veronica doesn't answer for maybe thirty seconds. When she speaks her voice is firm, or perhaps, resolute.

'I trust him.'

Frankie registers a slight increase in his heartbeat when he spots Veronica walking towards him along the pathway that leads from the Bayswater Road into Hyde Park. Seeing him, she flashes the crooked smile he saw the first time they met, at the fading of the twentieth century inside a flat he was trying to sell her in Shepherd's Bush.

He is sitting on a bench in the Italian Gardens facing the pool and fountains. As she approaches, he registers that she is still thin and graceful and walks with a certain sway, in a particular rhythm, slow and confident, that Frankie has always admired. Above all, for some reason, he loves her fleshy nose, at odds with the rakiness of her body – her flat, bony chest, her long, slim legs.

'Hello, Frankie,' she says as she approaches. Frankie is still dressed for business, in a two-piece made-to-measure suit that he has let out twice in the past ten years. She throws her arms open for a hug. He rises, enfolds himself, stays a second longer than he should. When they part, Veronica, now wary, takes an extra step back.

'Vronky. You're looking *good*. How was your session with . . . what's her face?'

'Elizabeth. *Elizabeth*. I've told you a thousand times. It's amazing how quickly you can annoy me.'

'Always with the compliments.'

Suddenly ill at ease, Veronica fumbles in her bag for a ciga-rette. She takes the carton out, offers one to Frankie who declines. They sit next to one another on the bench, a few careful feet apart.

'You don't smoke.'

'I'm trying to take it up. Stress,' she says, lighting the ciga-rette. Frankie watches the ember glow.

'How did the session go?'

'I haven't decided yet. To be frank I worry about the whole therapy thing. Sometimes I think it's a waste of time. And a client has made a complaint against me. But I can't discuss it, obviously.'

'I'm sure you're a brilliant therapist.'

'How would you know?'

'Because you care about people.'

Veronica pulls on the cigarette. Immediately not liking the taste, she stubs it out and grinds it under her heel.

'You're looking good too, Frankie. At least your fingernails are. Roxy's done a good job there.'

Frankie examines his fingernails and concludes that they do, indeed, look pretty tidy. He returns his gaze to Veronica, who is smiling broadly, apparently at nothing in particular. But there is a slight mocking tinge to the cast of her mouth.

'You're not annoyed? About me and Roxy?'

Veronica considers this. She isn't entirely sure how to answer because she has at this moment realized for the first time that she *is* slightly discomfited by the fact of their rela-tionship without quite knowing why.

'Why should I be annoyed? I've always liked Roxy, even

though we've lost touch since I moved to Brighton. The pair of you aren't an *obvious* match, but then it's funny how very different people can be attracted to one another.'

'Why not an obvious match?'

'I don't know, Frankie.'

Veronica scratches her nose with her little fingernail, a tic that Frankie remembers well. It turns his heart over.

'She just doesn't seem your type, I suppose.'

'What is my type?'

'Anyone who'll have you I expect.' But she says this smiling, this time without edge. 'Shall we take a walk around the fountains?'

'Hold on a minute.'

Frankie rises, takes some coins out of his pocket, throws them into the pool towards the base of the fountain, then closes his eyes for a couple of seconds.

'I thought I was the superstitious one,' says Veronica, getting up from the bench to join him.

'Clutching at straws. The god of the fountain is as good as anyone to try.'

'What did you wish for?'

'Obviously I can't tell you that or it will break the spell.'

They start to walk at a slow pace around the Italianate fountains. Frankie feels the urge to take Veronica's arm but hesitates. Then he decides to keep a safe distance. His over-extended hug has put him on guard against himself.

'So – what did you want to talk to me about?' says Veronica, glancing at his face, which is more open and vulnerable than it once was and traced with lines of sadness. It evokes a certain tenderness in her that she did not expect. In the end it is she who takes his arm. He looks at it, surprised, but gladly accepts the gesture.

'Do I have to want to talk to you about something? Can't we just meet up occasionally for a walk without a reason?'

'Sure. But you *did* say you wanted to talk to me about something.'

They leave the fountain area and start walking west, in the direction of Kensington Palace. Frankie smells her scent, a different one to the one she used to wear, more spicy than floral.

'How's Silas?'

'Busy being Silas.'

'Now he *does* seem your type.'

'He's got all the surface credentials, I suppose.'

'He's not perfect, then?'

'Nobody's perfect.'

'So how is he specifically not perfect?'

Veronica wags her finger playfully.

'Tut tut, Frankie – I'm not prepared to go there. I'm not going to discuss my relationship with Silas with you. Suffice to say – we rub along okay.'

'That's enough for you, is it?'

'So,' says Veronica, stopping for a moment and taking a deep breath. 'What did you want to talk about, then?'

'Our daughter.'

A dog chases a squirrel, hopelessly, as the squirrel casually climbs the nearest tree. The grass is muddy and drenched, the path strewn with dead leaves. Frankie sees a leaf skeleton at his feet. He lets Veronica's arm slide away from his, picks it up and examines it closely.

'What about her?'

He holds the skeleton up to the light and stares at it.

'It's such a beautiful thing,' he says. 'Like the ghost of a leaf.'

'When did you come over so poetic?'

Suddenly losing interest, he tosses the leaf aside.

'China won't *see* me, Veronica. I don't know what I'm going to do about it. She's my *daughter*. Without her I'm like . . . '

He points to the skeleton leaf as it skitters along the path in front of them.

'Like that leaf. Nothing moors me. I'm all bone.'

They start to walk again, inadvertently following the leaf as it skips, helpless in the wind.

'She's a teenager, Frankie. She'll grow out of it.'

'Can't you put in a word for me?'

'I *do* put words in for you.'

'You do?'

Veronica considers this.

'I've never spoken against you.'

'Never?'

'Not for a while, anyway,' she concludes, with the uneasy feeling that she *has* occasionally used their shared animus towards Frankie to bring them closer.

They continue walking in comfortable silence until they arrive at a refreshment hut on the east side of the Princess Diana Memorial playground.

'Cup of coffee?' says Frankie.

'Thanks.'

'Decaf flat white, right, soya milk. Correct?'

'You know me so well.'

'I used to.'

86

He fetches the two coffees and returns. Cradling their drinks, they stroll over to the Elfin Oak, fenced off in front of the playground. Frankie turns and stares at the equipment in the play area, deserted in the freezing weather.

'Do you remember I brought China here, the day my mum died?' he says. 'We played for a while. Under the water jets there. It was cold, even though it was summer. We laughed so much even though I was sad. So was she. I took her on the swings and she got frightened.'

Frankie feels a sting in his eyes. He turns to Veronica, hoping that she will notice the fraction of a tear, thinking she might start seeing him as sensitive.

'That China has disappeared for ever,' says Frankie.

'You sound bitter.'

'I'm just disappointed.'

'Everyone is disappearing all the time, Frankie.'

Frankie nods and takes a sip of his coffee.

'Thing is, Veronica. Listen. I've heard that China's not too happy living in Brighton.'

Veronica feels herself recoil slightly. The easy atmosphere between them tightens a notch.

'Who told you that?'

'Client confidentiality. Sorry. Is it true?'

Veronica turns and starts walking towards the Round Pond. In the distance, Frankie can see ducks, swans and pigeons crowding around an old man casting bread on the water. He follows her and catches up. They walk in silence for a few seconds.

'There's friction, like in any family. I think she does alright,' Veronica answers eventually.

87

'That's not what I've heard. I've heard Silas and Mason are driving her up the wall.'

'That's not any of your business, Frankie.'

'It is my business. She's my daughter. I worry about her. Even if she thinks I'm a waste of space.'

They arrive at the pond. Frankie reaches in his pocket and takes out what appears to be a half-eaten Danish pastry. He begins to crumble it and throw it towards the perimeter of the water. A flock of birds descends.

'There are stresses in any family,' says Veronica, watching the hysteria of the birds and the aloof dignity of the swans as they glide like emperors towards the site of the chaos.

'Such as?'

'I don't really want to say.'

'I hear Mason isn't the easiest kid in the world.'

'I can't really comment.'

'You're proper chatty, aren't you? Want a go?'

He hands the remainder of the pastry to Veronica, who throws the whole piece into the water. A swan picks it up in his beak, then spits it out.

'I'm just trying to be discreet, Frankie. I would be the same if I talked about you to Silas.'

'So — will you tell Silas that you've met me today?'

Veronica fidgets with the clip of her handbag.

'Why wouldn't I?'

'He might be the jealous type. I don't know.'

Veronica strokes some crumbs from the pastry off her sleeve and, finishing her coffee, deposits it in a litter bin.

'Frankie — what are we doing here? It's cold and I've got a train to catch.'

'It's just nice to see you, that's all.'

She turns towards him, regarding him fondly.

'It's nice for me too. What's happening at the agency?'

Frankie raises his eyes to the heavens.

'Same old same old. But they're going to offer me a partnership. Apparently.'

'Didn't they promise you that once before? And then stiffed you?'

'No, no, no. They really *are* this time. It was Ratchett that torpedoed it that time. Out of malice and greed. And he's dead. Thank God.'

'Frankie!'

'Yeh, well, he was a nob. I don't love Farley, but I think the promise is cast iron. He's a bit of a pompous muppet, but he's trustworthy in a way that Ratchett – God rest his stinking black soul – was very much not. It will mean a big hike in my salary. Very hard work, but a secure future.'

Veronica does up another two buttons on her coat against the cold. The wind is picking up force and scooping up water on the Round Pond into ripples and pools.

'Congratulations. You must be very pleased.'

'Thank you. I am, I suppose.'

'Still saving for the dream car?'

She throws him a sideways look that he knows well of old.

'Don't take the piss.'

'I'm not.'

'I can see from your face that you *are*. I know you think it's hilarious that I should be so invested in a particular car, but after the years I've been through – I don't know. It represents something to me. Getting back on my feet. Not being a . . . a *loser* anymore.'

Veronica pats him softly on the arm.

'Frankie – you're not a loser. You had some bad luck. That's all.'

'That's a change of story. I thought you thought it was all down to me.'

'Well, okay. You lied. You cut corners and got found out. But you *also* had some bad luck. 2008 was a lot of bad luck for a lot of people. Including me and China, of course.'

'I know. I'm sorry.'

Veronica, still touching his arm, rubs at the material of his jacket softly.

'I've told you before. You don't have to apologize anymore. It's water under the bridge. It makes no difference now.'

Franke takes a step away, suddenly businesslike. There is, after all, a reason for him meeting with Veronica today.

'It does as far as China is concerned. Which is why I wanted to talk to you.'

'Now we get to it. Come on, I really do have to go.'

She rubs her hands together against the cold. Her breath makes momentary clouds. Frankie stares at the clamouring birds squabbling as they consume the remaining crumbs of the pastry.

'I was wondering if you could talk her into coming to stay with me for a while? Maybe a month or two. I'm hoping we might begin at last to repair our relationship.'

Veronica shakes her head sadly.

'I wouldn't hold out too much hope. She's got a lot of baggage to unpack.'

'All the same – if she doesn't like Silas or Mason . . . '

'I didn't say that – did I?'

Frankie turns to face Veronica full on, but can hardly bear to look at her face since it fills him with longing.

'I just thought – with some gentle encouragement from you we could kill two birds with one stone. Take a bit of pressure off you and Silas. And China and I could get to know one another a bit better.'

'Frankie – China will do whatever she wants. She's nineteen years old. She won't listen to me. She's very strong-willed.'

'She worships you.'

'No – she doesn't. But we have a good relationship – yes.'

'I'm glad of that. Really I am. But she might listen to you if you tell her that . . . I don't know . . . that . . . '

Frankie suddenly runs out of thought.

'That she should try and keep in touch with her father more,' he blurts finally.

'"Should" isn't a word that goes down well with her.'

'Will you try?'

'No harm in trying. But I wouldn't hold your breath.'

Frankie nods, satisfied. He knows that Veronica will keep to her word.

'Now I really do have to go, Frankie.'

She takes a step forward and embraces Frankie. He brings his arms around and feels her angular shoulder blades with the tips of his fingers and he finds himself gently exploring them through the thick cloth. How well he remembers them, when he was allowed to touch them, to explore the bare skin. To kiss them. The hug lasts longer than either of them have planned. It is Veronica again who pulls away first.

'Bye, Frankie. Stay well. And give Roxy my love.'

'Sure. And tell Silas to fuck off from me.'

Veronica laughs.

'Same old Frankie.'

'No, actually. Not at all,' he answers. But she has swiftly turned away and is walking towards the southern entrance of the park so does not hear him.

Chapter Three

New Year's Day 2020: London

Frankie has noticed that Roxy is importing more and more of her clothes into his closet. It makes him uneasy. Apart from anything else, what was going to happen if China finally *did* decide to stay for a while? She would not appreciate seeing another woman's knickers in the laundry basket, metaphorically or literally.

He glances at Roxy, who is relaxing on the living room sofa, watching *Love Island* on the 55-inch TV and checking her phone. She is painting her fingernails bright green. Above the television, a framed Sebastião Salgado print of a Brazilian goldmine, hundreds of miners crawling like ants up and down a great mountain of mud. She has bleached her hair to pale blonde and cut it shorter. It makes her look both younger and older simultaneously.

'Shall we get a takeaway?' says Frankie.

'Again?'

'Why not?'

'Be nice if you cooked me something sometime.'

'Be nice if you cooked *me* something.'

'Because I'm the woman, you expect me to look after you.'

Frankie cannot muster an immediate counterpunch. He is still melancholic from his meeting with Veronica earlier that day. For some reason he cannot fathom, he has not told Roxy that he met with her.

'I've cooked for you loads over the last few weeks.'

'Beans on toast isn't cooking.'

'You haven't lifted a finger.'

'What time's the football on?' says Roxy, yawning.

'Do you *really* want to watch it? It's one shit team versus another shit team.'

'I didn't know QPR were playing.'

'Hilarious. What's the point anyway, since you spend most of the time staring at your phone rather than the match? Watching football with you is a very partial experience. Anyway, it's not QPR on the telly.'

Frankie turns towards the grapefruit-sized black globe on the coffee table, a Christmas gift from Roxy.

'Alexa.' The base of the unit flashes blue. 'What time is the Manchester United vs Arsenal game today?'

'I'm sorry, I don't have that information.'

'Alexa, you're a muppet.'

'Sorry this might not be what you want to hear, but I'm not sure what I did wrong.'

'I still get a kick out of that,' says Frankie as Roxy continues to scroll through her phone. 'Do you know if you tell Alexa that you love her she sings you a song?'

'You've been telling Alexa that you love her?' says Roxy, not looking up.

'She's the perfect woman. She always listens and she always says sorry. You're the perfect woman, aren't you, Alexa?'

'Sorry, I don't know that title.'

Finding Sky Sports, Roxy finishes painting her nails on the left hand, puts down the brush and scratches her nose with the other unpainted index finger.

'Takeaway it is, then,' she says.

Frankie picks up his phone. There are three texts, none of them from China. He has been thinking of driving down to Brighton to see her, but so far has had no response to his pleas for a day on which China was available.

'So when *are* you going to cook me a meal?' asks Roxy.

'Dunno,' says Frankie, fetching a beer from the fridge and settling down to watch the match, despite himself.

'How about the last Saturday of next month?'

Frankie sucks the beer down slowly, giving him time to think about whether there is a hidden significance to this question or this date. Finding none, he lowers the can.

'Is there something special about the last Saturday of next month?'

'It's our anniversary.'

Frankie burps and gives an incredulous laugh.

'Our *what?*'

'Six months since we started seeing each other.'

'But who's counting?'

'I am.'

'We've been seeing each other for the last twenty years.'

'You know. *Seeing*, seeing.'

Frankie casts his mind back to when they actually started their relationship. It had been quite unexpected. Their friendship, after Colin died, had been intermittent. Veronica was a closer friend to Roxy for the first few years after their divorce. But after Veronica moved to Brighton, the relationship had shifted in the direction of him and Roxy, if only because they lived close to one another. Towards the end of summer 2019 they had found themselves, to their mutual surprise, sharing a bed after an otherwise innocent movie and a Chinese meal with a little too much rice wine.

'A six-month anniversary of a first shag is a thing?'

'It is in my book.'

'You don't read books.'

'The book, Frankie,' she says, mock-melodramatic, 'of my *life*.'

He has always liked Roxy, he reflects. Up to a point. She seems to him everything Veronica is not. Crude, straightforward, rough at the edges, and unashamed about everything. Her philosophy was simple: take your pleasure where you can find it and don't worry too much about the consequences. Also – they share memories. Of Colin, of his mother, of the house he lived in with Veronica and China in North Kensington. Roxy's feels like a bridge to Frankie's past.

At the same time he can't escape the idea that in forming a relationship with her, he has moved down a notch on the social scale. Veronica had been a pathologist, a proper medical professional, when he met her, twenty years ago, and now she has a successful psychotherapy practice. The fact that Roxy had worked in a shop before she married Colin and now has a nail bar rankled with him, plus the fact that she has not a single A-level to her name.

Frankie condemns himself for being a snob, but can never quite push away the thought. Not that she was an idiot. Far from it. After Colin died and left her a chunk of money, she had tried to set up in business on her own. Gourmet popcorn. It had been a failure in the long run, but she had learned a lot about running businesses and there was plenty of money left.

Her next venture, the nail bar in Hammersmith, had been ahead of trend and she had started to make a profit almost immediately. Now she had three of them operating in west London. The pampering business was a good scam. She offered free prosecco to clients and her overheads were cheap, as were the Thai girls she got to work for next to nothing, mostly off the books. Nowadays she worked even harder than Frankie, who was labouring heavily to finally secure his partnership with Farley & Ratchett, so they had relatively little time to spend with one another.

'Knock knock,' says Roxy, uneasy with the growing tension generated by Frankie's lack of response.

'Really?'

'*Knock knock.*'

'Who's there?'

'Control freak.'

Before Frankie has got the full first syllable of the response out, Roxy interrupts.

'Now you say —"*control freak who?*"'

It takes Frankie a moment to get the joke.

'Pretty good,' says Frankie. 'Very hilarious.'

Roxy smiles to herself, satisfied.

'So what about next month?' Roxy presses.

Without enthusiasm, Frankie takes himself over to his laptop and checks his diary. That date is, to his faint disappointment, vacant.

'Why not? Looks like I've not got anything else on. I don't have to get you a gift or anything, do I? I'm not up on the etiquette for six-monthly shagaversaries.'

'I wouldn't turn down a bunch of daffs. But no need to go to town.'

Roxy turns her attention back to the television. Now it's *Bake Off*.

'Last Saturday of February it is, then. I'll nip down the garage for the flowers.'

'You're such a charmer. And no M&S gourmet meals for two on special offer.'

'One way or the other, it will be something.'

Roxy looks up from the TV and catches Frankie's gaze and holds it.

'Do you promise? Because you're always breaking our appointments.'

This is true. Frankie has become increasingly unreliable as his workload has got heavier.

'It's work, you know that. I can't always predict.'

'But this one time. Do you absolutely promise?'

Frankie hesitates, then gives a shrug.

'Yes. Sure. Whatever.'

'Pinky promise?'

She pouts and holds her little finger out to him.

'Oh, for God's sake.'

He reaches out his little finger and hooks it around hers.
'Pinky promise.'

February 2020: London

It is a gloomy Sunday morning. Nodge waters the plants on
the large, south-facing balcony overlooking the London skyline which is wreathed in clouds, pregnant with rain. Owen,
coming from the living room, positions himself behind Nodge
and put his arms seductively around his lower waist.

'I have to fertilize these plants,' says Nodge firmly.

'Never mind that. What about fertilizing *me*.'

'Would that I could.'

'I'm not entirely joking, Nodge. I mean, I am, but I'm not.'

'You'll have to wait a long time. I've not really got the
equipment. Neither have you.'

'Transphobic bitch.'

Nodge extracts himself from Owen's grasp, puts down the
watering can and turns. Owen's face is round, ruddy, a side
of beef with two blue-grey jewels inset. As he and Nodge have
grown closer they have come to resemble one another more
and more. Nodge supposes ruefully that within a decade they
will have joined the great grey mass of identical old people.
Overweight, bald, indifferent to appearance. Only JJ's persistent
individual style and remarkable crop of hair gives him hope.

'You know what I mean. I can't wait to be a father.'

'I know that, Owen. Neither can I. Once we've met
with Comfort at the end of the month, I reckon we'll be
properly set.'

Comfort, their adoption case worker, has been supportive

and steadily optimistic throughout the whole drawn-out process. They have formed a close relationship with her and the last time they met she informed them that the mood music from on high was 'universally positive'.

When Nodge returns to the front room, having finished watering the plants, Owen is sitting on the black armless sofa, staring blankly at a page of *Raised by Unicorns: Stories from People With LGBTQ + Parents*. Nodge takes a seat in the shaggy cream Yeti chair opposite.

'I can't concentrate,' says Owen.

He puts the book down and looks over at Nodge. Nodge comes and sits next to Owen on the sofa and takes his hand.

'You're not unhappy, are you, O?'

'No,' says Owen, staring ahead into space.

'We're doing pretty well, aren't we?'

'Sure,' says Owen, still not meeting his eye.

'But . . . ?' says Nodge.

'Something's missing.'

'I know,' says Nodge. 'I know it is. But it won't be when we two are finally three.'

'We already are.'

'Not counting JJ, that is.'

Nodge lowers his voice.

'How do you think it's working out – having him here? Do you mind very much?'

'Not at all. I like him a lot. I just wish he'd stop beating me at chess. And littering the balcony with cigarette stubs. And I wish he'd speak a bit louder; it drives me nuts. And I wish he would stop singing "A Wand'ring Minstrel, I" off-key.'

'He says he's going to give up,' says Nodge.

'Singing? That's a relief.'

'Smoking.'

'He also says that he's been saying that for thirty years,' says Owen.

'He'll be gone in a couple of weeks.'

'I'm in no hurry. As far as I'm concerned, three's company.'

Nodge looks puzzled.

'You mean two's a crowd?'

Later that afternoon, after the papers have been read and lunch, prepared by JJ, has been consumed, Owen and JJ are slightly drunkenly tussling over a game of chess. JJ is winning as usual and ten minutes into the game Owen is already fighting to keep his queen from being trapped. JJ is dressed formally in a shirt and tie – he says he still enjoys the formality of a Sunday. Owen is in trackie bottoms and a Stone Island sweatshirt.

'No! I didn't mean to do that!' says Owen, pulling his bishop back, having several seconds previously let go of it.

'Sure,' said JJ mildly. 'Player motivation is a key factor in this game.'

'Can I take it back?'

'Well, you *can* . . . but . . .'

'But then you would be cheating,' finishes Nodge, who is drying his hands after cleaning the kitchen area.

'Thanks for the support, *darling*,' mutters Owen.

'Honestly, Owen, you can take it back if you want,' says JJ. 'I'm not much fussed.'

'No, it's fine. If you want to take it that seriously,' he says sullenly.

'Oh, for God's sake, O. How old are you?' says Nodge, laughing.

Owen tries to hold on to his snit then feels it dissolve.

'I'm being ridiculous, aren't I?'

'Just a little bit.'

'It's just that JJ always wins and I thought I had a drop on him there for a while.'

'Go on,' says JJ. 'Take it back.'

'No, no,' says Owen. 'I've got over myself.'

He leaves the bishop where he has placed it. He is defeated in three moves. He knocks his king over and sighs.

'You're a slippery bastard, JJ.'

'I'm sorry, Owen,' whispers JJ. He genuinely does look regretful.

'Don't be,' says Owen. 'You can't help it if you're clever. And nice.'

'Ah, I'm not that nice. *You're* nice, letting me stay at your flat. It's a lovely space. As my old mother used to say, handsome is as handsome does.'

'I could have beaten you,' says Owen. 'I just make stupid mistakes.'

'We all make stupid mistakes,' says JJ softly. 'Sometimes they're just not as obvious as they are on the chess board.'

Chapter Four

February 2020: Brighton

China turns the handle on the door of her bedroom, having finished her job at Nando's three hours early since there had been a fire alert. A false alarm, but they closed the restaurant anyway and sent everyone home. The hours will be docked from her wages. She is still in her outfit, a black shirt with red trim, that makes her sweat however much anti-perspirant she applies. She has been feeling cheerful, thankful for the early release. The sight that greets her as she opens the door dissipates her mellow mood. She rocks back slightly on her flat heels.

Mason, a bulky chimpanzee, twitching and fidgeting, ginger hair sticking up like carrot greens, is sitting at her desk, eyes scouring an open book, small and red, that China recognizes as her diary. Mason has not even bothered to close the desk drawer where he has clearly been rummaging. He does not look up at the sound of her entering, although she presumes he must have been aware of it. His fidgeting slows slightly, his customarily blank face shows no reaction.

'What are you doing?'

Even as she tries to keep herself calm she can feel her emotions revving, straining at the thin membrane of self-will that keeps her voice from escalating into a screech. A few seconds pass before Mason finally looks up.

'Reading your diary. It's bare funny. Specially the dirty parts.'

He goes back to reading. China lowers her voice a notch, hoping that the suppression of her anger will condense it and impart an extra level of menace.

'Give. It. To. Me.'

Mason doesn't move. China takes a quick step and makes a lunge for the book but Mason, alert to the threat, ducks out of the way off the chair and onto the bed with surprising deftness given his lumpen physicality, still holding on to the diary.

'I didn't know you were a lezzer. Have you told your mum?' he says in his slightly odd, piping voice.

'How dare you.'

'Calm down. You got sand in your vag? Or is it you got the painters in?'

China, no longer able to control her fury, inches threateningly towards him. He slips off the bed and crouches on the other side. She tries to keep in the line between him and the escape route of the bedroom door. She circumnavigates the bed and closes in, inch by inch.

Mason realizes that the possibilities of escape are limited. At the same time, he registers the deadly look on China's face. She lunges again. He makes a dash for the door, over the top of the bed, but China swings her body round and catches him by the heel. He falls flat on the mattress and starts screaming.

'Dad! DAD.'

China tries to get a purchase on his leg and pull the diary from his hands, but he holds tight. The pages tear, leaving scraps on the floor.

'You're a carpet muncher,' yells Mason, wriggling furiously to free his foot from China's iron grasp.

China, climbing onto the bed, manages to secure Mason firmly by the collar of his polo shirt and finally take possession of the diary. Mason begins weeping, purely tactically as far as China is concerned.

'Dad!'

China, adrenaline and outrage driving her now, pulls him off the bed towards the small sink in the corner of the room, toiletries arranged along the rim. She feels strength flow through her so that the lumpish child feels light and easy to move. Mason looks up at her, frightened now. His usually half-closed, cunning eyes widen.

'What you going to do?'

Keeping one hand on the back of Mason's collar, as he writhes to break free, she grabs a small bar of soap that she had lifted from the Nando's bathroom a few weeks previously.

'Going to cry again for your daddy?'

'I want my mum.'

'She's dead.'

While his mouth is still open and before he has a chance to shut it, China slams the bar of soap into his mouth. She keeps her hand over his mouth to stop him spitting it out. Although he writhes and tries to escape, she holds him firm. Foam

105

begins appear at the edges of his mouth. His face turns red, his eyes are stretched wide with panic.

'Gaaaaaah!'

Then China hears Silas's normally quiet voice suddenly fill the room.

'China. What the frick are you doing?'

China turns and sees Silas framed in the doorway. Reluctantly she lets go of Mason, who spits out the soap on the floor. Silas takes two long steps towards China. His large, bulky body is tensed, his face is stone.

'He . . . ' Her voice dries, unnerved by Silas's body language. Despite his supposedly gentle demeanour, which she never quite believed in, he is 6'2" and strong from years of manual labour. Mason is bawling loudly now. Silas stops his advance towards China and leans down. Mason throws his arms around his father's neck, weeping bitterly and spluttering.

'She made me eat soap!'

Silas stands up again, Mason draped round his shoulders. His face is flushed, either from the sudden exertion – Mason is no featherweight – or anger. He snaps his head around to China and squints as if to bring her into focus.

'*Did you*, China?'

Silas looks at the spat-out bar of soap on the floor and puts his finger to a speck of foam at the corner of Mason's mouth. He tastes the finger.

'You did. You really did.'

He speaks in low, heavy tones. She has never heard him talk in this way before. China catches Mason's eye. He has stopped crying and he is now, out of the sight of his father, openly smirking.

'He read my diary.'

'So what? He's twelve. Years. Old. You're meant to be an adult.'

'He called me . . . he called me a . . . '

She can't bring herself to say the words, because it will reveal the private world of her diary to Silas.

'Dad, I didn't say anything!' said Mason, freshly tearful. 'I didn't know it was her diary. I just thought it had a pretty cover and it was a storybook. I didn't read any of it. I promise.'

'What did he call you, China?'

'He swore at me.'

'I didn't,' said Mason, crying loudly again. China ruefully reflects that this is true. She is trapped. It was her that swore.

'She called me the F-word.'

China has no answer. There is no point in denying it, as Silas had come through the door by then. Mason clings tightly to Silas's neck.

'You know this is child abuse, China – right?'

'Come off it, Silas. Anyway, it isn't soap. It's an organic oatmeal cleansing bar.'

'It's child abuse. I'm going to have to call the police. You've gone too far this time, China. You've committed a crime. I'm going to report you.'

'I thought you hated the police. I thought you thought we should defund them.'

China feels the situation spiralling out her control. She decides it is her turn to call Mayday.

'Mum!'

Already aware of the commotion and halfway up the stairs before China made her distress call, Veronica appears, her hair

TIM LOTT

wild, zip on her skirt undone, dressed in a business suit ready-
ing herself to conduct an afternoon therapy session.

'What's going on?' Her voice is flat, unconcerned. She
is used to crises like this. She pulls up the zip on her skirt.
Despite staying slim, she has put on an inch or two on the hips
over the last five years and it's an old skirt. It won't quite make
it to the top. She pushes her hair off her face in order to see
better and struggles again with the zip tab.

'Silas's calling the feds on me.'

'He's doing what?'

She yanks the zip up another inch, then gives up with half
an inch still to go.

'I'm going to have to invest in a new skirt.'

'She rammed a bar of soap down Mason's throat,' says Silas.

'It wasn't like that, Mum. It wasn't soap; it was a cleansing bar. I shouldn't have done it. But he was reading *my diary*.
There's very personal stuff in there.'

'I wasn't reading your diary. I didn't know it was your
diary,' Mason pipes up.

'*Did* you put soap in his mouth?' says Veronica, finally putting her skirt dilemma out of her mind.

'I didn't hurt him!'

'You shouldn't have done that, China,' says Silas. 'He's a
kid and we think he has a developmental disorder. He just said
he didn't read your diary. Mason may be a lot of things. A bit
unruly sometimes. But he's not a liar. I've always taught him
to tell the truth.'

'You must be joking,' says China, outraged at the size of the
lie. 'He's a fucking little . . . '

'She's swearing again,' says Mason.

'Like I say – I'm calling the police,' says Silas.

'There's no need for that, Silas. We can sort this out,' says Veronica, holding out a placatory hand, palm upward.

'This kind of thing can lead to permanent psychological damage. You're a therapist, you know that. That's why it's illegal,' says Silas. With Mason's arms still wrapped round his neck, he fishes his phone from his pocket.

Mason, catching China's eye, winks.

'You little bastard.'

'China. Stop making it worse!' hisses Veronica.

'He winked at me! Why are you taking his side?'

'So are you going to push another bar of soap down his throat?' says Silas.

'I didn't push it down his *throat*. Only into his mouth. Don't be so *dramatic*. It was only a tiny bar. He was rude to me.'

She is close to tears now.

'I *wasn't*.'

Silas starts dialling. Before he can react, Veronica darts forward and snatches the phone out of Silas's hands.

'There's no need for that, Silas. You're overreacting. I know China has misbehaved. But we'll figure something out between ourselves.'

'Mum! I haven't "misbehaved". I'm not a child. You're taking their side again.'

Silas stares at Veronica with a dead gaze. China thinks she can see pure hatred flash across his face. She watches as he conceals it with his well-seasoned mask of reason and compromise.

'I disagree.'

'Can we just take a few minutes to all calm down, please?

Let's talk about this,' says Veronica, in what China recognizes as her therapist's voice.

'There's nothing to discuss.'

Silas seems to bury his feet inches into the floorboards, presenting himself as an immovable object.

'Give me my phone back, please, Veronica.'

His voice is low, but cuts the air. Mason has finally disentangled himself from Silas, judging himself safe from China now, and stands beside his father, his face showing a mixture of self-pity and barely suppressed amusement.

'No,' says Veronica, stung now by China's accusation of partiality. She stands square to Silas. 'I won't'.

Mason who, it now appears, has been manoeuvring for position, suddenly sprints and grabs the phone out of Veronica's hand, turns back and hands it triumphantly to his father.

'Mason! Stop it. This is between me and your father.'

'She's a bloody lesbian,' blurts Mason, unable to resist the temptation any longer.

'How dare you!' says Veronica.

'Don't tell my son to stop it, Veronica. He was doing the right thing. After all, you snatched the phone out of *my* hands, didn't you? Why is what he did any different?'

'Because you were going to call the police!' Her voice suddenly takes on a puzzled tone. 'Anyway, why is he saying that China is a lesbian?'

'*Are* you a lesbian, China?' says Silas, his voice suddenly overflowing with concern. 'Because, you know. That's fine if you are.'

'It's none of your *business*.' China is choking back sobs now. 'Why do you think he thinks I am a lesbian? 'Cos he read it in *my diary*.'

Silas nods, counterfeiting patience.

'Well, as you say. Your gender and your sexuality is your own affair. However, I still have a duty to report child abuse.'

He starts to punch numbers into his phone, which he seems to know off by heart. This time, slapstick, it is China who lurches forward and grabs the phone. Before Silas can react she throws it out of the open first-floor window. There is a faint tinkling of breaking glass and plastic as it lands on the concrete patio below.

China thinks for a moment that Silas is going to hit her. She realizes that she wants him to hit her. Silas breathes heavily but doesn't move. Mason grins. This time, Veronica catches Mason's expression.

'If you've broken my phone, you'll pay for it,' says Silas. 'And even if you haven't you're going to pay for what you did to Mason.'

'You don't get to punish my daughter, Silas,' says Veronica.

'That's right. And you know what, Veronica? China doesn't get to punish my son. Come on, Mace. Some ice cream will take away the taste of that soap.'

Silas turns and walks slowly out of the room, Mason at his coat-tails. China watches them leave, helpless, as Mason flashes China one last infuriating smile. With that smile, China knows that the moment she has so often feared and anticipated has arrived.

February 2020: London

There is a buzz at the door of Nodge and Owen's flat. Not expecting anyone, Nodge walks to the door and calls out to the other side.

'Who is it?'

'Jiang Chiang.'

A woman's voice. Nodge looks puzzled, but opens the door anyway.

China is standing there holding her *Hunger Games* backpack in front of her and wearing a houndstooth coat with moth holes in the sleeve.

'Hello, Uncle Nodge.'

To China's surprise, Nodge doesn't move forward to greet her.

'China? What are you doing here?'

'Pleased to see me?'

Nodge just stares at her. Now China is positively disconcerted. She had expected a more or less ecstatic welcome.

'Can I come in?'

He hesitates again, then moves to one side.

'Of course. But why are you here? What happened?'

China takes a step forward and then, instead of moving further into the hallway, hurls herself into Nodge's chest and begins weeping. Nodge pats her gently on the back. He can feel the angles of her shoulder blades. She is too thin.

'I've run away from home.'

Nodge, Owen and China sit round the kitchen table, each nursing a fresh mug of herbal tea. China has taken off her coat to reveal a brown fifties' flared skirt and an orange polyester blouse that she found in a skip. They are both too big for her and they make her look even slighter than she actually is.

'We're so glad to see you, China,' says Owen, knitting the fingers of his hands together and resting them on the tabletop.

'We *are*,' says Nodge, who is still in his pyjamas, having done a night shift the evening before.

China smiles showing her gold tooth. When she allows herself it, she has an enormous smile, open, wide and somehow deeply innocent.

'I knew you would be. I knew I could rely on you both. I feel so comfortable with you. You're not like my mum and dad. *You* accept me for who I am.'

'Don't be too hard on Veronica and Frankie. They do their best,' says Nodge.

'Oh no! Mum's great, I'm not knocking her – really I'm not. But she doesn't understand what it's like for me to share a house with Silas and Mason. She's not there a lot of the time, and Silas usually works from home and Mason always seems to be under my feet and in my face. He's been trying to get rid of me for as long as I can remember.'

'But he's only . . . '

'Don't you dare say "he's only twelve".'

'China. He hasn't got a mum. If his dad is as big a dick as you say he is, he hasn't got much of a father either.'

'Whereas you have,' adds Owen cautiously, unlacing his hands.

'What's that meant to mean?' says China, her guard suddenly up, gold tooth disappearing beneath anxious white lips.

'Does Frankie know you're in London?' says Owen.

'Not yet.'

'How do you think he would feel if he knew that you had run away from Brighton to come and stay with us instead of him?' says Nodge.

'That's his problem.'

'It's my problem too. Frankie's been my friend for forty years. I can't keep this a secret from him.'

'Then don't,' says China. She takes the teabag out of the cup and squeezes it violently.

'Why don't you want to stay with him?' says Owen gently, trying to defuse China's visible anxiety. She barks a brief, humourless laugh.

'He's a racist for a start.'

'You're just like I used to be,' says Nodge.

'What's that, then?'

'A bit of a prig.'

China is stung by this remark, but is determined to show both Owen and Nodge that she is mature and in control of her emotions.

'So why aren't you like that now?' she says as calmly as she can manage.

'Because I've learned that people are complicated. Also, that self-righteousness is the perfect excuse for being cruel.'

'Being "laid back" is the perfect excuse for being indifferent to everything outside your own interests.'

Nodge is about to speak again but Owen, mindful of China's fretfulness, shoots him a reproving look and takes her hand.

'You've been brave. You must be tired. I can imagine what a terrible time you must have had. Listen – let's open a bottle of wine, have some supper, then go to bed and talk about it all in the morning. In fact, I think I've got a spliff stashed away somewhere. Do you get high, China?'

The gold tooth appears again.

'I certainly do.'

'Let's leave all the earnest stuff for tomorrow, then. I'm

going to make some supper and open a bottle. In the mean-time, why don't you go and have a bath?'

'That would be amazing.'

'Off you go, then. It's all La Labo soaps and shampoos; help yourself to as much as you want. There's a fresh bathrobe in the airing cupboard; help yourself to that too. As for supper — you're a vegetarian, right? I'll make something comforting.'

China wells up again. She is hormonal, on top of every-thing else.

'Thank you, Owen. Thank you, Nodge.'

'I'll show you to the spare bedroom.'

He indicates the stairs. She rises and walks up them unsteadily. Owen takes her backpack and follows her. It has rips and stains all over it and is surprisingly heavy.

'Christ, China, what have you got in here?'

'Pretty much everything I own, I suppose.'

They pass through the landing and enter the spare room. To China's surprise, although it is very neat and tidy, she notices that there is a pair of Japanese pyjamas hung over the back of the chair and a pair of men's shoes underneath. The shoes are patent leather, clearly expensive, and both flamboyant and somehow archaic. She registers that they are unlikely to be the property of her hosts.

'I'll change the bed for you, China.'

'Whose are the fancy shoes?'

'This is JJ's room. Remember? He's playing Nanki-Poo in *Mikado*.'

'JJ?'

'You struck lucky. He's away for the weekend. He's been living with us for a few weeks while his house is being renovated. I think Nodge told you before. Which is another reason why it's tricky for you to stay here. His house won't be finished for a while yet.'

China feels a sudden rush of dismay. Suddenly unsteady, she sits down on the bed.

'Oh. I mean . . . can't you . . . '

'We can't throw him out. Much as we both love you, it simply wouldn't be fair.'

'When's he back?'

'Tomorrow night. So you only get one night here, I'm afraid.'

China nods, and decides it will be impossible to complain. But she no longer has any idea what to do.

Owen returns to the living room several minutes later. Nodge is sitting at the dining table. His expression is serious, vexed.

'You know she can't stay here, don't you?' says Nodge as Owen sits down.

'Yes, I know she can't stay here.'

'You know why, don't you?'

'Because of JJ, obviously.'

'Not just because of JJ. Because of Frankie. I mean I love her. But I love Frankie too. I can't betray him.'

Owen covers Nodge's hand with his own.

'Perhaps you should call him and discuss it.'

Nodge enjoys the warmth of Owen's touch for a moment, then looks up at him with pleading eyes.

'I *can't*. Really, I can't, Owen. It would break his heart. It would say to him that China prefers me to him and that would be a blow he can't stand right now. He's not in a good place.

And it's not true either. China doesn't know it, because she's still only nineteen, but she loves Frankie. And Frankie *certainly* loves her. He never stops going on about her.'

'She loves you, too.'

'She loves *us*. Just not in the same way. We're just a symbol for her of – something or other,' says Nodge.

'She just needs to forgive him is all.'

'Easier said than done when you think you've had your childhood stolen from you. It helps to have a villain. Even though it wasn't all Frankie's fault.'

'I know that. But she's not mature enough to grasp that. Her mother was always her saviour. Now Veronica's let her down as well – at least as far as she's concerned – by getting involved with this Silas bloke and his kid. She's thinks she's got nowhere to go,' says Owen.

'But she does have somewhere to go. About a mile from here.'

Nodge can hear the gurgle of the bath drawing upstairs. His phone sounds. Nodge examines the screen and groans.

'Shit. It's Frankie. Right on cue. What am I going to tell him?'

'Don't answer.'

But Nodge has already hit 'accept'. Owen reaches over and presses the speaker button on the phone and sits back, putting a finger to his lips.

'Hi, Frankie.'

'Nodge! How are you?'

Frankie's voice sounds tired and vaguely sad.

'Good. I'm . . . good.'

'What's new?'

'Nothing much. How about you?'

'Nothing much. Just a bit bored.'

There is a pause. Frankie is waiting for the invitation that he expects. It not being forthcoming, he follows up.

'Wondering if you fancied a swift pint?'

Nodge, grimacing at Owen, decides to stall.

'Roxy not with you tonight?'

'That's sort of what I wanted to talk to you about. We're struggling.'

'Okay.'

There is another awkward pause. Nodge mouths 'What shall I say?' to Owen.

'So, what about it then?' Frankie continues. 'Even just a half. And a bag of crisps. The crisps are on me.'

Owen mimes making supper. Nodge frowns, then catches the drift.

'It's a bit difficult tonight, to be honest. Owen is just getting dinner ready. He's gone to a fair bit of trouble. You know what he's like.'

'Well, I could come over.'

Owen puts his head on his clasped hands and closes his eyes, miming sleep.

'I'm . . . a bit exhausted to tell you the truth.'

'I thought today was your day off.'

Nodge looks at Owen desperately, but this time he just shrugs. Nodge's eyes widen in panic.

'It varies,' he tries.

'But it's always Thursdays. For as long as I can remember.'

'Not anymore. Uber competition. I have to put in more hours than I used to.'

Owen puts his thumb up and Nodge returns the gesture.

'Right. So . . . '

Nodge and Owen exchange glances. They both hear the disappointment in Frankie's voice. Then China calls from upstairs.

'I can't find the towels!'

Owen rises and urgently makes his way up the stairs, making 'cut' gestures to Nodge with the side of his hand.

'Who was that?' says Frankie.

'The radio,' says Nodge. 'How about tomorrow night? Are you free then?'

'I can't. I'm having Roxy over. It's our anniversary, it appears.'

'Is it okay if you and I do Saturday, then?' says Nodge, trying to close the conversation.

'Fine, I suppose.'

'Great.'

There is another pause. Frankie is clearly waiting for Nodge to think again, but eventually gives up.

'Later, then,' says Frankie.

'Yeh. Later.'

Nodge, perhaps too quickly, hangs up. Owen has returned from upstairs, having found China a towel, and is sitting opposite him.

'Christ, I hated that!' says Nodge. 'I'm lying to him left, right and centre. He's my friend. What kind of friend lies like that?'

'A friend who wants to stop another friend getting hurt.'

'All the same.'

Nodge stares resentfully at the phone as if it had planned Frankie's call.

'Why did he have to call right at that moment?' says Nodge.

'You didn't have to answer.'

'Stop being annoying.'

'How am I being annoying?'

'By being right. Look, the long and short of it is, she can't stay here.'

'I agree. But where's she going to go?'

'Only one place she can,' says Nodge.

The following morning, China takes some convincing, a full-on back and forth with Owen and Nodge for at least an hour over granola, honey and yoghurt, but in the end, she accepts she has no choice but to give in.

'Alright. *Alright*. I'll try.'

'Good,' says Nodge, the relief plain in his voice.

'But if it doesn't work out . . . '

'Then you can come back here. At least Frankie will know you tried. But you've got to give it a proper go. A month at least. By then JJ will have gone.'

'A month?'

'At least. Then if you really think you can't stand it anymore, we'll happily put you up for a while. In fact we'd be delighted to.'

China looks sulky but she can tell by the firm set of Nodge's mouth that arguing isn't going to do any good.

'So, let's see you do what you've got to do, then,' says Nodge, nodding in the direction of her phone.

Reluctantly, China picks up the phone as if her arm contained ballast and hits the number for her father. The phone at the other end picks up almost before the first ring is completed.

*

The woman – it is almost impossible to tell her age – crouches in the doorway of a shuttered shop in Soho selling gay sex toys, fetish gear and fashion. She is filthy and she is, by her own estimation, as well as that of most passers-by, patently mad. Her eyes that stare so blankly at a space of nothingness in front of her, or roam wildly looking for something invisible, advertise the fact. She rocks back and forth and mumbles to herself constantly. She holds out a small plastic beaker in front of her. Half a dozen coins cluster at the base. Most people ignore her.

'She's just going to buy drugs with the money,' the woman hears one well-dressed passer-by say, to discourage her partner who has been half-heartedly reaching for his wallet.

The well-dressed woman is right. The woman wants money for drugs. It's the only thing she has ever wanted money for, or, at least, since she became the woman she is now. And that was so long ago.

She has sucked cock for drug money, she has been fucked for drug money, she has smuggled drugs for drug money. She has been in prison six times, she thinks, but in all honesty she has lost count. They are kind to her in there sometimes; she doesn't much mind. There is nothing left of her really – just bony scraps, but still she lives on somehow.

She is sitting in Old Compton Street with her knees up to her chin, a crumpled piece of cardboard in front of her, with 'Please take pity' on it. It was a bit Victorian, but she had discovered that it worked okay.

If she could remember how old she was, she might worry that she was getting old. As it was, the only clock was her skin, which was now mottled, whorled and yellow. The skin of a seventy-year-old. But she wasn't seventy — she was sure of it. Nothing like.

She turns and examines her face now, in the sheet of plate glass of the neighbouring delicatessen. It broadcasts back a double image. She can make out enough to prompt her to look away quickly. The decrepitude is not only unsightly but unprofitable. She can't even sell her body anymore. It has come to that.

She feels something warm between her legs and incuriously looks down. The escape of urine has formed a wet patch the size of a tea plate on the crotch of her jeans. She looks up again, unconcerned. She doesn't quite know who she is or even who she has been. The drugs have taken that away — the street drugs and the terrible depressions that the legal drugs had tried to erase, less and less successfully as time flowed through her, eroding her from the inside. Erasing her.

As she flops back against the shuttered shopfront she thinks to herself that she is living in a state of perfect equality. At her level — the level of legs and knees and ankles — everyone is the same. The shoes varied, of course, but she can no longer tell the expensive ones from the cheap ones. Her own shoes, dirty brown men's suede brogues, she had found in a skip. They are too big and hurt her feet. She will find a new pair, but at the moment her every thought is for her next fix.

She glances at the clock across the road. Her sight, like everything else, is fading, but she can tell that there are ten hours to go until she can make her connection. She doesn't have enough money. There are now four pound coins on the cardboard and some loose change. Not nearly enough.

She starts crying, a series of audible sobs. In truth, she is long beyond crying spontaneously. It is a performative act, an act of commerce. A weeping woman, even one as destroyed as she is, usually produces results. Sure enough, within a minute or so, a middle-aged man wearing a business suit bends down to her.

'Are you alright?' His voice is tender, quiet.

She nods, giving the impression of courage she hopes, then carries on crying.

'Can I get you some food?'

Fuck off, she thinks. She shakes her head. Her voice, when it emerges, is deliberately tiny.

'No, thank you.'

'Do you want to talk?'

She's had enough. Her voice comes out low and broken.

'Please, can you spare me some change?'

'I can buy you some food if you like.'

She shakes her head and the man hesitates, then walks away. Then, almost immediately, another punter, this one a woman, comes over and puts £5 in her cup. This is more like it. The street woman can't be bothered to thank her; she is also beyond gratitude. There is only pointless survival.

She has a limited amount of tears to manufacture, but she keeps doing the best she can, sometimes managing nothing more than a dry sobbing. After an hour, she has £40 and a ham sandwich from Pret. She decides to take a break. Gathering up her sleeping gear and her bright blue laundry bag, she begins stumbling towards the Strand where many of the others in the homeless diaspora congregate.

When she gets there, she recognizes only Davy Greenjacket. She doesn't like him very much. A huge man with no teeth and partly blind, who always wore the same stained green anorak, he would sometimes make a grab at her, although she suspects he wouldn't know what to do with her if she threw her ruined, naked body down in front of him. And she isn't about to try and find out. So she keeps walking, nodding to Davy as she goes. He stares through her.

The air is cool today but not unbearably cold and a thin sunshine comes through the clouds. She would have once thought it a beautiful day, but now her mind can't really settle on anything long enough to appreciate it one way or the other. It flicks between the past and the present, but rarely the future except in the case of meeting her connection. Nothing else has pleasure for her, not even food. Not even the brown sugar for that matter – it just stops her getting the horrors for a while.

She wonders idly if she should try suicide again, but knows it is just a fantasy, like the occasional one she had of getting back on her feet again. She knows she doesn't have the courage. An old blues song drifts into her head . . . *tired of living . . . scared of dying* . . . She can't remember the tune. She had liked the blues once. Hadn't she? Or was that someone else? Her thoughts are clouds that you can see through, that part and drift and disappear and are always pregnant with rain.

She becomes aware of the feel of the wet patch on her jeans – or rather the sharp smell that drifts up from it. There is a closed charity shop in this street and someone has put a bag outside it. She stops and rummages around, finding a pair of jeans with designer holes in them – stupid! – and a green frilly dress.

She explores further and locates a pair of men's flannel trousers. She sniffs them – they appear to be sufficiently clean.

In full view of anyone who happens to walk past, she roughly pulls off her jeans – no knickers, she never bothered with those anymore – throws the urine-soaked jeans into the gutter and pulls on the flannel trousers. They are far too big, but she keeps a bit of rope in her backpack and she ties this around the waist. It was good enough and the trousers were warm and dry. She always dresses as a man; it means far less hassle.

She unzips the laundry bag and takes a toothbrush and a tube of toothpaste out. For some reason, she has always tried to keep her teeth up to scratch even as everything else falls apart. She can't bear the taste of her own mouth nowadays. It is stale and smoky like a used firework.

She pulls a bottle of expensive mineral water from her jacket pocket, taken earlier from a bin, swills, douses the toothbrush and, for the next three minutes, brushes carefully. Then she sits back down and, refreshed, pulls out her cardboard sign and the plastic cup. She begins crying again with renewed gusto.

Chapter Five

February 2020: London

Frankie is sitting in the bath, staring at the ceiling while idly trying to fit his big toe into one of the taps, when his phone, balanced on the rim, starts vibrating. Seeing who is calling, he picks up immediately, albeit anxious that he might drop it into the water, which seethes with foaming pine-scented bath oil.

'Dad!'

He has failed to register in his excitement that it is a FaceTime call. He switches the video off.

'Sorry.'

'That's a sight I'm never going to be able to unsee.'

'This is a nice surprise.'

He tries to sound cheerful, but he knows he is coming across as anxious. China always puts him on his guard. Hearing the false note in his voice, he props himself up further and hits

127

the speaker button. Immediately, perhaps because he is nervous, he breaks wind in the water.

'What's that noise?'

'What noise?'

'Gurgling. Did you just fart?'

'No. To what do I owe the honour, my darling daughter?'

Nodge, off camera, watches her carefully as China rolls her eyes.

'Do you have to speak in that stupid way, Dad?'

'What stupid way? Hold on a minute.'

Putting the phone to one side, he pulls himself out the bath, pops the plug and starts vigorously drying himself.

'"To what do I owe the honour?" What are you, the Lord Mayor?'

'It's just an expression.'

China puts the phone on mute and turns to Nodge and Owen.

'He's annoying me already. And he's in the *bath*.'

She looks pleadingly at Nodge, hoping for a commuting of her sentence. Nodge simply nods towards the phone. China takes it off mute.

'China? Are you still there?'

'Yes, I'm still here. Dad, look. I want to ask you a favour.'

The sound of the water draining suddenly becomes very loud, so that Frankie can hardly hear what China is saying. Still naked, he turns the speaker off and puts the phone to his ear.

'Of course. Anything.'

China, glancing at Nodge again with a final pleading look, takes a deep breath. Owen, who has joined him, remains similarly unmoved.

'Can I come and stay with you for a little while?'

Frankie wraps the towel around his waist; it feels indecent to be naked while he is talking to his daughter even though she can't see him. The noise of the draining bath still makes it difficult to hear.

'Can you what?'

'I *said*, can I come and stay with you for a little while?'

Frankie feels a wave of exultation, but his pride prompts him to feign indifference.

'Well, this is very sudden. Any particular reason?'

'No, no particular reason. I'm just bored with Brighton and I want a break.'

Frankie puts the phone down and pulls on a pair of under-pants. Struggling with his jeans, getting one leg in without being able to find the entrance for the other, he topples over and falls on the bed, dropping the phone in the process.

'Shit!'

'Shit?'

Frankie grabs the phone and puts it back on speaker again while he tries to regain control of his trousers. The sound of the draining bath has subdued to a damp whisper.

'No, no. Not shit. I mean, when?'

There is a brief pause at the other end. Then China, seeing there is no escape under the steely gaze of Nodge, answers.

'Now.'

Frankie has both legs in the trousers now and is doing up his belt, but he stops in his tracks, leaving the buckle to dangle.

'What do you mean – *now*?'

'As in today.'

Frankie feels himself to be on the back foot. Roxy is coming for supper in a few hours' time and staying the night to celebrate their 'anniversary', so called. He fumbles with the buckle on his trousers, accepting reluctantly that it needs to be another notch looser, then sits gingerly on the edge of the bed, a furrow of concern burying itself in his forehead.

'Why the rush? What really happened?'

Nodge nods at her and rotates his open hand in the air to indicate that she should be honest. For the last time China gives him an imploring look, then her shoulders drop.

'To tell you the truth, I had a huge fight with Mum and Silas. I walked out. So I need to stay with you for a couple of weeks.'

Frankie feels a guilty glow of pleasure at this confirmation that life in Brighton was less rosy than Veronica advertised it.

'That's a shame. What was the fight about?'

'I'll tell you when I get there.'

Frankie's eyes dart around the bedroom as if hoping to find a solution inscribed on the walls. Finding nothing, his eyes rest on the cheap white IKEA wardrobe. The TV fixed on the wall shows his reflection in blackened colour.

'Well . . . ' says Frankie cautiously.

'What?' After being so reluctant to visit, now sensing a hitch, China feels an urgent need to claim her place.

'It's just that . . . Roxy is meant to be staying here tonight.'

'So what? Just cancel her.'

'I can't really.'

'Let's talk when I get there. I'm on the train now. Just going into a tunnel. About to cut off. But please, Dad. Just the two of us, okay?'

'But . . . '

'I'll explain everything later. See you in a little while. Bye.'

China hangs up. Nodge and Owen clap lightly and China bows.

Meanwhile, in the Golborne Road, Frankie stares at the phone and feels the acid of anxiety pooling in his gut.

Frankie, determined to be as good as his word after promising Roxy her anniversary dinner, has even bought a cookbook, *Cooking for Lovers*. He knows he's not a good cook, but ever since Veronica has gone, he has been doing his best to train himself. Cooking for one is a dispiriting business, however, so he's out of practice.

This time he's taken the afternoon off to prepare, gone shopping in several fancy supermarkets searching for ingredients that are obscure to him, Ras el Hanout and White Miso being two of the most tricky to source, taking him through the portals of food stores displaying many ingredients he hitherto never realized existed.

He has bought some beef filet – Roxy loves meat; cost an arm and a leg – some balsamic vinegar that was 15 sovs, just to dip a £5 focaccia in. He has sought out aromatic candles, purchased flowers, tidied and cleaned the flat and hoovered with his scratched and battered Henry. Roxy was scheduled to arrive at seven.

Then the phone call from China had come.

Now he stands and stares out of his bedroom window, trying to gather some scraps of resolve. Eventually, he sits down on the lattice chair in the corner of the room and, with a sense of acute trepidation, he FaceTimes Roxy. She picks up almost immediately. She is at the nail salon on the Uxbridge Road, a pale fluorescent light illuminating her face, casting menacing angles of shadow. Although Frankie hasn't said anything at all yet, he is aware that she is gazing piercingly into her camera, her face held close, as if already locked into combat mode.

'Hi, Rocks,' says Frankie, falteringly. Her telepathic abilities always unnerve him.

'You'd better not be calling to cancel our supper,' she says, then turns to her left and bellows to someone off camera.

'Busarakham! Tidy your station, it's a tip. Now!'

Frankie hears a murmur of apology from one of the tiny Thai girls Roxy employs, who passes into the camera field, dressed in a pure white outfit and scrambling in haste towards the massage bed that is her responsibility. Roxy's eyes swivel back to the camera phone in front of her. She stares again into the lens, waiting for Frankie to reply. Her business persona is so different from the sentimental and slightly frivolous woman he knows when she is off duty.

'Not exactly,' ventures Frankie.

'What you mean "Not exactly"?'

Roxy's eyes harden and she brings the phone still closer to her face. Frankie, seeming to see tiny yellow flames in the depths of her pupil, focuses on a corner of the screen so that her expression is only in peripheral vision.

'It's China.'

'What about her?'

To Frankie's momentary relief, Roxy's eyes are distracted again.

'Busarakham! Not like that, for fuck's sake. Use a clean cloth.'

Her gaze returns to Frankie, more intense than ever.

'She wants to come and stay,' says Frankie.

Roxy nods as if she has always been expecting some such foolery.

'Since when?'

'Since now.'

'I see. So when is she arriving?'

Her voice has coarsened, a far cry from the velvet pampering tones she uses for customers in the salon.

'That's the thing. In an hour or two – I think.'

Frankie takes his eyes of the screen altogether and lets his eyes focus on a white bird flying past the window. He makes a mental note to get some blinds fitted instead of the tatty curtains that, when open, leave the interior of the room open to the sight of anyone living in the flats on the opposite side of the road.

'Why aren't you looking at me, Frankie?'

The white bird disappears. He reluctantly draws his eyes back to the screen. Someone has turned a light off in the salon so now Roxy seems to peer out of the darkness.

'You *are* taking the piss? Right?' she says, her lips straight and thin.

'She just rang. Apparently she's had a big fight with Silas and Vronky.'

There is a beat before Roxy speaks again. The background seems to darken yet again, although Frankie doesn't know if this is just happening in his imagination. Roxy, meanwhile, appears – in the pool of remaining light – to be deathly white.

'So let me get this straight. China, who has been perfectly indifferent to you for the last five years – treats you, in fact, like a piece of garbage – rings up and tell you to drop everything because she's had a row with her mum. So you just roll over.'

133

Frankie now sits on the bed, stares at a small framed photo of China on the bedside table, three years old, gurning for the camera. The expression seems to mock Frankie.

'I never get to see her. Please try to understand. This is a chance for me, Roxy.'

'A chance for what?'

'To start to repair our relationship.'

'It can wait till tomorrow, surely?'

'She's on the train already.'

'She can stay in a hotel.'

'She's my *daughter*.'

'And I'm your *partner*.'

'Whaddya gonna do?' he mutters, unable to think of anything else to say.

'Frankie. You're not Tony Soprano,' snaps Roxy. 'More like Toni the ice cream man.'

'It's silly arguing about it,' says Frankie, now checking his watch, worried that China will actually ring on the door while he is talking to Roxy, forcing him to cut the call short. 'Why can't she just join us for supper? We can still have a nice time.'

'Very romantic. Supper with Titania McGrath. Well, at least I should learn something about my privilege. Which according to her I am fucking marinated in. Busarakham! Not that cloth! Oh, for God's sake, just go home, why don't you?'

Frankie hears a muttered assent at the other end and the Thai woman once again enters the camera field, head bowed, her expression cowed and apologetic.

'I know you and her don't see eye to eye over politics,' says Frankie. 'But you can get through one night, surely? You don't *have* to talk to her about illegal immigrants and the betrayal of the white working class.'

'Fine, Frankie. That's just fucking great.'

'I'll see if . . . ' But before he can finish, the screen goes blank. Roxy has cut off the call.

Now he's not even sure if Roxy is going to come or not. Dejectedly, he heads downstairs and into the small kitchen that is divided from the living room by a plasterboard wall. He starts half-heartedly assembling the ingredients for the meal. The prospect of the evening has sent his anxiety levels off the scale. He hasn't told China that he has failed to cancel his date with Roxy, worried that he might scare his daughter away.

But maybe, he thinks, with not much confidence, Roxy won't turn up, things will calm down between the two of them and everything will be fine. Trying to keep hold of this encouraging thought, he turns back to the food preparation. He finds himself focusing on chopping and slicing and grinding and crushing.

At six o'clock, there is a ring at the door. Frankie concludes that it has to be China because Roxy has house keys and China lost hers long ago or, more likely, threw them in a bin in a fit of pique. Opening the door, sure enough, he sees China stands there looking weary but not, for once, especially hostile. She is wearing baggy, shapeless clothes and her brown hair is strag-gled. On her hands, an assortment of cheap kitschy rings. Her nails are painted an array of different colours and she carries in front of her a large, heavy-looking *Hunger Games* backpack.

Frankie reaches forward and embraces her, but the backpack gets in the way and makes the gesture awkward. She tries to reach behind him all the same and he can feel the faint inter-mittent touch of her hands on the back of his jumper, hovering birds trying to land on a scorched surface.

'Look at you,' says Frankie, separating himself and taking the heavy backpack from her.

'Look at me. A proper sight.'

Frankie registers that she looks forlorn and tired. There are grey bags under her eyes and the sclera are the colour of dilute tea.

'You've lost weight.'

'You're looking a bit porky,' she responds, with a weak but not unfriendly smile.

'Thanks.'

She pulls the backpack out of Frankie's hands.

'I can manage, Dad.'

'No, really.'

'I said, I can manage. It's not the 1950s.'

'I was just trying to be helpful. Cup of tea?'

'I'd rather have coffee.'

China takes a step inside. She stops to look at the framed 10 x 8 photo on the side table by the front door – Frankie, China and Veronica outside the old house in North Kensington. China is maybe five years old. Veronica is staring at Frankie lovingly while China laughs, mouth wide open, hair in bunches. Frankie stares amicably at the camera, which is held by a friend of his who is a professional photographer. There is authority in Frankie's gaze – he is paying for the photograph and he is deter-mined that it conjure the right image. It is one of the few things he took from the family house before it was sold by auction. Veronica claimed what was left with Frankie's guilty assent.

'Nice picture.'

Frankie follows her gaze.

'Great days.'

'Were they? I don't remember.'

She bends down, and opens her bag searching for some painkillers, strewing detritus – clothes, packets of gum, a yellowed copy of *Death of a Salesman* – on the floor as she does so. Finding the blister pack she is searching for, she pops two co-codamol into her mouth.

'Got some water?'

She looks through the open door to the kitchen area and registers the exotic ingredients and chopped vegetables strewn about on the table as well as the aroma coming from the stove. Too lethargic to go to the sink, she swallows the tablets dry. Frankie heads into the kitchen and brings her back a cup of coffee that he had brewed earlier, reheating it in the microwave. The mug depicts a QPR shirt with the number 8 and the name 'Blue' on it, a present from Roxy at Christmas.

'Black, no sugar, right?'

She takes the cup and smells it critically. Coffee – AeroPress, cold press, siphon, Chemex – is her passion.

'What is this?'

'What do you mean "what is it"? It's coffee.'

'Where are the beans from?'

'Tesco.'

She slumps wearily at the cheap circular wooden living-room table – the living room doubles as a dining room, since the kitchen is too small for four people to sit round a table – casting her bag carelessly on the floor. There are four matching chairs, pine with curved white-painted backs, ranged round the table and she sits on the one facing the kitchen door. To China, it looks like a flat ready to flip at any time, like a thousand rentals in the surrounding area. Not pleasant or unpleasant. Just lacking any confidence, or flair, or meaning, or history. She puts the coffee mug on the table, ignoring the coaster in front of her, and imprinting a moist ring on the surface. She takes a water bottle out of the bag, unloading more overspill — peanuts, pencils — onto the floor, and drinks deeply. Then she looks back through to the kitchen.

'You shouldn't have gone to all this trouble. A bowl of pasta would have suited me. You know I'm not all that fussy about food. So long as it doesn't contain meat or fish.'

'Yes, well,' says Frankie warily. 'I need to talk to you about that.'

China notices a tray of diced meat on the kitchen table. It takes her a few seconds to parse its meaning.

'All this — it's not for *me*, is it?'

Frankie sits down on the chair on the opposite side of the dining table and faces China. He looks directly at her, but she will not meet his gaze. There is a vase with a spray of palely coloured paper flowers in the centre.

'You can't just turn up out of the blue and expect me to drop all my plans, China.'

China's puzzled frown turns into a complicated smile, part arch, part bitter.

'Of course not. Obviously you have more important things to do.'

'I was making an anniversary dinner for Roxy when you phoned.'

'Anniversary? You're not married. And you haven't even been hardly seeing one another you told me.'

'It's been six months. *Exactly* six months it turns out.'

'Is she even your proper girlfriend?'

'You know. She's my . . . main squeeze, I suppose.'

'Don't use that expression.'

'We're dating, yes.'

'So let me get this straight,' China says, pointlessly flattening down the crumpled front of her blouse with the palm of her hand. 'You haven't seen me since October. But you're having Roxy around for your "six-month" anniversary. Which isn't actually a thing. And you couldn't postpone.'

Frankie tries to reach over and take China's hand, but she pulls it away.

'To be honest, I'm not absolutely sure that she's coming.'

'How come?'

'Because she hung up on me after I told her that you were coming.'

He immediately realizes that phrasing it in this fashion is a misstep.

'Nice to feel welcome,' says China sourly.

'I thought you didn't want her to come!'

'It's not great when your father's girlfriend hangs up at the mention of his daughter's name.'

Frankie's struggle to find the right words to use with his daughter feels to him like picking through the pimientos de Padron Veronica used to serve at the big parties they would hold for their friends and neighbours in North Kensington. He would always try and avoid the spicy one, because it would give him heartburn, but there was no way of knowing which one it was and he would infallibly pick it, giving himself acid indigestion for the rest of the evening.

'It wasn't like that, China.'

China pulls a pack of sugarless gum out of the backpack, peels it with remarkable speed and dexterity, and pops it into her mouth. Her slow, cud-like chewing immediately gives her face an unpleasant, sullen appearance.

'It's complicated. I've been promising Roxy this for a long time.'

'So what, then? If she turns up the three of us are going to have a lovely romantic supper together?'

She blows a pink bubble and pops it, then draws the gum back into her mouth. Frankie finds this oddly revolting.

'It's not ideal, I know. But she probably won't come.'

'Why don't you ring her and ask her?' She pushes the wooden chair she is sitting on back on two legs. Also bought cheap from the junk market, she can feel that the legs are unsteady.

'Don't do that, China, you'll break it. I've tried to call her. Roxy's phone just goes to voicemail.'

China, still balancing on two chair legs, picks at a hangnail, then tugs at it harshly, pulling it off, exposing raw red skin.

'You'd rather I wasn't here — wouldn't you?'

Frankie stands, walks round the other side of the table and takes a tentative step towards his daughter. He wants to hold her. He wants to apologize. He wants to make everything right. But words, so powerful when selling houses, seem to shrink and fade like invisible ink when he is around his daughter.

'I'm so *very* glad you are here, China. I'm *delighted*. But let's just get past this first night, shall we?'

China's shoulders slump. She looks around the flat, so plain and bland and functional and ugly compared with Nodge and Owen's elegant, expensive minimalism or her mother's cosy shabby chic.

'Where are you dumping me, then?' she sighs.

Frankie gets up and gestures towards the stairs.

'There's a room for you up there. Next to my bedroom.'

China rises from the table and hauls up her backpack.

'Are you going to leave that stuff there?' Frankie says. There is now a corona of spilt items on the floor from China's bag.

'I'll pick them up later.'

Frankie silently, swiftly, gathers up the items himself, then leads her up the stairs. The two bedrooms are next to one another. A small bathroom stands to the right of the landing. Frankie ushers China into her room, which he has had little time to prepare, and drops the items he is carrying on the single foldout bed. Unlike at Nodge and Owen's, this spare room is tawdry, despite being clean and tidy. It has magnolia walls and a plain taupe carpet. Frankie had rushed out and bought a bunch of cheap luridly dyed tulips from the service station on the corner and thrust them in a vase that was too small for them on a table next to the bed. There is a flatpack desk and chair, a wooden litter bin, a folded laundry drying rack, a stand-up vacuum cleaner – the room is used largely for storage – and little else besides.

'I know it's not up to much at the moment.'

She sits down forlornly on the bed. Frankie carefully sits next to her, six inches away.

'So – tell me everything that happened.'

China feels herself softening. Then, to her own surprise, she begins to cry. She hates herself when she cries, it makes her feel weak, particularly in front of her father, but she can't hold it inside any longer.

'Oh, Dad, it's been horrible. We've all been fighting. Mason, he . . . '

She suddenly throws herself against Frankie's shoulder. Frankie is astonished but delighted at the novelty of his daughter looking for his emotional support. He tentatively puts his arm around her shoulder, feeling the curve of her thin shoulders. For once, China does not recoil. For the first time in years, he feels like a father. Then, from downstairs, there is the distinct sound of the front door opening. China immediately pulls herself away from Frankie's shoulder and urgently rubs at her cheeks to remove the tear tracks.

'Is that her?'

Feeling cheated and annoyed at Roxy's timing, Frankie irrationally decides that Roxy has planned this interruption.

'I suppose it must be,' he says, standing up awkwardly.

'But . . . I haven't told you what happened with me and Mason.' China's voice is still choked with tears.

Roxy's singsong voice broadcasts from the sitting room.

'Frankie! It's *moi*.'

Frankie calls down the stairs.

'I'll be just a moment.'

He hears the door slam behind Roxy, a little harder than necessary. The fact that Roxy doesn't acknowledge his call makes Frankie nervous. He knows her moods and signals and he is anxious to keep the peace. He hesitates, then makes his way towards the door to the landing.

'I'll just be a minute, China.'

China drops her head, then turns and wearily begins to unpack.

'Don't bother, Dad. Go and see your boo.'

Frankie stares at her, a trapped rabbit.

'I'll be right back,' he says, then scurries down the stairs. In the sitting room, Frankie sees Roxy is already relaxing on the sofa. She is done up to the nines. She wears a perfume so pungent it has already carried to the corner of the room where Frankie is standing. She cradles a bottle of Prosecco. Frankie notices that it is the cheap brand she purchases in bulk for the salon.

'Hello, lover,' says Roxy breathily. She rises from the sofa as he walks towards her, puts the bottle on the dining table and gives him a long kiss on the mouth. 'What time's the little madam getting here?' Her voice, it seems to Frankie, is pitched unnecessarily loud.

'She's already here. In the spare room,' Frankie hisses, glancing up the stairs. Then, in a more hushed tone: 'And the door's open.'

Roxy shrugs and slumps back onto the sofa.

'Let me just . . . I need to . . . ' Frankie turns and starts to make his way back towards the stairs.

'Aren't you going to fix me a drink?' says Roxy, in a clipped voice, not too different from the one she used when she was talking to her Thai masseuse earlier in the day. 'Something smells good.'

'I've been working hard on it.'

'Frankie – that's so thoughtful of you,' she says, her tone now sugared.

'I just need to . . . '

'Just fix me that drink, would you, Frankie? I've been on my feet all day.'

Frankie picks up the bottle of Prosecco from the table and, too violently, he pulls the cork out. It foams and spills. He struggles to find a cloth to mop up the mess, then grabs some flimsy kitchen towel. Eventually he manages to fill a glass and hands it to Roxy. Then he makes his way towards the stairs again.

'I'll be right back.'

'Did you get any munchies?'

'Some peanuts. Dry roasted.'

'Exotic. Be a darling and crack open a pack for me before you disappear.'

Frankie glances once again at the stairs. He hastily returns to the kitchen, rummages frantically in the cupboard and finds the peanut packet. He pours the nuts into a small bowl and hands it to Roxy, who takes them without any word of thanks, since she is now absorbed with examining her phone. At last he heads up the stairs and back to China's bedroom. Although he had left the door open, it is now shut. He knocks gently.

'China.'

There is no answer.

'China,' he repeats, in a slightly more forceful voice.

'What?' China mutters from the other side of the door, just loudly enough for Frankie to hear.

Frankie turns the knob and opens the door. China is lying on her back on the bed staring at the magnolia stippled ceiling. She has kicked off her shoes and Frankie can smell a faint cheesiness drifting from the soles of her naked feet, or possibly the socks that are lying on the floor at the foot of the bed.

'Sorry I took so long.'

'Don't worry about it,' says China wearily. 'I'm just so grateful that you can find any time at all for a "little madam" like me.'

Frankie sits down on the bed at China's feet. He feels the material of his trousers make light contact with her soles. The smell is more intense and he grimaces, but keeps his face away from China so she doesn't notice.

'Roxy didn't mean that,' he says, still facing away from her.

'Didn't she?'

'It's just her way. She's always taking the piss. Don't be offended. Tell me about Mason and Silas.'

He turns and risks a direct look at her. China pulls up her knees so her feet are no longer in touch with Frankie.

'The moment's passed. It always does.'

She surrounds her knees with her arms and links her hands.

'Roxy can wait.'

'Clearly not.'

Frankie is defeated by the simple irrefutability of this fact.

'Come and join us for supper, then,' he says lamely.

China wants to demur out of pique. But she cannot escape the fact that she is voraciously hungry. As Frankie leaves the room and heads down the stairs, she slowly gets up and rummages in her bag for a clean pair of socks. Then, deciding she can't be bothered, puts on the old ones instead.

Twenty minutes later, freshly showered, China makes her way down the stairs into the living room, dressed in a pillarbox-red tracksuit, the hood up. Frankie has made an illicit log fire – one of the reasons he bought the flat was that it had a small open hearth – and it blazes and crackles, lending character and warmth to an otherwise largely sterile space. China cannot be bothered to complain about the contribution he is making to air pollution, or quote the figures on how many children it kills every year. Anyway, the fire is nice.

Roxy rises from the sofa where she has been flicking through her copy of *Marie Claire* and takes a step towards China.

'China. How *are* you?'

'Fine,' China says, warily accepting Roxy's embrace.

'I haven't seen you in *such* a long time.'

Roxy waves her arm towards the open kitchen door where Frankie is working on preparing the meal.

'Would you like a drink?'

'Sure. Why not?'

'How about a Negroni? If that's not too controversial.'

'Is that meant to be funny?'

'Roxy . . .'

Frankie interjects, entering the living room from the kitchen. But China is too worn out to allow herself to rise to the bait.

'Yeh, that'll do.'

'I'll fix you one,' says Frankie. 'You two can catch up.'

He retreats to the relative safety of the kitchen, leaving China and Roxy alone together. Roxy rummages in her handbag, a Burberry two-tone canvas with a golden 'B' decorating the catch.

'I got something for you. To welcome you to London.'

Roxy retrieves a small blue velvet box and hands it to China. She takes it tentatively and turns it over in her hands.

'What's this?'

'You won't know unless you open it.'

Lifting the lid of the box, China sees an antique brass compass with a hinged lid and ring through a brass bulb at the top for attachment to, perhaps, a belt.

'Early nineteenth century or so I was told,' says Roxy.

China takes it out and examines it, taken aback. The last thing she expected was this kind of gesture from Roxy.

'It looks spenny,' says China, watching the glint of the pale gold colour in the overhead retracted ceiling bulbs.

'Oh, it didn't cost me anything. Colin gave it to me.'

China turns it over. On the back is an inscription – *To R. In case you ever get lost. Love, C.*

'I can't take this,' says China.

'It's fine. Honestly.'

'But surely – it must have a special meaning for you.'

'I don't much care for old things. But as I was leaving to come here, I suddenly thought you might like it. It's just been lying in an old junk box, so I dug it out.'

'I really can't accept it.'

China replaces the compass in the box and holds it out to Roxy, who pushes her hand away.

'Yes, you can. You probably need it. And I've got a houseful of mementoes for Colin. You'd be doing me a favour by taking it. If you really don't want it, feel free to sell it. I'm not the sentimental sort.'

China hesitates, then reaches over and embraces Roxy with a sudden genuine warmth of feeling.

'Thank you. That's very kind.'

'I thought you might need cheering up. I know it's not been easy for you.'

China takes the compass out again, jiggles it, watching the pointer dance to magnetic north.

'I remember when I was eighteen,' says Roxy, following China's gaze to the compass. 'My parents were divorced. They hated each other too. That was the hardest thing. So believe it or not, I have a good idea what you're going through.'

'I don't think my mum and dad hate each other.'

'That's a good thing, then,' says Roxy.

'Here it comes,' says Frankie, marching in from the kitchen carrying a steaming bowl of garlic rice.

'We were just talking about how you and Veronica get on nowadays,' says Roxy. 'I thought there was some tension.'

'I like Veronica. She's a wonderful person. I'll never regret marrying her,' says Frankie, placing the bowl on a coaster on the table.

'Don't get carried away,' says Roxy, her voice suddenly tart.

'Meaning what?' says Frankie, standing over the tureen and breathing in the aroma.

'Save a bit of affection for me.'

'I didn't *mean* anything by it,' says Frankie, looking up from the bowl. His crooked reading glasses, which he has been wearing to chop herbs, are steamed up. 'I just never thought Veronica was a bad person, that's all. It's sad when a marriage breaks up but a lot of them do, don't they? Not really any-one's fault.'

He takes off the glasses and wipes them with his apron.

Roxy gives an audible snort.

'You *really* think that. Not even after she . . . '

Frankie shoots her a furious look and Roxy stops. China, Frankie is relieved to notice, doesn't appear to be

148

listening. She is absorbed in examining the compass. But then she looks up.

'Don't let yourself of the hook so easily, Dad. You bankrupted the family, lied to Mum and got us thrown out of our home.'

'I know. I know I did. Is that new?' says Frankie, noticing the compass for the first time.

'Roxy gave it to me.'

'That was kind of her. Let me have a look.'

China hands him the compass. He turns it over in his hands, then notices the inscription on the back. He frowns.

'But . . . this was a birthday present for Roxy from Colin. I helped him to choose it.'

'I know but . . . ' China begins, suddenly feeling guilty. 'I tried to say . . . '

'I told China – I'm not sentimental,' says Roxy briskly. 'She's welcome to it.'

Frankie feels obscurely aggrieved. It feels like a betrayal of poor, dead Colin. He tries to tuck the feeling away and hands back the compass to China.

'That very generous. Um. I'll go and get the rest of the food and the cutlery.'

As soon as he has disappeared into the kitchen, China scrutinizes Roxy's face carefully.

'What did you mean?' says China.

'What did I mean by what?'

'You said, "not even after she . . . "? And then you stopped yourself.'

'Not even . . . after she filed for divorce,' says Roxy.

'That's not what you were going to say, though, is it?'

The fire, although blazing now, can do nothing to prevent the frost that is spreading through the room. Frankie, oblivious, returns with the cutlery and begins laying it out.

'What are you two gabbing about?'

'Roxy is denying she meant something that she clearly meant. And we're not "gabbing"; we're talking.'

'Right. Listen, the food is going to ruin if I don't go and baste the beef.'

'That's it. Run away. As usual. Go and tend to your dead animal,' says China.

'I don't know what Roxy is talking about. Sort it out with her. I've done you some teriyaki tofu to go with the rice.'

Frankie shoots Roxy a cautionary look and retreats to the kitchen once again.

'So, what were you *really* going to say?' persists China.

'I misspoke. A little too much vino. Let's leave it.'

China knows now she is being played. The frustration builds like a bubble of gum in her chest.

'Just *tell* me.'

'You should talk to your father about it.'

'*You're* the one that brought it up.'

Roxy says nothing, instead taking another deep swig of the wine.

'You should go easy on that stuff,' says China. 'You've already put away nearly a whole bottle.'

'What you going to do? Put me in detention?' says Roxy, now slightly woozy. 'Or is it off to the Lubyanka with a bullet in the back of my head?'

'Luby what?'

'Don't they teach you about communism at school?'

'I'm not at school anymore.'

Roxy can hear Frankie clattering unnecessarily in the kitchen, playing for time no doubt. She calculates that he isn't going to make a reappearance any sooner than he needs to. Roxy tries to get her thoughts straight and looks at China steadily.

'Listen, China, let's lighten up. I've got a great joke.'

'Please, Roxy. Don't tell me one of your jokes. I'm begging you.'

'So, an Irishman is looking for a job on a building site. And he goes to the foreman and the foreman says . . . '

'I'm not listening to this bigoted rubbish.'

'No, no, give it a chance. Anyway, I'm half-Irish myself so I can tell it. So, the foreman says, "Well, Paddy, I got to start by asking you, do you know the difference between a joist and girder?"'

'Roxy! Stop!'

'Just hold on. Give it a chance. And the Irishman says, "Well, isn't it that Joyce wrote *Finnegans Wake* and Goethe wrote *Faust*?"'

China feels her cresting anger break and resolve itself.

'I guess that's not so bad.'

'You probably didn't think I'd heard of Joyce and Goethe, did you?'

'No, I didn't. But what I do know is that all you're trying to do is get me off the subject of my mum and dad's separation.'

'Look, China,' says Roxy evenly. She feels herself sobering slightly. 'Talk to me straight, woman to woman. What do you know about your parents' break-up?'

China fingers the compass in her pocket. It now feels soiled somehow.

'Everything, I think. I've spoken to Mum about it a few times. They were married. Dad borrowed a whole load of money against the house without telling Mum. Then a property he owned was not properly insured and it burned down. He couldn't keep his loans afloat. Our house was repossessed. Mum divorced him because he had lied and because he had bankrupted us. We moved in with Grandma and Grandpa for a couple of years, then Mum met Silas, fell for him – for some reason – and we moved to Brighton to live in his house with him and Mason. End of story.'

'That's about all I know too.'

'So, what was it you were trying to say, then?' says China.

Frankie walks in brightly, carrying a tray of marinated Portobello mushrooms.

'Suppertime!'

He puts the tray down, picks up a glass and raises it in China's direction.

'To my beautiful China! China, I'm so glad you've come to stay. Stay as long as you like. I've missed you.'

China and Roxy exchange glances. They both rise and come and stand at the table, facing him.

'To China,' says Frankie, raising his glass higher.

Roxy raises her glass only a fraction of an inch. China lifts hers high above her head.

'To me. Hurrah.'

Her voice is not celebratory.

The supper goes poorly. The conversation is forced and punctuated with silences. Whatever it is that Roxy has left unsaid presses on China. Eventually Roxy rises from the table and announces that she is going to bed, leaving Frankie and China alone. Roxy offers to clear the table and wash up, but Frankie and China, both eager to defuse the tension, tell her not to bother. Once she has gone upstairs, they clear the table together in a silence that is almost companionable.

'Dad,' says China eventually, as she scrapes the leftovers of the food and piles the plates one on the other.

'China,' says Frankie, gathering the cutlery, deliberately making a noise as if hoping that it will impede any efforts on Roxy's part to eavesdrop.

'Do me a favour, will you?'

'Of course.'

He takes the cutlery into the kitchen, puts it in the dishwasher and returns. China is still standing there in exactly the position he left her. He starts picking up the coasters and putting them in a pile.

'Don't have sex with Roxy while I'm here.'

Frankie absently puts the coasters back down on the table.

'I beg your pardon?'

'I don't think I can make it much clearer. Don't have sex with Roxy tonight.'

He starts clearing the table again, trying to formulate a response. Eventually, now holding the coasters in his hand once more, rotating them nervously, he tries to block her.

'Is that any of your business?'

'Just *don't*.'

'I wasn't planning to.'

He puts the coasters on the cabinet behind him and begins gathering the dirty glasses.

'It's not the sort of thing you plan, though, is it?' says China.

She takes the plates to the kitchen and puts them into the dishwasher. Frankie follows her with the glasses.

'I wouldn't worry about it unduly, China,' he says over the clatter of crockery. 'My relationship with Roxy isn't one you would describe as being of unbridled passion.'

He looks round nervously to make sure that Roxy hasn't risen from bed and come into earshot, then shuts the dishwasher and switches it on. It begins to rumble.

'Hence the blue pills in the bathroom cabinet,' says China. Frankie blushes.

'I don't really want to talk about this with you. It's not appropriate.'

'What do you know about what's appropriate and what isn't? You called Roxy your "squeeze".'

'It was ironic.'

'I know it was *meant* to be ironic. But it was still inappropriate. Irony doesn't get you off the hook, all your semi-serious bantz.'

'What am I *meant* to call her? "Girlfriend" sounds stupid when we're both in our fifties. "Partner" sounds commercial. Do words really matter all that much?'

'Words are everything.'

'Are they?'

China doesn't answer, partly because she suddenly finds herself doubting that words *are* in fact everything. But anyway, they are important, especially when people use the wrong ones, whether deliberately, like Roxy, or out of ignorance, like her father. China takes a swig from her ever-present water bottle. Her third litre of the day. Frankie goes and stands and stares at the now-guttering fire. He throws another log on and jabs at it with a poker.

'Are we going to talk about it?' says China. She lowers

herself onto the sofa in front of the hearth. Frankie sits himself on the adjacent armchair.

'Are we going to talk about what?'

'What Roxy was saying, *implying*. That there was another reason why you and Mum split up — other than you being a liar and a bankrupt.'

Frankie stares at the fire, pauses carefully before replying.

'China, there are a thousand reasons why anything at all happens. Something as complicated as a marriage break-up — the list of reasons is endless.'

'So why can't I escape the feeling that something important is being kept from me?'

'We all have our secrets. You wouldn't like me to know all your secrets, would you?'

'This is different.'

Frankie feels the sudden strong urge to tell her the truth. It was a feeling he had learned to distrust. On the other hand, if he told her about Tony and made Veronica look worse in China's eyes, wouldn't he look like a better person relative to Veronica? But in the end it would just make China unhappy. And Veronica as well. He has no wish to do either.

'I'd just forget about it if I were you.'

'I can't. But clearly you're not going to tell me anything.'

'There's really nothing to tell.'

The fire sputters and fails again. China sighs, rises and makes her way silently towards the stairs.

'Goodnight, China,' says Frankie.

China doesn't answer. Frankie watches as she ascends the stairs and then hears her bedroom door close firmly behind her.

*

When Frankie enters his own bedroom, Roxy is still awake and sitting up in the bed. Frankie stares slightly resentfully at her as he gets undressed. She is massaging hand cream into her wrists.

'Why did you have to say that?' says Frankie.

'Say what?'

'About my break-up with Veronica. You knew what you were doing.'

Roxy squeezes out another blob and continues to rub, into her hands this time. Her eyes remain affixed to her fingers, which are stubby with beautifully painted and polished nails.

'Because, Frankie, she needs to know. That her mother isn't a saint. And I know you're too feeble to tell her the truth. So yes, I admit it – I was trying to force the issue a little bit. What's wrong with that?'

'It's not your place to decide what China should or shouldn't know.'

'What is my place exactly?'

'What's *that* supposed to mean?'

'What am I to you? A handy old-lady fuck?'

'No, that's . . .'

'Are we going somewhere? Is this all a waste of time?'

Roxy stops rubbing in the hand cream and looks up at Frankie, suddenly fierce.

'Why would it be a waste of time?'

'You never make love to me anymore. Don't you find me attractive?'

'Of course I do.'

Roxy pushes back the covers. She is wearing nothing. In the half-light her skin is pink and welcoming. She puts down the hand cream and parts her legs slightly.

'Come on, then. Show me how attractive you find me.'

Frankie, who has been unbuttoning his shirt, stops, his chest exposed with pepper-and-salt hair curling over the hem.

'I can't.'

'Oh, that again,' says Roxy wearily. 'Go and get your blue pill, then. I can wait twenty minutes.'

'No, I don't mean that. I just . . . *can't*.'

Roxy closes the gap between her legs and turns on her side.

'Why on earth not?'

Frankie swallows air. He had been hoping that Roxy would have fallen asleep. That he would somehow avoid this.

'Because I promised.'

'Promised who?'

'I promised China.'

'You did *what*?'

Frankie struggles to meet Roxy's gaze.

'I promised China that I wouldn't have sex with you while she was in the house.'

Roxy's gaze drifts away. She nods as if this satisfactorily completed some long-pondered-over equation.

'Let me get this straight,' she says without looking at Frankie, but putting her finger to her lips and nodding like a patient teacher trying to understand an unusually stupid pupil. 'You promised China you wouldn't have sex with me.'

'I mean – the bedrooms are adjacent. The walls are thin. You can be a bit, you know. Noisy. Surely you understand.'

Roxy seems to give this reasonable consideration. Then she nods firmly.

'Fair enough. We have to listen to what Madam says, don't we?'

'China, not "madam". And thank you for understanding.'

Frankie continues getting undressed. But he notices that an odd expression has fixed itself across Roxy's face. It is, all at once, sly, knowing and unfriendly.

'All the same,' she says. 'A woman is in charge of their own body. As a feminist, I'm sure China would sign up to that. Wouldn't you agree?'

'Of course you are. But you're not in charge of *my* body.'

'Righty ho, then,' says Roxy briskly. She parts her legs again, puts her hand down between them. Then she begins to play with herself, swivelling her hips slowly, then moaning, at first softly and then very quickly louder. At the same time she raises and lowers her rump on the bed so that the thin base creaks audibly.

'What the hell are you doing?'

'Oh! Frankie,' moans Roxy, now picking up her iPhone with her free hand and idly scrolling through her messages. 'Oh my GOD.'

'Stop it! You're being a child.'

Roxy slams her behind harder against the mattress and groans louder, at the same time deftly tapping out the answer to one of the messages.

'FRANKIE. OH, FRANKIE.'

On the other side of the wall, China lays in her bed, muscles rigid, her fingers in her ears, an expression of disgust spread across her features. She picks the antique compass from where it lies on her side table and presses on the ancient glass with her thumbs until it cracks. The glass cuts her. A speck of blood blossoms.

*

The next morning, after Roxy has left for work and China is still in bed, Frankie, wearing baggy pyjamas and chewing on a piece of Marmite toast, decides to phone Veronica to get the full briefing on China's sudden appearance. However, it is Silas who picks up, on his way across the living room to measure a rotting sash window frame due for replacement. Veronica has left her phone on top of the upright piano that Silas sometimes uses for composing songs. He flicks the phone onto speaker.

'Silas? It's Frankie.'

'Hey, bud. How's everything?'

His voice, as ever, is affable and bland.

'Yeh,' says Frankie curtly. He has no interest in being Silas's bud. 'Is Vronky there?'

'She's just nipped out to the garden for a moment. I can call her. How you getting on in the big smoke?'

Silas feels himself reluctant to enable conversation between Veronica and Frankie. There is a trace of intimacy that endures between the divorced couple that he finds unsettling. His fingernail clicks anxiously on the protruding tip of the metal measuring tape he grips in his left hand.

'What's going on with China?' says Frankie.

'It is what it is, you know.'

'What the fuck does that mean?'

Frankie's customarily brusque manner with him always makes Silas uneasy. He looks out into the garden searching for Veronica, but cannot see her. Out of his field of vision, she is smoking a Silk Cut behind the apple tree, letting the smoke dissipate beyond the corona of the rotating lawn sprinkler.

'I'm just trying to locate Veronica. Can't see her at the moment.'

'China's turned up on my doorstep. Says she's been kicked out.'

'She hasn't been kicked out. She left of her own accord.'

'She told me she had a big fight with you and Veronica.'

'Not really licensed to discuss this stuff, bud,' says Silas.

'Why not?'

'You know. It is what it is.'

He looks out in the garden once more, eager to divest himself of Veronica's phone, which he holds between his fingertips as if it were dangerously hot. Veronica has appeared by the rosebush, beating the air with one hand while the other holds a trowel. She is wearing a pair of yellow shorts and a grubby 'Wild Feminist' T-shirt that she only uses for gardening.

'I can see Veronica now.'

Silas waves to her energetically and stabs his finger at the phone, as if the intensity of the waving and pointing can increase the likelihood of being seen. It seems to work. Veronica looks up, sees Silas and raises her hand in acknowledgement. She starts walking towards the door, popping a piece of strong mint chewing gum in her mouth on the way, meanwhile pulling on a battered Barbour jacket and zipping it up in case the cigarette smoke has adhered itself to the T-shirt.

'I'll put you on to her. Stay well, Frankie.'

'Yeh.'

A few seconds later Frankie can hear Silas muffling the phone and saying something inaudible to which Veronica makes no reply. She takes the phone, puts it to her ear and switches off the speaker function for privacy. Her voice is strung tight, pitched slightly higher than usual.

'Frankie! China's with you?'

'Don't sound so surprised. I'm her father after all.'

'She didn't tell us where she was going. I thought she'd come back.'

'Doesn't look like it.'

'How do you feel about it?'

'Don't do the analyst thing on me.'

'You must be pleased to see her.'

Veronica takes the gum out of her mouth and casts it in the wastepaper bin. She can still taste cigarette smoke.

'A bit of notice would have been nice. Why didn't you call me after she walked out on you?'

'Like I said – I thought she was going to a friend.'

'And you still didn't think it was worth calling me, when our daughter has run away from home?'

'I didn't want to worry you.'

'I'm certainly worried now. Her and Roxy have already had aggravation.'

Veronica feels oddly heartened by this. Although theoretically she would like Roxy and China to get along, for China's sake, in reality she finds the idea of them developing a strong relationship uncomfortable.

'Oh dear. Is she alright?'

'Who? Roxy?'

'No, not Roxy. My daughter.'

'*Our* daughter.'

'Our daughter. Of course. Sorry. How is she?'

Frankie surveys the living room. China's mess is everywhere. It seems however often he clears it up, within five minutes of her presence, devastation ensues.

'Untidy.'

Veronica gives a rich chuckle. Frankie savours the sound, the unabashed lustiness of her laughter.

'Tell me about it. Our house is tidier now than it has been for years.'

'She was untidy when she was five,' says Frankie, smiling himself. 'Remember when we came home and she had emptied all the bedroom drawers out?'

'Oh God, yes? And I had, you know, a thingy in there . . . '

'A vibrator.'

Veronica laughs again.

'A Rampant Rabbit,' continues Frankie. 'That's right. What did you tell her it was? I've forgotten.'

'A swizzle stick.'

Now they are both laughing. Silas is standing a few feet away measuring the window and looking perplexed. He stops and starts scratching the back of his ear with his fingernail.

'Honestly though, Vronky. I'm really pleased she's come to see me. But what went wrong? I hate to see her this unhappy. Why won't she talk to me?'

'She's a teenager, Frankie. She doesn't even talk to me.'

'I want to be a good father to her.'

It's a little late for that, thinks Veronica.

'It's a long conversation. I'm not in an entirely private space at the moment.'

'Wim Hof earwigging you, is he?'

'Who's Wim Hof?'

'A sort of cartoon action man. China watches his YouTube. Actually, he looks a bit like Silas, only twice the size. Immerses himself in freezing water to show how hard he is.'

Veronica starts laughing again. She looks across the room at Silas. The ear-scratching has become intense.

'I'll call you back in a while, tell you all about it. We can have a proper talk then. But I'm sure she'll be fine. You won't have to put up with it too long. She's off to uni in September apart from anything else.'

'She can stay here as long as she wants. But I have to admit, it's tricky what with Roxy and all.'

Veronica suddenly has an image of Frankie and Roxy between the sheets together and takes her gaze away from Silas to look out in the garden, hoping it will distract her. The apple tree, she thinks, is dying. It leans to one side and the bark is brittle. Silas is noisily going through his toolbox in search of something or other. Veronica lowers her voice.

'Can I say something, Frankie? It's a bit tactless, though.'

'That's never stopped you before.'

'To be honest, I still can't quite imagine you and Roxy together.'

Frankie finishes his toast, swallowing the last mouthful. It feels rough and dry on the back of his throat and he swills some coffee to clear it.

'You said that before – in Hyde Park. I can't see why not. We're cut from the same cloth after all,' he says, wiping the back of his mouth with his pyjama sleeve.

'What do you mean?'

'Common as muck innit.'

Frankie can hear sounds of movement coming from upstairs in China's room. He feels suddenly anxious about Roxy's performance the previous night and wonders if China will have the front to upbraid him for the noises coming from their

163

bedroom, which he is certain she would have heard unless she had earphones in or had fallen asleep. He's not looking forward to having to explain.

'I'm sure you're much happier now you've got your posh boyfriend and all his books,' he says, keeping one eye on China's door.

'Silas? All he reads is about great military battles and gruesome thrillers.'

'I've been reading better stuff lately, you know. Some of the classics.'

'*We're Going on a Bear Hunt*?'

'*Crime and Punishment. Madame Ovary.*'

'*Bovary.*'

'It was a joke. I'm not that dumb, Veronica. Also, *Death of a Salesman.*'

'You're reading plays now?'

'It's China's.'

'What do you think?'

'Bit depressing, to be honest. Look, have you got any advice for me? How can I work this thing out with China?'

'I wish I knew. Since she's just walked out on me, I'm not sure I've got any easy answers. She's volatile, what can I say?'

'But what exactly happened?'

Veronica glances at Silas, still loitering on the other side of the room. He has finished rummaging in the toolbox and has surfaced with a pair of pliers, but he isn't doing anything with them. Instead, he is staring out the window at the garden, as if in a reverie. Veronica is sure that he has been listening in.

'I've got to rush. I've got a hot yoga session in twenty minutes.'

'What's that?'

'It's like yoga only in a 104-degree room. It flushes out toxins.'

'Don't talk to me about toxins. China's terrified of those too. She drinks about a gallon of water a day to try and flush the bastards out.'

'I'll call you later. Okay?'

'Sure, Vronky. Watch out for yourself. And watch out for those toxins. They're a menace.'

'It's the things you can't see that get you in the end, Frankie.'

Veronica cuts the call off. Silas snaps out of his pretend reverie. Still holding the pliers, he takes a couple of steps towards her.

'What were you saying about me, Veronica?'

'Nosy, nosy.'

'I couldn't help but hear some of the conversation. I don't only read books on military battles. Or thrillers.'

'*Stalingrad*?'

'That's one book about one battle. It's a very respectable literary study.'

'Still boys with guns, though. What's the other one you've got on the go? *Girl with the Dragon Tattoo*?'

'It's very well written. But yes, I do like books that crack on with the plot. Is that a crime?'

'And feature plenty of violence.'

'I suppose you're right.'

'I usually am.'

'I am trying to be a better man, Veronica,' says Silas, his mouth going weak. 'I know us – we men – have got a lot to answer for.'

'So go and sweep the kitchen floor, then,' says Veronica.

Silas hesitates, then puts the pliers back in the toolbox and heads to the kitchen where he starts on the floor with the broom, pushing it in quick, angry thrusts, hunting down dirt, matter out of place, with venomous precision.

Chapter Six

February 2020: London

Nodge steers his black cab towards the adoption agency. Owen spreads himself across the back seat. The glass partition is open between them. It is a three-mile journey from Kensal Rise to Harlesden. Neither of them speak until Nodge pulls up in the street outside the ugly red-brick low rise that houses the adoption agency.

'This is it, then,' says Owen as Nodge lines up the vehicle against the kerb.

'Nervous?' says Nodge, his head screwed round to watch for the kerb.

Nodge cuts the engine and gathers his bits and pieces – a book by Alexei Sayle about growing up in the Communist Party, a half-consumed Dime bar, a pen and a thick notepad with 'Adoption Info' scrawled on the front.

'I wouldn't say that.'

'Good.'

'More like bricking it.'

Having straightened the cab to his satisfaction, Nodge switches off the engine, pulls himself out of the driver's seat and opens the rear door for Owen. Owen is still dressed in his John Lewis uniform, dark blue suit, plain tie, white plastic badge on the lapel. Owen notices that he still has a lanyard round his neck, takes it off and puts it in his pocket. He has come directly from the branch at the Westfield store, from where he has taken the remainder of the afternoon off. He lowers his head and steps out tentatively onto the pavement as if there were hidden assailants waiting to strike.

'Don't worry, O. Everything will be alright,' says Nodge, shutting the door and locking the cab.

'You don't *know* that.'

'Obviously I don't know that. I'm trying to be encouraging, aren't I?'

They brush one another's lips with a kiss. An old black man wearing a vicar's dog collar with white hair sticking up like bedsprings is passing. He slows down and stares. Owen pulls gently away from Nodge.

'Thanks, Nodge. You're a sweetheart.'

'I love you too, Owen. And if this doesn't happen – well, we still have one another.'

'And that's a lot.'

'It is. We are very lucky. '

'But I so want to be a father. It's like an ache that just won't leave my body.'

'I'm scared too.'

'You always seem so calm.'

'Of course I'm scared. I want this just as much as you do.'

'Do you? Do you *really*?'

They stand staring at one another for a second. Nodge wonders if Owen is trying to say something. He turns away and puts some change in the meter. He checks his watch. There is still five minutes before their appointment. They enter the building through double glass doors into a shabby hallway, then make their way up a flight of stairs to the adoption office on the first floor. It is situated on the other side of a plain grey door with inlaid smoked glass panels. Nodge presses the entry buzzer and the lock clicks open. Making their way inside, he is reassured by the familiar posters of joyful adults holding or playing with gleeful, healthy young children. Encouragingly, several are same-sex parents.

The atmosphere today feels unusually sepulchral to both Owen and Nodge. The room is chilly and the receptionist, whom neither of them have seen before, with stiff short hair and a blue-white cotton blouse lacking a single crease, gives a frosty stare when she looks up from her desk. Is she prejudiced about gay adoption? It is unlikely, given the job she has, but you never can tell. They have learned how people hide their hatred. Nodge notices a small silver cross on a necklace round her neck. This increases his suspicion.

They sit and wait, lowering themselves heavily onto hard chairs as if time is pressing down on them like a low-pressure storm front. Exactly on the stroke of two o'clock, according to the electric clock humming behind the receptionist's desk, a buzzer sounds. The intercom crackles, although Nodge can't quite understand what is being said. Apparently, however, they

are being summoned, since the receptionist gestures indifferently towards the door to her right.

Nodge and Owen are surprised by the punctuality. Their
appointments here, as a rule, run at least fifteen minutes late.
They rise and cautiously approach the door. They have negoti-
ated this portal many times before, each time with a growing
sense of apprehension – not because they are scared of failure,
but because they are getting closer and closer to success and
the nearer they get, the more they fear disappointment.

Entering the office, they see Comfort Brakespeare, an
imposing, bulky Ugandan woman with kind, constantly roaming black eyes, sitting behind her desk, fidgeting with a pencil.
They have met her a half a dozen times before and like her very
much. She is always cheerful, helpful and positive. Today she
wears a large headscarf in brilliant emerald and glasses with
fashionable thick black octagonal frames.

'Hi, Comfort,' says Nodge.

'Hi, Comfort,' says Owen.

She nods and smiles. Her eyes stop roaming and settle on
the desk in front of her, on which there are several buff files
with sheets of papers protruding. Her laptop is switched on –
blue light reflects onto her slightly leathery skin. Her eyes flick
between the screen and the paperwork periodically. Without
looking up, Comfort gestures for Nodge and Owen to sit
down. When she finally raises her head to meet their gaze,
Nodge tries to read her expression, but finds nothing scrut-
able. They lower themselves onto the proffered chairs.

'Hello, Owen. Hello, Jon. How are you both?' Her rich,
treacly accent is reassuring.

'Nervous,' says Nodge.

'Of course,' says Comfort. She fidgets with the papers on her desk. 'Can I offer either of you a coffee? Or a glass of water?'

'No, thanks.'

'Not for me.'

She clicks on her computer mouse a few times and purses her lips.

'Is everything okay?' blurts Nodge.

'You mean regarding your application to adopt?'

No, regarding your new headscarf, you muppet, thinks Nodge savagely. It is only at this point that he realizes how on edge he is. However, his voice when he speaks remains polite.

'Yes, of course.'

There is a slow, indrawn breath through the nostrils from Comfort.

'I guess you want me to get to the matter of the decision as quickly as possible.'

Is she just doing all this neutrality/glumness for effect, wonders Nodge. Was it like the old game show, *Who Wants to Be a Millionaire?*, when Chris Tarrant looks depressed before he tells them they'd won half a million sovs?

'Yes,' say Nodge and Owen, more or less in unison.

'The thing is, there's been a complication,' says Comfort finally, after a long pause. She opens one of the files on her desk and sifts through the papers inside.

'A complication?' says Nodge. 'I thought we were more or less good to go. You said there were just one or two formalities left to complete.'

'That's right. And now the agency has completed those formalities.'

'What were these formalities exactly?'

171

'One of them was a final police check.'

'Spit it out, then,' says Owen. But instead of responding, Comfort looks directly at Nodge. She pushes a piece of paper over the desk to him.

'Are you aware of this, Mr Drysdale?'

The sudden formality of the address frightens Nodge. Puzzled, he takes the paper and examines it. He feels his heart sicken slowly as he comprehends the words on the paper.

'I suppose so,' he says, voice parched.

'What is it?' says Owen, leaning forward. Nodge's body goes slack as he passes the paper to Owen. Owen slowly reads, shaking his head more and more insistently as he does so. Nodge, who has been staring at the floor, turns cautiously towards him.

'Don't be angry with me, Owen,' Nodge whispers, as if Comfort, two feet away, could be kept from hearing him.

'You have a conviction for possession of drugs,' says Owen.

'It was a long time ago. I wasn't even old enough to vote. Which is why I didn't mention it on the form. It's meant to be deleted from my records.'

'It was for twenty tabs of ecstasy.'

'I didn't know it was twenty tabs. A so-called friend slipped them in my pocket when we were stopped by the filth — sorry, police.'

Owen's forehead crumples into ragged patterns of confusion. Nodge looks at the beloved creases in Owen's skin.

'I don't *care* about the ecstasy. I care that you never told me.'

Nodge says nothing, but looks wretched. When Owen speaks again, his voice has shifted from puzzlement to anger.

'Why? Why didn't you tell me? Or, for that matter, why didn't you tell *her*?'

He waves the paper in the direction of Comfort, who is silently drumming her fingers on the desk and looking as if she wished she could be somewhere else.

'I thought the bust would have been wiped or expired or that it would simply be lost,' says Nodge weakly. 'Christ, it was more than thirty years ago.'

'But having a historic offence isn't a bar to adoption. Is it? Not when the individual was still technically a child?' says Owen, looking at Comfort hopefully.

'It isn't necessarily a bar, no. Especially an offence that took place so long ago. You were, what?' she looks at the papers on her desk again. 'Seventeen?'

'Sixteen,' says Nodge, his gaze returning to the floor in front of him.

'So it probably wouldn't have counted against you. Other than that, your record appears to be clean.'

'What's the "complication", then?' says Nodge.

'The complication is that you never told us about it. The panel looks very seriously on being deceived. It puts the whole trustworthiness of any candidate into question.'

Owen hands the charge sheet back to Comfort.

'How complicated is it, then?'

'Very complicated.'

Comfort takes off her glasses. They are strong glasses, Nodge can see from the impenetrability of the lenses. With a lurch in his stomach, he realizes that she doesn't want to see the expressions on Nodge and Owen's faces when she speaks again.

'This is a very sad matter, because from my perspective, I think you both would make excellent adoptive parents. Considerate, thoughtful, responsible, hardworking, loving, in a long, stable relationship. I was looking forward to giving you the good news. But then this came through yesterday. Now it's out of my hands.'

There is a pause during which Owen and Nodge appear to have been stricken into sitting statues. Finally, Comfort passes judgement and pronounces the sentence.

'I'm afraid we are going to have to reject your application to adopt. There's nothing I can do about it. I'm sorry, because there are so many children that could benefit from your care and support. But that's the system, I'm afraid.'

'I see,' says Nodge, his voice like cracks in ice, spreading.

'The rules say that you can try to apply again in eighteen months. If you declare the offence openly this time, you might have better luck.'

The deed done, Comfort replaces her glasses on her nose and stands up, avoiding the gaze of either of the men.

'So. Good luck to you both in the future, anyway.'

She holds out her hand. Nodge stands, swaying like a drunken man, dully takes her hand and forlornly shakes it.

'Thank you, Comfort,' he says. 'You have always been good to us and on our side, and I am very thankful for that. I don't doubt if you had any choice in the matter, you would give us the benefit of the doubt. I'm sorry we've let you down.'

'You haven't let me down. I'm just sorry that . . . well . . . '

'She's sorry that you've let us *all* down,' says Owen in a small, hard voice. He too shakes Comfort's hand, manages a thin smile, then turns and walks out the door without waiting for Nodge to follow him.

During the time it takes to walk back to the cab, neither Owen nor Nodge speak. The air sits on their shoulders like a heavy, damp blanket. Nodge climbs into the cab and focuses his gaze straight ahead at the road. Instead of getting in the back, Owen comes round to the driver's side and puts his face close up to the glass. Nodge slides the window down.

'I think I'd rather walk,' says Owen.

'Don't be stupid. It's going to rain in a minute.'

'I'm not stupid. You're stupid. In fact, you're a fucking idiot.'

Nodge cannot meet Owen's eyes.

'I know. I know I am. I'm sorry. Get in the back of the cab. We can talk about this later.'

Owen takes a step back, away from the cab.

'I can't.'

'Why not.'

'I'm too angry.'

'But I . . . '

Before Nodge can finish his sentence Owen is scuttling away from him along the road, head down. He is zigzagging on the pavement. He looks like he could bump into a lamp post any moment. Nodge swings the cab round in a 360-degree circle, and pulls it up beside Owen, against the flow of traffic. A motorcyclist has to swerve and curses at Nodge before continuing his journey.

'Owen. Get in. Please!'

Specks of heavy drizzle have begun to explode on the cab

175

windscreen. Owen, rain beginning to slam into his face, stares momentarily at Nodge, then suddenly wheels to the right and disappears down an alley. Nodge considers parking and following him, but decides there is no point. He turns the cab around again and heads towards home.

In his gut he is aware of a new feeling, mixing and curdling with the disappointment and shame. It is something he has not experienced for a long time – the sour gnawing of fear.

March 2020: Brighton

Veronica, Silas and Mason sit around the rustic kitchen table, picking at supper. Mason is tapping his knife on the distressed oak surface, an effect painstakingly achieved by Silas with wax, sandpaper and steel wool. Veronica, concentrating hard, manages to ignore the irritating noise.

'You look a bit down, Veronica,' says Silas.

'It's nothing really,' says Veronica, inclining her head towards Mason and hoping that Silas will take the hint.

'Is everything okay? At the therapy practice, I mean.'

Veronica gives up trying to send Silas signals. He's either being obtuse or simply ignoring her.

'I suppose so. I mean – I had this one client, Vincent. I told you about him.'

'Did you? I can't remember. Mason, aren't you going to eat that?'

Mason pushes some lentils around his plate, but does not raise his fork to his mouth. He taps on the table more vigorously.

'I've told you a couple of times. He walked out on me, said I was wasting his time. He's made a complaint to BACP.

It's been eating away at me somehow. Perhaps at some level because I'm afraid he's right. The thing about therapy is that it's so, I don't know, evanescent. Are you healing? Are you helping? Are you doing nothing at all?'

'I'm sure you— Mason, you need to use a knife to cut that.'

Mason is hacking at the sausage with the tines of his fork.

'Please, Mason. Stop that,' says Veronica, regarding the vacant fourth seat that she is facing. With his left hand, Mason continues banging the table at precisely the same volume with the same infuriating frequency. Silas coughs, putting his hand over his mouth and apologizing. He has to clear his throat before he speaks.

'Buddy,' says Silas in a voice that contains a pleading note. The tapping becomes quieter, but does not disappear. Silas tears a chunk off the ciabatta loaf and dips it in the olive oil and balsamic.

'This balsamic is good,' he says, chewing the bread.

'Waitrose,' says Veronica.

'How much did it cost?'

'I don't recall.'

Silas considers this and decides to let it rest or, at least, leave it for a more opportune moment.

'Look, Veronica. I'm sure you do make a difference to your clients,' he says absently, cutting into his own food.

'There's no real way of knowing.'

Silas nods as if this settles the matter to his satisfaction.

'You don't really care about what I do at work, do you, Silas? You pretend you do, but you don't.'

Silas prepares his 'that's not fair' face.

Suddenly the tapping from Mason feels like hammer blows

to her head. Veronica reaches over and snatches the knife out of his hand.

'Fuck you!' says Mason, jumping down from the table.

'Mason — language, please,' says Veronica.

'"Language, please",' he mimics infuriatingly. 'You're not my mother, bitch!'

He runs out of the room, kicking at the kitchen cupboard hard as he passes it and rattling the crockery within. Veronica and Silas remain facing one another at an angle. Silas begins coughing again, more violently this time. He scratches his earlobe and takes a sip of water. Mason's steps sound on the staircase as he runs upstairs to his room.

'He's just acting out,' says Silas.

'Does that forgive everything? Don't there have to be consequences?'

'You mean punish him?'

'That exactly what I mean.'

'I'm not sure punishment is that effective as a positive behavioural strategy. Rewarding good behaviour is always better than sanctions against bad. All the research says so. I'll certainly talk to him about it, though.'

'You'll talk to him about him calling me a bitch and telling me to fuck off?'

'I certainly will.'

'How about him going to bed without any supper?'

Silas looks down at his cutlery. Another coughing fit strikes. He waits until it ends.

'It is what it is, Veronica. I'm not sure that getting nasty about it is a good long-term solution.'

Veronica takes a long swig of wine from her glass.

'This isn't working,' says Veronica, slamming the glass down so hard Silas fears it is going to shatter.

'What isn't?'

'You, me and Mason.'

Silas looks startled. His eyes droop; he shifts into puppy-dog mode.

'Come on, Vronky. I know he's got a few problems. Just wait till we hear from the ADHD Centre. It might be something we can treat.'

'He drove my daughter out of the house. He's abusive towards me.'

'That's not really fair. China has issues of her own.'

'What's *that* supposed to mean?'

'You can't completely blame a twelve-year-old boy for the fact that China has left the house. All teenagers go through a difficult time. And China comes from . . .'

Silas hesitates nervously, tries to recalibrate the thought. Veronica pre-empts him.

'A broken home? Is that what you were about to say?'

'I was trying to think of a better way of phrasing it. China is part of a melded family. Like Mason. Like all of us.'

'A broken home is a more accurate way of saying it, though, isn't it?'

Veronica stares resentfully at her supper, as if it was her food that was broken. Italian sausages with Puy lentils, red wine and garlic.

'Aren't you going to eat that?' says Silas. 'It's from the cookbook you gave me for Christmas.'

'I'm not really hungry.'

'Mason hasn't eaten any of his either. He must be starving.'

Silas, carefully, as if fearing sabotage, picks up Mason's plate. Veronica looks at him sharply.

'I hope that's going in the bin.'

'Mason needs to eat. Anyway, these sausages were expensive.'

'For Christ's sake, Silas. He just had a tantrum and stormed off. You can't reward him by taking him his supper in his room. And do you *ever* stop thinking about money?'

'I wouldn't be a good father if he didn't eat. And it's not fair of you to bring up money. Things are a bit tight at the moment.'

'What makes you think you're a good father in the first place?'

The words slip out, half deliberate, half not. She is surprised to discover that she finds them intoxicating. Silas holds the shallow plate uneasily balanced in front of him, uncertain what to do with it.

'I do try my best, Vronky.'

She bites into a sausage. There is a faint taste of blood – the sausage is undercooked. She bolts it down and starts speaking again before she has fully finished the mouthful.

'You're a shitty father. You spoil him. You don't provide him with any boundaries. You put him before our relationship, which is not going to have a good outcome. You can't control him. He manipulates you. On top of that, it's not that "things" are tight. It's that *you* are tight. You won't even give him pocket money.'

Veronica takes another bite of the sausage. She licks her lips. She likes the slight rawness. She stares at Silas, challenging him to commit himself to a course of action.

'I try to be kind. And he doesn't need pocket money. He'd just waste it on sweets.'

'Being kind can also be thought of as weakness.'

'What am I *meant* to do?'

'Not take him his meal for one thing.'

'Veronica. Pumpkin. Are you feeling okay?'

'What's that meant to mean?'

'You were saying the other day that your periods were drying up.'

'*Drying up?* What am I, a fucking well?'

'I didn't know how to put it. I think you're overreacting.'

'So it's just "hormones", right? They're not "drying up". They've become slightly more irregular.'

She stirs the flatleaf parsley into the lentils.

'I didn't mean that. I was just wondering if you were feeling unwell. What with you not eating your supper.'

'I'm eating it now, aren't I?'

Silas begins coughing again. He stares at Mason's plate, still held in front of him with one hand, the other over his mouth. When the coughing has receded, he takes a careful step in the direction of Mason's room.

'Seems to me that you're the one that should be worrying about your health,' says Veronica, plucking up some bread and dipping it in the lentils. She stares at a framed poster above the sink, a nineteenth-century illustration of common vegetables. She thinks how good it would be to stab the dull, inert potato with a sharp fork.

'I'm fine. Just a tickle. Something went down the wrong way. Look, I'm sorry, Veronica. I swear to God, the last thing I want to do is upset you. But he's my son. Try and imagine if it was China.'

Veronica takes another swallow of wine. It tastes sour in her mouth. When she speaks again it is softly but distinctly.

'Screw you.'

Silas looks down at Mason's plate as if the solution to his dilemma was buried among the lentils, then back up at Veronica who is pouring herself another glass, right to the rim.

'If this is the way you feel, why did you get together with me in the first place? You knew I had a son. You knew it wasn't always going to be easy.'

Drinking again, Veronica feels her head swimming. She tries to bring her therapeutic training into play, to hold the space safely, but her words, when they emerge, still bear the taint of bitterness.

'Because I thought you were *honest*. I'd had enough of lies with Frankie.'

'I *am* honest.'

'Maybe you are. But you're also wound round that kid's finger.'

Silas stares at her. His expression, temporarily aggrieved, returns to its noncommittal default. Then he slowly turns towards the stairs and makes his way up, holding the plate in one hand, a knife and fork in the other.

Veronica watches him walking away from her. She thinks of calling after him, but says nothing. She seems to feel something inside fracture. It is as if, inside her, continents are drifting.

When Owen finally comes home — it isn't until after eleven that night — Nodge has gone from feeling guilty to feeling furious. JJ is watching TV, quietly sharing the sitting room with Nodge. There are aromatic candles burning and the lights are down low.

'Where the hell have you been?' says Nodge to Owen in a

low, controlled voice, as he sees his husband enter unsteadily through the front door. He rises from the sofa.

'Just walking,' says Owen quietly. He is soaked through with the rain and his cheeks are pale with cold.

'And drinking.'

'Walking and drinking.'

Owen simply stands there, dripping, as if he is waiting for someone to tell him his next move.

'Ought I to go?' says JJ, noticing the shambolic figure standing in the doorway. 'Sounds like you've got one or two matters to discuss between you, haha.'

'We're fine,' says Owen.

'Pull the other one; it's got bells on. As my old mother used to say.'

'Would you mind very much, JJ?' says Nodge, politely gesturing towards the door to JJ's room.

'Not at all, not at all, sorry to be taking up the space. You alright, Owen?'

'I'm just on top of the world, JJ. Hasn't Nodge told you about it?'

'We've barely spoken. Most of the time I've been in my room doing my accounts and playing chess on my computer. I got so bored I thought I'd come in here for a bit of junk TV.'

As he speaks, JJ gathers his things – a cigarette pack, his phone and a book on chess strategy – and then retreats to his room, closing the door behind him. A few seconds later, the strains of 'A Wand'ring Minstrel, I' can be heard, even more off-key than usual.

Nodge turns to Owen, who has now removed his coat,

hanging it on the hook behind the door. He is wiping his hair dry with a tea towel.

'Why didn't you answer your phone? I've been sick to death with worry,' says Nodge, taking a step towards him.

'Out of battery.' Owen folds the tea towel and, looking around, seemingly unsure what to do with it, puts it pointlessly in his pocket. Nodge knows this is a lie since he had heard a ring tone on the first few occasions he tried to call him. Owen seems slumped, as if vertebrae have been removed from his back. Nodge can't bear it. He reaches over to give Owen a hug, but Owen takes a step back.

'Don't ever do that again,' says Nodge, but in a softer tone now, disarmed by Owen's sunken diffidence. 'Don't disappear like that.'

'Only if you promise never to hide a drugs offence from me.'

'Have a shower, put on some fresh clothes and sit down here with me. I'll fetch you a drink.'

Owen walks unsteadily towards their bedroom. His shoes, which he normally removes at the doorway, are still wet and leave imprints of the sole on the vintage rug. Nodge stares at the traces, as if they represent a trail of some kind that needs to be interpreted. Each footprint becomes fainter as they move away from him.

Thirty minutes later, Owen emerges from the bedroom wearing expensive blue Brooks Brothers pyjamas and a pair of Mahabis classic slippers in slate grey. He has sprayed some cologne under his chin. His just-washed hair, fresh from being towelled, sticks up in sprigs on top of his head. Nodge is sitting on the sofa and Owen lowers himself into the space next to him. Nodge reaches over and flattens the sprigs affectionately with his palm. Then he gets up, fetches two glasses of Picpoul and hands one to Owen. Owen takes it, but stares at it without taking a swallow. Nodge sits down again, feeling the chill of the wine coming through the warm glass.

'Are we okay, O?' says Nodge.

'Not really.'

'I'm really sorry about the . . . '

Owen jerks his head up.

'You knew they would find out. Didn't you? You've never wanted to have a child. That's why you sabotaged the whole thing.'

'Owen . . . '

'Don't "Owen" me. I *know* you, Nodge.'

'It's the opposite! I didn't want them to find out! Of course I didn't.'

'Then why didn't you tell *me* about it?'

Nodge searches for an answer, but cannot locate one.

'I'll tell you why, Nodge,' says Owen, his face flushed now with anger as well as drink. 'You didn't tell me because you knew I would make damn sure you declared it to the adoption agency.'

'Oh, come off it.'

Owen swigs a mouthful of wine and jabs a finger at Nodge's face.

'We could have talked to Comfort about it. She has always been on our side. She would have advised us. A five-minute search on the internet would probably have told us we were okay.'

'I didn't think. I'm sorry. I fucked up. What else can I say?'

Owen takes his gaze away from Nodge and stares down at

the rug. Nodge has cleaned it and amorphous wet marks have replaced the defined treads left by Owen's shoes. Normally houseproud, Owen shows no interest in the damp spots. He puts his wine down on the table, next to a small rare cactus, then clenches his arms defensively across his chest.

'The thing is, Nodge . . . '

He looks up at Nodge again. His breath still smells of alcohol, which mixes with the sage of his cologne, but his eyes look sober.

'I just don't know if we can sustain this relationship if we don't have a child.'

Owen takes Nodge's hand and notices that it is shaking. His eyes are steady as they look at Nodge now, while Nodge's are suddenly watery and afraid.

'It's not that I don't love you, Nodge. I do. It's just that – I don't know. We're running out of purpose. We buy nice things. We go to nice events. We have nice dinner parties and go to fun clubs. We even have good sex.'

'But?'

Owen strokes the back of Nodge's hand with a single finger.

'But it's not enough anymore.'

Nodge feels something at his core begin to shrink and tremble. He digs inside himself to find some words to parry this blow, but nothing seems sturdy enough. The words when they come pull in two directions, half attack, half defence. His shaky, uncertain delivery underlines the division.

'It's enough for *me*.'

This seems merely to curdle Owen's melancholy into pique.

'It's not enough for *ME*. I mean — you've already *had* kids in a sense.'

'Who? Florence and Dilly?'

'Your nieces, yes. And then there's China. She's like your own daughter. She's mad about you.'

'That's not my fault. And she loves you too.'

'I want the same as you've had. I want the next step. I want a child.'

Nodge weighs his words carefully before speaking again.

'And if you can't have one?'

Owen shakes his head very slightly, but otherwise remains absolutely still.

'I don't know. I guess I'll be unhappy.'

'Then I'll be unhappy.'

'Then we'll both be unhappy.'

'*Then* what shall we do?'

Owen looks at him with a pleading look on his face as if hoping that Nodge has the answer.

'I just don't know, Nodge. I just don't know. Perhaps we ought to spend some time apart.'

Before Nodge has a chance to reply, JJ walks brightly into the room, still humming his song from *The Mikado*.

'Are you alright, boys? Fancy a quick game of chess, Owen? Might take your mind off your troubles.'

Nodge is about to wave him away, but Owen immediately rises, seemingly grateful for the interruption.

'I don't mind if I do. But go easy on me. JJ, are you wearing a *cravat*?'

'Old school. You wouldn't appreciate the finer things. Inspired by Oscar Wilde.'

'Peter Wyngarde more like,' says Owen.

'What would you know of Saint Peter? You're too young by far.'

'I know my heritage.'

'Owen . . .' says Nodge, desperate to continue their conversation.

'I'll bring the board in, then, shall I?' says JJ.

'No, let's go to your room. It's cosier there.'

'Well, if you say so.' He glances at Nodge with concern. 'No problem, I suppose.'

Without saying another word to Nodge, Owen follows JJ into the spare room, leaving Nodge, stunned and alone, slumped on the sofa, staring at the blank, silent screen of the television.

March 2020: London

Frankie is sitting on an armchair in the living room with China. She sits on the sofa in silence, apart from the insistent tattoo of her finger against the screen of her phone. Frankie struggles to discover a way of opening a father–daughter conversation. The hoped-for regeneration of his relationship with China is proving more difficult than he had imagined. Eventually, he decides to go with something neutral. He is always on the lookout now for causing offence.

'So – have you got a boyfriend at the moment?'

'What makes you think I want a boyfriend?' snaps China without looking up from her phone. 'How do you know I don't want a girlfriend?'

'Do you?'

'Would it matter if I did?'

'Not at all. I've got no problem with lezz . . . with people who are same-sex attracted.'

'I'm not a lesbian.'

'Thank Christ for that,' Frankie answers before he can censor himself. China takes a break from her phone and glares at him.

'I think I like boys *and* girls actually.'

'Oh, okay. Swing both ways, then.'

China looks disgusted.

'You know . . . so you're . . . bisexual, right?' ventures Frankie, flailing.

'Actually, I'm pansexual – if anything.'

'Yeh, no. Of course.'

'You don't know what I'm talking about, do you?'

Frankie concedes defeat. He wishes he hadn't started the conversation in the first place.

'No. What *are* you talking about?'

'It's not for me to educate you. It's tiring. Go and do some homework.'

China returns to her phone. Frankie goes to his laptop on the dining table. He resentfully takes note of the coffee mug stain that China left on the day she arrived and which has proved impossible to remove. He checks Google for 'Pansexual'. After a few minutes, China goes to refill her water bottle, drinking a glass at the sink when she gets there.

'I think you're meant to be about half made of water,' says Frankie. 'You seem to be pushing for total saturation.'

China pours another glass and drinks it in one.

Five minutes later, at the completion of his online research, Frankie doesn't feel much the wiser. But he does not want to get into another battle of definitions. China has returned to her seat on the sofa. Before she can pick up her phone again, Frankie decides to shoot for sympathy rather than risking more conflict.

'I don't think I understand the world anymore.'

'Let me clarify things for you, then,' says China briskly. 'You're the enemy.'

'I am?'

He looks at his daughter. She stares at him blankly. It settles on him that she isn't joking.

'But I'm your father.'

'What you are is an old, white, cis man who thinks the world is still his. It isn't anymore.'

'I don't think the world is mine.'

'Then you've got something right for a change.'

'I never did. It never was.'

'You just don't get it, do you?'

'No,' says Frankie sadly. 'I really don't. Not any of it.'

The streets around London's Theatreland have mysteriously emptied. The woman sits alone. She is always alone, but this is pure, distilled solitude. There is something about it she likes. The peace. The streets have become her own. And yet there is an edge of isolation that disconcerts her. She wonders if it is like this everywhere.

Perhaps things will be better where she grew up. It had been home, once. Although home wasn't a word she really understands anymore.

It has been a cold winter, they were all cold winters, even when they weren't. But the weather now is beautiful. She enjoys the clear air, the gaping spaces in the streets. No one to spit at her. No one to ignore her. No one to patronize her with their pity, insult her with their money.

But then again. Her supplier has gone to ground and it is impossible to score. Now when she weeps it is not only for real, but there is no one there to see. Her plastic cup is empty. People from the council come round, they always come round every night, them and the charities and the police, and try to arrest her or get her into a hostel and at first she refused — they're cesspits those hostels, and dangerous. Men have fiddled with her in such places; they gave her no money for the groping; they thought they could have it for free.

She takes out her mobile phone. She keeps it well hidden from the punters as well as the other homeless people. The punters didn't like to see you had things like that, or even clean, nice clothes. If they were going to give you money, they wanted to make sure that you really needed it, that you were suffering, that you weren't someone who just *wants* it. She agrees with them sometimes. Too many ponces on the street, gypsies, Albanians, darkies, gangs, scumbags. Yeh, she knows about them, she could handle herself, keeps a shiv down her boot just in case. Has used it once or twice.

There are a few friends from the streets that she thinks might be still around, but she either gets no answer or a dead tone when she rings them. Her oldest friends, the ones from before she ended up on the street, gave up on her long ago; they had to face that she was beyond repair. She was angry at the time, but now she thinks that perhaps they were right. *No perhaps about it*, she thinks, and laughs joylessly, an empty rustling sound with no one to hear it, a tree falling in an empty wood.

She hasn't always been mad. She remembers a time when she had a home, even a partner. Then there were the drugs, but she can't blame the drugs completely, not entirely. After all, she took them. She didn't have to, did she? That's what he said anyway. Oh, she was a bad person alright, the worst person.

Fuck them all.

She looks up, for want of anything better to do. There is a sign up above her, an advertising hoarding with a giant tick. It instructs her quite plainly to 'Just Do It'. *Okay then.* She takes off her trousers and pisses in the street. There is no one to see. Some new plague apparently. Well, it would clean some of the scum away, she supposed; there was scum everywhere. She supposed she was scum too, but she had stopped caring long ago.

London, she decides, is finished. Time to go home.

She trudges without enthusiasm in what she senses is the direction of Victoria Coach Station.

Ugly Sue's phone has been dead for months, but perhaps she's still there and they can keep one another company.

PART TWO

Infection

Day 1 of Lockdown, 23 March 2020

'He's only gone and done it.'

Frankie stares at the untypically serious image of Boris Johnson on the TV screen.

'At least we've got plenty of toilet paper,' says China.

'So this is it. We're stuck here for the next three months.'

'Or forever. If they don't find a vaccine, what are we going to do? I'll go mad if I have to stay inside all the time.'

'Same for me. They've closed the offices.'

China and Frankie sit adjacent to one another; Frankie on the plain grey sofa, with grey cushions, China on the matching armchair. Frankie drums his fingers on the rectangular smoked-glass coffee table. China yawns and stretches. She gets up and walks over to the dartboard that Frankie has affixed to the back of the kitchen door and starts idly throwing arrows. Every one misses and lodges in the protective corkboard behind.

'I'm already bored,' she says, dawdling to collect the darts and try again.

'Look on the bright side. It will be an opportunity for us to get to know one another better.'

China launches the darts again, this time scoring twenty-two, then raises her arms and stretches.

'Is that a thing?' says Frankie.

China looks down. She realizes that Frankie is waving his hand in the general direction of China's exposed armpit.

'Is *what* a thing?'

'Hairy pits.'

China snaps her arms down and crosses them over her chest.

'You're body-shaming me.'

'I'm just asking if it's the fashion now for girls to leave their underarms unshaven.'

'It's got nothing *to do* with fashion. No one would ask you why you don't shave *your* armpits. It's just men laying down the rules again for how women should present themselves.'

'I was just asking.'

China hugs her arms around her body tighter and stares at the dartboard.

'But what I don't understand is . . . I mean, Roxy told me . . . that a lot of young girls now . . . '

'*Girls!* I'm a woman. We're all women. We're not "girls" or "ladies".'

'*Women* then. A lot of women . . . even women with hairy armpits . . . shave themselves . . . you know . . . down *there*. So, what's the difference? Why not shave the pits, but shave the bits?'

China takes a brisk step towards the front door.

'I'm going out for a walk.'

'I'll come too.'

'I'd rather you didn't.'

She marches straight out of the front door, leaving it open behind her, and down the stairs to the street. He listens to her trainers pound on the stairs. On the floor, next to the open door to the flat, are two large plastic bags containing an assortment of

DIY materials. Frankie gets up, closes the door and rummages in the bags. Sandpaper, paint, putty, a drill, varnish, a socket set. He has already decided that if lockdown came he would use some of the time to refurbish his flat. He takes no pleasure in DIY, but feels he needs something to fill this strange aperture that is opening in his life.

He decides to start with the banister. He takes a sheet of rough sandpaper out of one of the bags and, without further preparation or laying down a dustsheet, he begins to rub the worn, stained surface of the varnish. He checks the clock and decides to stick at it for the next sixty minutes.

Five minutes later, he is back on the sofa watching *Antiques Roadshow*.

Day 12, 4 April 2020

8:05 a.m.

Frankie wakes up. Tries to go back to sleep. Fails. Tosses and turns. Gets up, pulls the curtains closer, tries to stop the light coming through the window. Fails. Gives up and goes downstairs to make himself a cup of tea. Reads *The Times* online, sport first. Goes on Facebook. No messages. Scrolls his Twitter feed. Reads the news. Can't think of anything to Tweet. Stares out the window. Picks up the book China has told him to read. *A Girl Is a Half-Formed Thing*. Finds it boring. The narrator seems very disturbed. A nut. He puts it down after fifty pages. Most books he puts down after fifty pages. If that.

10 a.m.

Frankie makes toast with peanut butter. Skippy, smooth not crunchy. Spills butter on his dressing gown. Tries to remove it carefully with his finger. Unsuccessful. Looks out the window again. Plumps up the cushions on the sofa. Picks up China's mess from the previous night – socks, notepads, plates, a still half-full can of Brewdog IPA. He gets some peanut butter on the cushions while he's trying to clean them. Wipes the cushions. It spreads the peanut butter further. Frankie gives up. Wipes down the kitchen work surfaces, sprays a heavy dose of disinfectant, pours bleach down the sink. Doesn't like the smell, too much like semen. Makes mental note not to mention the comparison to China.

10:30 a.m.

So many hours in the day. They stretch like a dreary windswept path towards a barely visible, always receding horizon. Once time just ate itself up. Now it just sits there, a stubborn lump, refusing to shift. Frankie decides to go out for a walk. Soon. Maybe do some food shopping? But shopping is the high point of the day. He doesn't want to squander it. Decides to leave it till later. Maybe go out for a cycle?

11:03 a.m.

China comes slowly down the stairs and into the living room. She is wearing a onesie with bear ears. It's ironic, apparently. Frankie offers a cheery greeting. China says nothing, nods slightly and heads for the fridge. She is wearing earbuds. She has soaked some oats to make Bircher muesli and left them overnight. She takes the mush out of the fridge and sniffs it, then makes herself a coffee without offering Frankie one. Frankie tries to make conversation about breakfast food, remarking that in his day Coco Pops were considered exotic. She remains unresponsive since she can't hear him and will not remove her earbuds. They are connected to her phone which is in turn connected to Spotify. She is listening to Lana Del Rey. Lowering herself onto the sofa and spooning the cereal into her mouth, she spills scraps of the muesli on the cushion that Frankie has just been cleaning.

11:25 a.m.

China finally takes the buds out of her ears. Frankie is now watching morning TV, *Homes Under the Hammer*. China speaks for the first time, asks Frankie if he has read *A Girl Is a Half-Formed Thing* yet. Frankie says that it's 'interesting'. China checks Instagram and TikTok. Despite lockdown there are still videos of happy people lip-synching and dancing in their bedrooms, eating bananas or posting videos of chipmunks. She wonders why Kardashian never did anything funny. She is surprised to register that she misses the inert, indifferent presence of her stepfather's cat.

She posts a TikTok video of her miming to Aldous Harding's 'The Barrel', trying to imitate the hand movements in the video for the song, but she ends up just feeling silly and deletes the post. She listens to Mitski, Glass Animals, James Blake, Dusty Springfield.

12:30 p.m.

Frankie resolves, finally, to go out for a cycle. It is a perfect blue day, the sky like a porcelain plate. He dresses in Lycra, Muddy Fox top and cycling tights, which makes him bulge in the wrong places. Spotting him, China mimes vomiting. Frankie pretends not to notice. Before leaving, he picks up the dirty crockery that she has left on the floor of the living room, complaining loudly.

China takes no notice.

1 p.m.

While Frankie is out, China calls Veronica. Silas answers and China is curt with him. When Veronica comes to the phone, China can hear Mason screaming in the background. They talk about nothing for there is nothing to talk about. Nothing has happened.

2 p.m.

Frankie returns sweating from his cycle ride and goes upstairs to take a shower. China is making lunch for them both, mainly grains, tofu and fresh steamed veg. Frankie, returning from the shower in his dressing gown, is unexcited by the offering but feigns enthusiasm. He eats the food appreciatively but in silence, then tops up, secretly, in his bedroom with a biltong, a supersized Mars Bar and two packets of Quavers.

3 p.m.

Frankie sits in his room and listens to his heritage iPod playing mainly music from the 1990s – Pulp, Blur, the Verve, Oasis. He returns to the living room and waxes nostalgic about Tony Blair to China, who condemns Blair as a war criminal. Before Frankie can develop his case for New Labour, China, not listening, heads upstairs to change and get ready for a run.

4 p.m.

Frankie finally gets round to doing some background work for Farley & Ratchett – mainly accounts, plus some rough valuations guessed at via webcam and floor measurements.

5 p.m.

Frankie begins to prepare supper. He decides to make some spaghetti with tomato sauce to which he will add proper meatballs for himself and veggie ones for China.

6:30 p.m.

Frankie starts to watch TV. He exists on a diet of gangster, fantasy and sci-fi movies. China binge-watches *Gilmore Girls* in her room.

9:30–10 p.m.

Not tired, Frankie goes to bed, just to try to block out some hours with sleep. China sneaks a quick joint out of the window of her room.

11 p.m.

Frankie and China are both asleep. Outside, an urban fox prowls the dustbins, eyes glinting in the streetlights.

Day 15, 7 April 2020

Frankie stares at the glitching image of Roxy on FaceTime. She has a moisturizing mask on which, in Frankie's mind, makes her look like the Ed Gein character in *Texas Chainsaw Massacre*.

'Can't you wipe that stuff off?'

'Why?'

'It's distracting.'

'It's how I stay so young and beautiful.'

Frankie has started rubbing down the banisters again, sitting on the stairs in his pyjamas. A thin film of dust has settled on the floor where he has been at work. He thought he would have had the banisters painted a week ago, but he still hasn't even finished the prep.

'You look terrifying.'

'You and your silver tongue. I miss you.'

'I miss you too,' he responds automatically.

'Do you?' says Roxy.

'Have you got some paracetamol in? In case you catch the virus? Apparently it helps.'

Frankie, three-quarters of the way up the stairs, looks dejectedly at the still-uncompleted section of the banister. He wonders if he could just get away with painting the bit he has already rubbed down, then dismisses the thought and carries on rubbing desultorily. He had asked China to help him. She hasn't taken up the offer.

'That reminds me of a joke.'

'Is there anything that doesn't?'

'So, a man walks into the pharmacy and asks the pharmacist, "Do you have any acetylsalicylic acid?" "Do you mean aspirin?" says the pharmacist. "That's it," says the man. "I can never remember that word."'

'Up to your usual standard at least.'

Frankie catches his finger on a splinter and flinches as a sliver of dirty wood slides under his fingernail. He tries to pull it out with his teeth.

'Listen, darling. I've had an idea,' says Roxy.

'Why have I got a feeling that I'm not going to like it?'

The splinter is out and is stained with blood. He stares at it as if hypnotized. Weary of the sanding now, he leaves the sandpaper and makes his way down the stairs, disposing of the bloody splinter on the way in the bin, deciding that he has earned himself a break.

'Why don't I come and stay over at your place? Just for one night.'

Frankie stops in his tracks, sits down again, this time on the bottom step, and stares at the white, greasy mask that fills his phone screen.

'I can think of a couple of reasons. Such as the existence of a worldwide deadly virus and the fact that it would be against the law and you would be putting myself and my daughter at risk.'

He looks down at the gap in the stair runner and notices an ant, which he idly crushes with his thumb. He briefly examines the black mess and then flicks it away, wondering why ant blood isn't also red. But what colour is it? For that matter, do they even have blood?

'I'll have a test before I come. Make sure I'm negative.'

'It's all I can do to keep China obeying the rules as it is. She's desperate to go and hang out with her friends. If I do what you want me to do, then she can do what she likes.'

'She does what she likes anyway.'

'Not really. She's quite responsible in some ways. Very, very untidy, but with an ineradicable streak of piety.'

Frankie notes that there is another ant in the space where he terminated the previous one. And another. He follows the trail from the stairs and sees a river of ants, running all the way to the kitchen. The organic mess that China has been leaving behind her every day, he concludes, has finally produced consequences.

'We wouldn't have to tell her.'

'We're not exactly going to be able to hide you. She's not deaf, dumb and blind. I think she might notice you at some point. Fuck!'

'What the matter?'

'Fucking ants all over the shop.'

He crushes a few more. Others immediately take their place. Roxy starts peeling off the mask, revealing a sweating but fresh-looking face underneath displaying full, pink lips.

'What time does she go to bed?'

'Early, as a rule. Partly out of boredom and partly because she wants to have her own space for a while, and I'm always trying to get her to watch old Quentin Tarantino movies with me.'

'Ten o'clock?'

'More or less.'

'Does she ever come out of her room again after she goes to bed?'

Frankie idly squashes a few more ants and wipes the mess off his thumb with a tissue he keeps in his pocket.

'Where are you going with this, Roxy?'

'Where do you think I'm going?'

He stands up and starts stamping on the trail of ants leading into the kitchen. She finishes wiping off her mask.

'What the hell are you doing, Frankie? Are you having some kind of epileptic fit?'

'I'm killing ants.'

'How many ants does it take to fill an apartment?'

'What?'

'Tenants.'

'What?'

'Ten-ants.'

'Yeh. Why do you want to know about China's bed-time habits?'

'I bet she doesn't get up again until late the next day.'

Frankie follows the trail to the kitchen and to a spot behind a cupboard where he can now see that China has dropped a half-eaten energy bar with honey. It is coated with a seething army of insects.

'*No*. No *way*, Roxy. It's a betrayal of trust for one thing,' he says, murdering as many ants as he can with his stockinged foot.

'Frankie the Fib. Betraying someone's trust. God forbid.'

205

'Betraying *China's* trust. My daughter. Which is not exactly maximal as it is, but we are gradually mending things.'

'I haven't seen any sign of it.'

'You haven't been here, have you?'

He tentatively picks up the energy bar and drops it into the bin. Several ants make a run for it onto his finger, and he flicks them away.

'How do you get rid of ants? There's so many of them.'

'Ant poison. Or a tiny machine gun. Come on, Frankie.'

She licks her lips and adopts a singsong voice.

'I'll make it worth your while. Anything for a laugh, eh, isn't it?'

'No.'

'You could just tell her I'm staying over for one night.'

'She wouldn't stand for it.'

'So, it's what she wants instead of what I want again, is it?'

'It's not a competition,' says Frankie, giving up on the ants and slumping into an armchair, defeated by both the banister and the insects.

'It feels like one.'

'To you it does,' says Frankie.

'So what if it is a competition? Everything's a competition. We live in a capitalist economy. You of all people should know that. China's a teenager. She still believes in fairness and equality and all that bollocks.'

'Is it bollocks?'

Roxy's voice softens again. Frankie closes his eyes and sees a constellation of yellow specks on a red background. His hands are oddly cold and he thrusts them down the side of the cushion for warmth.

'It'll just be for one night. I'm getting lonely. In fact, I'm going *postal*. I'll turn up at eleven, well past her bedtime, and I'll get up and go before eight. She'll never know I was here.'

'She'll work it out. China's not stupid.'

'I'm not stupid either. I'll be careful.'

'I don't know, Roxy. It doesn't sound like a great idea to me.'

Feeling something sticky with his fingers, Frankie pulls his hand out to reveal a green jelly sweet. Jelly sweets have been China's favourite since she was an infant. Further exploration uncovers a red one, two more green ones and, in their vicinity, several dozen more foraging ants.

'That doesn't mean it *isn't* a good idea,' says Roxy. 'Don't tell me that you wouldn't like to have me in your bed for a night.'

'I don't think I can do it, Roxy.'

Roxy simply stares at him. Without another word being spoken, Frankie knows that he has lost another battle.

Day 25, 17 April 2020

'I'm going for a run,' announces China.

She is wearing tight, very short Nike nylon running shorts, a Nike polypropylene long-sleeve top that stops at her midriff, a gilet and Nike trainers. She turns to examine her face in the wall mirror and pokes her hair into place.

'There was I thinking you were going to a banquet at the Guildhall.'

Frankie looks down at his hairy spreading gut and the remains of the cheese on toast he has just consumed for lunch. He looks up at China, who is now bending over with perfect flexibility and adjusting her left shoelace. He notices for the first time the tattoo of a tree on her lower back.

'What's the tattoo all about?'

'It's a tree, Dad.'

She stands up and stretches.

'Why a tree?'

'I'm sure if you think about it enough you'll work it out.'

Frankie ponders this, but comes up with nothing. He continues to express bewilderment. China turns and faces him.

'It's my name, Dad.'

'Your name's China. China Blue.'

'I'm taking Mum's name. Tree.'

'But why?'

'I like it better. And I don't see why I should have to take a man's name. What's all this shit all over the floor?' she says, noticing the frosting of white ant powder.

'Cocaine,' says Frankie, feeling a surge of bitterness in his throat. 'What do you think it is?'

China notices one stumbling escapee from the tiny apocalypse jerking its way towards a crack in the floorboards where it disappears.

'We have ants?'

'I can't believe you haven't noticed them. They're everywhere.'

China finishes lacing, stands and starts jogging on the spot.

'Can I come with you?' says Frankie on impulse, slapping his stomach with the flat of his hand. Something has been triggered by the tree tattoo. He feels excluded.

'You want to have another heart attack?'

'I just want a gentle run. I need to do something. It wasn't a heart attack. I had ischemia. That was five years ago. They sorted it. I'm good as new.'

He gets up and does a couple of star jumps, almost losing his balance and falling.

'Why do you need to go with me? You'll slow me down. Best you go on your own.'

Frankie tries to touch his toes but gets no closer than just beneath his knees.

'I wouldn't mind a bit of company while I exercise. It will motivate me. I'm turning into a slob.'

'I won't be much company. I won't be able to hear you,' she says, holding out her earbuds.

Frankie pushes as hard as he can towards his toes, but can get no further. He gives up and stands up straight again, puffing.

'You could always take them out.'

China stretches out her calf muscles. She is lithe, even bony, no spare flesh on her.

'Being seen running with a fat dad is a bit uncool. Even with one who isn't fat.'

'The streets are empty. Who's to see?'

'I am.'

'Then don't look.'

She looks up and registers her father's hopeful expression, softens.

'Go on, then — if you must. But don't try "bonding" with me. And get a move on.'

'What's the rush? It's not exactly like either of us have got a lot to do.'

'I'm mentally prepared. Now I'm going to have to wind down, having warmed up.'

'You warm up to run?'

'Stretches. You can hurt your muscles. Especially when you're old.'

'Just hold on here a minute.'

Frankie skips up the stairs, while China flops onto the sofa and checks Instagram on her phone. People are still managing to have a better time than her, it seems. She throws off a selfie of herself in her running kit, grinning, captioning it 'great opportunity to get fit'. She takes seven photos before she finds one she deems sufficiently joyful and flattering. She adjusts the colour and contrast, crops the frame and finally posts it. Then she starts to wait for some likes to appear. Only one has – from her mother – when Frankie appears at the top of the stairs, ten minutes later, wearing a faded Strokes T-shirt, a pair of ill-fitting cotton shorts and battered trainers with thick white towelling socks. He has a headband on that pushes his thin hair back, revealing the scar left by his attempt to get rid, by plastic surgery, of the port wine facial mark he was born with. The T-shirt is too tight and his belly bulges. He holds a transparent sports bottle full of yellow liquid. He makes his way friskily down the stairs.

'Why the bottle of piss?' says China, already regretting her invitation.

'Lucozade.'

'You look ridiculous.'

'Right. I'm ready,' says Frankie, pumping his knees up and down. The kneecaps are pale, the calves hairy. 'Where are we going?'

'You're going to last about three minutes.'

'Don't underestimate me. Many have made that mistake before.'

'Have you stretched out?'

'Not so much.'

'Be it on your own head.'

'What's the route?'

'I usually run down the Golborne Road to Latimer Road, up towards Little Wormwood Scrubs, do a few rounds of the park then head back.'

Frankie nods briskly and starts to jog on the spot.

'Let's Do It, as I believe your sponsors recommend.'

They head down the stairs and onto the main road. Frankie still hasn't got over his astonishment at how empty it is of traffic and people since lockdown. He sniffs the air. It is sweet and pleasant. Since the restaurant downstairs has closed, even the flat is fresh and fragrant. He can hear the birds. He takes a swig of the Lucozade. It goes up his nose and makes him sneeze.

'Well, this is nice.'

'What is?' says China, beginning to jog at a gentle pace in front of him. She has yet to put her earbuds in.

'Doing something together. Father and daughter.'

'We're together all day.'

'But this is actually *doing* something. Slow down a bit.'

Frankie's breath is already coming heavy. He stares again at the tree tattoo on China's back and feels a new determination to prove his worth.

'I'm barely running, Dad.'

'Just give me a chance to adjust.'

China slows her pace fractionally as they make their way down the deserted road, the shops all closed apart from the cash 'n' carry which has a substantial queue outside. After five minutes, Frankie is panting pitifully.

'Do you want to stop?' says China, removing an earbud, not looking round but hearing the rasping and heaving of Frankie's breath.

'What makes you think that?' says Frankie determinedly. He takes a desperate swig of air. China keeps a steady pace. Up to and past Portobello they enter Chesterton Road, tree-lined, vaguely suburban. He sees the top of Grenfell Tower, still with its green-hearted mask of shame and the legend 'Forever in our Hearts'. China has hardly broken sweat. Turning, she sees Frankie's T-shirt is soaked with perspiration. His face is red and what's left of his hair is matted under the headband.

'Keep going,' gasps Frankie, forcing a smile. He has made a promise to himself that he is going to surprise China – prove that he isn't past it after all. But he is beginning to wonder if he isn't going to end up making the reverse point.

They pass the borders of the St Quintin estate, within 500 metres of the house where they once all lived together, then they make the gates of Little Wormwood Scrubs on Dalgarno Gardens, flanking the spreading blocks of the Peabody Estate to the north-east of the park. Perspiration runs down Frankie's forehead and cheeks despite the sweat band and into his eyes, blurring his vision. His breath is coming so heavy now, he feels that his lungs are going to start bleeding.

'Dad,' shouts China, looking over her shoulder, still jogging. 'I think you should stop for a while.'

'I'm fine.' Frankie pushes on. 'Just need to get through the wall.'

'You've only been running fifteen minutes. There isn't usually a wall at fifteen minutes.'

'It's been all wall since we started.'

Frankie slows still further and falls thirty yards behind China. He makes a resolution to at least do one lap of the park, but twenty seconds later he flings himself down on a bench, his chest burning. He even has to wait a minute before he can take a swig of the sweet warm yellow liquid in his bottle. China runs on, either oblivious or indifferent. Frankie watches as she jogs into the distance.

Watching her fluidity of movement, he feels a burst of pride and love. She is so strong, so at ease with her body. So determined. So young.

At the same time, he has a strange epiphany. He seems momentarily to realize that she is not just his daughter, but a complete human being, with terrors, feelings and an entire universe of personhood inside her skin.

It frightens him because it momentarily reveals to him how vulnerable she is. She is not just a thorn in his side. It was too easy to think of her that way. He had watched, since the divorce, her innocence and trust gradually dissipating. He knew that he had a role in that dissipation, in accelerating it and intensifying it, and he also knew that it was the most precious thing that she possessed. And he had helped destroy it.

After a while, a young woman, similar in height to China, emerges from the tree line on the far side of the park. Frankie automatically thinks how attractive she is. He realizes in the same instant that it actually is China – she has shed her track top and taken the hair band off.

Ashamed, he slots her urgently back into her correct conceptual pigeonhole. China was right. *What a vile thing it is to be a man.* He watches her speed up as she realizes that Frankie is watching her. He thinks of his own flabby body. It is a wreck. He must do better. His breath more or less returning to normal now, he rises from the bench, grits his teeth and jogs towards the gate, estimating that they will arrive there at about the same time. As he makes it to the gate – puffing again already – China comes towards him with a broad grin on her face.

'How you doing, old man?'

Frankie puts a thumb up. He is determined to make it back to the flat. Following in China's slipstream, he tries to keep pace. This time, for some reason, it doesn't feel so bad, although he is still breathing with difficulty. Maybe he has got to the other side of the wall after all. He manages to keep running albeit at half China's pace until they arrive back at the front door, Frankie only stopping once or twice on the way to catch his breath. China has already used the latch key and is waiting for him at the foot of the stairs.

'Alright, crock?'

Frankie nods, unable to find the breath to reply.

'Sorry,' he says eventually as they make their way up the stairs.

'What for?' says China. She is already breathing normally again.

'Slowing you down. Being old. Being me.'

They make their way up the stairs and go through the front door. China sits and begins pulling off her trainers. She raises one to her nose and inhales.

'Ripe.'

She prises the other trainer off and throws them both on the floor without thought. Other detritus left by her includes three coffee cups, two notepads, three books, a pair of knickers, a pair of legwarmers and two dirty plates.

'You did well,' she says to Frankie. Frankie, still trying to recover, doesn't respond. She peels off her socks and throws them after the shoes. After a few seconds she looks up.

'We can try again tomorrow if you like. Just get some decent running kit. It's like I'm in training with Homer Simpson.'

Frankie smiles. Minutes later, he is ordering shorts, trainers and a running vest from Amazon.

Day 27, 19 April 2020

Frankie rises from bed at five past nine. China is still asleep. He makes himself a cup of coffee and settles down to read the news on his laptop. Afterwards, he cleans and tidies the room assiduously, as he does every morning. Tidiness not only keeps chaos at bay; it gives him something to do. Dusting, sweeping, polishing the surfaces. He cleans up China's mess, complaining loudly, hoping that China is in earshot, not that it will make any difference one way or another. Then he makes a cup of tea and stares out the window as he does every day, wondering how he is going to fill the stretch of hours ahead.

By 10:25, the sun has worked its way around the sky and penetrated the front room. It dazzles him. Up until this moment, he has hated the lockdown. He had dreaded it coming and panicked when it arrived. All day long and all night long with nothing to do but watch TV, drink and fight with China.

But right now, at this moment, as he stands and stares out of his window into perfect spring sunlight and an uncluttered sky, denuded of aircraft, he decides that lockdown isn't so bad. In fact, he now realizes that he rather likes it.

In the wake of this insight, as if it has jemmied open a secret door, an unexpected trail of revelation comes. Ever since he left school, more than thirty years ago, life has been activity – working, striving, trying to get ahead, battling to keep one step in front of the next person who was, in turn, trying to bring him down with their own momentum. The need for money, the need for praise, the need for success. At weekends, the need to sort out the house, look after the kid, do some DIY, mow the lawn, do some washing. Even play was relentless and competitive, watching football an ordeal. It was endless.

At this moment, it occurs to him that he has been chasing nothing at all. Or nothing worth chasing anyway. He was running for a finish line that didn't exist. That never did exist.

Or he was on that line already. Which was also, somehow, the starting line as well. He would be here, precisely *here*, until the real finish came – as it came, out of the blue, nearly fifteen years ago, to Colin. In that sense, life was all one moment. Wasn't it?

He sinks deeper into his own mind, unanswerable questions spawning like a virus. Where had all the hunger for tomorrow got him? His drive towards future success had led him into bankruptcy. Until the lockdown happened he had been on the same old cycle – trying to get a partnership in F&R, buying a flash new car, getting himself rich again. Rich-ish, anyway. Admittedly he had given up on getting a trophy girlfriend – Roxy was hardly that – but why did he need a girlfriend at all? Weren't girlfriends just another promise of the fool's gold of the future? Why not just sit here, staring out of the window? He isn't achieving anything, but then again, he isn't doing anyone any harm.

He opens the window. He can hear birdsong. Of course he cannot identify the bird; it is just a fucking bird. But the song is liquid, melodious, delightful.

He had started the day with the question he has asked every day since lockdown began. *What am I going to do?* But for the first time today, he thinks to himself instead, *Why do I have to do anything?*

He rocks back on his heels slightly and listens to the birdsong as it changes rhythm and pitch and watches the shape of the shadows on the wall. He is still bored, but so what? Is it a crime to be bored?

He hears footsteps on the stairs behind him, pulling him out of his thoughts. He turns – China, descending, nods at Frankie, goes straight to the kitchen and makes herself a cup of tea and some wholemeal toast. Frankie watches her silently instead of gabbling as he usually does, trying to make conversation as he usually does, and refrains, for once, from complaining about the mess she was even now scattering behind her.

After a minute or so, China returns to the living room, *Death of a Salesman* in one hand and the cup of tea balanced finely on the plate that holds the toast. Frankie finds himself regarding her from a viewpoint of unaccustomed tranquillity.

My daughter.

My beautiful daughter.

He continues to watch, in a reverie, as she sits on the sofa and bolts down her breakfast, concluding with a loud burp. *Death of a Salesman* is balanced on the arm of the sofa. Then, leaving the soiled plate and cup where she has put them on the coffee table, she rises from the sofa and reaches for a brass gong that sits on the sideboard.

She strikes the gong gently with an attached metal stick with a rubber bulb on the end. It chimes once, sending a throb and a vibration into the air. She sits down cross-legged, as she does every day around this time. She lights an incense stick, takes a deep breath and closes her eyes.

'Mind if I join you?' says Frankie.

'You hate meditation,' China answers, without opening her eyes. Frankie takes this as assent or, at least, not refusal. He tries sitting cross-legged but finds it uncomfortable and sits instead with his eyes closed on a straight-backed dining chair. He tries to relax. He knows he's meant to watch his thoughts, but he can't get a sense of watching anything other than the pinky-white blurs behind his eyelids. As far as Frankie is concerned, he *is* his thoughts. He can't get past the flotsam and jetsam and find his way into the clear stream.

After twenty minutes, China opens her eyes and sounds the gong again. Frankie is still sitting on the chair with his eyes closed. Slowly he opens them.

'You meditated too?' she says.

He nods.

'How do you feel?' says China.

Frankie considers this carefully.

'I'm not sure what the point is.'

'The point is that there is no point.'

On this day, at this moment, he determines not to argue with her. On this beautiful blue morning with the birds and the flowers and the clear air. What is there to fight about, after all? It was all an illusion – ambition, hope, worldly status.

'What's the matter with *you*?' says China, perplexed by

Frankie's uncharacteristically calm demeanour. She picks up *Death of a Salesman*, sits on the sofa and starts to read.

'Nothing,' says Frankie softly. He smiles. China looks up again, discomfited.

'Why are you staring at me like that? Why aren't you saying anything? Why are you grinning like a weirdo?'

'I haven't got anything to say.'

'That's never stopped you before.'

'So what's the book about?' says Frankie.

'It's about a man who wants to be special when he is very ordinary,' says China, returning her eyes to the book. 'A man who wants to be a good parent, when he doesn't know how to be.'

'Sound likes a real page-turner. What happens in the end?'

'I don't want to spoil it for you.'

'It's "literature", so endings don't matter, right?'

'He kills himself if you really want to know.'

Frankie nods and rises from the hard chair to sit down in the armchair that faces the window. China, unable to concentrate, now gets up and heads back towards the kitchen, teacup in one hand, book in the other. On the way, she trips slightly on a heavy barbell left on the carpet that she uses for weight training and, losing her balance, a remnant of tea from her mug dribbles onto the carpet. Normally Frankie would have run to get a cloth, complaining loudly, but now he just sits there, continuing to smile.

'Sorry,' says China, taken aback at Frankie's lack of reaction.

'That's okay.'

China shrugs and returns the mug to the sink. Still hungry, she spreads a croissant with some jam and sits down on the sofa again. She makes no effort to get a cloth and remove the tea stain from the carpet. Normally, her indifference would have infuriated Frankie, but he continues to regard her benignly.

China picks up her phone and begins texting. The croissant, as she bites into it, distributes crumbs all over the sofa that Frankie has just hoovered and cleaned. A blob of strawberry jam follows the crumbs. Frankie – though it is now becoming more of a struggle – holds fast to his sense of tranquillity.

China slops the tea again. This time a large drop falls on the sofa rather than the carpet. She ignores it and carries on texting. Frankie realizes that the robe he is wearing is working itself open. He hasn't put on pants so quickly pulls it back together. China, he is relieved, doesn't appear to notice.

My beautiful . . . daughter . . .

Now indulging in a complex manoeuvre that involves her tea, her phone and her croissant, China topples the remnants of the tea onto a brand-new book that Frankie had been reading and enjoying, a Robert Harris blockbuster. Unable to contain himself any longer, Frankie rises to his feet.

'For fuck's sake!' he breathes, keeping his voice as neutral as he can manage.

'Keep your shirt on, boomer,' says China, without looking up from the phone. Now she feels comfortable, on familiar ground again.

'Go and clear that mess up, and the tea you already dropped on the carpet.'

'In a minute. I'm just answering this.'

'No. Now!'

'Chill the fuck out. It's only a bit of cloth.'

All the same she reluctantly rises from the sofa, puts down what is left of the tea and the croissant and goes into the kitchen returning with a dampened J-cloth. She makes a cursory rub of the stain on the carpet, then a similarly token attempt on the mark on the sofa. She puts the wet cloth down on the arm of the sofa and picks up her phone again.

'That's not good enough.'

'It's fine,' says China, smiling at a GIF of a virtual white bear hugging a virtual brown bear that a friend has just sent. Frankie purses his lips but feels helpless – China always makes him feel so helpless.

China, he realizes, returning to finish the clean-up, is now sitting on the stains she has made with the tea on the sofa.

'Can you move, please?'

China, still texting, shifts a few inches to the left.

'A bit more.'

Still texting, she moves a bit more. Frankie begins to dab at the stains.

'I don't think they're going to come out,' he mutters after a few minutes of careful dabbing.

China finishes her texting session and looks down at the damp patch to her left.

'I don't know why you get so stressed.'

'Me – stressed?'

'Yes – you, stressed.'

Patience finally exhausted, Frankie throws the wet cloth on the floor.

'At least I'm not sticking compass points into my fucking arm.'

Stunned into silence, China can do no more than stare at him blankly.

'Look, I didn't mean . . . ' says Frankie.

China has turned pale. When she speaks again, Frankie can barely hear her.

'You're an insensitive bastard. And Nodge is a snake for telling you.'

'Don't blame Nodge. He thought I needed to know.'

China gets up and stamps up the stairs back to her bedroom, slamming the door behind her.

Frankie feels blindsided. He had been so completely in the right and China so completely in the wrong. He had exercised patience and forbearance. All that it turned out to mean was the explosion, when it came, was even worse than usual. He had actually been beginning to enjoy the martyrdom of mopping up the tea stains. Now he has lost his right to complain, simply by pointing out an uncomfortable fact.

Perhaps it wasn't the right moment to have mentioned it, though, he reflects. Now he has cast himself once more in the familiar role of villain. He shouts up the stairs at the closed bedroom door, but his voice comes out reedy and weak.

'I'm sorry, China. I was upset. I didn't mean to . . . you know . . . *say* that.'

The door remains firmly closed. He stares at the banister.

It looks worse now than when he started.

Day 37, 29 April 2020

Nodge shouts goodbye to Owen and JJ as he heads out to take the cab on his shift. They do not reply, but then Nodge never hears JJ reply because his voice is so soft and Owen is taking a shower.

There's not much trade to be had during lockdown. Most of the cabbies queue up at Paddington or Euston for hours hoping for a lucky run that might earn them 50 sovs for a run out to the airport.

After cruising the empty streets fruitlessly for forty-five minutes, the heavens open and pavements are shiny with rain. A hand shoots up from one of the few pedestrians scattered on the pavement and Nodge picks her up, sharp-suited, a businesswoman by the looks of it. She barks an address at the north end of Ladbroke Grove and he goes back the way he came, ending up more or less where he started an hour previously. She pays the fare in cash – no tip – and climbs out into the rain brandishing her umbrella like a sabre.

As he was hoping to take a break for a walk in Regent's Park later, he decides to consult his phone for the weather. Checking his jacket resting on the left-hand seat, he realizes that the phone isn't there. He remembers now that he changed jackets at the last moment before he went out. The phone would have been in the other one. He remembers because he was wearing the same jacket that morning when he had an animated phone conversation with China. She was complaining once more that he, Nodge, had given one of her guiltiest secrets away to her father. He had apologized, but he still insisted he had done the right thing. If her self-harm had worsened and he had never said anything to Frankie, he could not have forgiven himself. Now she assures him the episode is over and he believes her.

Nodge is only a few hundred yards from the flat so he decides to go and collect his phone. Parking outside, he makes his way up the stairwell and quietly lets himself in. In front of him, Owen and JJ appear to be playing a game of chess at the kitchen table. Music is playing quite loudly, a 1950s recording of *The Mikado*. JJ's face is creased in intense concentration. They don't seem to notice his entrance.

Without speaking, Nodge looks around for his jacket and sees that it is hanging on the back of the front door. He turns to announce himself to JJ and Owen, noticing that JJ has his eyes closed now for some reason. Presumably a bout of intense concentration. Then he sees that beneath the chess table, Owen's hand is firmly grasping JJ's erect cock.

Owen has a slightly disengaged smile on his face. Nodge coughs as he takes his phone out of his jacket. Owen looks up. His smile evaporates and his hand is sharply withdrawn.

Now JJ also becomes aware of Nodge. His eyes widen and he tries furiously to tuck his cock back into his trousers, but struggles since it is still fully erect.

Nodge says nothing. There is something about the moment he savours. The utter clarity of it, the inability to deny what is there in plain sight.

JJ's eyes fix on him. Nodge returns his gaze.

'Nodge, now listen, feller, it's not what you think,' says JJ in even more of a whisper than usual, having finally managed to get purchase on the zip of his trousers. The more stressed he is, the quieter JJ talks. Nodge can hardly hear him. Nodge, still holding the phone he has taken out of his jacket pocket, puts it in his shoulder bag.

'Forgot it,' he says, smiling. He takes a step towards them both and examines the chess board.

'Bishop to C7 and mate,' he says. He is savouring his own *sangfroid*.

'Nodge, I . . . ' mutters Owen, a bloom of pink flush spreading over his features. Owen, reflects Nodge, feeling oddly calm, never blushes.

'I wasn't talking to you, Owen. It isn't your move.'

Nodge turns again to face JJ, who suddenly looks older than his sixty-five years and very tired. Nodge can hear the sad friction of his zipper as he finishes closing it.

'Talk about shutting the stable door after the horse has bolted,' says Nodge.

'It was just a hand job, Nodge,' says Owen. 'No harm done really. He'd only just started.'

'That makes all the difference, then,' says Nodge.

'It's my fault. I badgered him into it,' whispers JJ. 'Got him to pity me. Anyway, as my old mother used to say . . . '

Nodge puts his finger to his lips to stop JJ babbling. When he speaks again his voice is cold and even and clear.

'Fuck you. And fuck your old Irish mother.'

The narrative stands frozen. No one seems to know what the next line should be. In the end, it is Nodge that breaks the silence. He continues to stare at JJ, who shrinks under his gaze, seeming to sink lower and lower in his chair.

'I am going out on my shift now, JJ. I will be back in six hours. When I get back I want you out of here. Everything of yours gone. If it isn't gone, it's going out the window.'

'But . . . ' ventures JJ.

'And so are you, you treacherous old cunt.'

'Ah, come now,' says JJ pitifully. 'The lockdown rules say you can't . . . '

'You'll have to take your chances,' says Nodge briskly. He turns to Owen. 'I'll talk to you about this later.'

'But, Nodge,' continues JJ desperately. 'See – the house isn't finished yet, there's still builders all over the shop.'

'I don't care,' says Nodge evenly, 'if your house doesn't have a wall. Or is missing four walls. Or four walls, the roof and the kitchen sink. I want you out. And take your chess pieces with you.'

He reaches over and picks up JJ's king.

'You're lucky I don't stick this up your wrinkled old arse. Only you'd probably enjoy it.'

He puts the king back down and knocks it over. He pauses, then he knocks over the whole chessboard, scattering pieces on the floor. He pivots on his heel and leaves the flat, closing the door with a slam.

Outside, on the stairwell, he finds himself breathing so heavily that he thinks he is going to blackout, fall and tumble down the winding stairs.

Six hours later, at the end of his shift, Nodge walks through the front door again. He has ignored the interminable phone calls that both JJ and Owen have tried to make to him.

Owen emerges from JJ's bedroom and sits down heavily in the sitting-room armchair.

'We need to talk,' says Owen.

There is something unexpectedly defiant in his voice that unsettles Nodge.

'Has JJ gone?'

Owen nods.

'We certainly do need to talk,' says Nodge curtly. 'What the hell do you think you were doing?'

Owen shrugs — as if indifferent. Again, the defiance. Nodge, puzzled, sits down on the sofa opposite him.

'It was just a hand job, Nodge,' says Owen gently as Nodge adjusts a cushion behind his back. 'Not even that. He just wanted me to touch him. He's an old man. He never gets his rocks off. He was letting off steam. Is it such a big deal?'

'I'm not even going to answer that.'

Owen looks at him steadily. Still, to Nodge's consternation, no trace of shame reveals itself.

'You know that I love you, don't you?' says Owen.

'You've got a funny way of showing it.'

'But even so, this isn't working.'

Nodge wonders innocently what Owen is trying to get at. He is confused at what is happening because he unexpectedly feels on the defensive. This wasn't in the script. *He* was the outraged, betrayed, innocent one, Owen the unfaithful, remorseful lover pleading for forgiveness.

'*What* isn't working?'

'Us.'

Nodge studies Owen's face. Instead of its usual equanimity, it is suddenly stricken, pulled taut into a grimace of pain and resignation. Nodge reacts with a bolt of acid in his gut.

'What are you talking about?'

'I want a child, Nodge,' Owen snaps. Then, more softly, with careful pauses inserted for emphasis. 'I. Want. A. Child.'

'I *know*. So do I. You know that.'

'Not like *I* want one.'

'That's not fair.'

'It's true, though.'

'I admit it: you're enough for me.'

'You're not enough for me.'

Nodge begins to rock back and forth slowly on the sofa. Owen's face softens. He sits down next to Nodge and takes his hand. Nodge looks up. He sees that Owen's face is wet with tears. This frightens him more deeply still.

'I really do love you,' says Owen.

'You've already said that.'

'And I'm not angry anymore that you kept that drugs offence from me. Ultimately it doesn't make any difference.'

Nodge pulls his hand away, a surge of anger pulsing through him.

'Why are you bringing this up? Aren't we meant to be discussing you wanking off JJ? Isn't that the injustice that is currently at hand?'

'What's done is done. We can't adopt. That's it.'

Nodge feels Owen take his hand again. He does not pull it away.

'But, JJ . . . '

'It's a side issue, Nodge. I have to be a father. I *have* to be. I've wanted it for so long. I don't know how to let go of it. I've tried. God knows, I've tried.'

'So – putting aside for the moment the apparently irrelevant matter of JJ's cock – what's the solution?'

'I don't know.'

There is such bleakness in his tone. What is at stake dawns on Nodge. When he speaks again, it is as a supplicant, not an accuser.

'I mean, maybe we could pretend to live apart and you could apply as a single parent and then we could gradually, you know, sneak the child into our life,' says Nodge.

'I know you don't really want a child. Not *really*. I know you're only doing it for me. That's the problem. It wouldn't work. Both of us have got to be equally committed.'

'So, what are you saying?'

There is a long pause before Owen answers.

'JJ wants a child as much as I do. And his credentials are impeccable. He's a doctor. He's wealthy. He's got a big house with a garden.'

Nodge suppresses a desire to vomit.

'Credentials? A garden? What is this, a fucking loan assessment meeting? To find out if you can afford to invest in a new lifestyle feature?'

Owen can't meet Nodge's eye. His voice now shows traces of shame, but he remains determined.

'I didn't mean it to sound like that.'

'What did you mean it to sound like?'

'Like a practical arrangement.'

Nodge can't deny that what Owen is saying has some truth to it. He doesn't really – not *really* – want a child, although he is prepared to embrace it for Owen's sake. He already has his two nieces and his goddaughter, China. Owen has no one – apart from Nodge.

He sees with terrible clarity the truth – that he is blocking the path of Owen's unquenchable and entirely valid need.

'I don't know what to say,' said Nodge eventually. He feels the sudden ashen taste of the world suppurating in his mouth.

'You don't have to say anything.'

'Are you . . . are you going to move in with JJ?'

Owen answers immediately. It is clearly a question he has considered, realizes Nodge, even discussed with JJ.

'I don't know. He wants me to. If we get the go-ahead for an adoption then I will. Because it's got to be best for the child. And I can't keep putting you and myself first. Because if I did, I would want us to stay together. But I have to put the child first.'

When he hears his own voice as he speaks again, Nodge sounds to his own ears like a robot has taken possession of his vocal chords, so coldly and mechanically does he deliver the words.

'And if you and JJ are not allowed to adopt?'

Owen shrugs.

'We'll see.'

Nodge considers this. When he speaks again, it no longer seems like he is speaking but some voice beyond or behind him.

'I think you should go and stay with JJ,' says Nodge. 'After all, he's probably still got a bit of steam that wants letting off,' he adds, bitterly.

To his dismay, Owen, instead of contradicting him, nods.

'Okay.'

'I wasn't being serious,' says Nodge.

'I'm not going to argue with you. You're right. We can't carry on like this.'

'But,' says Nodge, looking around the room as if for an exit, 'JJ's house isn't finished.'

'It is, though,' says Owen. 'He was just using that as an excuse to stay on. He's lonely there. He liked being with us. He likes you very much, Nodge.'

'That's nice to hear. Good old JJ. And that's very nice of you to go and give him some support and relief in his old age.'

'You're right about something else. It was more than just a hand job.'

'What was it, then?'

'A symptom.'

Slowly Owen rises and makes his way to their bedroom without another word. Nodge watches him through the open door as he begins to pack clothes into the leather suitcase Nodge bought him for his forty-fifth birthday.

The bell sounds, taking Frankie by surprise. He hasn't ordered anything from Amazon or Deliveroo and he never received unannounced visitors even before the lockdown started. He speaks cautiously into the intercom.

'Who is it?'

'Nodge.'

Frankie, puzzled, buzzes him in from outside and opens the flat door. Watching him trudge up the stairs, Frankie sees that he is wearing a Covid mask decorated with a 'Joker' smiling mouth.

'What's with the creepy mask?' he says, taking a step backwards as Nodge reaches the landing.

'Owen bought it for me as a joke. It was the only one I could find.'

Frankie notices that Nodge's eyes are red-rimmed and streaming. In the forty years he has known Nodge, he has never seen him cry, not even at Colin's funeral.

'Did somebody die?' says Frankie half-jokingly, gesturing for him to come in. He feels immediately that it is a ridiculous remark, then worries that his speculation might be true.

Nodge just stands there staring at Frankie. Awkwardly, Frankie takes a step forward and tentatively puts his arms around Nodge. Nodge lowers his head onto Frankie's shoulder, still silently weeping. Frankie looks blankly down the stairwell, feeling at the same time embarrassed and shame at being embarrassed.

'This isn't Covid-safe,' he says, uneasy at the feel of his arms circling the bulk of Nodge. It's a remark as idiotic as his previous one, he decides. He notices that Nodge smells strongly of whiskey. 'Are you drunk?'

'Yes,' says Nodge in a pitiful voice. Frankie suddenly wants to push him away.

'But it's only one o'clock in the afternoon.'

Nodge says nothing, he just continues to hold on to Frankie.

'I think you had better come in,' says Frankie after ten seconds frozen in this unfamiliar embrace.

'Not allowed.'

'We can go out on the balcony at the back. I'll put a mask on.'

Nodge lets himself out of Frankie's leaden embrace. He follows Frankie into the living room and onto the small iron balcony with slow, heavy steps. Frankie pulls on a well-used disposable cheap mask that he finds in his pocket. It stinks of sweat, breath and bacteria. The balcony does not have a pleasant aspect. It faces a block of brutalist flats that cut out most of the light. One floor below is the cluttered backyard of a restaurant. Although the restaurant is closed, a member of the kitchen staff, a young man wearing a hairnet, sits on a chair below, smoking a cigarette.

'Where's China?' says Nodge dully.

'Veronica's come up to London to have a socially distanced stroll with her. They're schlepping up Portobello.'

Nodge lowers himself on a wire two-seater with cushions. Frankie can't quite decide whether to sit next to him and put his arm round him or sit opposite him. In the end, he does neither and remains standing. An odour of garlic and onions mixed with cigarette smoke drifts up from the patio below.

'Do you want a cup of tea?'

Nodge shakes his head.

'You reek of booze.'

'I'm aware.'

'How did you get here?'

'Drove.'

'In this condition? You could have lost your cabbie's badge. For Christ's sake, Nodge. What's happened?'

Nodge looks up at him from his slumped position on the two-seater. There are damp patches on his rumpled fawn T-shirt.

'Owen left,' Nodge whispers, finally.

'What do you mean, "Owen left"? Left where?'

'He left me. He's gone off with someone else.'

Frankie lowers himself onto the single chair facing the two-seater. He feels like too much air has left his body or that the traces of cigarette smoke floating up from below are making it difficult to breathe. Not only is Nodge always the most solid of his friends, unshakeable and emotionally tough, Nodge's relationship with Owen was also the most assured, the most secure, the most untouchable he had ever encountered. It almost gave him faith in the possibility of love.

He reaches into his pocket and hands a paper tissue he finds there to Nodge. Nodge takes it and wipes his face vigorously, until the thin tissue dissolves into scraps. It's as if Nodge is clawing at his face, not wiping it. The terrible Joker grin leers out at Frankie, who pulls off his own mask, unable to bear the stink any longer. Nodge seems to gain purchase on himself. He throws the tissue carelessly to the balcony floor and stares at the sky.

'He wanted to adopt a child. He couldn't, so long as he was with me. So he went off with JJ.'

233

Frankie rummages in his memory before he can come up with an image to match the name.

'The old Irish bloke who dressed like he was auditioning for a pensioner's version of *Queer Eye*?'

'That's him.'

'Just like that? No explanation?'

Nodge shifts on the lightly mildewed cushion.

'There was a trigger. I came back early from my shift because I'd forgotten my phone. JJ and Owen were playing chess.'

'That doesn't sound too bad.'

'No, it doesn't. Until I realized that Owen was wanking JJ off under the table.'

'Well,' says Frankie, once again caught off balance and answering without thinking. 'That certainly gives a new meaning to bashing the bishop.'

Nodge looks up sharply.

'Frankie,' says Nodge, a note of annoyance creeping into his otherwise wrung-out voice. 'Why have you always got to try and make everything into a joke?'

'I don't know. Just trying to lighten the mood,' he says helplessly. 'Why . . . JJ of all people?'

Nodge fidgets with the mask which is making his face itch.

'Because apart from anything else, he's a lovely, lovely man,' says Nodge, working the stubble with his fingernail and raising his gaze to the sky again as if he cannot bear to look at Frankie. 'More to the point, he's someone who desperately wants children. That seems to be the key factor for Owen.'

Frankie turns and glances over the balcony at the man beneath, who is now scratching his groin.

'Don't *you* desperately want children too?'

'Not as much as Owen does. And he senses that. He's very perceptive. I can't fool him. In fact . . . '

Nodge stops.

'In fact what?'

'In fact . . . he seems to suspect that I deliberately undermined the adoption process.'

'That's ridiculous. How would you do that?'

Nodge stands up, stretches his legs and leans against the balcony wall. The man on the patio has gone inside, leaving a jumble of cooking oil cans and some wooden crates.

'Do you remember when I got pulled for having those E's in my pocket?'

'What – back in the seventies? Course I do. Seemed funny at the time.'

Nodge hawks and, unable to find anything to do with the spit, propels a gobbet of sputum onto the patio below.

'I didn't mention it in the adoption application. And they found out.'

'I wouldn't spit on the patio if I were you. Antanias might consider it disrespectful. He owns a lot of knives. Also he fuck-ing hates gays.'

'Sorry,' says Nodge absentmindedly. 'I wasn't thinking.'

'So, did you?'

'Did I what?'

'Did you deliberately undermine the adoption?'

Nodge hawks again, this time spitting on a fading pot plant.

'Of course not.'

Frankie doesn't respond. Nodge goes back to looking at the sky, still standing up, and Frankie realizes that he cannot bear to meet Frankie's eye. When Nodge starts talking again it is facing into the empty air.

'I can barely remember the details. I certainly thought it would have long expired as anything relevant to the adoption. I sort of . . . forgot about it.'

'But didn't you mention it to Owen when you were applying?'

Nodge suddenly looks furious, turns to him with a fierce grimace on his face.

'For fuck's sake, Frankie. I came here for a bit of support, not a bollocking.'

Nodge rips his Joker mask off now, seemingly worn out by the constriction. He holds it balled in his fist. Frankie can see now that he hasn't shaved. There is a heavy shadow of stubble round his jaw.

'Fucking stupid masks.'

'You didn't mention it to him, then.'

Nodge is quiet again.

'No, I didn't, I suppose.'

Frankie is aware of himself picking his words very carefully.

'Is it even remotely possible that you . . . I don't know . . . *chose* to forget. Unconsciously, so to speak?'

'I think I will have that cup of tea,' says Nodge, turning his face towards the front room.

Frankie, somewhat relieved to stop sharing space with Nodge, goes to the kitchen and puts the kettle on. When he returns with the tea, Nodge is sitting again. His body language has changed. It is slumped. There is an air of apology leeching from it.

'I suppose it's possible,' says Nodge forlornly, taking the mug, 'that I might have chosen to forget.'

Frankie takes a sip of his own tea. He feels a rising tide of sympathy for his friend wash over him. He sits down and faces him.

'Look, Nodge. Before we go any further, I want to tell you that you are the best, kindest, most solid and loyal person I have ever met. If Owen has left you for this . . . JJ or whatever his name is . . . then he's a fool and an idiot and a shit-for-brains.'

Nodge manages a slight smile of gratitude.

'Thank you, Frankie. I appreciate that. But I'm not sure that he is a fool. I even think he might be right. I never wanted a child in the way Owen did. You have to be fully committed to be a parent, don't you?'

'I wasn't,' says Frankie.

Nodge looks puzzled.

'I've never told anyone this, Nodge, but I sort of encouraged Veronica to have an abortion when she was pregnant with China. It was only at the last moment I realized that our relationship might never recover. And also that, because I loved Veronica, I knew I would never, ever regret having a child with her. And I didn't. But at the time the last thing I wanted was a child.'

Nodge seems excited by Frankie's grasp of his dilemma.

'I'm the same. I'm *afraid*, Frankie. Of the responsibility. Of the fact that it might damage my relationship with Owen, that all the attention will go on the child. I am selfish, selfish, selfish. And this is where it has got me.'

He begins to weep softly again.

'Sorry, sorry.'

He wipes his eyes with the tissue he has just spat in.

Frankie rises and puts his hand round Nodge's shoulder.

237

'It's not too late. Owen loves you, doesn't he?'

Nodge nods furiously, as if the vigour of his nodding will make his answer more true.

'I think so. But he was angry that I deceived him. So very angry.'

'*If* you did . . .'

'He was desperate to move on. And JJ was there, and he was available and keen and ready. And I was a coward.'

'Well,' says Frankie briskly. 'If he loves you then there's still hope.'

'There isn't. It's too late. I've blown it.'

'He's only just gone, hasn't he?'

'Today.'

'It's a bit soon to be writing off your marriage, then. Look, should I tell China when she gets back?' says Frankie.

'Leave it a bit,' says Nodge. 'I don't want to upset her. It might shake out, who knows.'

Nodge doesn't look like he believes it for a moment.

It is an eerie experience walking down the Portobello Road on a bright Wednesday in spring to find it almost entirely deserted. Veronica and China find themselves unusually quiet even though they have not seen one another face to face for nearly two months. There is something about the closed shops, the gaps left by the absent tourists and locals, the unaccustomed stillness that presses the air towards emptiness as if the silence – a silence born of unseen death – is somehow sacred.

It is not only that peculiar aura which robs them of words. Both are unsure what is expected of them. Veronica fears her own need. China is torn by guilt at abandoning her mother and is haunted by the idea that she made a mistake in running away to London.

So they simply walk, companionably, with only scattered, hungry pigeons for company as the road unfolds on either side of them – the Spanish School, the frescos of Joe Strummer and carnival scenes, the vacant market spaces under the Westway, Honest John's record shop, Portobello Wholefoods. All closed. Veronica's heels click on the pavement, while China's trainers drag at the cracks in the stones.

The day, again, is beautiful and clear. It has been in some senses an enchanted time to be in the city. There is no invisible smog, little noise, a peace unimaginable other than at the breaking of dawn or the small hours of darkness.

'How's it going with Mason?' ventures China finally when they reach the gates of the refuse depository on the far side of the flyover.

Veronica pauses to reply, then catches the stench of waste from the dustbins and continues walking southward.

'Not easy. I'm having to home-school him – obviously. You can imagine how much fun that is. But my practice has had to close – temporarily I hope – so I've got time on my hands. It's tough, though.'

'Why isn't his father schooling him?'

'He's out doing carpentry work under the radar. Only way we can earn any money at the moment.'

'Why is it so difficult? As if I can't imagine.'

'He won't sit still for a moment. He can't concentrate. Silas is thinking of putting him on medication. He's yet to be formally diagnosed with ADHD, but most of the symptoms seem to be there. The GP thinks it's probable anyway.

'So now he's got a handy excuse.'

'He's difficult, I know. God, do I know. But if he's got ADHD then it's not really his fault. He's really not a bad kid at heart. I think he misses you, believe it or not.'

'If you're giving me the choice, no, I don't believe it. Is ADHD even *real*? I was reading up about it. Some doctors say it's not actually a thing.'

'Doctors used to say that about depression. Anyway, Mason's *behaviour* is real, whatever else is the case. Maybe Ritalin will help. Or Adderall.'

'Or a smack round the head. Everyone's ADHD now anyway, thanks to TikTok. Including me probably. Why is he any different?'

'TikTok isn't a developmental disorder. It's a bad habit.'

They approach Gregg's bakery, which is one of the few shops actually open. Outside, an ancient grey-haired Rastafarian thumping a single drum with the heel of his hand is sitting cross-legged on the pavement torturing 'No Woman No Cry' to the point of agony. His eyes are closed, his face raised blissfully to the heavens. There are no passers-by to top up the small polystyrene cup in front of him. He stops momentarily and opens his eyes. Veronica reaches into her pocket and drops in a few coins. When she turns back to China, she can see that she has started crying. Veronica embraces her. On cue, the Rasta starts singing 'No Woman No Cry' again, even more tunelessly than before.

China steps back, wiping her face and laughing.

'What's he going to sing next? "Stop Your Sobbing"?'

Veronica laughs too, puts her arm through China's and they continue walking.

'Why were you crying, Chi?'

'Mum, I only intended to come here for a short while. But I felt too stupid before to ask you if I could come back again.'

'I know. I understand.'

'I'm sorry, Mum. Really I am.'

'I've missed you.'

'I've missed you too. I *do* miss you. I can't take this much longer. Dad's driving me up the wall.'

They pass the Electric Cinema. The French bakery, 50 yards south, is open, and they stop and get some coffee and brioche. Veronica dips her pastry into her coffee and drops the dissolving sugary blob into her mouth. She swallows and nods in satisfaction at the taste of sweet mush, then turns back to China.

'I know you think all my attention goes on Mason and Silas instead of you. But I have to try and make this work. I don't want another broken relationship.'

China stiffens, feels a bolt of bitterness tarnish the sugar from the brioche in the back of her throat.

'That's right. Put them first.'

'I don't.'

'Then why don't you stand up for me?'

'I do.'

'The water pistol? The diary?'

'I stood up for you when Silas snatched your phone.'

'For once. He's a bully. '

Veronica feels an urge to join China in attacking Silas, but manages to hold herself back. She counts herself as a loyal person. But whom should she be loyal to?

'Don't talk about Silas like that. Please.'

'Why? Do you love him?'

'What sort of question is that?'

'What sort of answer is that? Did you love Dad?'

'Of course.'

'Do you still?'

'It's not a matter of love, China. Some things can't be repaired.'

For no reason she can understand, China now feels protective of her father.

'You only got together with Dad in the first place because you wanted to get away from your mother.'

'That's not true!'

'Isn't it?'

There is a brief silence before China, finishing her brioche, speaks again.

'Mum, I want to come home.'

These are the words that Veronica has been waiting to hear. She has suspected that China's pride and stubbornness have prevented her returning to Brighton. Her spirits momentarily lift, then subside, as the reality of the situation sinks in.

'Despite everything?'

China turns to Veronica.

'I'm sorry I ran off, Mum. It was all getting too much for me. I've thought of coming back before, but I wasn't sure I could cope being locked into one house with Silas and Mason.'

'Well – you're probably not wrong. Tell you the truth, things are a bit difficult with Silas at the moment. He's been sick. You know that, right? With Covid. It's horrible. He says it's like having an alien creature inside you. But he's quite fit and healthy. Or was. And he's only fifty. He should be okay soon enough. Seems to hit the oldies worse. It really puts them on their backs.'

'Or kills them.'

'Yes, thank you for that thought. Or kills them, quite.'

'I didn't mean to be snippy. Sorry. I hope he's alright.'

'I'm sure he'll be fine.'

A thought, hitherto kept hidden by China from herself, rises to the surface.

'Could *you* get it?'

Veronica throws her coffee cup into an empty bin and wipes her lips with a napkin. They start to drift across Portobello Road to the other pavement in the direction of the Hummingbird Bakery.

'I've already had it.'

'What?'

'But very mildly.'

China stops dead in the middle of the road.

'Mum! Why didn't you tell me! What happened?'

'I ran a temperature, had a slight cough, felt a bit knackered. But otherwise, it wasn't even as bad as the flu. Apparently, you can have it without having any symptoms at all. Anyway, I don't think Silas is going to drop dead anytime soon. He *is* probably infectious, though. So . . .'

'So?'

'So, as I say, it's probably best you stay away for a while. It will only be a week or two, I'm sure. Anyway, I'm sure they will find an antidote soon.'

A lone car makes its way slowly towards them and they cross to the other pavement.

'But what if they never find an antidote? I heard on the TV there was no guarantee. This could be it. Forever.'

'I don't think so.' But Veronica can't keep the doubt out of her voice. 'In any case, I think you'll be good to come back in a few weeks. You can join our bubble.'

China considers this carefully. She can endure Frankie that long, she decides.

'And Mason might be drugged up by then?'

'He will probably have started some medication, yes.'

'Hallelujah.'

'Amen.'

The agreement is made. They turn and begin the walk back towards the Golborne Road and Frankie's flat, where Nodge, unbeknownst to China, has now made both his entrance and exit.

As they walk past the drummer, this time he is singing 'Could You Be Loved'.

Day 68, 30 May 2020

Frankie gets the text message, as promised, at 10 p.m. on the dot.

Is it safe?

Frankie texts back.

I'm still not sure about this.

Is she in bed?

I think so.

I'm coming up then.

Frankie's nerves feel like catgut on an overstrung tennis racquet. China disappeared into her room at about 9 o'clock as usual. She very rarely leaves her room after retiring, falling asleep early, out of boredom as much as anything. At least this is what she tells Frankie, although it is often to sneak a night-time spliff. But it isn't unheard of for her to suddenly resurface. On this particular evening, Frankie has several times put his ear to her door and on the last occasion could just about make out her ritual night-time listening, an audiobook, *Gmorning, Gnight* by Lin-Manuel Miranda. This is usually the cue for her to sleep.

About one minute after he has received the text message, he hears a key turn in the front-door Yale. Roxy's head cautiously pokes itself through the gap between the door and the frame. She puts a hand through in front of her, gives the thumb up and shoots Frankie a questioning look. Frankie glances up the stairs at China's door. He beckons urgently, mouthing the word 'quickly'. Roxy pushes through the door and closes it softly behind her. She is dressed as if for a night out – with heavy makeup, a black cocktail dress and high heels. Her hair has been fresh dyed brassy blonde. He can smell her perfume from where he stands, five yards away to the side of the dining table.

'You smell like a brothel,' he mutters, glancing again up at the stairs that lead to the bedrooms.

'I just wanted to look nice for you.'

'Get a move on,' says Frankie, beckoning urgently. 'Up the stairs and into my room. Hurry. And take your shoes off first. Take them with you.'

Roxy tries to remove one of her shoes, but as she does so, she falls forward, unbalanced by the manoeuvre. She topples on her other high heel and puts her arm reflexively out for support. Her capacious frosted-pink handbag collides with a framed photo of the Blue family when it was intact – Frankie and Veronica and China outside the house in North Kensington. It falls to the floor with a clatter. Glass chips scatter across the carpet.

'For fuck's sake!' breathes Frankie. He glances anxiously up the stairs at China's closed door and freezes to see if there is any movement. Roxy stays close to the door to the flat, ready to swiftly retreat if China appears at the top of the stairs.

After he feels enough time has safely passed – both Frankie and Roxy stuck in tableau – Frankie ushers Roxy into the room. Removing her other shoe and tiptoeing carefully, she climbs the stairs and disappears from his view.

After waiting again to see if there is any sound from China, Frankie picks up the photograph. There is a crack in the glass that seems to separate China from her parents. It's only now that he hears the creak of a door and, with a rising sense of panic, he sees China appear at the top of the stairs. She can only have missed Roxy on the landing by seconds. China looks bleary-eyed but otherwise perfectly alert. She is wearing leopard-print pyjamas. Frankie imagines her as a wild animal, stalking.

'What was that noise?'

'I accidentally knocked something off the table. Go back to bed.'

China registers that he is holding the picture frame.

'You haven't broken that, have you?'

Softly, catlike, she starts make her way down the stairs.

'It's fine. Go back to bed.'

But China continues into the living room as Frankie cautiously replaces the damaged picture on the sideboard. China takes a few quick steps towards the door, takes the frame from the sideboard and examines it. She is wearing no slippers.

'Careful, there are bits of glass on the floor. The photo isn't damaged. I'll fix the frame, don't worry.'

China carefully scrutinizes the photo, which is now lopsided on the other side of the cracked glass.

'You look so much younger.'

'It was ten or so years ago. You look younger too.'

China looks momentarily sad.

'Mum actually looks happy. Haven't seen that for a while.'

'We *were* happy. Sometimes.'

China looks up sharply from the photo and sniffs the air.

'What's that smell?'

'What smell?'

'Like woodsmoke.'

'Aftershave.'

'Are you going out somewhere?'

'I was bored. I found it in my cupboard, thought I'd give myself a little spray.'

'Smells familiar.'

'Why wouldn't it?'

He hears a floorboard creak from above. Roxy must be moving in the bedroom, but China doesn't seem to notice.

'It's not too bad actually,' says China, still inhaling the smell of Roxy's perfume.

'Glad it meets with your approval. Now can you . . . '

'Can I try a bit?'

Frankie gets on his knees and starts picking up the scraps of glass.

'It's aftershave, not perfume. You don't shave, do you? Except . . . ' He has the sense not to finish the sentence.

'What does it matter? A smell is a smell.'

He locates five shards in all, rises and drops them in the battered wire mesh bin that the office was throwing out and which he reclaimed.

'It's very expensive.'

'You won't let me try a bit of your leftover aftershave?'

'I'd rather you didn't. I've only got a tiny bit left.'

He examines the other contents of the bin. A tax demand. Three pizza flyers. A milkshake cup with liquid leaking from it. A Coke can which conceals an old roach of China's last joint.

'God – and I thought Silas was tight. What's it called, then?'

Frankie, once again, feels himself in a panic. Turning away from the bin, he notices a painting behind China's head – an *art sauvage* portrait of a green forest bought when he and Veronica were in Costa Rica on their honeymoon.

'Tropical . . . no . . . Forest Green.'

'"Tropical" or "Forest Green?"'

'Tropical Forest Green.'

'Never heard of it.'

'That's something you don't know, then.'

China catches sight of her reflection in the wall mirror. Her hair is tangled and matted.

'Fuck. I look like Medusa.'

'You look fine,' says Frankie automatically.

'I think I left my hairbrush in your room,' says China brightly. 'Do you mind if I . . . ?'

'I'll get it for you,' Frankie says quickly, darting up the stairs ahead of China.

When he reaches his room, Roxy is on the bed, already in her underwear. She gives him a seductive smile. He puts his finger urgently to his lips and makes a *shhh*-ing sound. He sees, to his consternation, that she is brushing her hair with China's hairbrush.

'Give it to me,' Frankie hisses. Roxy frowns, but holds on to the brush.

'Nearly finished,' she whispers back.

'Now.'

Frankie is trying desperately to control the volume of his voice. He looks back at the door, terrified that China will open it. Roxy shrugs and hands him the brush. He swivels and heads out the door, closing it behind him, and back down the stairs into the living room. China is standing where Frankie left her.

'That smell gets everywhere,' she says, holding the brush up to her nose. 'Tropical Forest Green, eh?'

'Forest what?' says Frankie.

'The aftershave?'

'It's a bit too pungent for me, I think.'

China narrows her eyes. Frankie tenses. Then, to his relief, she turns and heads briskly back up the stairs.

'Night, Dad.'

'Night, China.'

Just before she reaches the landing she turns again.

'Just one more thing.'

'What?'

Frankie is now following her, making his way up the stairs.

'Someone asked me if I want to go on the Black Lives Matter march tomorrow.'

'Why are you telling me? Why do you care what I think about it? Do you want to go?' says Frankie. He is only half-listening, distracted by the presence of Roxy a few yards away behind a thin wooden partition.

'Yes, I really, really want to go. I'm very excited about it.'

'Okay, then.'

He stops and checks the paintwork on the banister. Disappointingly, there are drip marks showing on the fresh coat.

'But I'm not going to.'

'Right.'

Frankie hears another faint clatter from his bedroom. Now his concentration is shot completely. China's words come to him as if through a lengthy tunnel. However, she doesn't seem to register the noise.

'Do you want to know why?' says China. Her face, puzzlingly to Frankie, shows irritation. He nods absently, eyes fixed on his bedroom door.

'Because I don't want to put you into danger of Covid from my making close contact with other people.'

'Okay.'

Frankie continues making his way up the stairs. China looks at him, trying to discern some awareness of the sacrifice she has made for his sake. His face is blank.

'No need to thank me.'

'Thank you,' he says, oblivious to her disdain, and heads into the bathroom, closing the door behind him.

China shakes her head forlornly and goes into her room, closing the door behind her. She checks her phone. There is a message from an old friend from her days living in North Kensington.

Are you still not coming? Everyl is going to be there.

China hesitates for some time, trying to decide how to respond.

Maybe she should go after all.

After several seconds considering this possibility, sorely tempted, she texts back.

I can't put my dad at risk. Even though he doesn't seem to give a shit.

Is he very old?

No. He had a dodgy heart a few years back, though. Can't take the risk.

'*Dutiful daughter!*' comes the reply followed by a rolling eyes emoji.

Frankie, having brushed his teeth and emptied his bladder, the stream weak and partial, emerges from the bathroom and swiftly enters his bedroom. There is a flimsy bolt on the inside of the door, inherited from the last owner. He slides it shut behind him.

'Won't she want to know why it's locked?' says Roxy. She is wearing a black silk slip and black hold-ups.

'Better that than she just walks in here.'

'I thought she never came out of her room after ten o'clock.'

'Almost never. Then you knocked over the fucking photograph.'

'You told me to hurry.'

'I didn't tell you to break a picture frame.'

Roxy gives a moue and reaches into her handbag.

'Be nice, Frankie. We're by ourselves at last. I haven't seen you for a month. Look.'

She produces a bottle of Hatozaki Japanese whiskey out of her bag.

'Your favourite. Go and get some glasses.'

'I'm not going out there again. Too dangerous.'

He takes the bottle and swigs directly from the neck.

'Very romantic.'

'Cheers,' says Frankie, handing the bottle back to Roxy. 'That hit the spot.'

She takes the bottle from him and takes a swig herself. Then she hands the bottle back to Frankie again, leans back and idly lets her hand linger near the crotch of her panties.

'I'm lubed.'

Frankie upends the bottle again, then puts it on the bedside table.

'I need to unwind a bit, Rocks.'

'I'll unwind you.'

She licks her lips. Frankie, still glancing furtively at the bolted door, takes off his T-shirt, pants and trousers and climbs into bed beside Roxy. Immediately, she starts kissing him and draws her right hand down towards his cock. Her mouth tastes of whiskey and iron.

'Not much of a party going on down there, is there?' says Roxy after several minutes of fruitless exploration.

'Give me a chance.'

'I'm giving you a chance.'

She is pumping with her fist at Frankie's limp penis but getting no results.

'Sorry,' says Frankie. 'I feel like I'm being tested. I've got a lot on my mind.'

Roxy pulls back her hand.

'You've got nothing on your mind! You've been stuck here for two months doing fuck all.'

Frankie sits up and stares at his limp, drooping member.

'I'm *nervous*. What with China being on the other side of that wall. I told you this was a bad idea.'

'We can try again in a little while. Have you taken some Viagra?'

'Didn't think I would need it.'

'Well – you apparently do.'

Reluctant to leave the room again, he nevertheless unbolts then carefully opens the bedroom door. He returns to the bathroom and finds the blister pack he keeps hidden from China's view behind a bottle of indigestion medicine. There are two left. He pops one, swallowing it dry. Replacing the blister pack, he stops and regards the cabinet ruefully before closing the door. What was sadder than the middle-aged man's bathroom cupboard? The tubes of ointment. The muscle strain lotions. The elasticated bandages.

Thirty minutes later, he has managed to achieve enough tumescence for a brief, semi-hard penetration and a swift, unsatisfying orgasm.

'I've had better,' says Roxy afterwards, still playing idly with herself, trying to finish off.

'There's such a thing as the male menopause,' says Frankie.

'Yeh. And unicorns,' says Roxy, giving up, turning over on her stomach and closing her eyes.

The next morning, Roxy sneaks out successfully at 6 a.m., before even Frankie has woken up. He wakes hours later to an otherwise empty bed. When he goes downstairs and enters the kitchen to make himself a cup of tea, China is already there at the dining table, brushing her hair.

Frankie makes himself some toast and contemplates another day with absolutely nothing to do. His mood is good, feeling that last night he deftly avoided a situation that could have gone badly wrong.

Making his way back into the living room, he notices the unfinished banister again. He can't face going back to it for some reason. He decides he might start a different job, just to break the monotony. In a flurry of enthusiasm, when lockdown had first started, he had gone to Homebase and bought shelves, brackets, tins of paint, varnish, paintbrushes. Most of them are still sat in the loft where he had stored them, untouched.

He pours himself a cup of tea, then makes his way up the stairs towards the loft. Once on the landing, he pulls down the loft ladder and starts to climb, leaving the half-drunk tea at the bottom. A few moments later he hears footsteps and senses China's presence at the bottom of the ladder. Ignoring it, he pushes open the hatch and climbs in. Then he hears China's footsteps on the ladder behind him. Bent low, tiptoeing between the wooden joints, he scrabbles about looking for a Homebase bag. China's head appears through the hatch. She is still holding her hairbrush out in front of her.

'I'll be down in a minute. Just looking for a paint roller.'

'Can you take a look at this hairbrush for me?'

He can't read the expression on her face but something in her eyes, reflected in the light coming from below on the landing, makes his stomach gripe.

'Why?'

'Just have a look, will you?'

'Is this urgent for some reason?'

'It could be.'

'How can a hairbrush be urgent?'

'Take a look.'

Frankie reluctantly edges towards her and takes the brush out of her hand. The light is weak in the attic, despite the 100-watt bulb in the corner. He glances at it.

'Looks normal to me.'

'Take another look.'

Frankie does. This time he sees, quite clearly, three or four strands of bleached blonde hair.

'Nope. Nothing.'

He hands the brush back to China.

'Is there anything you want to tell me?'

'What would I want to tell you? Look – I've got to find this roller. I've wasted too much time during lockdown. I want to do something constructive for once.'

'Seems to me you were doing something quite constructive last night.'

'Meaning?'

China picks out the blonde hairs and holds them up to Frankie.

'See that?'

'A few old strands of your hair. So what?'

'I haven't had blonde hair for three years. I pulled all the blonde hairs out of the brush when I went back to being natural. And no one else ever uses my brush. So how come it has blonde hair stuck in it this morning?'

'Maybe you missed a few strands.'

'I liked that aftershave you were putting on last night. "Tropical Forest Green", wasn't it?'

'I think that's what it was called.'

'I went on the internet this morning. There's no after-shave called Forest Green or Tropical Forest Green or Tropical Green.'

'Maybe I got the name wrong.'

'Where's the bottle?'

'I threw it away.'

'Where? I thought you said there was some left?'

'I was wrong. I took it out with the rubbish this morning. Think the bin men have already been.'

'They come tomorrow.'

'I thought it was today. I'm sure it was today.'

China stops picking at the brush. She has several blonde strands in her hand.

'Roxy has blonde hair.'

Frankie says nothing. China's head abruptly disappears from the hatch again. Frankie mechanically picks up the bits and pieces he needs to start painting the bathroom. It takes him longer than he expects to locate them all. After twenty minutes, he brings the rolling tray and brush downstairs so he can wash the roller in the sink, and sees China working on a large piece of material laid out on the floor of the living room. She has at least put an old sheet underneath to protect the carpet from paint splashes. She is holding a spray paint can in one hand.

'What's that?'

'This? Oh, it's called "Tropical Forest Green".'

'It looks like a banner.'

Frankie watches as she shakes the paint can and scrawls the legend 'I CAN'T' carelessly across the fabric.

'You can't what?'

'Breathe.'

She finishes the banner with these seven letters and turns it over, where he can see the legend 'ACAB' sprayed in the same hand.

'It stands for "All Coppers Are Bastards".'

'I'm sure some of them are nice. You're going on the march?'

China nods without looking up.

'Isn't that dangerous?'

'Not for me, mate. I'm young and healthy.'

'Is that the point?'

'What is the point, then? That it's dangerous for *you*?'

China stops working on the banner and looks up at her father through narrowed eyes.

'I suppose so,' says Frankie. 'Anyway, you said last night . . . '

'And it's not dangerous to actually spend the night with someone who could easily be carrying the virus? Who could not only give it to you, but to me as well?'

Her eyes are blazing now. Frankie puts the roller and paint tray down on the dining-room table. His voice, when he speaks again, is low and fractured.

'I'm sorry. Roxy . . . she was very insistent.'

'That's okay, then,' says China, giving him a final contemptuous glance.

'She had a test before she came. She's negative.'

'Have you actually seen this test?'

'No. But she said . . . '

'She's just been party to an elaborate deception. Why should I think she is any more trustworthy than you? She's irresponsible and immature. She's not far off sixty and she still takes drugs and gets blasted every Friday night. At least she did before lockdown. I wouldn't trust her as far as I could throw her. Which is about as far as where you are now.'

'Look, China, you're wrong about Roxy. She's a good person. She'd never take a risk with my health.'

'Or with mine.'

'Look . . . '

Now China rises from the floor and faces Frankie directly, gesticulating with the aerosol can as if about to spray him.

'The point is, you lied. Again. Like you always do.'

Frankie gazes down on the banner which China has also decorated with a red magic marker frame around the borders.

'Are you *really* going to go on the march?'

'Absolutely.'

She shakes the can. Frankie can hear the ball bearing rolling around inside.

'Wanna come with me? Make a stand for once in your life for something.'

'For some armed robber three thousand miles away?'

China throws the aerosol at his face. It misses, but only because he instinctively ducks.

'You really don't get it, do you? Just go away, will you? Go away and leave me alone.'

Frankie nods but doesn't move.

'Why are you still standing there?'

Frankie hesitates before speaking again.

'Do you really want me to come with you?'

China's face contorts. She stares at Frankie incredulously.

'Are you offering to come?'

'Yes – if you like.'

She laughs – with genuine amusement, which makes Frankie feel more unsettled then any forced laughter might.

'No, Dad. I wasn't serious. I'd rather die of Covid than die of embarrassment. You stay at home and watch the world on telly, like you always do. You stay at home and watch the world burn, black people die, transgender people get murdered while you count your pennies, do up your expensive houses that you bought cheap and watch old movies while drinking bottles of nice wine. Like you always do. You and all the rest of you old white fuckers. Talking of which, I'm going back to Mum's.'

'What? When?'

'First chance I get.'

'But we were just getting to know one another.'

'Exactly.'

Day 72, 3 June 2020

Since her return from the BLM march, the atmosphere between China and Frankie has been choked with tension. Frankie is still trying to make amends for sanctioning Roxy's illicit visit and as a result is vigorously cleaning China's grubby, untidy room, which he usually leaves untouched out of simple resignation. China has made little attempt to make it any more homely since she arrived. It still resembles what it originally was – a room essentially for storage – only now it languishes under several layers of laundry, half-drunk coffee mugs and scattered footwear.

Frankie picks up the last of the pairs of sweatpants on the floor to put them in the wicker laundry basket and a plastic wrap the size of a baby's fist falls out of one of the pockets. Inside there are green stalks and leaves. Even the fact that it is triple wrapped does little to block the sour smell leaking from it.

Normally, he would have just returned it to the pocket – he is under no illusions about China's self-medicating habit – but for some reason he feels in a mischievous mood. He makes his way downstairs holding the wrap in his hand.

'What's this?' says Frankie, brandishing the baggie.

China, sitting on the grey sofa, still in her leopard-print pyjamas, looks up from the book she is reading.

'What's it look like? And what are you doing snooping around among my stuff?'

'I wasn't snooping among your stuff. I was tidying up your shit.'

'Just put it back where you found it.'

Frankie holds on to the bag and sits down on the chair opposite.

'Is this what I think it is?'

'What are you going to do?' says China, turning her gaze back to the book again. 'Confiscate it? I'm nineteen. I can do what I want.'

'Are you into this stuff? I'm not exactly a stickler about drugs, but I've read that for teenagers it can mash up your brain pretty badly.'

'I haven't really had an opportunity to be into it. Stuck here and all.'

'Then why is it in your pocket?'

She wearily looks up again.

'I had a couple of spliffs when I went out for a walk. So hand me over to the feds why don't you?'

She holds up her hand for her stash. Frankie hands it over and China, slipping it in her pocket, returns, once more, to the book.

'Look, China. I'm not quite as straitlaced as you think I am.'

'Who said I thought you were straitlaced? You get bladdered often enough. As if that was better than a little weed,' says China, finally giving up on the book and giving her attention to Frankie. She doesn't know why, but she can't help but feel defensive as well as innocent. Like she had been caught shoplifting something small from a big chain store.

'I used to take quite a lot of drugs when I was your age,' says Frankie. 'There was nothing else to do.'

China, despite herself, finds herself interested in her father's druggie years. She had always known that Frankie had been far from innocent in his teenage days. Nodge had told her all about it, but somehow being confronted with it now nonplusses her.

'What kind of drugs?'

Frankie wonders if he should change the subject, worried what Veronica will make of the conversation. After all, weren't parents meant to be role models for their children? But at the same time, he senses a small gap through which he might drive some toothpick of intimacy. After the Roxy fiasco and the subsequent BLM march, father and daughter relations seemed to have struck an all-time low.

'I smoked grass from time to time. When I could get hold of it.'

China throws her legs up on the sofa and pushes a cushion behind her head.

'How often is "from time to time"?'

'Pretty much every weekend. Don't forget I grew up in The Bush. The streets smelled of skunk all the time. Now it's all gussied up, you don't get it so much. All Saints in Notting Hill was the frontline. But Shepherd's Bush was *a* frontline.'

China's laugh sounds almost enunciated. *Yargh Yargh Yargh.* She makes a peace sign.

'*Frankie the stoner.* "Don't bogart that joint". "Pass me the bong". "I'm so wasted, man".'

'I think it damaged my brain pretty thoroughly anyway. Probably why I ended up as an estate agent.'

'That explains that, then. What else did you take?'

China has now given Frankie her full attention and it's his turn to feel uncomfortable. He decides to press on all the same, sitting forward on the chair, closing the space between them.

'Pretty much everything, I guess.'

China laughs again, not so much out of pure amusement but incredulity.

'What? Like – junk?'

'No, no, no. Nothing like that. But – I don't know. Speed. E. Amyl nitrite. Shrooms. Coke. Acid.'

China, shifting on the sofa, finds that she has mixed feelings about this confession. She is curious. On the other hand, it wasn't something dads were meant to do. Like sex. China had never done coke or acid. She thought of them as serious drugs. Adopting a neutral tone, she fixes her eyes on Frankie's face, which is open, although cautious.

'What was coke like?'

'I had a friend called Tony once. Diamond Tony. Not a very nice man. He had a hairdressing business. Ended up going bankrupt and living on the streets because he was so into the snow. It's a bad drug.'

China nods, in the manner of a formal investigation between a case worker and client.

'Is it fun, though?'

'Of course it was fun, or I wouldn't have taken it, would I? But not for very long. And it makes you very depressed afterwards. If you're too inside of it, you have to get a new nose. In the end it's like tearing up £50 notes and flushing them down the toilet.'

China takes her nose between two of her fingers and waggles the tip.

'I wouldn't mind a new nose.'

'Don't say that. Honestly, though, Chi. Don't get into gack. It's not a good place to go.'

Because of the frankness of these confessions, China finds herself taking her father seriously for what feels like the first time in years. Frankie, sensing this, decides to push the borders further, stung as he is by her habitual portrayal of him – even before the BLM march – as a naive, narrow-minded member of the *Daily Mail*-reading petit bourgeoisie. He leans even further forward in the chair and lowers his voice.

'Once, when I was a teenager, I did this kind of natural high. It was called Morning Glory. It was flower seeds.'

China almost doubles up with laughter on the couch, bringing her knees up to her chest and hugging them.

'Flower seeds! Shut up!'

Frankie looks around the room as if to check if someone is listening, then continues.

'It was called getting an organic high. Not very different from 'shrooms only more horrible. The seeds were called Heavenly Blue. I was round Uncle Nodge's house with him and we took a load of these things. They were disgusting. And we drank a lot of cheap red wine, too. Bull's Blood, it was called. Also disgusting.'

'What did they do to your poor adolescent head?' says China, stretching out again.

'Apart from making me feel sick? They lowered my inhibitions. Uncle Nodge and me . . . '

Frankie suddenly feels that he pushing at the borders of his relationship with his daughter too far.

'It doesn't matter,' he says. 'Listen, I'm going to finish up your room.'

He rises and begins to head towards the stairs. China rises too, as if she has caught the odour of something she doesn't want to lose the scent of.

'How did it lower your inhibitions?'

'You don't want to know.'

'Whatever it is, I won't mind.'

'I wish I hadn't said anything.'

'I don't know what you think you could say about what you did thirty years ago that could shock me.'

They stand face to face, separated only by inches of air.

'We had sex. Sort of. I mean, not . . . You know. But there was. Contact.'

China feels her blink rate accelerating and a faint but swiftly growing tightness in her stomach.

'Who had sex?'

'Me and Nodge.'

China stares at her father as if hypnotized. He seems to be transforming in her mind as she speaks.

'Shut up!'

'You did ask,' says Frankie, taking a step towards the safety of upstairs.

'Shut up. Shut up. Shut up.'

Now she is blocking his way.

'Aren't you being just a tad homophobic here, China? I mean if I said I'd had . . . contact . . . with a woman, would you . . . ?'

'Fuck off!'

Before Frankie can make it to the stairs, she runs past him, bumping him quite hard on the way. She marches into her room and slams the door behind her so hard the plasterboard wall seems to shake.

She emerges half an hour later. She finds Frankie staring out of the window, wondering if he has finally destroyed the last vestiges of his relationship with his daughter. China sits herself on the sofa and stares in his direction. He turns and looks at her, but she doesn't actually seem to meet his eye.

'Too much information?' he ventures.

'*Much* too much.'

But any hostility in her voice seems to have evaporated.

'I've never told anyone that before. Nobody. Ever. Not even your mother,' says Frankie, taking a step closer.

China hesitates before replying. She feels disoriented, unsure but oddly flattered by being taken into his confidence. Frankie sits on the floor in front of her as if awaiting judgement from a higher power.

'Do you want a cup of tea?' she says.

'Sure. I guess so. Thanks.'

Slowly, as if feeling her way, China gets up and goes into the kitchen, gets one of Frankie's QPR blue-and-white striped mugs, drops a teabag in it, boils the kettle then pours the water over the bag, watching the steam from the mug rise and disappear into nothing. This is what her life is like, she decides. She returns a few minutes later with the cup for Frankie.

'So, what – are you *gay*?' she says, handing the cup to him.

'I don't think so,' says Frankie, taking the cup carefully. 'It was the only time it ever happened with anyone. I never felt attracted to men. It was just one of those things.'

'Did you . . . did you *enjoy* it?'

She sits back on the sofa.

'I sort of did. Yes. Though I would never admit that to anyone.'

'Except me.'

'You didn't want a cup of tea yourself?' says Frankie, anxious now to move on and away from the subject.

'I think I need something stronger.'

'You won't tell anyone, will you?' he says. He suddenly feels acutely vulnerable. China fidgets nervously in her pockets. She feels the baggie there which she had forgotten about. She rolls it between her fingers, then brings it out and waggles it in front of his face.

'Tell you what. Shall I roll one?'

Frankie, not quite knowing how to respond, takes a sip of the tea, playing for time. In the end, he says nothing.

'Just to help me through these difficult teenage years?'

Frankie puts the tea down on the coffee table.

He smiles.

Half an hour later, the room is seamed with the rich smell of grass. China reclines on the sofa, a saucer doubling as an ashtray balanced on the arm. Frankie crouches on a brown leather footstool. China is staring intently at Frankie's nostrils.

'You're making me uncomfortable,' says Frankie.

'There's bristles in there. Like a toothbrush. A toothbrush up your nose. Two toothbrushes.'

'I was young once,' says Frankie.

'You ain't now, old man.'

'Got hair coming out of all the wrong places.'

'And no longer coming out of the right places.'

Frankie carries on ineffectively rolling a spliff, spilling tobacco and weed on the carpet.

'Hair's a funny thing.'

'Ker – a – tin,' says China. 'Is what they call it.'

'Fuzzy stuff all over you and, like, on your *face*. What's the point of face hair? What's its *significance*? Or ear hair for that matter. Or hair hair.'

China shrugs and nods, contemplating the question deeply.

'I've got hair on my back too,' says Frankie.

He suddenly seems puzzled.

'Have I got hair on my back?'

'It's your back,' says China.

Frankie gazes at China. Her eyes are glazed.

'I can't see it. Can I?'

There is a moment's pause, then they both burst into laughter.

'Like the back of my head. Or any of my head. I mean, where is my head? I can't see it.'

'Top of your neck. You ever had a beard?'

Now Frankie has lit the saggy spliff and is trying to draw on it. Having managed to shallowly inhale, he passes it to China.

'Your mother – God bless her little cotton socks – didn't like them.'

'Silas has a beard, though.'

'No, he doesn't.'

'He did when he met Mum. This spliff is a mess.'

She tries to tighten up the paper with a few licks and presses with her fingers.

'That's better.'

Frankie affectionately mimics her in a high-pitched whiny voice.

'*Silas has a beard*. That manky old stuffed teddy bear. That soft toy. That lame-o. Have you ever had a beard?'

China squints through the smoke, now satisfied with the draw she is getting.

'Not so far as I can . . . '

She pauses. The next word seems to elude her.

'Recall,' she says eventually.

'But why not?'

'Why not — what?'

Frankie screws up his face, trying to solve the conundrum.

'Everything's mixed together now — isn't it? Male, female. Trans, straight. Sex, intersex. Pansex. Not that I know what intersex is. Or Pansex.'

China hands Frankie the repaired joint and he takes it.

'Don't use that word.'

'Sex?' says Frankie, taking a puff. 'Why're Zoomers grossed out by the idea that their parents had sex? It's not as if there wasn't *evidence*.'

China puts her fingers in her ears and makes a *la-la-la* sound. Frankie takes another puff and hands China back the joint. She takes it and inhales deeply, then balances it on the edge of the saucer. A few moments later, when China has stopped *la-la*-ing and removed her fingers from her ears, Frankie speaks again.

'This stuff is potent. I've got a whitey coming.'

'A *whitey*?'

She wrinkles her nose in disgust. She licks her lips. She suddenly feels starving.

'I've got the munchies very bad, Dad.'

China throws her legs up on the footstool and stretches out her arms.

'*Bad Dad.* That's what you is.'

'Haha,' says Frankie. 'Then you're a . . . *whiner, China.*'

She picks up the joint from the makeshift ashtray.

'I mean you're not *really* a bad dad. Not in general,' she says, sucking on the soggy roach. 'Apart from abandoning us. And bankrupting us. You're bad for smoking weed with your nineteen-year-old daughter, though.'

'I expect I'll forgive myself. I'll see what we've got to cure those munchies.'

Frankie shakily makes his way to the kitchen. He returns a minute later with two Crunchie bars and a Terry's Chocolate Orange. He starts to clumsily take the silver paper off the chocolate orange.

'Now I'm feeling menolcholic,' he says.

'Melancholic.'

'Like a melon with stomach pain.'

The scraps of foil fall to the carpet floor and he stuffs a segment of the chocolate orange into his mouth.

'Why the feeling of . . . melon?' says China as he hands her the remainder of the orange. His fingers are sticky and brown with chocolate.

'*Why?* Good question. Why? Yes. Precisely.'

Frankie racks his brain for a reply that makes some sense. Or anything at all that might make any sense at all.

'Because I still love your mum. That's why.'

China shifts in her chair, snaps off half the chocolate orange and bites it.

'Even I can see that, mate. Even when I'm bare lit.'

'Didn't think it showed. Your face is covered in brown stuff.'

'Why wouldn't you love her?' says China, wiping her mouth with her pyjama sleeve. 'She's a great woman.'

'I know.'

'But then if she's such a great woman – why did you leave her? Leave *us*.'

Frankie feels himself abruptly begin to come down from the high.

'She didn't love me anymore, China. And . . . '

'And what?'

China examines the chocolate stain on her pyjama sleeve, while consuming what is left of the chocolate orange.

'It doesn't matter.'

She hands him the remainder of the smouldering joint.

'Actually it does matter. It *does*,' says Frankie.

Seeing there is only roach left, he stubs the joint out. He stares past the TV screen now to the cracked glass that covers the photo of them all together in the house in North Kensington.

His voice drops to a whisper.

'She slept with someone else, China.'

China laughs, joining in what she takes to be a joke.

'Old friend of mine,' continues Frankie, still in a low voice. 'Tony Diamonte. "Diamond Tony", we used to call him. That's what Roxy was driving at. After she gave you the compass for a present. Which was nice of her, I suppose I should acknowledge. Yeh, she's not so bad.'

China stares blearily back at Frankie.

'Sorry. Tuned out there for a moment. Something about diamonds?'

'Bad piece of work. Attractive. Nice skin. Like an olive. Fat lips. Like a fish. All the women chased him.'

'Who chased what?'

'Diamond Tony! I just *said*. He was the one I knew who became a you-know. *Cokehead*. He wasn't a friend. He was a *fiend*. Veronica met him at the drugs reba . . . rebahil . . . drying out centre.'

'Rehabilitation.'

'Rehabilitation centre that what . . . she did her training at. She worked in a rehab . . . place. Centre.'

China tries to concentrate.

'Why are you talking about this . . . dryout . . . thing?'

'I just *told* you. She slept with him.'

'Who slept with who?'

'Him.'

China gathers up the scraps of conversation that she has only been half-listening to.

'Mum slept with this . . . diamond . . . person? How long . . . before she met you?'

'You're not *listening*. She slept with Tony just before Veronica and I chucked in the tea towel.'

'Chucked in the tea towel?'

'Separated.'

China's feeling of woozy goodwill starts to evaporate.

'Bullshit. Bullshit. Bullshit.'

Frankie simply grunts.

'Who's Tony again?' says China.

'Diamond Tony! I just told you.'

Comprehension finally dawning, China sits up rigid on the sofa.

'Mum would never do nothing. Like that. Not ever. You split up because you lied . . . and cheated.'

'Yeh, no. You're right, though.'

China now hears her own voice rising in pitch. Her head clears.

'Also, *Dad*, you are famous for being a fucking liar. "Frankie the Fib", isn't it?'

'Yeh, that's it. Frankie the Fib.'

She rises from the sofa and kicks Frankie, hard on the leg with her bare foot.

'Don't you slag off my MUM.'

'Still love her. Doesn't it.'

Frankie finds that he is weeping.

'Well,' says China, icily calm. 'She's well rid of you. If you ask me.'

China picks up what is left of the joint, examines it, tries to light it again, fails. Then she goes upstairs and sits alone in her room.

The world in front of her eyes is spinning.

One more joint and four episodes of *Rick and Morty* and Frankie is passed out on the sofa. His T-shirt has ridden up to show his bare midriff and pot belly. There are two Crunchie wrappers scattered on the floor, foil from the chocolate orange and an empty vanilla ice cream pot. He has an old tartan blanket, which smells of flour and mould, covering part of his chest.

China comes downstairs to the front room to collect what is left of her stash. She whispers his name in his ear, but Frankie is beyond responding. He just manages to nod his head very slightly to indicate that he's heard her. Then he begins to snore, a tiny cement mixer.

China pulls the blanket up to his shoulders and over his belly, tucks the edges around his back. She notices there is a smear of chocolate at the edge of his mouth and gently wipes it off with the corner of her pyjama top.

Day 73, 4 June 2020

Frankie eventually stumbles into bed an hour after midnight, falling immediately unconscious. When he wakes it is still dark. The illuminated digital clock reads 03:03. His throat hurts and he feels nauseous. He coughs and finds it hard to stop, but puts that down to the spliffs he shared with China. Then he feels he is burning up and has a weird sensation like a small engine is running in his chest, throwing off painful sparks. At the same time, it is as if he has smoked a menthol cigarette. His lungs feel very alive and receptive, tingly almost.

He drifts back to sleep, but when he wakes again his whole body is aching, especially in his lower back. He can hardly sit up. He drags himself out of bed and makes himself a cup of tea and a slice of toast. He can neither smell nor taste the toast or the tea. The menthol feeling is now in his nasal cavity.

He slumps into an armchair, frightened that he has been infected with Covid. What is he going to do? Get a test, he supposes. You had to ring 111 if it got too serious. It was probably fine. Maybe the flu. Could be lots of things. He doesn't believe his own reassuring thoughts.

China appears in the doorway wearing black pyjamas and yawning. She has heard his coughing and, unable to sleep herself, has come to join him.

'What's the matter with you, old man? Can't take a bit of spliff?'

'I think I've got it. I feel terrible. Exhausted. Aching all over. Can't move. Coughing. Can't taste anything. Sore throat.'

He starts a hacking cough again. It continues for thirty seconds before he can catch his breath. China sits down opposite him.

'But where could you have got the Rona?'

He raises his head heavily to look at her. China can't help but register a glimmer of accusation in his eyes.

'I wore a mask all the time to the demo, Dad. I don't have any symptoms.'

'You can still pass it on.'

'I was careful. It's too soon for you to have symptoms.'

Frankie tries to rise from the chair, but he feels too exhausted to move and slumps back down.

'Nobody knows anything about this fucking bug. I saw the pictures on the TV of the demonstration. It wouldn't matter how careful you were.'

He forces a smile as a shadow of panic flickers over China's features.

'One less old white man, eh?' says Frankie.

'I didn't *mean* that. Couldn't it have been Roxy?'

'I told you. She got tested before she came. Negative.'

Frankie gingerly stands in order to return his mug to the dishwasher. Then he collapses on the carpet in front of the fireplace, the remaining contents of the cup spreading in pools across the tiled hearth.

He cannot stop sweating. He sleeps most of the time. Sometimes, he finds, pineapple juice helps the pain in his throat. Paracetamol doesn't help. Almost worse than the physical symptoms are the way he has been driven in upon himself. As his body languishes, the silent voice in his head gets louder.

Frankie feels life trickle weakly through him like the last remains of tepid water in a bathtub. He is no longer living life; it is living him, and it can let go of him at any moment. He feels he is little more than a corpse, faintly animated by some power he didn't understand.

The shining hum of simply *being* that he usually experiences, wordlessly, as the backing to everything is now obscured by a mind full of insects. Hornets, dragonflies, moths, midges, fireflies. Clouds of them. They confuse him. Sometimes he captures one and begins to examine it, only to see another crash into it and render it meaningless. Some sting, some fly harmlessly by. Many rise up from the blackness of his past. Others seem to come from nowhere and recede into nowhere, still others drift towards him from the future.

The stingers – the hornets – come from the past. The dragonflies are beautiful and important. If he can only capture a dragonfly, hold it in his mind, he knows he will find relief from the unceasing confusion. They whisper to him rather than just buzzing and fuming. Sometimes he traps one. But as soon as it is caught, the dragonfly fades and begins to decay. One or two, though, remain perpetually bright and whisper from a distance. They whisper the names of those whom he loves.

The attempt to get a test is impossible. No one even answers the phone. When they do, they tell him to ring back only when he can't get a sentence out without losing breath. They seem to only want to admit him when he's as good as dead in any case. They are terrified of overflowing hospitals. He wants someone to make the decision for him – the responsibility is too great.

Anyway, thinks Frankie, in his coherent moments, they can't do anything about it, other than put you on a ventilator. If they do that you're as good as dead. 50/50 chance of copping it. If you recover you're still going to be fucked up. He decides he doesn't want to go to hospital when he can hardly get out of bed. It is like there is an enormous weight on his chest and snakes of sharp metal writhing inside him.

He feels possessed. His breath is short and harsh. Sometimes he can't get hold of it at all. He is vaguely aware of China coming in with some hot Ribena and Night Nurse. Frankie feels like he is coughing his insides out, that his actual lungs are going to start rising up through his throat and that fleshy shreds will appear in the air.

'Is it bad?' he hears China say through the buzzing insects and the murk of his mind.

Frankie nods and tries to sit up so he can take the medicine and drink the Ribena. China helps him, propping a pillow behind his head.

'It comes and goes, they say,' says China. 'For a lot of people, it disappears in a few days.'

Frankie tries to answer, but sinks into another fit of coughing. China sits down on the bed next to him and begins to softly weep.

'Stop it,' croaks Frankie as soon as he can catch a breath.

'It's my fault.'

'I could have caught it anywhere. Down the shops, on the bus – anywhere.'

'You never get buses and I'm the one who usually goes to the shop. It was me. It has to be me.'

He then launches into a fit of coughing that lasts several minutes. China can do nothing but sit and hold his hand, and feel the tears run down her face.

'Should I phone Mum?' says China after Frankie has recovered enough to pay attention again.

Frankie shakes his head furiously. He doesn't want Veronica to have to bear his burden.

Day 78, 9 June 2020

Frankie is sitting in a hot bath, one of the few places that gives him any relief. The steam seems to loosen his lungs. He feels most of the time as if he has been kicked by a horse. If he breathes in anything other than the most shallow manner, he experiences unbearable pain.

But now, five days after the first symptoms appearing, Frankie feels better. He can snatch enough sleep to refresh himself, the cough has nearly disappeared and he can walk around the flat without fear of falling over.

'Do you think you've recovered?' says China, anxiously watching his halting progress across the floor.

'I *feel* better.'

'Then maybe you are.'

'Maybe I am. Perhaps I can go out for a walk.'

'You're meant to self-isolate.'

She puts her arms around Frankie and refuses to let go. He is too ill to hug her back.

Day 79, 10 June 2020

The illness comes fully back again, this time with renewed, terrible force. China, sitting next to Frankie in his bed, watches him struggle to breathe. Without consulting Frankie, she picks up her phone and calls 111, her hand shaking. When she eventually gets an answer, after twenty minutes, someone at the other end reads a list of set questions which China responds to. She is then peremptorily informed they will get a call back soon.

Two hours later the call comes. Someone very stressed is at the other end of the line. Their voice is tight, their tone impatient. China offers the phone to Frankie, but he can barely get enough breath to speak. So China talks the man at the other end of the line through Frankie's symptoms.

'He says his chest feels like it is full of concrete . . . He can barely even cough and when a cough does come, it hurts, does nothing to clear his chest . . . Yes, just at the top of the lungs he says, the rest is all bunged up . . . Pain in the back and chest . . . '

The man, it is clear to China, is not a doctor, possibly not even a nurse, just someone lightly trained in triage. He sounds as terrified as China feels. It is clear that the panic China has been reading about – the fear of the hospitals becoming over-whelmed – is setting the tone of the conversation. She cannot escape the idea that the last thing the man wants to do is admit Frankie into a Covid ward.

Eventually he asks to speak to Frankie and China passes the

phone. After a few routine yes-or-no questions which Frankie can barely find the breath to answer, the man, who says his name is Alan, asks Frankie if he has enough breath to finish a sentence.

Frankie finds that he cannot.

'I . . . don't . . . think . . .'

He falls silent.

There is a long pause before the assessor speaks again.

'So, are you saying you need an ambulance?' Alan asks in a wavering voice.

Frankie is torn. He thinks he may die. He wants an expert to tell him what he should do, not this . . . pen pusher. If he goes to hospital he may end up on oxygen, and the next step could be intubation. Fifty per cent of those put on respirators die. They die alone. Frankie doesn't want to die, but he particularly doesn't want to die alone. He has seen all the terrifying newsreel of the hospital wards, the doctors and nurses swaddled and invisible behind protective gowns and masks. A completely alien world.

He feels very scared.

Eventually he manages to answer, while China chews her nails to the nub.

'I'll . . . stick . . . it . . .'

There is another long pause.

'Out . . .'

With that, he passes the phone back to China and collapses onto the bed, too tired to move. China ends the conversation with the plainly relieved Alan, then sits and stares at the prone Frankie and then at a random spot on the floor, where she can see a single ant marching purposefully along.

Frankie's hair is thin and unwashed, as well as too long after nearly three months of growth. He has a rough, ungroomed beard. Particles of food from the last attempt he made to eat remain lodged in the stubble.

He feels like he has swallowed — and is continuing to swallow — broken glass mixed with glue.

He thinks he can feel the virus inside him moving under his skin, probing for weakness, for space where it can further breed, choke and destroy. A sense of paralysis has come upon him which started at the bottom of his lungs and has been moving relentlessly upward. When it can go no further upward he believes he will be dead.

China, sitting by his bed, listens to her father start to cough violently. His face is red with effort.

Later, at his request, she reads him children's books, bought on Amazon, books he remembers from childhood — *The Magician's Nephew*, *Fantastic Mr Fox* and, when he is particularly far away, *The Moomins*. They seem to comfort him.

She holds his hand and tells him, without very much conviction, not to be afraid.

Her hopes that he might recover without going into hospital — if at all — are fading. The previous night, she lay awake, listening as Frankie struggled to breathe. It sounded like a drowning man.

On FaceTime, Nodge makes sympathetic noises. Her mother cries. China has told her of the infection, despite Frankie's wishes. But there is nothing anyone can do. They cannot even come to the flat.

China asks if she should call 111 again, but Frankie shakes his head weakly. He thinks hospital is a death sentence. She considers ringing without his permission. Because how much worse can this get? Frankie's hair is matted and there is a light sheen of sweat on his skin. His face, having been bright red a few minutes ago, now looks pallid and weary, making him seem maybe ten years older than his fifty years.

His hand is hanging limply over the bed. She looks at his face, at the faint scarring below his hairline. Somehow she finds the scar unbearably moving. She takes Frankie's hand. Instead of feeling clammy, as she had expected, it feels dry as parchment.

He turns his head to look at her with yellowish rheumy eyes. A faint smile filters through before vanishing in another blizzard of coughs. She holds fiercely on to his hand. The guilt she feels from going on the march is now with her every moment of the day, an impossible burden. She broods and broods. Finally, to displace the guilt, she experiences a rush of compensatory fury. She stares at Frankie, who is reclined on the pillow with his eyes closed.

'Why did you let me go on that stupid march?' she hears herself snap. 'You know that's what a father is for? To set boundaries. You never set me any boundaries. You never cared enough about me to set boundaries. And now look what you're doing to me! You're saddling me with a burden that isn't really mine. Same as the fact you took our house away and sent Mum away. And you left *me* and it was *my* fault I know because . . . because . . . '

Her voice drains of anger, trails to almost nothing.

'I don't know why . . . '

For a moment Frankie seems to stop breathing. A wave of panic hits China.

'Dad!' she almost shouts, her anger returning, then falling away, as she sees the faint flicker of eyelid. Frankie lies back with his eyes now closed. He nods faintly. China starts crying, her whole body shaking.

'I'm sorry. I'm sorry. I'm sorry, Dad. I shouldn't have gone on the march. I was such a selfish, immature bitch.'

Frankie's voice emerges as a croak. He finds he cannot speak. He reaches weakly for a pen and paper on his side table and manages to scribble a few words. It takes some seconds for China to finally decipher the agonized scrawl on the paper.

not your fault.

Frankie eventually falls asleep and China, wiping away tears, goes downstairs to make a vitamin drink. As she reaches the bottom step, her phone vibrates. She takes it out, glances at the caller display and hits the speak button.

'Hi, China. How are you?'

China stares at the image of Roxy. She is taken aback. Roxy has never called her before. Her face is tired-looking, grooved with worry, clean of makeup. She is wearing a grubby white T-shirt and her nails are ragged.

'How did you get this number?'

She is aware that she must sound rude, but doesn't really care.

'Veronica gave it to me,' says Roxy. Her dyed blonde hair is grown out showing greasy roots.

'You talked to Mum?'

'I rang her when I couldn't get an answer from Frankie. I wanted to see how he was,' says Roxy. China can now see in the background some of her flat – a full-length mirror on a stand, a large framed photo of her dressed as a box of popcorn, and a dummy's head with a wig on it. China feels herself soften. She has had few chances to unpack her dilemma, and Roxy is an opportunity for unburdening, even though she doesn't fully trust her.

'He's very ill, Roxy. And it's all my fault.'

China hears her own voice and becomes conscious that it is parched and cracked with misery and self-pity.

'Veronica told me. How did he get it?'

China finds that she can't meet Roxy's eye.

'I went on the BLM march. I must have picked it up and given it to him.'

Roxy doesn't respond, just stares neutrally into the phone camera.

'Say something, then,' says China finally.

'What do you want me to say?'

'I don't know. How about "China, you're a selfish bitch"? That would do for a start.'

Roxy continues staring. She puts her face slightly closer to the camera. China can see the lines of age and worry, normally concealed under makeup, clearly.

'Given how much you've been looking after him, it would be hard to make that one stick. How soon after the march did he get symptoms?'

'Two days. Maybe three at most.'

Roxy's head nods slowly and she comes still closer to the camera. Now her pale face fills the screen.

'That's too soon, I would have thought. It usually takes longer than that to incubate. Up to a week.'

China, who is sitting at the living-room table, dejectedly flicks a scrap of granola that spilt from her dish that morning onto the floor where it collides with a used tissue.

'I know you want to make me feel better, Roxy. But it couldn't have been anyone else. I've basically murdered my dad.'

She feels grief welling up within her.

'Come on, China. Don't be so melodramatic.'

China wipes her face with the back of her sleeve. She doesn't want to cry in front of Roxy. She is determined to show her strength.

'That's better,' says Roxy. 'Anyway. It could easily have been me.'

China pulls her sleeve away from her face sharply.

'In fact, I'm pretty sure it *was* me,' says Roxy in a low voice. But China waves the remark away with the back of her hand.

'You had a test before you came. Dad told me. You're just trying to make me feel better.'

Roxy doesn't answer. Now China sits forward at the table. She feels herself gripping the phone tightly.

'You did have a test, didn't you?'

There is again a long pause before Roxy finally answers.

'I didn't have a test, China,' Roxy says. 'I couldn't get one. No one can get one.'

'Shut *up*.'

'But I thought I'd been pretty safe, since I'd been properly self-isolating. So I took a chance. I came to the flat anyway. Frankie's symptoms started about five days later. That's a much more plausible timetable. Also – I developed a temperature and a sore throat after I stayed. But the symptoms disappeared quite quickly, so I wrote them off. Wishful thinking. Yeh, so, the thing is, it was me, China. It has to have been. I'm really very sorry.'

'You're kidding, right? You're making this up.'

'No. I'm telling the truth. On my life.'

'Right. Right. Right.'

Momentarily, China considers hanging up. Then she says, 'You selfish cunt.'

Roxy's drooping expression of apology gives way to mild defiance. She recoils from the screen slightly.

'Well, fair enough – it was a bit cunty. But you did go on the BLM march – didn't you? She who is without sin and all that. You just got luckier than me.'

'Yeh, whatever. Listen to me, Roxy. I don't ever want you to show your face round here again.'

'I'm not sure that's your choice.'

'You knew it was a possibility that you might have it. And you *actually* came and spent the night with my dad. Put not only him at risk, but also me. And God knows who else. All so you could have a bit of fun.'

'China, it's not that simple . . . '

Now China does hang up, breathing heavily, her rage accompanied, however, by a momentary flood of deep relief.

Then she remembers that her father is still barely hanging onto life and her anxiety returns as strongly as before.

Day 80, 11 June 2020

Roxy, lying in her bed, all black satin sheets and brass bedsteads, picks up on a phone call from Veronica. She props herself up on a cushion. No greeting is proffered. She can hear the anger in Veronica's voice tearing through the ether. Veronica is sitting at the piano in her living room randomly pressing the keys, clashing notes discordant in the air.

'Is it true that you gave the virus to Frankie?'

'No, it's not,' says Roxy, putting another cushion behind her so she is more upright.

'Don't talk shit. China told me.'

'I lied to China.'

Roxy takes a cigarette out of a side drawer and lights it. She has been smoking again since lockdown. Something to do.

'You did what?'

'I lied to her. I lied through my teeth.'

She blows out a cloud of smoke at the camera. Veronica abruptly stops hitting the keys.

'Why on earth would you lie to China?'

Roxy searches for an ashtray, can't locate one, and lets the ash drop on the floorboards.

'Because I knew how much China would be suffering. I wanted to help her.'

Veronica's fingers now hover uncertainly over the piano keys.

'You're just trying to wriggle out of responsibility.'

Roxy sucks deeply on the cigarette. Her eyes are dull, listless.

'How does that work, then, Veronica? By confessing my guilt? How's that wriggling out of responsibility? All I'm saying is that it isn't like I told her.'

'You can't get tests unless you are a doctor or something.'

'I did get offered a test, because I'm immuno-compromised. I have congenital IgA deficiency. Inherited from my father. I was all clear.'

'How do I know you're telling the truth?'

'You don't. Does it matter? The point is China has to believe it was me.'

Veronica goes silent, unable or unwilling to process this new information. Yet she finds herself suddenly certain that Roxy is telling the truth.

'Don't tell China. Let her hate me. And Frankie,' says Roxy, ending the silence that follows. She finally spots an old shell that she picked up on a beach somewhere, and stubs the cigarette out into it. She waves away the smoke with her hand. 'I just don't want you to hate me too.'

'But if what you are saying is true . . . then China hates you for something that isn't true. Or probably not true. She's going to try and stop you seeing Frankie again. If he lives. And Frankie won't want anything to do with you.'

Roxy smiles sadly. She takes some hand cream from the bed-side table and begins to rub it into her palms.

'Yes, but at least he won't resent China for giving it to him. And of course he's going to live. Don't be so gloomy. Anyway, it's okay if Frankie doesn't want to see me again. I've known for a while that he's not that into me. I keep trying to keep the fact away from myself, but I can't really ignore it any longer. He's too scared to dump me, but he doesn't really want me. He doesn't really love me. He never has.'

'I'm sure that's not true,' says Veronica, uncertainly, confused by the transition she has had to make from righteous anger to sympathy, even gratitude.

'There's only one woman, other than China, who he loves. I'm sure you're perfectly aware who that is.'

She examines her ragged fingernails and shakes her head in despair.

'I need to get these seen to. But who's going to even see them? It doesn't matter. Nothing matters really nowadays, does it?'

It dawns on Veronica, after a few seconds, what Roxy is saying. She almost laughs at the absurdity of the notion.

'That's just silly, Rocks. We've been apart for ten years.'

'Love doesn't go off with time, Veronica. Not the proper kind.'

'But . . .'

Roxy cuts her off, raising her hand.

'Tell China that you hauled me over the coals and tore a proper strip off me. I can't let China go through what she's going through any longer. Not on top of all the worry about her dad. I just *can't*. And I hope to God that Frankie is going to be alright. I'm actually praying for him. When I don't even believe in God. Not after Colin I don't. Not that I did anyway in the first place, I suppose. So it wasn't that big a loss.'

Veronica stares at her phone for a couple of seconds, then finally speaks.

'I'm . . . I'm sorry I haven't been in touch with you more often, Roxy. It was tardy.'

'Well – it was all a bit awkward, wasn't it? Things change. And you're fifty miles away. Look, I guess I should be going. We'll meet again and all that. Stay well, Vronky.'

'You too, Rocks.'

'Do me one more favour. Before you go, can I tell you a psychotherapist joke? You know. Since you are one.'

'Oh God. You never grow up, do you?'

'Does anyone?'

Veronica groans.

'Go ahead then. If you really have to.'

'It's a good one. How many psychotherapists does it take to change a lightbulb?'

'One — but they really have to want to change it,' says Veronica.

She has heard a version of the same joke multiple times.

'Not funny?' says Roxy.

'Up to your usual standard,' says Veronica.

Roxy cuts off the call.

Day 81, 12 June 2020

China hears a knock on her door and a voice drift through the thin stripped pine panelling. The door opens. It's Frankie in his pyjamas. He looks astonishingly normal. He is smiling, albeit weakly. China throws the bedclothes aside and jumps out of the camp bed. She is about to throw herself into his arms but something, a residual reticence, stops her. Instead she stands in front of him, very close. He touches her gently on the shoulder.

'I'm feeling much better.'

China puts her hand on top of her father's, then takes it away again.

'You should go back to bed. You thought you were better the last time.'

Frankie does a little skip to show how well he's feeling.

'No, but this time, I think . . . I think I really am. I can feel it. Do you want a cup of tea?'

He starts to turn and head towards the stairs.

'I'll make it,' says China quickly, stepping in front of him. 'Get back into bed, Dad. Straightaway. I don't want you falling over again.'

She hazards a quick, tentative hug.

'Thank you,' says Frankie as she pulls away.

289

'Don't get too used to it,' says China. But she is smiling all the same.

As Frankie makes his way back towards his bedroom, he casts his eyes down the stairs around the detritus distributed by China all over the floor over the past few days. Paper plates, takeaway containers, a half-drunk bottle of sour milk, sweet wrappers, orange peel, plastic spoons and a blister pack of contraceptive pills.

'This place is a pigsty. What have you been doing in here?'

'I've been trying to look after you, Dad,' says China, now halfway down the stairs, not looking back. She holds onto the still-unfinished banister and feels a splinter poke into her palm. 'Now you're better you should finish this fucking banister.'

'That doesn't mean you have to leave half-eaten sandwiches on the floor and – my God! Look at this!'

He is peering into a bowl of vegetarian chilli left on the landing which China had been meaning to clean up for some days. 'It's actually going green.'

'It was green in the first place,' says China as she reaches the bottom of the stairs and heads towards the kitchen, pulling the splinter out on the way.

'Not *that* shade of green. Not the sort that comes in colonies and settlements.'

'Welcome back. It hasn't been the same without you.'

'I mean you really are taking the piss, China.'

China disappears into the kitchen but calls through the open doorway.

'Why don't you just go back to bed? It makes things easier. Just don't die, okay?'

'I don't intend to. You'd never forgive me.'

'Damn right I wouldn't.'

'If I don't die, will you make an effort to be a bit tidier?'

'I'll think about it,' says China, putting the kettle on.

21 June 2020

Frankie is finally clear of the virus. He has been well enough to consult with his GP and has been given a clean bill of health. Outside, the shops on Golborne Road are open again after three months of shuttering. He sits next to China, close, on the grey sofa. They are both in their pyjamas. China as usual is checking her phone. She is arranging a picnic outside with her friends in Holland Park. The living room is relatively tidy. For once, it is China who has done the tidying.

'Did you enjoy being a carer?' says Frankie when she is finished.

'It was a blast,' says China, plugging her phone into the charger.

'Good training for when I go senile.'

'Hasn't that already happened?'

Frankie turns to China and she lets him take her hand.

'I'm sorry to have been such a burden.'

China, feeling uncomfortable now, gently takes the hand away and pats Frankie on the knee.

'Doesn't matter. That's what daughters are for, isn't it? To save their fathers from extinction. Temporarily at least.'

She takes a brush from next to the fireplace and starts to sweep out the embers scattered on the surround.

'You must have felt very alone.'

The ash gathered in a shovel, she empties it into the fireplace.

'I'll clear this out properly a bit later,' she says.

'Did you have much support?'

'I had Mum to talk to.'

She replaces the cleaning tools and stares out of the window onto the Golborne Road, which is beginning to fill up with shoppers and tourists.

'That must have helped.'

Frankie picks up his own phone and examines it for messages.

'Did Roxy get in touch at all? I've been trying to ring her, but been getting no reply.'

'I'm not surprised.'

China takes a seat on the armchair opposite Frankie. She picks with her fingernail at a particle of toast that has been left on the arm that morning.

'What do you mean?'

Instead of flicking the particle on the floor, she reaches over and puts it in the bin next to the chair.

'Roxy rang me. The thing is this. It was her that gave you the virus – not me.'

Frankie's eyes dart around the room. They finally come to rest on the silver cup on the mantelpiece.

'No, that's not true. She told me she had two tests, both negative.'

'When I talked to her, she told me that she not only hadn't had any tests, but that she had had a temperature. Even before she came to see you.'

'No, no, that's wrong.'

'She didn't say anything before because she knew you would be angry and that you would probably dump her.'

Frankie lets this settle.

'She's absolutely right.'

'Just keep away from her, Dad. She was never any good.'

China picks up the bin, takes it into the kitchen and empties it into the dustbin. When she returns to the living room Frankie is sitting in exactly the same position. China sits next to him.

'Are you sad? About Roxy, I mean?'

Frankie shakes himself out of his reverie.

'Not really. She always got on my nerves, to be honest. It's a bit of a relief to be able to get rid of her without feeling guilty about it. What about Nodge? Did you talk to him much?'

'He was a great strength for me. Very supportive and loving. As always.'

'How did he seem to be – in general?' says Frankie, aware that China might still be unaware of the split between Owen and Nodge.

'Fine, as far as I could make out.'

China, sensing something amiss, gives Frankie a sideways look.

'Did you speak to Owen?' says Frankie.

China crumples her brow in puzzlement.

'Funnily enough, all the times I called Nodge, Owen wasn't there. Or that old bloke who's been living with them. JJ, is it? I asked to speak to Owen a couple of times, but he was always out on his daily walk. Actually, come to think of it, that's not like Owen at all. He was always very keen to talk.'

'Right. So Nodge didn't tell you, then?' says Frankie in a flat tone.

22 June 2020

China knocks on the door of the immaculate Edwardian ter-
raced house on the fringes of Queen's Park. It is Owen that
answers the vintage pale blue door with the deco stained-glass
panel. He is wearing tailored shorts and an oversized T-shirt that
reads 'Can't Hide My Pride'. His face registers consternation at
the sight of China, who looks frail and tired. She is wearing outsize corduroy trousers which are too long for her and cover her
trainers, and an emerald green silk blouse with a single, penny-
sized coffee stain down the front.

'China girl! What a surprise.'

She glares at him fiercely. He takes a slight step backwards.

'Why didn't you tell me about . . . '

She waves her hand vaguely in the direction of the interior of
the house.

' . . . this?'

Instead of inviting her in, Owen keeps the door half closed.

'You had other things on your mind. I didn't want to trouble
you. I hear Frankie's out of the woods now. That's great news,
isn't it?'

'That's not what I'm here to talk to you about.'

'I suspected as much.'

A single cough comes from upstairs.

'Is that him?'

'JJ. Yes.'

'Your . . . lover.'

'Yes.'

'You know you're committing adultery, don't you? I'm very
angry with you, Owen. Nodge – your husband, incidentally,

294

as well as my beloved godfather – is going out of his head with grief. But doubtless, you know that already.'

Owen doesn't make any response. China crosses her arms.

'You actually haven't talked to him?'

A Siamese cat, lithe and slightly sinister, winds its way through between Owen's legs and stares at China through vast green eyes with resentment.

'Boo! Get back inside!'

Owen manoeuvres the squealing cat back into the living room and shuts the door behind it. After a second or two, he returns to the still only half-open front door.

'I thought talking to Nodge would just exacerbate the wounds. Clean break and all that. You know.'

'Bullshit,' says China, taking a step up from the path onto the polished red doorstep. 'You just couldn't face the mess you'd left behind you.'

'That's not really fair.'

'How long are you going to keep me out here? Can I come in?'

'Well . . . it's not really allowed . . . with the virus and . . . '

'Where's JJ?'

'In bed. He's not feeling well.'

China, taking a mask out of her bag, puts it on and simply pushes the door fully open. Owen gives way. She walks through the hall into the living room. The house, she notes, is surprisingly suburban. Chintz, pale, thick carpets and English landscapes on the wall, even a George Stubbs reproduction of a bucking chestnut horse. A vase of fresh flowers sits on a faux-antique coffee table next to an outsize book on English country houses. There is a sunburst mirror and a grandfather clock. She nearly trips over a footstool with a frilly trim.

'I hope this is all meant to be ironic,' says China.

'JJ has very eclectic taste.'

'That's one word for it.'

She makes her way across the living room and walks through the open sliding glass doors that lead into the garden. She takes a seat on a bamboo garden chair with a cream cushion. Owen follows her, also now wearing a mask, and opens his mouth to speak, but China speaks before he can get anything out.

'Let me come to the point. Have you fallen out of love with Nodge?'

'That's typically direct of you,' says Owen, sitting down on the adjacent chair. The garden is small but lush, with huge banks of roses and bursting blooming peonies.

'Have you?'

'No,' says Owen, staring at the ground. There is a puddle of water where the sprinkler has been operating.

'Are you in love with this man – JJ or whatever his name is?'

Owen puts his finger to his lips, glances upstairs towards the bedroom where she presumes JJ is sleeping. Owen checks that the bedroom window is closed, moves a little closer to China and lowers his voice.

'Not really.'

'So what the hell are you doing living with him, then?'

'Well, it's like this . . .'

'On second thoughts don't bother explaining. Dad told me all about it.'

Owen picks off a scrap of dandelion fluff that has blown onto his navy blue shorts.

'I'm sorry, China. I didn't think enough of the impact it would have on you.'

'Everything has an impact on everyone.'

'But I can't see what I can do about it.'

He is having trouble removing the final flowers of the dandelion. The sound of violent coughing emerges through the window upstairs. Owen glances up again.

"Rona?' says China, raising an eyebrow and following his gaze.

'He's got none of the other symptoms. Testing negative. Probably just a cough.'

'Old people get ill. He's too old to be a father, Owen.'

Owen slaps at the remains of the dandelion. He suddenly looks haughty and defensive.

'Better an old father than a reluctant father. Or a father who is going to be disqualified by the system. Anyway, they say that you can't go back,' he finishes sullenly.

'Who are "they"? Do "they" have an office somewhere?'

'You know what I mean.'

He is still examining his shorts, although they are perfectly clean now. China fixes her eyes on Owen's 'Can't Hide my Pride' T-shirt.

'Ironic,' she says.

'Meaning what?'

'Meaning you should be ashamed of yourself.'

Owen stares off into the garden where a mower sits among half-cut grass. A sprinkler is distributing a thin spray of water that separates into a perfect rainbow under the powerful sunshine.

'Look at the colours,' says Owen faintly.

'Do you know where a rainbow is, Owen?' says China.

Owen turns away from the sprinkler.

'What do you mean?'

'It's in your head. It's a construction of your mind.'

Coughing emerges from the window upstairs, more frantic now. JJ sounds as if he is gasping for breath.

'I'm going to have to go and attend to him. Anyway, I'm not sure why we're talking about rainbows.'

He rises from the chair.

'Sit down again, Owen. I'm sure he'll survive a few minutes longer. The point is this. I think I have a solution to your problems.'

In the distance, the sprinkler falters and the rainbow, only a second ago so bright and real to both of them, dematerializes.

23 June 2020

The woman has been moved into temporary accommodation during the lockdown, a room little more than the size of a walk-in wardrobe with a single bed, a sink and an adjacent communal toilet in a badly converted office block. Her room also has a small window that shows, on this day, a patch of blue sky.

She knows this arrangement is going to be temporary. The moment the virus finally reaches a safe enough level, she will be back on the street again. It's all window dressing for the council and the government or the charities or whoever it was that made these decisions. Apparently, it didn't look good for homeless people to be on the streets of Brighton during the Rona, so they had scooped her up and put her here. She doesn't care one way or the other.

Yet somehow confinement to a bed in a dry room has made the endless scramble of her thoughts, always chasing after one another in the dark and crashing against invisible walls, seem to become still and begin to clarify. Perhaps that was also because it has been nearly impossible to get any drugs or beg any money. After a bad couple of days – no, weeks – the drizzling mud that had saturated her mind for so long had become patchy, allowing her to glimpse scraps of clear sky.

Flashes of memory come into her head sometimes that make her desperate for a fix, but now she can't escape the sear of the lightning. Her madness had protected her for so long – her madness and the drugs and the drinks and the pain – that letting go of it, even a small bit, was a form of agony.

A picture now forms in her head of a child. It is little more than a baby. It looks at her in a certain way, a way that makes her uncomfortable, makes her scared. Was she meant to love it, to care for it? She didn't know how.

Darknesses that had been buried or forgotten come back to her whenever the image of the child visits, fogging her mind and driving her into a race to outpace the blackness, a race into alcohol, into whatever she can get her hands on. In the past, when drugs erased the child from her awareness, it was a relief. She could get on with the project of dismantling herself without interference. She could learn to forget everything again, make it all un-happen, at least inside her head, where it counted.

She sees in her mind a blank, and then a hospital wall, and then a picture of her on the street and then the rest of her life, a flight from reality that ends here. Here where there was no reality, only need, but right at this moment, in her tiny room, the reality is creeping back. She doesn't like the feeling – and yet there was something there that she could recognize was calling to her. She cannot help but turn her gaze inward as long-forgotten truths beckon, threaten and summon her.

The world is empty and the people she meets in the corridor are unfriendly and distant and wearing masks – without drugs to hold the community together, all the street people have retreated into their private nightmares. No sharing of needles or bottles. No mumbled sentimental declarations of eternal fealty.

Fealty. Where had that word come from? Who had she once been – to use a word like 'fealty'? Whoever that person was, she had long gone, and the woman wasn't sure that she wanted to meet her again. *Be* her again. Yet the silence, and the dry, warm room, and the circle of blue above her head – it kept pulling on a thread somewhere, and the thread seems to be attached to a bow that was slipping loose. A million bows and knots, all of them slipping, loosening.

I don't like it I don't want it, she repeats to herself. But it seems she can't escape. If she goes back to the street, they would scoop her up again, and she would end up here, or somewhere else where thoughts could chase her and her oblivion run away from her.

She has even begun to wash her clothes – there is a laundry room – and dry them on the bathroom radiator which never turns off, even in summer. It is odd not to smell of piss and sweat anymore. One day, two nights ago, she took a bath and washed her hair with the hard soap they left out for the tenants. When she left the bath, to use the small thin towel she had been given, and looked in the cracked, stained mirror, she got a shock, because in front of her was something like a person, something like the woman she half-remembered once being.

It won't last, it can't, because nothing does, but also the people from the council had been bringing her medication for months and for once she found herself being organized enough to take it every day.

More light, light that hurt but somehow cannot be resisted, floods into her mind. It stabs at her brain; it aggravates and picks at the shredded remnants in the cage of her chest. She keeps taking the medication, keeps gazing at the patch of blue. Something is taking shape inside her, a certain kind of sequence of thoughts that are beginning to discern and tabulate their own order.

She listens to the television blaring from the room of the resident next door, an ancient Somali man, some rubbish or other; she has never much liked television.

Here it comes again. Memory, seeping, rising. Why doesn't she like television? Everyone likes television. Everyone on the street talks about some crap they had once come upon, slumped on a dredgy sofa and watched like the zombies they were. Like she is. Or had been. Is.

There is a book in the drawer in the room. It is a Gideon Bible. On impulse, she opens the first page and begins to read. It is the first book she has read for many years, not that 'years' mean anything to her, those numbers and figures that, like months and days, marked the passage of time.

Time. You didn't move through it; it moved through you. It is moving through her now, like a gathering tide, like a flood, dislodging screens and blockages and prising open thick, heavy curtains that had cut her off and protected her for so long so long so long.

A name keeps coming into her head, and she can see the shape of the letters, and she can imagine the face behind the letters, and she can feel the feeling that comes with the face, but she cannot . . . not . . . quite . . . put . . . her . . . finger on it – or her or him. Or maybe she just doesn't want to put her finger on anything that would let in more light. Or take her finger off something that has so long been blocked.

She examines her pinky finger. There is a mark of skin there that is more indented, darker, than the rest of the skin of her finger, she sees, as it catches the light.

PART THREE

Recovery

July 2020: London

Frankie inspects his tailored suit, brilliant white shirt and green shot silk tie in the plate-glass window of Farley & Ratchett. The ghostly tramp of lockdown has been exorcized. He is satisfied that he looks as he was pre-lockdown – professional, smart, able, efficient. On this day, he has indulged in an expensive shave, haircut and scalp massage at George Trumper in Piccadilly – a treat to himself after so long confined to quarters. The F&R office has opened again, and after working there for two weeks, having fully recovered from the virus, Frankie can sense the tide of life flowing in his direction.

F&R suffered during the lockdown. Margins are now tight. One of the most senior salespeople has got seriously ill and isn't coming back for the foreseeable future. Long Covid, apparently; that was a thing now. Frankie knows that Simon Farley needs him. He needs the business and he needs Frankie's experience and expertise to guide them back into the good times.

Farley had long promised Frankie a partnership and knew Frankie wouldn't stay around if he wasn't offered one. The lockdown and the departure of the ailing salesman had high-lighted Frankie's importance to the firm. Frankie's summons to 'an important meeting about an important question' had come yesterday, and by the pleased and anticipatory tone in

Farley's voice, Frankie had little doubt what the meeting was concerning.

As Frankie walks through the shining glass entrance into the immaculately clean, tidy and polished office, Farley, behind his desk at the back of the room, raises his head and greets him with a special estate agent's smile, full of carefully prepared warmth. Behind the smile, there is just business, only ever business.

'Hello, Frankie,' says Farley amiably. Farley is so amiable Frankie almost considers it a form of mental illness. He has, for as long as Frankie can remember, worn a Marks & Spencer brown suit. He considers designer garb an expensive indulgence and believes that 'dressing down' gives him the common touch with clients. He is also wearing his perpetual brown brogues which tend to squeak rhythmically when he walks.

'Simon.'

Farley half-rises from his chair, holds out a hand and Frankie shakes it. Farley takes a bottle of hand sanitizer out of his pocket, drips it on his hands and rubs them vigorously together. Those seated in the rest of the office sneak glances at the two of them through the transparent screen of Farley's partitioned office space. They have an idea what is going on because Farley mentioned it in confidence to Jane – once the office help, now underperforming only Frankie on the sales roster as a senior agent. To Frankie's resentment, she has leapfrogged him to become a junior partner in the firm. Jane has trouble keeping secrets and the perceptible buzz in the office indicates the news has leaked.

Feelings on the shopfloor are mixed. Frankie is liked, but, like the fictional Bernard who Frankie had read about in *Death of a Salesman* after China had thrust it into his hand, not *well* liked.

But then no one at F&R *really* likes one another; they just tolerate each other as they manoeuvred for position, power and wealth. As a consequence, there is a certain amount of natural jealousy towards the idea of Frankie prospering.

Frankie glances to his right. The faces in the office are pressed to phones, while all the hands tap at keyboards. The mouths move, broadcasting whispers – imprecating, supplicating, manipulating. He wonders with a shock if what they seem to him – shallow, artificial, uncomplicated in their greed – is also what they see when they look at Frankie.

An unwelcome question pops unbidden into his head. *What has he become?* Thirty years of graft and selling and negotiating and schmoozing and where has it got him? The prospect of a partnership in a small and lately declining estate agency business. Here's where he would stay until he was fifty-five, sixty, sixty-five. Then retirement. Then death.

Farley rises and beckons him out of the cubicle and towards the more private back office which was more or less unchanged since they had moved into the premises a decade ago. As they enter, Frankie notices that it is looking tired and shabby, but then what was the point of keeping up appearances when no one was going to witness them, when those appearances would accrue no profit?

Farley sits himself plumply behind his desk and indicates the chair on the other side. Frankie lowers himself into the space and blankly examines the strip-lit room, windowless apart from a tiny pane of glass showing a square of uncertain blue sky way above Farley's head.

As the chair takes his weight, Frankie realizes how much he hates this room – its careful neutrality, its uncared-for utilitarian air, its self-aggrandizing desk legend — *'A desk is a dangerous place from which to view the world'* — *John le Carré* — its smell of stale air and chemical stain remover. Simultaneously, to his mild surprise, he realizes that he hates Farley too — whereas before, he had thought he was only indifferent to him, imagining him always as nothing more than a means to an end.

Perhaps he hates himself as well. Because wasn't it true that Farley was him and he was Farley, and Farley was Ratchett, and Ratchett was Jane, and they all together made up this office, all backstage scenery for the accumulation of wealth through deception and charm?

This is his destiny. He will work, now, as a partner within these walls for the rest of his useful life, selling empty space, pretending he needed the money, taking the money, spending the money on things he didn't need. Occasionally ogling women clients behind dark glasses, occasionally meeting up with China, perpetually longing for something he couldn't name or describe. It seemed he was always trying to get back to where he was.

Now he realizes he isn't even where he is.

'So, Frankie. I expect you know what I wanted to see you about?'

'Was it to ask about my birthday present?'

Frankie's fifty-first is a few weeks away. Farley laughs, indulging the joke.

'I've already decided on your present. As I'm sure you can guess.'

Farley puffs himself up a little. He is enjoying this. His moment of generosity and largesse, of, even, forgiveness for the prodigal son. The fatted calf is to be slaughtered and cooked.

'I'm excited,' says Frankie in a flat voice. Farley picks up a paperweight shaped like a pyramid – who used paperweights anymore? – and taps it pointlessly on the desk. It makes a hollow sound, not the solid tap Frankie might have expected.

'So – Frankie. You've worked very hard for the firm and you've done good honest work for a long time now. We have had our ups and downs and we have been through some rough waters together.'

'Yes. We've had ups and downs in rough waters.'

'And sometimes . . . ' says Farley.

'And sometimes we've dived beneath the roaring waves and seen the monsters roaming with glistening teeth,' says Frankie, a slight petulance creeping, unbidden, into his tone.

Farley looks faintly irritated at the interruption. His gracious giving of this gift is not providing him with the buzz, or the response, he had expected.

'I was going to say, and sometimes we had the wind in our sails. Whatever the case, let me get to the nub. Frankie, I want to offer you a partnership in Farley & Ratchett,' he announces grandly.

Frankie sits back in the chair, spreads the fingers of both hands and put the tips together, but says nothing.

'On the standard terms. You'll be on equal shares with Jane. There'll be bonuses every year and a 20 per cent share in the business. You'll have to work hard – it's extra responsibility, but I know that you *will* work hard, 24/7. You've shown your capacity for hard graft over and over again. I know you've had a long wait for this, Frankie, probably too long, but I hope now it will all be worth it.'

Frankie keeps his fingers together and flexes them once more, feeling the joints under the skin slide back and forth.

He marvels how his spongy, material brain can magically will such a thing.

'Shame Ratchett couldn't be here to see this,' says Frankie.

'Yes, good old Nick.'

'Good old Nick,' says Frankie.

'Well, then,' says Farley. He reaches out his hand to shake Frankie's. 'Congratulations.'

Frankie doesn't move or say anything. For the first time, Farley appears flustered, unable to work out what to say. Finally he settles for:

'I think your old friend Ralph Gwynne would be proud of us today.'

Frankie grins automatically as Farley's hand hovers over the table.

'I'm sure he would,' says Frankie softly, half to himself.

Would he fuck, decides Frankie a moment later.

'I'll save you the hand gel,' says Frankie, keeping his fingers pressed together. He stares at the single patch of blue above Farley's head. Farley, after a few puzzled moments, lets his hand drop.

'You don't seem particularly excited,' says Farley.

'I don't – do I?

'Any particular reason?'

'To be honest my relative indifference comes as much as a surprise to me as it does you. Truth is, I've just realized something that I should have realized a long time ago.'

Farley's phone pings. He reaches and checks it, then replaces it on the desk.

'I'm going to have to go in a minute, Frankie.'

'Something urgent?'

'A golf game with one of the local councillors. Very useful contact. Now. Shall we sign the papers?'

Farley picks at the corner of the buff file on his desk with his fingernail, then opens it.

'Not really.'

Farley closes the file again and then checks his watch.

'Of course. You'll want to see a lawyer, of course.'

'It's not that so much. It's more that I don't want to be . . .'

Frankie pauses, recognizing the precipice he stands on and feeling giddy.

'Be a what?'

'Be a partner,' says Frankie, steadying himself.

Farley stares at him blankly.

'Truth is, I don't want to be an estate agent at all.'

Farley gives a small, nervous laugh and shifts on his chair. For once his legendary amiability seems to be abandoning him.

'So a career in ballet calls? What the fuck are you talking about, Frankie?'

Farley is tapping his finger on the buff file in a furious tattoo.

'What I said. I've had enough.'

Farley looks seriously fazed and turns his attention to the pointless paperweight, which he now cradles like a precious jewel.

'Is it the terms of the contract? Because I'm sure we can talk about it. It's not set in stone. You know, Jane will take it badly, but . . . I don't know . . . I can up it to . . . what? Twenty-five per cent?'

'No, I don't think so.'

'You're serious?'

Farley puts the paperweight down and pulls on his knuckles so that Frankie can hear them crack.

'Let me just check.'

Frankie stands there for a moment to see if there are any contradictory impulses working within him. He finds only a single unyielding stream of pure resolution.

'I am completely serious.'

'But what are you going to do instead?'

Frankie frowns and considers this. It seems a reasonable question.

'I haven't got a clue.'

'So you're just going to – walk out of here? Right now. With no job to go to. No future. No security.'

Farley's face has turned a light shade of scarlet which is deepening by the moment.

'That's about the size of it.'

Frankie stands up and takes a step towards the office door. To his surprise, he feels entirely calm and focused.

'If you walk out that door you're not coming back,' says Farley, standing now, his suit crumpled, knuckles cracking furiously. Frankie fishes in his pocket, finds his office keys and throws them on Farley's desk. He turns again and closes the door behind him.

Walking past the staring, puzzled faces of the agents in the main office, he steps out into the street. To his surprise, the space feels very different from the space he stood in, examining his reflection thirty minutes previously.

Bigger. Wider. Freer.

Above all, more uncertain.

A few hours later and Nodge, Owen and China are sitting with Frankie in the pub garden of the Duke of Wellington in Brook

Green, less than a mile from the office. Frankie has summoned them all to give them the news, the public utterance rendering the reality more finally real. Unable to hold back, he told China what he had done when he phoned her to summon her to the pub. Now, as he picks up the pint of beer that Nodge had bought him, his hand is shaking slightly. The three others all stare at him. He cannot read their expressions.

'Oh God, what have I done?' says Frankie softly into his beer. 'Maybe I should go back there right now and beg Farley for the partnership again. Tell him it was a hangover from the virus. That I'm not thinking straight.'

Nodge is picking at a bag of pork scratchings. He offers one to Owen, who refuses, tapping his lockdown belly.

'Why *did* you do it?' says China.

'It was like there was a magnet inside of me,' says Frankie. 'Pulling me away from the job. I could have ignored it, but . . .'

'But you didn't,' says China.

'Frankie,' says Nodge. 'Can I tell you something? You're thinking completely straight. For once.'

China leans over from where she is sitting on the chair next to Frankie and kisses him on the cheek. She is wearing, for the first time Frankie can remember, a simple black cotton dress instead of running shorts or sweatpants.

'I'm so proud of you, old man,' she says.

'You are?' says Frankie. Feeling up until now bewildered and helpless, he takes a long pull on his pint, his second so far, along with two whiskey chasers.

'Never thought I'd say it,' says China.

'Thank you,' says Frankie, dazed but suddenly, unexpectedly happy – a happiness he feels begin to grow and spread within him, suffocating the doubt and fear that had been coiling inside him only a few moments before.

'Me too,' says Owen.

'Oh, *you*,' says Frankie, not sure what else to say. 'You're just joining in.'

'I still feel proud, though,' says Owen.

'But – how am I going to survive?'

He steals a pork scratching from Nodge and crunches down. It is too hard, almost breaks a filling. He spits it out into his hand and drops it on the ground.

'Your round,' says China, who has just finished her J2O mixed with vodka. She holds her glass up to Frankie. Frankie reaches for his wallet and finds that it contains no cash. He knows that his company credit card, the only one he carries with him, will already have been cancelled.

'I'm a bit broke, to tell you the truth. I suppose I'd better get used to it.'

'Come off it,' says China. 'I happen to know that you have saved up at least eighty grand to buy yourself a fancy Merc. So cut it out with the self-pity.'

'Think I might have to make do with one of those new electric scooters now,' Frankie says. 'Seriously, though, I'm frightened, I think.'

'Of loneliness? Of financial insecurity?' says China.

'I'm more afraid of not having a place to go to every morning,' says Frankie. 'Even if it was populated by vultures and creeps.'

'You do have a place to go,' says China. 'In fact, you're already there. Wherever you go, there you are. Didn't you find that out during lockdown?'

'I'm buying then – since poor Frankie's down to his last 80K,' says Owen. He takes the orders and heads for the bar. Nodge at the same time rises to head for the men's room. Left alone with Frankie, China reaches in her shoulder bag.

'I've brought something for you,' she says.

She brings out a small black velvet bag. From within she produces the antique compass that Colin had once given Roxy, who had in turn given it to China. There is still a crack in the glass from when China damaged it the night Roxy gave it to her.

'It's in case you ever lose your way,' says China, handing it to him. He closes his hand over hers before he takes the compass. He fumbles for his reading glasses so he can see it clearly, and puts them on, but the compass figures are still blurred since his eyes are clouded with water. He feels ashamed. He doesn't know if it's the compass, or his resignation, or his rising tears.

'What's the matter now?' says Owen, returning with the drinks. 'You're not having second thoughts again, are you?'

'No. It's nothing. Absolutely nothing,' says Frankie, rubbing his eyes with the back of his sleeve. He puts the compass back in its bag and slides it into his pocket, mouthing a 'thank you' to China. 'Apart from the fact that I'm unemployed, with no prospects and heading for my fifty-first birthday without a pot to piss in.'

'Apart from the 80K,' says China. 'And the flat in a highly desirable area that you happen to own. Drama queen. Look – I have to get off,' she says, standing up and draining her J2O.

'Where to?' says Nodge, appearing from behind her, his hand still fumbling to close his zip.

'She's heading back to Brighton for a while,' says Frankie, standing up and holding out his arms towards China.

'I've got some catching up to do,' says China, hugging Frankie and then Nodge, and bending down to give Owen a kiss on the cheek. 'Unfinished melded family business.'

She departs with a wave. Frankie feels the compass in his pocket and thinks momentarily of his friend, poor dead Colin. Then he turns his attention to Owen and Nodge who are sitting next to one another, holding hands. Both look profoundly content. Frankie takes a sip of the beer that Owen has placed in front of him.

'So anyway – enough about me. Tell me: how did China arrange this reconciliation? Between you two? Last I heard you were pretty frosty with one another.'

Nodge and Owen exchange faintly nervous looks.

'I suppose we'd better tell you. Although I'm not sure you're going to like it. Or if this is the right moment to tell you the truth,' says Nodge.

'What do you mean?'

Frankie takes a deeper draught of the beer and wipes his mouth with the back of his suit sleeve.

'China told us to wait until she'd left the pub to tell you. I don't think she wanted to be dragged into it. Although it was all down to her in the first place.'

Frankie drains most of his beer and replaces the glass on the table. A persistent wasp buzzes around the rim of the glass.

'I don't like the sound of this.'

Owen tries to wave the wasp away but it remains persistent.

'The long and short of it is,' says Owen, belting back a double scotch, 'China offered to act as a surrogate.'

Frankie looks confused and stares at the door through which China had departed a few minutes previously, as if she might return and explain this puzzle.

'A surrogate what?'

'A surrogate mother,' says Nodge.

'What's that when it's at home?'

'It means that China would take sperm from me and/or Nodge . . . '

'Or both of us,' adds Owen.

'And carry our child for us. When she had given birth, we could then adopt.'

Frankie takes a moment to absorb this. He slowly gets to his feet, his feeling of rising goodwill having suddenly dissipated. He takes his reading glasses off and puts them slowly in his pocket.

'Are you fucking kidding me?'

'Frankie . . . ' says Nodge. Frankie's head is whirling and not only because of the alcohol he has imbibed. Owen and Nodge appear as indistinct blurs.

'You must be out of your fucking tree. My nineteen-year-old daughter is going to have my best friend's baby? It's *sick*. I can't believe that you . . . '

Frankie's voice dries in his throat. Nodge holds out the flat of his hand in front of him.

'Frankie. *Whoa*. Obviously we didn't say yes. *Obviously*.'

'I said no to China even before I told Nodge about the offer,' adds Owen. 'He was just as opposed to the idea as me. It was never going to happen. Ever. I swear.'

'We both swear,' says Nodge.

Frankie finds himself placated. He lowers himself back slowly down into the pub garden chair, picks up his drink and pulls on it, despite the fact there is now a dead wasp in the glass which he narrowly avoids swallowing.

'So why . . . what . . . why *are* you two back together again, then?'

'I'm not sure,' says Owen, taking the glass out of Frankie's hand and fishing out the wasp. 'I think it has something to do with the gesture that China made — even though we couldn't accept her offer.'

'That degree of love. The sacrifice involved,' says Nodge. 'It was just so extraordinary. You have an amazing daughter, Frankie.'

'For the first time I think I began to understand what love could mean,' says Owen as Frankie gazes at the lager-soaked body of the insect on the ground, where Owen has flicked it. 'Love for her godfather in this case. But it set an example. It moved me. Tremendously. Both of us. That she would carry our child as a gift. Simply to save Nodge from heartbreak.

'After she said that, I thought to myself, "Nodge would prob-ably do the same for me." I mean if he had a womb. Perhaps he did do the same for me in offering to become a father when he didn't really want to. And then I thought, suddenly, that being with JJ instead of my . . . my *husband* was ridiculous and a betrayal and a madness. The day after I sent China away — having, as I say, utterly and immediately but with much thanks refused her offer — I rang Nodge and asked if he would forgive me and let me come home.'

'I said I would think about it,' says Nodge, staring softly at Owen.

'What you actually said was, "God yes, Owen, please. I beg you, come home this minute."'

'Yeh, maybe thinking about it, maybe it was something more like that,' says Nodge.

'What about you two having a child, though?' says Frankie.

'We can apply again in a little over a year. This time Nodge will tell the truth. According to Comfort, we're in with a good chance. She's going to give us her highest recommendation.'

Frankie chews this over silently. His phone buzzes. He checks it – it is Farley. Frankie briskly switches the phone off.

'What about this JJ, then, or whatever his name is?' he says.

'He understood,' says Owen. 'He knew deep in his heart he was too old to be having a child. It was wishful thinking. It got him carried away.'

'You're all still friends, then, are you?'

'Amazingly – yes,' says Nodge. 'He might even babysit sometimes. He's a hell of a terrific human being, even after, you know, what happened at the chess table.'

'Oh yeh,' says Frankie. 'Bashing the bishop.'

'Terrible Nanki-Poo, though,' says Owen, laughing. 'Thank God the lockdown at least saved West London that embarrassment.'

Frankie joins in the laughter even though he doesn't have a clue what Owen is talking about.

'I heard from China that he might have Covid,' says Frankie. 'Apparently he was coughing something terrible when she went round to see Owen that day.'

'He doesn't have Covid,' says Owen.

'Thank God for that. It's no picnic, I can tell you.'

'He has an underlying condition, though,' says Nodge.

'Yes,' says Owen. 'Death.'

Frankie looks from one to the other, perplexed.

'Lung cancer,' says Nodge. 'Smoking sixty a day for forty years finally caught up with him. He's got maybe a year to live. Maybe less.'

Frankie finds this hard to register. No sense of compassion rises up to greet the news. There has been so much death over the past few months – albeit among strangers he has never met. He just feels numb.

'That's a shit sandwich. How did he take it?'

Owen's willpower breaks and he takes a handful of Nodge's pork scratchings, feeling the tang of the salt, the chew of the fat on his tongue.

'Remarkably well. Life and death is all the same to him, he always says. Or at least his mother used to say.'

'His mother used to say a lot,' says Nodge.

'He saw in the end, especially after he was diagnosed, that he wouldn't have made an ideal father,' says Owen. 'He even helped me to pack my stuff to come back to Nodge's.'

'Poor guy,' says Nodge.

'Well,' says Frankie finally, as if to close the matter, shrugging his shoulders and glancing at the dead wasp on the floor. 'Whaddya gonna do?'

'Goodbye, then, Dad.'

China stands by the doorway to Frankie's flat, her suitcase packed. The *Hunger Games* backpack has gone to the charity shop. Frankie bought some grown-up luggage for her online as a gift.

The banisters are finally finished. They shine in the afternoon light.

'Your room is still a mess.'

'Yeh, I know. But it's the last time.'

Frankie stares at her mock-reproachfully. She raises her eyes to the heavens.

'I'll give it a quick clear up, then.'

China actually puts her suitcase down and moves towards the stairs. Frankie blocks her way.

'It doesn't matter.'

She pauses, nods, then picks up the suitcase again.

'You can't wait to get rid of me, can you?'

'I won't miss your chaos. But I'll miss you, China girl. I'll miss you terribly.'

China lifts the suitcase to check its weight. She seems to be leaving with a far less heavy load than she arrived with.

'I'll miss you too, Dad.'

'I'm sure you won't,' Frankie says briskly. 'Anyway, you're only an hour away.'

'Until September. Then I'll be three hours away, in Newcastle.'

'There's always Zoom.'

'Not the same, is it?'

China opens the door of the flat with her free hand. She turns back to Frankie.

'Thanks for not dying, Dad.'

'You're welcome. Thanks for sticking with me while I nearly did.'

'I didn't have much choice – did I?'

China drops her suitcase, then she puts her arms around Frankie's neck and feels herself hang there, as she once had as a child. Then she takes a step backwards, firmly, as if making the step unretractable.

'See you, then – old man.'

Frankie nods. China turns and closes the door softly behind her. Frankie stares at the closed door, hears her footsteps on the stair, waits for them to fade into nothing.

*

August 2020: Brighton

In the bedroom she shares with Silas — an uneasy mix between Veronica's fondness for shabby chic and Silas's preference for clutter-free clean lines — Veronica finishes reading the email that has just arrived in her inbox. There are unnecessary vintage scatter cushions on the bed (Veronica) and a workstation in the corner (Silas). Veronica prefers to use this otherwise unwelcome surface when Mason is on the loose in the rest of the house and she is not in her office. She sits on an imitation of a Rennie Mackintosh chair and leans forward as if the physical movement could bring the emotional content of the email closer. It is one of thirty she has received that morning, but the sender's name and the subject line that reads 'Forgiveness' sounds a klaxon in her mind. She opens it immediately, feelings of hope and anxiety jostling for position within her.

Dear Veronica,

I am belatedly writing to apologize for my behaviour at the end of last year when I stormed out of our last meeting. I was unacceptably rude if not positively insulting.

During the lockdown period, I have done a lot of reflecting on my mental health and how you have helped me with my endeavours to build a healthy relationship between myself and other people. I think when I was seeing you I was actually in the throes of a breakdown, and I behaved in an irrational manner despite all your sincere attempts to make me see that I was heading for a fall.

I realize now, having come out the other side of that breakdown, that the time I spent with you was profoundly useful. Or could have been if I had had more sense. I hope very much that you will consider taking me on as a client again, now that lockdown has finally ended and I seem to have recovered from this 'episode'. I will understand if you choose not to, but I confess I think I will find it hard to find another therapist as sympathetic, understanding and wise as I have found you to be. But if you can forgive me at least, it would mean a lot.

I have finally discovered for myself what you have so assiduously tried to teach me. That real life is in the mind and if you get that right, everything else follows.

I have, of course, withdrawn my ill-considered and rash complaint to the BACP.

Sincerely

Vincent Canby

Shakily, she begins her reply:

Dear Vincent,

Thank you so much for this, Vincent. You can't imagine what a load it is off my mind. I must admit I was shaken by your . . .

She pauses. Is real life in the mind? *Did* she try to teach him that?

As she considers how to continue, she hears footsteps on the front path then the sound of the front door opening downstairs. She shuts the laptop. The guest is anything but unexpected. Veronica feels a surge of excitement pulse through her.

Downstairs, China has entered the living room, suitcase in hand. China dreads Mason's hyperactive fussing and Silas's condescension. But she is excited to see her mother in person again.

She looks around the room and becomes aware of the contrast with the barren space of Frankie's flat. The old piano in the corner where Silas practised, the yin/yang poster, the ceiling rose with its vintage chandelier hanging. One of the walls papered with a shoal of fish in blue. An Indian embroidered footstool. Five floor-to-ceiling bookcases, all stacked.

Was this her home? Did she have a home anymore? Even if she did, she was leaving it soon to go to university. She felt herself reeling at the immensity and jeopardy of the future while at the same time relieved to again be in this welcoming, shabby but warm space.

'Where is everyone?' China calls tentatively. She expects her mother to answer, but it is Mason who appears first, walking into the room from the kitchen where he has been making himself the same marmite and white bread sandwich he eats every day.

He says nothing, just stands in the doorway of the kitchen holding the limp sandwich. He seems to China oddly nervous and reluctant. China smiles stiffly. Mason seems to be waiting for something. Unsure of herself, China nevertheless cautiously holds out her arms. Mason drops the sandwich on the living room table, runs towards her arms at full pelt and enfolds himself.

China, in the grip of the embrace, sees Veronica appear on the stairs. Her hair is tied up and she is wearing the old men's pyjamas that she favours when relaxing at home.

'That's a sight I never expected to see,' Veronica says. Mason is still holding on to China's waist fiercely. Veronica, laughing, makes her way down the stairs. Mason disentangles himself and Veronica takes up the space in the circle of China's arms.

'Good to have you back, China.'

'I'm glad to be here, Mum. So glad.'

'Do you want a cup of tea?' says Mason, looking at them both hopefully. Mason, it occurs to China, has never offered to make a cup of tea in all the time they had lived together previously.

'Love one.'

'Mum?'

'Thank you.'

Mason disappears into the kitchen. China stares after him in astonishment, then turns to Veronica, who goes to sit on the sofa where she kicks off her slippers.

'He calls you "Mum" now?'

'Is that okay with you?'

'Why shouldn't it be? If it makes him feel safer.'

'Good. Come and sit down with me.'

China, dragging her suitcase behind her, makes her way to the sofa and sits next to her mother. Veronica grabs her hand and China holds on tight.

'So. How did it go with your dad?' says Veronica, her face shining.

'Long story.'

China, who had been anxious about arriving, now feels enveloped by a sense of belonging, of welcome. Of home.

'Headlines?'

'You've heard most of it. The Covid was pretty bad. I mean he wouldn't go to the hospital. I would have done, left to myself. In the end he came out of it, but it was pretty much touch and go. He didn't want me to tell you that he was ill at all. I had to do it without his permission in the end. He didn't want to worry you.'

'That doesn't sound like Frankie,' says Veronica. She feels moisture on China's palm and rubs her own palm against it as if the perspiration could be absorbed by her own pores.

'Maybe Dad isn't the person you think he is. He certainly isn't the person I thought he was.'

China weighs her words carefully.

'He still loves you, Mum. I can tell. It's obvious.'

Mason walks back into the room holding two mugs of tea. China takes hers and ventures a sip. She makes a face at the bitter stewed flavour. Seeing her expression, instead of flaring up as China expects him to, Mason grins.

'Yeh, sorry. I haven't quite got the hang of it yet. I'll improve. What's wrong with Mum?'

He looks towards Veronica, who is completely ignoring the cup of tea Mason holds out to her.

'She's just had a bit of a shock. She'll come out of it. Where's your dad anyway?'

Veronica takes the tea.

'Oh, him? He's out on a job. Should be back soon,' says Mason.

'How are you two getting on?'

'Not bad, considering.'

'Considering what?'

'That he's my dad?'

China laughs. Bracing herself, she takes another sip of the tea.

'Yeh, I get that. You know, this tea really isn't that bad.'

'Liar.'

Mason glances at Veronica, who has put the tea on the coffee table in front of her, untouched.

'I've got some homework to do, China. Sorry to disappear so soon. I'm glad you're back.'

With that, Mason makes his way upstairs. China settles herself into the sofa and turns back to Veronica.

'Can you believe that Roxy could have been so thoughtless? Getting together with Frankie when she didn't know if she was positive or not. She might have killed him.'

'To be honest, I can't believe he got together with Roxy in the first place,' says Veronica.

'Why shouldn't they have? You weren't friends anymore. They were both lonely.'

China suddenly looks fierce, seasoned, even wise. Veronica seems to see a woman sitting next to her rather than a girl. It unnerves her, even saddens her, while making her feel both proud and slightly defensive.

'When did *you* suddenly become so understanding?'

'Perhaps I'm starting to grow up a bit. Perhaps you should do the same.'

'Cheeky cow.'

Veronica gives her a play kick on the ankle with the tips of her fluffy slippers.

'I guess I've been patronizing Dad for long enough. Thought maybe it was time I gave you a turn. In some ways, you're quite similar, you know.'

Now Veronica goes from being playful to feeling oddly offended. She crumples her face and prods China in the ribs with a finger, still playful, but with an edge.

'China, Frankie's a *liar*. I would never behave like him. It's different. We're different.'

'*Are* you all that different?'

Now all trace of playfulness has departed Veronica. Her voice betrays an edge of anger.

'Yes! He betrayed me. Betrayed *us*.'

'And you've never betrayed him?'

China holds Veronica steadily in her gaze.

'Of course not!'

'Never?'

Veronica is suddenly feeling less certain of her ground. China stares at her now directly in the eyes. Veronica's eyes can't hold hers and slide away.

'Not in any *major* way.'

China lets that sit there for a while. She nods slowly, as if her weighing of the evidence has been completed. She is about to speak again when the door opens. Silas walks in, wearing a pair of dirty jeans and a T-shirt under a thin Timberland canvas jacket. He breaks into a cautious smile as he makes his way towards mother and daughter on the sofa. China rises and gives him a hug.

'How have you been, Silas?'

'It is what it is. Pretty good on the whole, considering. You?'

'Ups and downs – you know.'

The conversation seems to dry almost immediately. China was intending to leave this for later, but to fill the awkward silence, she reaches into her bag and brings out a long object wrapped in brown paper.

'Guess what this is . . . ' says China.

'An anti-tank weapon?' says Silas. 'An umbrella? A length of 4x2?'

China slowly unwraps the parcel to reveal the Nerf Super Soaker Mark 4. Veronica covers her face with her hands. Silas doesn't move.

'Before you say anything,' says China, 'I'm showing it to you first so that I can get your approval before I give it to Mason. If you don't want me to, that's fine, I can take it back to the shop, no harm done. But I thought it would be a nice gesture.'

Silas nods, but otherwise doesn't give any sign of a response.

'Right,' says China, suddenly dejected. 'I guess that's the way things still are then.'

Silas still says nothing. Desperate to fill the gap, China speaks as she slowly wraps up the Super Soaker again.

'Mason seems to have changed.'

'Oh, he has,' says Silas. 'Unquestionably.'

He lowers himself into one of the armchairs and puts his feet up on the footstool.

'What happened?'

'You left. He was very upset about it. He thought you going was his fault.'

China pauses in her wrapping.

'I thought he was glad to be rid of me.'

'Not at all. He cares about you, China. You're the closest thing he has to a sister. That's why he fought with you so much.'

Silas kicks off his shoes, revealing thick brown knitted socks with a hole in one toe. China stares at the revealed inch of flesh and toenail.

'Don't tell me he's transformed just because he missed me a bit.'

'No,' says Silas, throwing his head back to rest on the back of the chair. 'He's also been taking Ritalin. It's made a remarkable difference. He's calmed down, matured, become more thoughtful.

How much is the drugs, how much is you leaving, how much is just growing up a bit I don't know. But the change is obvious. His schoolwork has improved. He even makes cups of tea.'

China glances at her and Veronica's undrunk mugs on the table.

'Bad ones,' says China.

Silas follows her gaze and gives one of his tight little grins.

'Very bad ones. But he's working on it.'

Silas's eyes go back to the Super Soaker. The smile widens and eases. He turns to China.

'Thanks for the gift, China. I'm sure he'll love it.'

'Love what?' says Mason, appearing at the top of the stairs and making his way down, his feet hammering on the carpet.

Silas nods towards the still only partially wrapped Super Soaker that China is holding.

'Look what China got for you,' says Silas.

China tears off what's left of the paper and holds it out to Mason. Mason stares at the lurid plastic toy, his face a blank.

'Uh, thanks,' he says, slowly taking it from China.

'You don't seem too thrilled,' says Silas, sitting forward on his chair.

'Well, I'm *grateful*,' says Mason, taking the water gun and holding it limply. 'But . . . '

He stops as if trying to understand his own lack of enthusiasm, then continues. His smile, once vaguely malevolent, is sheepish and even apologetic.

'I guess I've outgrown water pistols a bit is all.'

Kardashian wanders into the room. She glances at China indifferently, curls up on the sofa and falls asleep.

*

The end of the lockdown means the end of the woman's free, government-sponsored room. It is temporary hostels and shelters from now on, or park benches or shop doorways. Once she wouldn't have cared, but the long stretch in this room of her own and the regular ingestion of her medications – and the lack of availability of her drugs of choice, which were pretty much any drugs at all – seem to have shifted some ancient blockage in her brain.

It isn't an entirely pleasant shift. Somehow, as memory seeps back, it brings with it pain, a dark wrenching in her heart and chest, a glowing red-hot lining of guilt. Yet somehow this new – or perhaps old – suffering feels healthier to her than the endless scrambling and puzzling of her mind that had paralyzed her for so long.

She sits now, on the steps of this shopping centre, with her begging cup in front of her. She isn't getting much success. She wonders if it is because she is clean now and her clothes are decent. She simply isn't wretched enough anymore to elicit pity.

It is a warm day and she becomes aware of a sensation she hasn't felt in a long time rising like a dawn across the black starless skies of her long waking night. Not happiness – that was a distant memory, so distant that it was barely a memory at all, more an unconfirmed rumour. This was more like a low-key suggestion of an intimation of peace. The strange voices no longer drummed so loudly in her ears, no wild birds flew, dipping, swooping and colliding endlessly inside her head. Her restlessness had alleviated, if not ceased. She wasn't afraid 24/7. Her thoughts were stringing themselves together in a sort of rough order, although they still faltered and started and backed up into themselves.

She knew what her name was now. Her name was Sarah Hilyard. She had grown up in Kemp Town, Brighton. Bad things happened to her when she was a child. Her father had done them. And her grandfather. She had tried to hide these things away from herself, tried to hide them from other people, tried to be normal. Succeeded for a while. But the wreckage always drifted to the surface sooner or later.

She noticed again the dark ring mark on her finger. She had once been married, perhaps. Or not married but coupled. With someone. More than for just a night or two. Someone who had cared for her, perhaps loved her. Perhaps even did not abuse her.

A well-dressed man comes over and puts twenty pence in her cup. Once she would have thrown it back at him in disgust. Instead, she nods and politely says thank you. He doesn't reply.

The cars cruise by in front of her, intermittently stopping at the traffic lights by the pelican crossing. On such a bright day, people have their car windows open. Perhaps she would have better luck at the crossing. Perhaps she would have enough luck that she could find, sooner or later, a way off the street. She realizes that at the moment, she actually wants to find that way.

She walks towards the traffic lights. She won't hassle the drivers, that isn't her style anymore. She will simply hold her hand out and smile when they stop and ask if they have a few coins to spare. If they shake their heads, she will politely move on to the next car.

There is bubble wrap all over the floor, pulled excitedly from the new bed that has arrived for China. Even though she is going to university in a few months, the arrival of the bed feels important. It is hers; it will occupy her room when she returns during the holidays, it will mark her space. The old bed, still covered in peeling stickers of the Powerpuff Girls and fading unicorns, sits in pieces in the front garden waiting for collection by the local council. Silas has spent the morning putting the new bed together, and now China is reclining on the soft yielding mattress, wondering why she took so long to get rid of the old one. Silas pokes his head through the door of the bedroom.

'Shall we go into town today?' says Silas cheerfully. 'The shops are open again.'

He is in an expansive mood. To China, who is used to his mordant 'only grown-up in the room' act, he seems unfamiliar, vaguely unreal.

Mason appears behind Silas.

'Yes, please,' says Mason.

The Mason China remembers would never insert the 'p' word into any of his demands, but since the medication has become effective he appears not only to have calmed down but become more civil.

'I'd like to go as well,' says China, having left the bed, and now standing at the top of the stairs. 'If that's okay.'

The three of them make their way down the stairs, and Veronica enters from the kitchen dressed for summer, in a thin cotton dress with blue daisies printed on it and a wide-brimmed straw hat with a green ribbon round the crown.

'Did someone say we're going shopping?' says Veronica.

'I just thought it might be good to go into town,' says Silas. 'We're all sick to death being cooped up in here. We're finally allowed. Maybe we could get a pizza.'

'A pizza would be good,' says Veronica.

'Chicken tandoori stuffed crust,' says Mason.

'Disgusting,' says China.

333

Mason sticks his tongue out at her and China sticks hers out back, putting her hands behind her ears, open-palmed and waggling the fingers and going cross-eyed.

'We're agreed, then,' says Silas. 'Let's get our stuff and head off in, what, five minutes?'

'Call it ten,' says Veronica.

'Call it fifteen,' says China.

'Pizza,' says Mason.

'I'm going to buy some new clothes,' says Veronica. She has £60 cash in her purse, the money she took from Vincent Canby at the end of the previous year, which she has kept sacred in her drawer. Today she has decided to liberate it.

Then Silas does something neither China nor Veronica has seen him do. He takes out a credit card and hands it to Veronica.

'Treat yourself. Anything you want. The code is 7762. We haven't spent hardly anything for the last three months. Time to indulge. Anyway, it's your birthday soon. Think of this as an early gift.'

'My God!'

'Don't go mad, though.'

He suddenly looks worried.

She kisses him briefly on the cheek.

'I know better than to take advantage.'

She resolves to spend no more than a few hundred pounds. Even that will be pushing her luck, knowing Silas. But that should be enough to get her a couple of blouses and maybe a decent pair of shoes.

They approach the town centre, the silver Volvo polished and shining. It was one of the ways Silas had kept himself occupied over the past few months. They have decided to drive the short distance as Silas wants to buy some heavy hardware – a work-bench and a vice.

There isn't much parking to be had – it seems much of Brighton has had the same idea as the family, as well as day-trippers, released finally from captivity. The two car parks they had tried so far were full and on-street parking impos-sible as usual.

'I'm getting sick of this,' says Silas softly after cruising for fifteen minutes looking for a spot.

'Pizza!' says Mason in a sharp, whiny voice. His calm demean-our, as well as his day's dose of Ritalin, appear to be wearing off.

'I think there are spaces in that one,' says Veronica, as they turn the corner into the main road. Sure enough, the illumin-ated green sign outside the car park shows thirteen spaces free.

'We should have walked,' says Silas.

'It'll have to do,' says Veronica.

There is a set of lights and a pelican crossing to navigate before they get to the entrance. The lights turn red at the last moment. Silas nearly shoots them, terrified he is going to miss the car park space, but he is as always worried about hidden cameras, which he believes are everywhere, part of the surveillance state he vehemently opposes, so at the last moment he brakes. Mason, China and Veronica are thrown forward in their seats.

'Christ, Silas!' says Veronica.

'All good,' mutters Silas.

The car rests, the engine ticks over, then cuts out to save on carbon imprint.

'Do you have any change?'

A soft, weary voice comes at Silas's right shoulder. Silas turns.

Without looking at the woman's face he feels in his pocket for change, but there isn't any. Nobody uses cash anymore after the virus.

'No, I'm really sorry,' says Silas, now glancing briefly at the figure to his right. Their eyes meet.

'Sigh,' says the voice.

Without another word, he accelerates away, the light still on red. Instead of pulling into the car park, he drives straight past the entrance.

'What are you doing?' says Veronica.

'Dad!' says Mason.

'I am sure we can get closer to the shopping centre than this.'

China looks at him, puzzled.

'That street woman called you Si,' she says.

Silas laughs, but it contains a false note.

'No, she didn't. She said "Sigh". She was slurring. Probably mad.'

All of them – Mason, Veronica and China – stare at Silas.

'I don't know who she was,' says Silas, unsettled. 'Whatever she may or may not have said.'

'Then you drive past the car park without stopping after we'd been looking for a space for half an hour. It doesn't make any sense,' says China.

'The two events aren't connected. Correlation isn't causation.'

Silas's pedantic side always rises to the surface when he feels under pressure.

'What's going on?' says Veronica.

'Nothing's going on,' says Silas, a note of impatience in his voice now. 'An old crazy woman puts her hand out for some money and makes a sighing noise because I couldn't give her any money. Then I decided we could find something closer to the centre. And look – there's a space.'

There is indeed a space that a Mini has just pulled out of. Silas, sliding into it too quickly, gently collides with the bumper of the car in front.

'Sugar!'

Veronica looks at China inquiringly. She shrugs. They both know that Silas never rushes his parking. He has never been known to strike any other cars, either stationary or moving, and takes a pride in the fact.

He backs up quickly and straightens the wheels.

'There we are, then,' he announces, as if a great thing has been achieved. 'Everybody out.'

He leaves the driver's seat and cursorily examines the bumper of the car he has made contact with.

'No harm done,' he says unconvincingly. China feels sure she can see a small dent in the other car.

Across the way there is, to Mason's delight, a Pizza Express. 'Sick!'

'I *am* the best dad in the world,' says Silas, turning away from the scene of the crime.

Mason jumps out of the back seat. Veronica and China follow them across the road to the restaurant. But Veronica stops at the threshold as Silas holds open the door.

'I'm not hungry.'

'Come on!' says Silas as Mason breaks away and charges past him into the restaurant.

'No really, I'm fine. And we've been under one another's feet for long enough, don't you think? Like three months?'

'Okay — let's forget about the pizza,' says Silas, feeling irritated but sensing that he needs at this moment to be magnanimous.

'Mason is already in there,' says Veronica firmly. 'He's desperate for a pizza. Anyway, I'm gagging for a bit of retail therapy.'

She takes Silas's card out of her pocket and waves it joyfully in front of his face. Silas shrugs.

'Fair enough. Don't go mad.'

'So you already said. Several times.'

'Meet you at the shopping centre afterwards by the Boots.'

'I'll WhatsApp you.'

Once Silas, Mason and China have disappeared into the restaurant, Veronica doubles back and heads towards the crossing where the strange woman had spoken to them through the window.

She finds the woman still working the junction. She is standing at the kerbside, politely asking drivers for change. There are thick streaks of grey in her tangled hair. Veronica pulls a five-pound note from her pocket and, coming from behind the woman, pushes it into her cup.

'Thank you,' says the woman, turning. There is no flicker of recognition. Veronica guesses that despite the yellowing skin and cold sore on her lip that the woman had been attractive once. There is some light in her eyes that is not yet destroyed. The woman turns back to approach the next car which is slowing before the lights.

'Can I speak to you for a moment?' says Veronica.

The woman turns again and looks at her without curiosity.

'Are you from the social?'

'No. I was in the car,' says Veronica. 'With the man that you called "Si".'

The woman looks at her steadily. Her eyes have become watery.

'Do you want to sit down for a bit?' says Veronica, indicating a wooden bench on the pavement behind them. The woman hesitates before answering. It is a long while since anyone requested her company. Quietly, almost resignedly, she comes and sits on the bench, still holding her plastic cup. She examines the coins inside, takes out a button and throws it on the pavement. Veronica sits next to her.

'So, what do you want to know?' says the woman, unwrapping a Twix bar that she produces from her pocket. 'Lunch,' she adds, conspiratorially.

'Why did you call him Si?'

The woman shrugs, finishes removing the wrapper and takes a bite. She begins chewing slowly. Now she looks up as if addressing a small patch of air in front of her face.

'He reminded me of someone.'

'Who did he remind you of?'

'Someone called Si.'

She takes another bite of the Twix and wipes a crumb from her parched lips.

'Short for Simon?'

'Silas.'

Veronica looks at her shoes, which are a pair of old black trainers with the sole peeling and bird shit on the upper of the left shoe.

'But the man in the car was fatter and he didn't have so much hair. No beard. Also the Silas I knew wouldn't have just driven off like that. What is his name actually? The man in the car?' says the woman, still chewing and looking up for the first time at Veronica. Her eyes are the colour of cigarette ash.

'Silas,' says Veronica.

The woman stops chewing and crumples the empty Twix packet in her hand. Her face changes, darkens, droops.

'There was a boy,' says the woman eventually. 'In the back seat.'

'Mason,' says Veronica.

The woman nods.

'Macy,' she says.

Veronica, to fill the time as much as anything else, heads for the shops and, only half concentrating, begins shopping. She doesn't really notice what she is buying, but she registers that it is expensive. Normally she doesn't go much beyond Jigsaw for her clothes, but now she goes into Armani, Prada, Max Mara, savouring the churchlike atmosphere of faux-reverence and the ridiculous liveried doormen.

She spends £1,200 on an outfit. All of it suits her perfectly, she thinks. She is astonished with herself. She has never spent more than a few hundred pounds on a shopping trip before. She is certainly not used to spending Silas's money without a knot of guilt and anxiety in her stomach.

She has received a text message from Silas, asking her to meet back at the parked car. When she gets there, China and Mason are in the back and there is a space for her in the front. She throws her bags into the back, then seats herself next to Silas. Silas and China chatter with Mason, who has bought a handheld computer game that China is playing with him. They giggle as Silas turns to the wheel and they start the journey back. Silas concentrates on driving as usual, but after a while he notices how uncharacteristically quiet Veronica is being.

'Are you okay?' he asks without taking his eyes off the road.

'I'm perfectly fine.'

'What did you buy?'

'Just some clothes. A jacket. A skirt. Two blouses. A pair of shoes.'

They stop at some traffic lights. Silas cranes his neck to look at the bags on the seat behind. He looks anxious.

'Quite a haul.'

'I'll say.'

'Expensive?'

'Not for what it was. The shoes were a bit pricy.'

'How much.'

'£600,' says Veronica.

Veronica sees his Adam's apple work its way up and down.

'Jesus! For everything, I hope.'

'Just for the shoes.'

Veronica, who has been holding her handbag on her lap, reaches into it and takes out a packet of cigarettes. She slides one from the pack and lights it. A cloud of smoke drifts from her mouth and into Silas's face.

'Veronica!'

'Oh, sorry,' says Veronica sweetly. She winds the window half down and continues to smoke.

'Mum, are you *smoking*?' says China.

'Yup,' says Veronica, taking another deep drag. China shrugs and goes back to playing the computer game. The lights change to green, but Silas doesn't move the car. Instead, he stares at Veronica in astonishment.

'What are you doing?'

'I'm smoking a cigarette, Silas. What are you doing?'

He pulls over to the side of the road, reaches behind him and pulls out one of Veronica's shopping bags, inside which is an elegant cardboard box.

'Manolo Blahnik. Crimson leather. They're really quite beautiful,' says Veronica.

China and Mason, not listening, carry on playing the game in the back. Veronica notices, with satisfaction, that Silas's lips have gone white.

'Then there was the jacket, which was £500. And, oh my God, the skirt. So beautiful. And not that bad for what it was. £300.'

'Have you gone entirely insane?'

'I don't know. Have I?'

'Where are you getting all this money from?'

'From your credit card. You told me to treat myself.'

China finally looks up.

'Mum. That cigarette stinks.'

'Sorry, darling.' Veronica flings it out of the window – on the driver's side. It narrowly misses Silas's face.

'Silas looks like he's about to have a conniption. Is he alright?' says China, still only mildly interested.

'He's fine. Aren't you, Silas?'

Silas says nothing. China and Mason return to playing the game. When finally Silas speaks again, it is in a hiss.

'We need to talk.'

'We do.'

'All that stuff has to go back.'

'I suppose that would be possible. So long as it's undamaged.'

Silas shoots a hard look at her, then returns his gaze to the road.

'What's that supposed to mean?'

'I've put a tiny cigarette burn into each one of them. Not that noticeable, but the shop will notice them. Except the shoes. I liked those too much to actually harm them.'

'That makes no sense.'

His eyes are bulging like grapes.

'Why would you set fire to the clothes you just spent hundreds of pounds on?'

'Oh, spite, I suppose. Also because now you can't take them back and get a refund.'

'But that's crazy.'

'Not everything that doesn't make sense to you is crazy, Silas.'

When they arrive home, Mason and China emerge first from the car and head up the path. As Veronica gets out and moves to follow them, Silas grabs her arm.

'Let go, Silas. You're hurting me.'

He tightens his grip.

'What are you playing at?'

'What are *you* playing at, Silas?'

'I don't know what you mean.'

'Don't you? I went back and found that woman who talked to you at the traffic lights.'

Silas immediately lets go of Veronica's arm. His face, a moment before full of solid rage, collapses like a building dynamited in slow motion.

'She seemed a nice woman. Terrible mess, though. I wonder how she got that way?'

Silas stares at her, but does not speak.

'I think we'd better go inside,' says Veronica, picking up her shopping bags.

Inside, China registers the tension between Veronica and Silas when Silas simply heads upstairs without a word after China asks him if he wants a cup of tea. Veronica's face, she notices, is dark and angry.

'I wish everyone could just be happy,' says China, pausing and fishing for teabags at the back of the larder.

Kardashian pads across the room, settles herself on the sofa and closes her eyes.

'You want to know what happiness looks like?' says Veronica. 'Happiness looks like that.'

She points to Kardashian who appears, once more, to be insensible.

Ten minutes later, Silas sits on the bed in their bedroom, the door closed. He is holding one of the six scatter cushions as if for protection. Downstairs, China is preparing supper, cheerfully assisted by Mason.

'Who was that woman?' says Veronica, carefully inspecting Silas's face for signs of deceit. 'I want to hear it from you.'

'I don't know.'

'I can't really express to you how off-the-scale angry I am with you at this moment. Don't make it worse. I'll ask you again. And don't forget, I already know the answer. This time tell the truth. Who was that woman?'

Silas puts his face in the cushion then takes it out again.

'She looked like someone I used to know.'

'You seemed awfully keen to get away from her.'

'She seemed a bit loopy.'

'I don't know. When I got speaking to her she seemed pretty sane. In a bad way, I suppose, but sane.'

Silas looks up at Veronica. As usual, his eyes are sliding away from hers, not even catching her gaze for a moment. His face is naked now. It is, she suddenly realizes, a small boy's face hidden behind the mask of a grown-up. His eyes are red-rimmed.

'What did she tell you?'

'These are the crucial details, I think. She told me that she thinks she was married once. To – let me remember this correctly. Oh yes. To you. You had a child together. After the child was born, she suffered severe postnatal depression. After that happened, you abandoned her. You got a court order to keep her away from her own child. After you disappeared, she went back on to drugs. "Back on to" because she was into drugs before she had the child. In fact, you *both* were into drugs. In fact, *you* got her into drugs in the first place.'

'That's not . . .'

Veronica holds up a hand to stop him.

'Not your turn yet. She came from a terrible background, a broken home. She was abused as a child. She was self-medicating with alcohol and you introduced her to heroin. She became a junkie. So did you. You recovered but she didn't, even after she got pregnant. At that point, you became a heroic father, returning from the brink, and she became a fallen woman. She ended up broken, on the streets, anonymous, a nobody.'

'Okay,' says Silas, pointlessly zipping and unzipping the cushion cover.

Veronica looms above the slumping figure in front of her.

'Is that all you've got to say? That poor bloody woman. How she must have suffered.'

Silas picks up another cushion and starts picking at the snake motif that is embroidered onto it.

'It was much more complicated than it sounds.'

345

'How much more complicated?'

For the first time, Silas's voice contains a note of defiance.

'She was abusive. Dangerous. Out of control. I couldn't risk her being around Mason.'

'How long did you help her try to recover after she suffered post-natal depression?'

Silas slowly shakes his head.

'The doctors said . . . that it was likely to be chronic. That she was too damaged.'

'How long?'

'Veronica . . .'

'How long?'

'I thought it was best that we make a clean break. And so did the courts,' he adds, defiant once more. But still his eyes slide. A silence falls. Eventually Veronica leans forward and puts her mouth near to Silas's ear.

'Do you know why I have put up with you all these years, Silas?'

'Put up with me? That's harsh.'

His voice is meek again.

'I'll tell you. Because for all your faults – and there are many, many of them. Your meanness. Your cruelty to China. Your inability to create boundaries for Mason. Your pomposity and self-righteousness. Shall I continue?'

'I'd rather you didn't.'

'I've started so I'll finish. The fact that you are shit in bed. Your fucking vegetarian lasagne. And the way you try to be the victim in *everything* you do. But all the same I chose to be with you. Do you know why?'

'I expect you're going to tell me.'

'Because despite everything else, I thought you were *honest*.'

She allows the word to float in the air for a few seconds before continuing.

'My marriage died because it was full of lies. I decided never to let that happen to me again. Never. I believed in you. I believed *you*.'

'I *am* honest, Veronica. It was just . . .'

'Just this one little thing? That you'd been married before? That Mason had a mother? That the mother was living on the streets? That you had abandoned her to her fate? Is that what the word "just" represents? That's making it do an awful lot of work.'

Silas tries to take Veronica's hand but she pulls it away violently.

'I made a mistake. But I still think it was best for Mason.'

'I don't care. The point is, you didn't tell me about it.'

Now, lost for anything further to say, she picks up an empty Habitat vase sitting on the bedstand and throws it against the wall. Amazingly, it doesn't shatter but bounces back and sits limply on the floor as if stunned.

'You didn't tell me *anything*, Silas. After I trusted you.'

'Okay,' says Silas flatly. 'Guilty. So. What do we do now? How do we fix this?'

'Always the practical one, aren't you?'

'Nothing wrong with being practical, is there? We could see a therapist perhaps,' he says hopefully. He stands and picks up the vase and replaces it on the bedstand, adjusts it so it lies in the centre of the space.

'You don't get it do you? You *lied* to me.'

'I never *said* anything.'

'You can lie just as much by not saying anything.'

Instead of returning to sit on the bed, Silas goes to sit at the workstation. He glances at Veronica's still-open email with its subject line, 'Forgiveness', but it does not register, and he idly closes the laptop so that Veronica doesn't think he is snooping. For the first time when he looks back at Veronica, he allows his eyes to meet hers for an instant before they glide away once again, mercury on glass.

'Listen, Veronica. Mason has become very attached to you. I wanted you to be a mother figure for him and you have been. I think he has learned to love you.'

'Why are you bringing this up now?'

'I'm just trying to make you see the implication if you . . . if you . . . '

'Leave you?'

Silas nods.

'So now you're trying emotional blackmail. You must be scared.'

Silas suddenly looks as if he is about to weep. His expression contorts into slightly forced wretchedness.

'I am.'

Veronica regards him coolly, as if looking at a complete stranger.

'You'd better get used to it. You might benefit from getting to know what it feels like to be scared. How some people are scared every day of their lives. What it makes them do.'

They go downstairs to the kitchen without saying another word. Mason and China have disappeared. After a while, Silas goes to the fridge searching for a snack. But when he closes the door, he is holding one of China's bottles of Budvar. He hasn't touched a drop of alcohol since Veronica has known him.

He reaches for the bottle opener.

'You touch a drop of that stuff and I'm out the door,' says Veronica.

'It's for you,' says Silas, prising off the cap.

'So, what are you going to do?' says Veronica.

'About what?' says Silas, handing her the bottle.

'About *her.*'

For the first time, Silas looks Veronica directly in the eye and holds her gaze.

'I'm going to go and find her again tomorrow. And I'm going to try and help her.'

'Correct answer,' says Veronica, her voice steely.

She feels the beer, cold and startling, in her throat.

Later that same evening, Sarah Hilyard waits for the coach near the Brighton seafront, in the shabby mess that is Pool Valley Coach Station. She is clean, and her clothes are tidy – a pair of jeans she has bought in Primark and a simple white blouse from a charity shop. Her backpack is still stuffed, but the contents are clean and in some semblance of order.

She knows she cannot stay here on the coast. The past is too heavy a burden and she isn't ready to confront it. Silas was right to drive away from her. She knows that the woman will come looking for her – perhaps with Silas. Perhaps with Mason, too.

She can't face it.

She climbs on. The driver smiles at her and she smiles back. She hasn't smiled like that – so casually, so reflexively – for a long time. She takes her seat and puts her knapsack on the rack above her head. Inside, there is a full supply of medication she has been taking every day. And every day, she feels clearer. She has no plans, but she also feels the weight of no unexploded bombs inside her either. The urge to self-destruct has been fading. What will happen in London is unknown, but it is at least a known unknown. Brighton is her past. *You can't go back*, she decides firmly.

She thinks once more of Mason, sitting in the back of the car by the traffic lights, as the coach pulls away. He has grown so handsome and strong. The women sitting with him seemed like good women. The woman who came and talked to her was a good woman too. Sarah was sure of it.

Mason was in good hands.

The coach heads out of the Brighton Road towards the motorway, which is the part of this journey she has always liked most. She loves the ring road, the sense that she is just going round and round, and round and round, a life of circling without the pain of leaving or arriving.

But she is getting somewhere all the same, she now feels convinced of it.

August 2020: Brighton

Frankie and China are spread on beach towels on the hard pebbles of Brighton beach. It is a perfectly still day – there is barely a ripple in the waters of the English Channel. The temperature is touching 30 degrees centigrade. Frankie sits up and begins to rub himself over with factor-20 sun lotion. All around them there are seething crowds, but they have carved out territory for themselves with a strategically placed windbreaker. Previously, they spent an hour on the Palace Pier, eating doughnuts and chips and crashing bumper cars into one another. China has changed her mind about the Palace Pier – now it seems an affirmation of life, brash and cheerful, while the West Pier seems to her just a mess of untidy black bones.

'I'm getting burned here,' says Frankie. China doesn't reply. She turns over onto her back to top up the tan she has been developing over the summer.

'You be careful too, China. We've been out here for hours. You could get sunstroke.'

He looks at her bare back where the tree tattoo is pebbled with droplets of perspiration. China is oblivious. She is listening to Kanye on her AirPods, which Frankie has not noticed are thrust into her ears, and looking at the Vice website on her phone. She has a large bottle of water which she periodically pulls on. Frankie leans over closer.

'China! Can you hear me?'

She takes an AirPod out of one ear. Her skin gleams with youth in the sun.

'Sorry.'

'I said, you should be careful not to get sunstroke. Or you might set your tree on fire.'

China nods and tries to twist round to see the small of her back.

'Yeh, you're right.'

Frankie examines the tattoo. He squints carefully at what he had previously thought was black ink.

'Is that tree *blue* . . . ?'

'In a certain light, I suppose,' she says.

Frankie cranes closer. The tattoo ink is definitely dark blue, he notes, with a rush of excitement. Not black, as he had previously thought. A Blue Tree.

China checks her retro digital watch. Her phone pings with a text. She reads it and gives a short laugh.

'Who's that?'

'Silas asking if I want a lift to my friend's house later. He's suddenly got a lot nicer for some reason. Weird. Shall we go for a swim?'

'It's cold in there. I only signed up for sunbathing,' says Frankie, cracking open a can of beer that he has stored in a cooler pack. 'How's everything at home? How you getting along with Mason?'

China squeezes the last of her sun lotion onto her collarbone.

'He's turning into a pretty good kid. We have a laugh, actually.'

'You always said he was a nightmare.'

China drops the empty lotion bottle into her bag and rubs the remaining lotion into her hands.

'He was hurting. When you hurt, you turn into a nightmare. So then you can make sure other people hurt as much as you do.'

Frankie takes a swig of the beer and gives a gentle burp.

'Pardon me. And how's your Mum getting on with wossisname?'

'Up and down.'

China tells him the story of their shopping trip – Veronica lighting a cigarette in the car, infuriating Silas to the point of apoplexy.

Frankie considers this, sucking down the last of his beer.

'That *is* strange. What did Silas do?'

China stretches out, arching her back. A daisy-decorated football comes over from the nearby family group where the mother is playing with her infant daughter, who has kicked the ball in their direction. China gently rolls it back and the girl smiles and waves. China waves back.

'He went fucking mental. And then – and this is the strange thing – a bit later he quietened right down. Hasn't quite been the same arrogant, condescending prick since. It's as if he was on probation or something. I don't know. Come on, Dad, let's have a swim.'

'I told you. It's cold in there,' says Frankie, performing a mock shiver.

'Don't be such a baby. Mum goes in the middle of winter.'

'Mum goes in the middle of winter,' repeats Frankie in a mocking baby voice.

China frowns, then gets up and slides her possessions under the towel. In the distance she can see low white clouds gathering.

'By the way, Dad, thanks for offering to pay my tuition fees for uni.'

'Sure you won't change your mind?'

'You're going to need that money now you don't have a job. Student loans are cheap. Anyway, it's time I struck out on my own. I've got to make my own way.'

'I'll still give you something. Maybe help with the rent.'

China shrugs and turns towards the sea.

'Come on, then. Before the sun goes.'

Frankie follows her gaze to the ocean. The low clouds seem to be drifting towards them at speed. He decides to rise to the challenge.

'You are the most important person in the world to me, China,' he says, getting to his feet.

'You're definitely one of the most important people in the world to me. Along with my mum, my friends and Kardashian.'

'And Nodge,' says Frankie.

China suddenly looks earnest.

'No. Not Nodge. I mean, obviously I *like* him more than you.'

'Of course. What's not to like? So how come I have risen above him in the charts?'

China flicks a gobbet of sun cream that is still on her finger in the direction of Frankie and it lands on his stomach.

'Because he's not my dad. And you are.'

Frankie grins, rubs in the sun cream and leaps to his feet.

'I'll show you what a baby I am.'

Without waiting for China, he runs to the water's edge, China chasing him. He is about to throw himself in, but, feeling the sudden cold on his ankles, slams to a stop and begins to pick his way, very slowly, through the pebbles, as the water rises to the level of his knees. Then China is next to him, hurling herself in recklessly. She surfaces from the trough of an incoming wave.

'Fraidy cat.'

Frankie feels embarrassed, but he hates cold-water swimming – he always has. He inches a little further forward. Now the water comes up to his thighs. China emerges from the ocean in front of him, glistening with water. She flicks a handful at Frankie's chest.

'Old man!'

'Don't!' yells Frankie. 'I mean it! I need to do this in my own time.'

He immerses himself to his waist, all the time shivering and sharply drawing breath, while China dives and bobs around him. The crowd in the sea is almost as thick as the crowd on the beach, but about fifty feet further out, the crowd line breaks, and the sea is almost empty apart from a few dotted swimmers and surfboarders.

Frankie finally works up the courage to take the plunge and thrusts his whole body under. The water, despite the heat of the day, feels shocking. His breathing increases and he breaks into a fast crawl away from the beach in order to get his metabolism working.

Before he knows it, he has broken the crowd line and his skin has adjusted to the cold. He feels elated – refreshed by the water and bolstered by his own courage. He can see China twenty feet behind him moving towards him in long, slow strokes. The water is so calm, he kicks backwards to see if he can simply float on his back. But he finds himself tensing up, scared of sinking and choking on salty water. China, from nowhere, surfaces in front of him.

'The fuss you make!'

'I'm here, aren't I? In the sea, freezing my nuts off.'

She flips on her back and floats easily, as the sun beats down on her salty body. The sound of the crowd is fading now; they can hear only seagull squawks and the movement of breeze on the water.

'How do you do that? I've never been able to do that,' says Frankie, doggy-paddling in front of her.

'Do what?' says China, spouting a spume of sea water from her mouth. 'I'm not doing anything.'

'Float on your back. I always sink or tip over. I think it's because I have fat legs.'

'You have fat everything. Nothing to do with your legs, Dad. You're too rigid. You have to trust the sea to carry you.'

Frankie looks back at the crowd near the beach and

worries momentarily that there might be a stray shark this far from shore.

'Is that from the little book of Dalai Lama quotes?'

'Pradesh Ji.'

'Tibetan?'

'My primary school swimming teacher. Paddington.'

Frankie turns on his back in the water again, this time determining to let his body go limp. At first he is scared to do so, sure that he will sink beneath the surface. And he does. But then he realizes that he can't be *determined* to go limp because that is the opposite of relaxing. So he just lets his mind go blank. Thoughtlessly, he feels himself let go of himself. Sure enough and to his amazement, he immediately floats. His eyes take in the blue expanse of the sky above which has now turned milky.

'See?' says China. 'Easy. If you don't try.'

Frankie savours the feeling as he bobs up and down.

'You're right. This is great. I could lie here all day just looking at the sky and getting a . . . '

At that moment, a low wave appears out of nowhere and lands on Frankie, sending him sputtering into a ball of flailing limbs and pumping lungs. When he emerges, choking on a lungful of saltwater, China is doggy-paddling in his direction, laughing uncontrollably. Frankie, momentarily furious – he feels not only China has tricked him, but the sea, the wind, the wave – again feels himself relaxing. His hurt pride subsides and he finds himself laughing too. China drapes herself around his neck and whispers in his ear.

'Silly old man.'

'I am,' says Frankie. 'I am a silly old man.'

With that, he flips himself on his back again and floats with perfect ease. They lie there together side by side until the low ocean mist which has been approaching covers them and the beach, sending them and the sunbathers scurrying with their towels towards the car park as visibility suddenly closes down. They fumble their way back to their towels, pack up their stuff and return to the car, both shivering in the sudden chill.

September 2020: Brighton

'So I guess this is it,' says China. 'The great cliché of the parents and the departing train scene.'

Frankie and China are standing on the platform of Brighton railway station. China has a valise full of clothes. Frankie drove her up to the university campus a week ago and took the bulk of her stuff. These are her final bits and pieces. Frankie is catching a later train to return to his flat in London.

'You're all grown up,' says Frankie. He can feel a tear stinging at the corner of his eye.

'I love you, Chi,' says Veronica, reaching out and throwing her arms around her daughter. China hugs her back fiercely. They stay clenched together for almost a minute before separating.

'Mason was terribly upset at you leaving,' says Veronica.

'I'll be back. I'll miss him too. A bit. Occasionally. Probably. I dare say,' says China.

China turns to her father.

'Bye, old man.'

Frankie hugs her and plants a kiss on her cheek which she wipes off with the back of her hand.

'Go on. You'll miss your train,' says Frankie. 'And don't take drugs or get involved in prostitution.'

'Sex work,' says China.

'Whatever it's called, don't do it.'

'It's just as valid a profession as estate agency.'

'I wouldn't disagree there. Anyway, I'm not an estate agent anymore.'

'So who are you, then?'

Frankie finds that he has no answer.

China turns and starts to walk away. Frankie and Veronica take a long last look at their child – whom they grasp now, fully and finally, is no longer a child – as she heads towards the platform. A whistle sounds. They watch as she boards the train, turning and giving a final wave.

Frankie feels the smallness of the space between him and Veronica. He can hear that she is sobbing. She puts her head on Frankie's shoulder briefly, then removes it as if embarrassed. The train begins to pull away. Frankie feels his hand close to Veronica's. He can feel her heat. On impulse he takes it. Briefly her hand closes around his. Then she gently slides it away.

'Veronica . . . ' says Frankie carefully.

He looks into her eyes. They are exactly the eyes he saw when he first looked into them, more than twenty years ago, grey green with a dark inner ring of flecks. He wonders if it is the same person peering out from behind them as it was then. He wonders the same about the mysterious space behind his own eyes. He opens his mouth to speak, but Veronica holds her hand up to stop him.

'Don't,' she says in a voice that, although warm, is firm.

She starts to walk towards the station exit and he follows her.

Outside it has begun to rain, but the rain is somehow light and refreshing rather than oppressive and unwelcome.

'I didn't say anything. I didn't do anything,' says Frankie, struggling to catch up with her.

'What you don't do and what you don't say is as important as what you do do and do say.'

'But I still . . . '

'I know what you're driving at. But the past is another country, Frankie.'

'So is Tahiti.'

'What the hell does that mean?'

Frankie isn't sure. He tries to work it out.

'I'd still like to go there,' he says finally.

Veronica takes an umbrella out of her bag, opens it and sighs loudly. She looks Frankie in the eyes. Something smoulders there in the depths, but Frankie cannot tell what it is.

'You can't put the rain back in the sky, Frankie.'

With that she smiles, the smoulder turning into a bright, brief flash of light, then turns her back and starts to walk away towards the Palace Pier in the distance.

Frankie watches her retreat. Then he switches his focus to the sea beyond her. There in the distance, the sun beats on the water. A faint haze seems to hang over waves on the horizon. Perhaps a sea fog is gathering again and heading inland. But as he stares at the horizon, Frankie is sure he sees the vapour from the sea rising distinctly upwards, lofting towards darkening clouds, where the mist will surely once more turn into rain.

Acknowledgements

Clare Alexander, my legendary agent.
Suzanne Baboneau, my indispensable editor.